A
QUEEN'S
MATCH

BY KATHARINE McGEE

The American Royals series

American Royals

Majesty

Rivals

Reign

Inheritance (A Prequel Novella)

A Queen's Game series

A Queen's Game

A Queen's Match

A QUEEN'S MATCH

KATHARINE McGEE

Random House New York

Random House Books for Young Readers
An imprint of Random House Children's Books
A division of Penguin Random House LLC
1745 Broadway, New York, NY 10019
penguinrandomhouse.com
GetUnderlined.com

Produced by Alloy Entertainment
alloyentertainment.com

Library of Congress Cataloging-in-Publication Data is available upon request.
ISBN 978-0-593-71074-6 (hardcover)—ISBN 978-0-593-71076-0 (ebook)

The text of this book is set in 11.25-point Goudy Old Style MT Pro.

Manufactured in the United States of America
1st Printing

The authorized representative in the EU for product safety and compliance is Penguin Random House Ireland, Morrison Chambers, 32 Nassau Street, Dublin D02 YH68, Ireland, https://eu-contact.penguin.ie.

Random House Children's Books supports the First Amendment and celebrates the right to read.

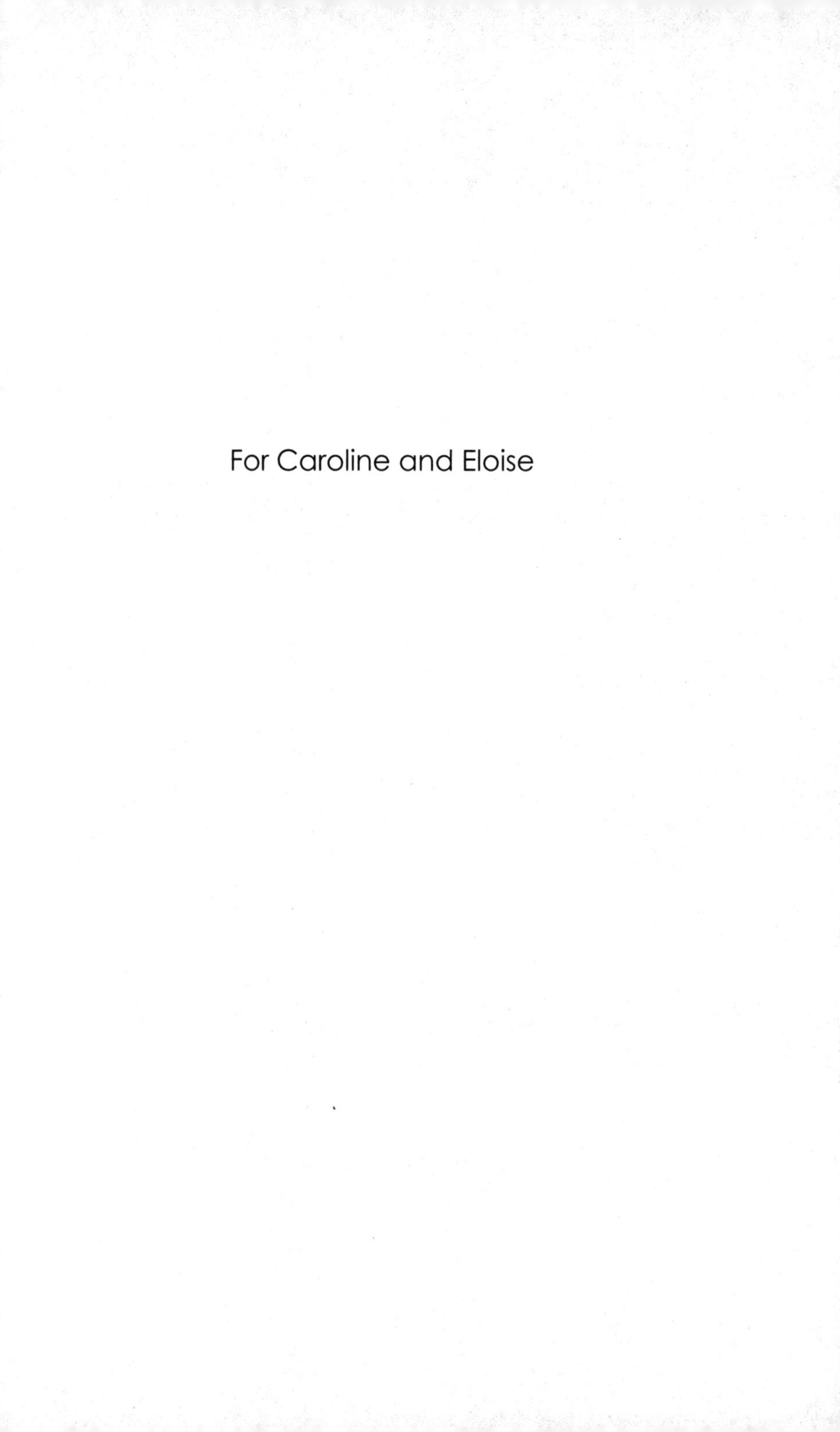

For Caroline and Eloise

A
QUEEN'S
MATCH

CHAPTER ONE

Hélène

"COME ON, AMÉLIE!" HÉLÈNE SHIFTED HER WEIGHT, HER FEET warm on the platform's wooden boards. Bathing machines were like carriages designed for discomfort. Or perhaps they were more like closets on wheels? Behind them, plodding toward the shore on a sleepy-looking dray horse, was the coachman who'd driven their bathing machine into the surf. A lot of work, all so that the Orléans sisters could swim without compromising their virtue.

As if Hélène had any virtue left to compromise.

It was maddeningly slow, being bundled into that ridiculous machine and dragged into the ocean. But Hélène had swallowed her complaints. Amélie's husband, Carlos, the Crown Prince of Portugal, had tried to be thoughtful by arranging this outing. And it was hardly his fault that men were allowed to stroll around the beach in one-piece bathing costumes while women had to keep themselves hidden.

Hélène lowered herself onto the top step of the ladder and shivered. The water was chillier than she'd expected.

"They should make these costumes warmer," Amélie grumbled, nudging open the door of the bathing machine. Like Hélène, she was dressed in a white camisole and bloomers: not the beautiful silk bloomers they wore under their gowns, but a simple pair made of cotton.

"You'll warm up once you get in the water," Hélène fibbed.

Amélie lifted a skeptical eyebrow, wrapping her arms around herself in the ocean breeze. So Hélène dived in.

The water closed over her head, cold and dark. It was so blissfully quiet that she couldn't hear anything but the far-off roar of the surf, murmuring like a distant heartbeat.

Here in the water, Hélène could forget it all. The mistakes she'd made, the secrecy and the joy and the unbearable pain she'd endured over the past year and a half: when she had fallen in love with Prince Eddy, then lost him.

As she broke the surface, Hélène looked up. Amélie was still standing on the back platform, watching her closely.

"I'll join you," Amélie declared, and began descending the ladder built into the back of the machine. The water wasn't deep; Hélène could dig her toes into the sandy bottom.

Amélie drifted toward her, moving her arms in circular motions to keep her head above the surface. "You look like a little mermaid with your hair all wet," she teased. *Une petite sirène,* she'd said; the sisters were speaking French, as they always did together.

Hélène bristled at the phrase; it made her think of that awful Hans Christian Andersen story. "I don't like the little mermaid." What a foolish decision, to give up everything for a man. Small surprise that the prince had left the mermaid the moment her back was turned, breaking her heart forever.

Though, to be fair, Hélène's heartbreak came from the fact that *she* was the one who'd left *Eddy.*

"You're right, of course. You're more like Mélusine than the little mermaid," Amélie amended.

Mélusine, the water spirit who had married a mortal man, a beloved French children's story. The ancient House of Anjou had claimed her as their ancestor; and since the Anjou were earlier French kings, succeeded by the Valois, then by the Bourbons, then by Hélène's own family, the Orléans—well, perhaps she was an ancestor of Hélène's, too.

Though Hélène was really a princess in name only. If history had played out differently, her father, Philippe, might have sat on the French throne; but France was a republic now. The Orléans family lived in exile in England.

"It's been so long since I went swimming," Amélie said eagerly. "Remember when we all used to go into the canal?"

"Philippe pretended to be an eel." Hélène elongated her body to mimic her brother's movements, pleased when Amélie smiled. "That feels like so long ago," she added softly. She didn't miss France, exactly, but she missed the simplicity of childhood. She missed those summers at the château in Normandy, before her family's exile.

Swimming like this—without heavy lace dragging her steps, without a corset constricting her movement—she felt a bit like a child again.

Hélène plunged beneath the surface and stayed submerged as long as she could, until her lungs were in agony.

When she emerged, her sister sighed. "Are you ready to tell me what's wrong?"

Hélène kicked her feet above the surface, staring at the pale half-moons of her toenails to avoid Amélie's gaze. "What do you mean?"

"You're hiding from something. And as much as I love having you here, you'll have to go back eventually, and face whatever—or *who*ever—it is."

Hélène had been with her sister for months, since Prince Constantine and Princess Sophie's wedding in Athens. The morning after the wedding, Hélène had asked her parents if they could stop in Portugal to visit Amélie and her baby. Her parents had been surprised; they knew that Hélène was secretly engaged to Prince Eddy of England. Didn't she want to return to London and make a wedding announcement? But Hélène had been adamant. She needed her sister.

After a few weeks in Lisbon, Marie Isabelle and Philippe had returned to England, but Hélène had lingered. Now it was April, and she still had no plans to return.

Eventually, Amélie had suggested that they go to Albufeira, on the southern coast, so that Hélène could "see the Mediterranean." As if her sister hadn't just been at a royal wedding in the Mediterranean. Clearly, Amélie had sensed that something was amiss, and hoped that the ocean air, and solitude, might help.

Hélène kept floating, buffeted by the sway of the waves. The air smelled of salt and lemons. Overhead, the sky was a brilliant blue.

Eddy is looking at this very same sun, Hélène thought, and instantly felt ridiculous. That was the kind of sappy thing that heroines of operas sang about—right before they died of a broken heart.

"It was Prince Eddy," she heard herself say.

Amélie's mouth fell open in surprise. "Prince Eddy, as in the future King of England?"

"We don't know any other Prince Eddys. So, yes."

It was a sign of Amélie's shock that she didn't chastise Hélène for the sarcasm. She just stared at her, droplets of water gathering in her dark eyebrows. "All those letters you got were from *him?*"

Eddy knew Hélène well enough to guess she would run to her sister. He'd written a series of letters to her in Portugal, begging her to change her mind.

If only Hélène could risk a reply.

"You'd better start at the beginning," Amélie said incredulously. So Hélène told her.

She explained how last year, she and Eddy had begun seeing each other in secret. They met up late at night, at the rooms he kept in London for that exact purpose, or at crowded parties, where they stole away for a few illicit moments. Eddy wasn't the first man Hélène had been involved with—earlier, she'd had an affair with Laurent, her family's coachman.

"*Laurent?*" Amélie interrupted. "I had no idea!"

"It started after you were married." Hélène waited for Amélie to scold her, but her sister just lifted a hand from the water, gesturing for her to continue.

Eventually, Hélène and Eddy had realized that their relationship was far more than a fling. They loved each other. When Eddy proposed, Hélène had been elated—except that Eddy wasn't free to marry. At least not according to his grandmother Queen Victoria, who had already matched him with Princess Alix of Hesse. And Her Majesty's opinion was the only one that mattered.

Eddy's request to court Hélène had been met with laughter at first. As his grandmother had reminded him, Hélène was a princess without a country, a princess whose value on the marriage market was a matter of constant debate. But then Hélène had done the impossible, and convinced Queen Victoria to give them her blessing.

Until May of Teck ruined everything.

Somehow May had intercepted a letter from Laurent to Hélène. She was now using it as blackmail, threatening to show the highly incriminating letter to Queen Victoria unless Hélène ended things with Eddy.

So at the wedding in Athens, Hélène had told Eddy that she'd changed her mind, and couldn't convert to the Church of England, as she'd promised. As a future Queen of England would need to do.

Eddy hadn't flinched. He'd just reached for her hand and said, *I'll renounce my place in the line of succession.*

He'd offered to give up the throne for her, and still Hélène had turned him down.

She wanted so desperately to tell him the truth. But she feared that it would ruin everything—that Eddy's impulsive temper would get the better of him, and he would confront May head-on. He might succeed in exposing May's cruelty, but in the process, he would inevitably expose Hélène's secret. And then she could relinquish any hope of marrying him; because a formerly Catholic queen was one thing, but a queen who was not a virgin . . . Queen Victoria would *never* allow it.

No, Hélène needed to keep this mess to herself, and let Eddy go on thinking that she'd left him. It was their only hope of ever being together.

When she finished her story, Amélie was silent. Hélène braced herself for her sister's judgment. She doubted that her sister had even *kissed* Carlos before their wedding night, let alone slept with him—and as for Laurent, Amélie wouldn't have dreamed of it.

But to Hélène's surprise, her sister swam forward and flung her wet arms around Hélène's shoulders, her tiptoes perched on the ocean floor.

"You cannot keep blaming yourself," Amélie murmured. "Do not regret anything you did out of love, all right?"

Hélène's eyes stung. It must be from the salt water, because she couldn't be shedding any more tears over her mistakes.

When Amélie drew back, her hair had utterly fallen from its knot, damp tresses floating like seaweed over the waves. "I can't believe May did such a thing! You know, I used to feel *sorry* for her, showing up at parties in those awful old dresses. When, the entire time, she wasn't just a shy relation of the Waleses; she was a—a lying, two-faced *snake*!"

Hélène was a bit startled to hear such vehemence from Amélie, who rarely spoke ill of anyone. "Now you understand why I can't go home."

"But that's exactly why you must. Did you hear what you just said? You called England *home*."

Hélène hadn't even registered her own words. She had lived in England since she was fourteen, yet she'd never thought of it as home until now. Until she fell in love with Eddy.

It hurt, thinking of him—of how his eyes lit on hers across a crowded ballroom. The impatient warmth in his voice when he said her name. The sensation that the world had become sharper, or brighter, or somehow vaster, simply because he was in it.

"You love him," Amélie observed, watching Hélène's face.

"I do."

A cloud scuttled across the sun, breaking the light that danced over the ocean. Hélène splayed her fingers on the water as if she might catch the shadows in her grasp.

"If you love him, you cannot let May win. You need to take action," Amélie told her.

"But the only safe action is to do nothing!" Hélène splashed her hands angrily into the water. "If anyone learned about me and Laurent, I'd be ruined, and our family in the bargain. Papa would never get his throne back."

"Why not?"

"Because I would have shattered our reputation!"

"You should have more faith in our family." There was a new determination in Amélie's voice. "People have been trying to destroy us for centuries, yet here we are! We survived burning palaces and revolutions; we survived mad kings and corrupt kings and a hundred years of war with England. You really think that one little affair with a coachman would bring down our dynasty, when even the guillotine didn't end us?"

Hélène stared at Amélie with something like awe. "You can be quite frightening, you know."

"Motherhood tends to make women into the scariest versions of themselves," Amélie said ruefully. Her hand drifted to her belly, and Hélène's eyebrows shot up.

"You're pregnant again?"

"I think so. It's still early days, though."

Hélène hugged her sister again, more gently this time; even as a strange, bittersweet sensation seized her. She adored her sister, but it felt like their lives were diverging. Amélie was so settled, happy with her husband and her son, and now another baby on the way. While Hélène was confused about most everything.

"Speaking with maternal wisdom, you need to go back," Amélie insisted.

Hélène blew out a breath. "I'm scared. As long as May knows about me and Laurent, I don't dare antagonize her."

"You mean, as long as May has *proof* about you and Laurent. Without the letter, her allegations are nothing but slander, and will hurt her as much as they hurt you."

Amélie was right. Without Laurent's letter, all May could do was gossip—and Hélène could fight against that.

"You need to let May think she's won," Amélie mused aloud. "Once she believes you've given up on Eddy, she'll lower her guard. Then you can find a way to outwit her, and get your letter back."

Hélène turned and began swimming with strong, clean strokes toward the shore, no longer caring about the ridiculous bathing machine. What did it matter if anyone happened to see her in her wet bloomers?

"What are you doing?" Amélie called out.

"I'm going to England!" Hélène needed to pack her things, book herself on the next ship to Portsmouth. And she should write to Alix. The two of them had exchanged a few letters since that night in Athens, when they had confessed their secrets while watching the fireworks.

Well, *Hélène* had confessed her secrets. Alix had explained that she loved someone whose parents disapproved of her, but she'd never admitted his name.

Hélène heard an exasperated laugh behind her. Amélie was splashing along in her wake, the bathing machine left behind like the hull of an abandoned ship. Then the two sisters were running, waves breaking around them as they sprinted, dripping wet, onto the beach.

Amélie was right. The Orléans dynasty was made of fighters, of survivors.

If May of Teck wanted a fight—well then, a fight Hélène would give her.

CHAPTER TWO

May

MAY OF TECK PRIDED HERSELF ON SEIZING EVERY CHANCE TO further her own cause, even if it meant attending an industrial fair.

"Oh, look, ice cream!" Princess Maud tugged May toward a cart with a striped umbrella. May forced an agreeable smile, though she hadn't come to an exposition hall in South Kensington to eat dessert. She was here because this event was sponsored by the Prince of Wales, and she'd hoped that meant Eddy might come, too.

So far, all she'd done was stroll the exhibit hall with Eddy's sister Maud, feigning interest in galvanized electrical wire and new types of phonographs.

"Can I offer you some ice cream? I've kept it stored for over ten days in my new icebox, without replenishing the ice!" The man at the cart prattled on about some new insulation he'd invented, explaining that iceboxes would someday be powered by electricity. "Then we won't need to haul ice down from the mountains at all!"

"Electrically powered iceboxes. Can you imagine?" Maud murmured, reaching for a cup of ice cream.

May couldn't imagine. Her family was down to a single

icebox. The ice delivery cart—laden with slabs of ice packed in straw, which were chiseled off at each house and charged by weight—now only drove by White Lodge once a week. The Tecks had to store all their perishables in the same tiny icebox, cramming the dairy alongside the meats. It was one of her father's many complaints that their butter smelled like fish.

She turned to Maud, ignoring the man's offer of ice cream. "You must be so excited for your parents' party next month. To be married twenty-five years! What a milestone."

May's parents had celebrated their own silver anniversary with a luncheon they couldn't afford. They hadn't given each other gifts—they had long ago stopped doing so—but Her Majesty had given a lovely watch bracelet to Mary Adelaide. May sometimes caught her father staring at it with a sour expression, as if he blamed the bracelet for everything that had gone wrong in his marriage.

By contrast, the Waleses would mark their quarter century of marriage with a formal ball at Marlborough House, which half of Europe's royalty would probably attend.

"It's always quite awful when Mother throws a ball," Maud admitted. "Just yesterday she and Father were arguing about how big the tent should be."

May doubted that Maud would call her parents' discussion an *argument* if she knew what went on in the Teck house. Then she registered the rest of Maud's sentence. A tent, for an evening party? The Waleses must be planning an even larger guest list than she'd realized.

For a fleeting moment, May missed her friend Agnes, an American heiress with a wicked sense of humor and a closet full of breathtaking gowns. Agnes would have lent her the perfect dress for this party.

Except that Agnes wasn't actually May's friend. From the beginning Agnes had been using her as a stepping stone: hoping May could propel her upward in her endless, relentless social climb.

"If there's a tent, your parents must be expecting guests from out of town," she said carefully. This was what she really wanted to know—which other princesses would be in attendance at the silver anniversary.

In other words, who her competition for Eddy might be.

"Mormor and Morfar," Maud replied, using awful Danish nicknames for her maternal grandparents, the King and Queen of Denmark. "Aunt Minnie said she hopes to come, but I'm afraid she'll end up stuck in St. Petersburg. And of course there's no chance of Uncle Sasha making the journey."

May felt a stab of jealousy, hearing Maud refer to the Tsar Alexander as *Uncle Sasha*. She wasn't as excruciatingly royal as Maud, but she was part of the royal family, too—her great-grandfather was King George III! Yet she felt excluded from the network that Maud spoke of so effortlessly, this skein of intertwined connections that gave Maud access to every crowned head in Europe.

"What about Alix?" May asked.

Maud handed her empty bowl and spoon back to the ice cream man, who dropped them into a tub of soapy water. She shrugged. "Perhaps? No one ever knows when Alix and her brother are coming from Darmstadt."

May wasn't especially worried about Alix. Last year, she had ensured that the Hessian princess would never marry

Eddy by spreading word about Alix's fainting spells. A harsh move, perhaps, but Alix did suffer from a weak constitution. It didn't count as gossip if it was true. . . . Right?

May knew she wasn't anyone's first choice as future queen. Queen Victoria would have preferred Alix; Eddy had wanted Hélène. But neither princess was currently in London. Her Majesty had already slid further down the list of eligible brides than she'd expected—surely, eventually, she would remember that May was an option too?

Of course, it all came down to the question of Hélène.

May hadn't seen her in months, since the wedding of Princess Sophie and Prince Constantine. She suspected that Hélène was hiding with one of her relatives, probably her sister, worried that May would reveal her explosive secret.

May hadn't actually been the one to blackmail Hélène; Agnes had written the letter without telling her. But now it was done. Given Hélène's continued absence from London, May couldn't help feeling just the slightest bit grateful for Agnes's interference.

At the sound of a commotion, May and Maud glanced over. A man with a thick mustache waved enthusiastically from a platform several feet above the ground.

"The Otis elevator! The safest lift in the world, as seen at the World's Fair in Paris!" The man gestured to the machine on his left. It resembled a closet with three walls, connected to a series of pulleys and ropes and wheels.

"I've heard of elevators! They are like dumbwaiters, but for people," May exclaimed, momentarily forgetting to hide the fact that she read the newspapers. Luckily, Maud didn't seem to notice.

"What a strange contraption." Maud tilted her head, studying it. "I can't imagine anyone would choose that box over a staircase. It looks quite devoid of air."

May could have pointed out that one side of the elevator box was open, letting in plenty of air, or that many people found it impossible to walk up a staircase. In fact, Queen Victoria had taken to riding in her wheelchair more often lately.

But May was distracted by a flash of dark hair near the elevator. "Your brother is here?"

"I didn't know George was coming!" Maud followed May's gaze, and cast her a puzzled look. "I'm sorry, did you mean Eddy?"

"Yes, Eddy," May said awkwardly. She must not have been very discreet last year, when she and George had developed a friendship—which May had, for a foolish moment, thought was more.

At least George himself seemed ignorant of her feelings. He had made it abundantly clear that his inclinations toward May were strictly friendly, that he wanted to marry his younger cousin Missy once she came of age. And he would almost certainly get permission to do so. George was a second son, and could follow his heart.

Eddy, on the other hand, would have to marry whomever his grandmother selected for him. May just needed to ensure that Queen Victoria chose *her.*

"Father dragged Eddy along," Maud explained after a beat. "Said that if he had to deal with these freakish scientific types all afternoon, then Eddy did, too. I think he was surprised that I wanted to come," Maud added, "though I'm glad you suggested it."

May craned her neck. Sure enough, the Prince of Wales stood a few steps behind his son, his features glazed with boredom. Or perhaps he was simply nursing a hangover.

Through wordless agreement, she and Maud started toward the man at the elevator.

"Of course, powered hoists have been around for years, used to lift building materials in construction," the man with the mustache called out. "The elevator is something different! Imagine how high buildings might soar if we were no longer limited to staircases." He grinned. "Now, who is willing to test this marvelous invention?"

A crowd of several dozen people stood around the elevator in a loose semicircle. Men in morning suits glanced at one other with amused expressions, as if daring their friends to complete the challenge; women gasped in shock and held tight to their parasols or their children's hands.

"I'll do it." Prince Eddy stepped forward.

The crowd roared in approval. May wondered how many of them recognized the young man before them, in his lightweight gray coat with a checked vest beneath, as their future king. It wasn't as if the newspapers printed his photograph with any regularity.

"Thank you, sir!" The elevator man beamed. That *sir*, instead of the customary *Your Royal Highness*, revealed his total cluelessness about Eddy's identity.

But Eddy didn't flinch. He smiled slightly, as if the lack of title didn't bother him—as if he was almost pleased by it.

"Anyone else?" the man asked, scanning the crowds once more.

Before May could quite think it through, she lifted a hand into the air. "I volunteer as well."

"May!" Maud grabbed at her wrist. "What are you doing? You aren't acting like yourself!"

She *wasn't* acting like herself, truth be told. And perhaps that was a good thing. If she wanted to get Eddy's attention, May needed to stop acting like herself and start acting like Hélène.

There was no doubt in May's mind that the French princess would have climbed up there without hesitation.

She met Eddy's gaze, and was gratified to see that she'd surprised him.

"Welcome aboard." The man held out a hand, helping her to step up next to Eddy on the enclosed platform.

They heard the hissing sound of a steam engine. Then the gears overhead turned, lifting the elevator box off the ground.

May had never believed in magic; she'd always rolled her eyes at children's stories about fairies and mermaids. But rising into the air like this made her think, uncharacteristically, of a magic carpet.

"We're flying," she whispered.

"You aren't frightened?" Eddy must have been talking to May, though his eyes were fixed on the distance.

"Not really." There were plenty of things in this world to be frightened of. An elevator machine simply wasn't one of them.

Eddy turned. "Is that why you volunteered to come up, then? Because you wanted to fly?"

I'm here because it gives me an otherwise-impossible opportunity to be alone with you.

"I came for the same reason you did," she declared. "I was curious."

Eddy gave a huff of what might have been amusement. "You give me more credit than I deserve. I volunteered to ride the elevator because I wanted to get away from my father."

They were at least fifteen feet above the ground now. May could see the tops of the gentlemen's hats, little gleaming black circles when viewed from above, a stark contrast to the women's bonnets with their curling pastel ribbons.

"Why are you avoiding your father?"

It was a bold question. But something about this situation—looking down on the crowds from the vantage point of birds—made it feel less intrusive than normal.

"He's been rather hard to deal with lately. He and Grandmother are trying to pin me down on the subject of . . ." Eddy hesitated. "My future."

May knew what that meant. They were pushing him to marry.

"I should think your future is rather clear. You'll be king someday," she replied, her tone falsely flippant.

"I think the more pressing question is, who will be the queen?"

May couldn't help a sharp intake of breath at his bluntness.

"There was—there is—someone. But I'm not sure she will have me." Eddy seemed to have half forgotten that May was here; he was staring into the distance again, his words quiet. "She loves me; I know she does. There are just so many obstacles."

He was clearly talking about Hélène. May felt a wave of relief that her strategy had worked, and she'd successfully scared off the French princess.

"And now Her Majesty is trying to suggest other . . . options?" May asked as tactfully as she could.

"Exactly. You know what she can be like." Eddy flashed her a grateful look.

May resisted the urge to grab him by the shoulders and shake him. *I'm right here*, she wanted to scream. *Don't you see?* But of course, Eddy never saw much of anything, even when it was directly in front of him.

The elevator machine was still ascending. May dared a glance down at the ground, then regretted it.

"It helps if you pick a focal point. Something distant, like that lantern on the far wall," Eddy suggested. "Don't look down, or it will only make you more afraid."

May kept her gaze fixed on the ironwork lantern he'd indicated, trying to ignore her sudden prickling of fear. "Is this something you learned when you climbed the Himalayas?"

"On sailboats. I like climbing up to untie the knots. I've never actually climbed the Himalayas," Eddy added, "though I did climb the pyramids at Giza. From the top you can see the Sphinx."

"Did she ask you a riddle?"

"Who?"

Once again, May had blundered, letting her cleverness slip out. She should have known a reference to mythology would have been lost on Eddy.

"Are the pyramids haunted?" she asked, rapidly changing tack. "I've heard there are ghosts there."

"You believe in ghosts?" Eddy teased.

"Of course I do. I heard them at Balmoral last summer."

That startled a laugh from him. "I'm sure it was Grandfather.

He haunts the ballroom, where all those deer heads he shot still hang."

"Are you sure he doesn't haunt the upstairs corridor? Because my room was absolutely frigid."

"That's just how Scotland feels at night. You'll get used to it." Before she could wonder what Eddy meant by that—did he think she'd be invited again this year?—he sighed. "Sometimes I think this whole country is founded on ghosts. We all seem to be doing things for the benefit of people who are long since dead."

Now it was May's turn to glance at him in surprise. That might have been the most eloquent thing she'd ever heard Eddy say.

"When you're king, everything you do will be for the living. Mostly for people you've never met."

The elevator came to a stop. May tried, and failed, to keep her gaze on the iron lantern Eddy had indicated. They were just so high. Even with walls surrounding three sides of this box, she felt like she might tumble to the ground at any minute.

"Our fearless volunteers are forty feet aboveground!" the elevator man shouted. "And now I will demonstrate the safety brakes that make the Otis model so unique."

May's head whipped toward Eddy. "Safety brakes?"

"It'll be fine," Eddy said, which wasn't particularly helpful. "Remember when you thought it was magic?"

"That was when we were still close to the ground!"

May was too high up to see the elevator man, but later she would hear Maud recount how he had drawn a sword ("A real old-fashioned one, like my grandfather used to have!"), waved the sword with a dramatic flourish, and cut the cable holding the elevator aloft.

All she knew in that moment was that the floor had fallen out from beneath her.

May's skirts swooped upward, her stomach flying up to somewhere in her throat. She closed her eyes, scrabbling for anything to grab hold of—

The box shuddered to a screeching halt, and May realized that her body was pressed against Eddy's, her hands grabbing the walls to either side of his waist.

"It's perfectly safe!" the elevator man boomed. "Even if the cord is damaged, the safety brakes will engage, ensuring that no one falls to the ground. . . ."

May rapidly disentangled herself from Eddy and took a step back, only to realize with surprise that he was smiling. Inexplicably, he'd thought that was *fun*.

Hélène would probably have thought the same thing.

"I take it the safety brakes were more than you bargained for?" His voice was teasing, but gently so.

"A little," she admitted. "But I'm glad I did it."

When the elevator car descended, everyone swept forward, peppering them with questions and exclaiming how brave they'd been. Eddy's identity must have been revealed while he and May were in the air, because there was also a lot of bowing and *Your Royal Highness*ing. Eddy's little adventure had, May thought, helped deflect attention from how useless the Prince of Wales was as a royal scientific patron.

"You were up so high! How did it feel?" Maud asked, hurrying toward May. "Did it give you a new perspective on things?"

May stole a glance back at Eddy. As if he felt her eyes on him, he met her gaze and grinned knowingly. There was nothing romantic or intimate about it; it was the sort of look you might give a friend, someone with whom you had shared a joke.

Well, she had to start somewhere.

May turned to answer Maud's question. "How astute of you. Yes, being in the elevator gave me an entirely new perspective."

CHAPTER THREE

Alix

"CAN I JOIN YOU?"

Alix of Hesse set aside the sketchbook she'd been holding. "Of course," she told her brother, who dropped down to sit next to her. Insects buzzed in the air around them, which was filled with the fresh growing scents of spring, tender green shoots peeking up through the earth.

"How long have you been out here?" Ernie asked.

"A few hours?" When she'd come into the gardens, the sun had hovered above the ivy-covered brick wall; now it was nearly overhead. But then, Alix was always losing track of time. She would fall headfirst into whatever she was doing, a novel or a sketch or a piece on the piano, and the hours melted away like candle wax.

That must be one of the reasons she'd made a poor impression at the Russian court. Everything there ran on such a regimented schedule: meals served at the stroke of the hour, appointments carved into little thirty-minute blocks. It was maddening.

Ernie leaned over to study her sketch. "Did you start this last night?"

Belatedly, Alix realized that she'd drawn the scene before

her with heavy strokes of charcoal. Moody shadows crept across its surface, a bruised sky looming overhead—nothing like the sunny garden that surrounded them.

"I wanted to draw a stormy day," she replied, though Ernie wasn't fooled. He knew the reason her mind felt turbulent, alternating between hope and despair.

Alix hurried to change the subject, nodding in the direction of the stables. "Were you out riding this morning?"

"Oh—no," Ernie said, almost evasively. "But I might go later, if you want to join."

"Maybe." Alix fiddled with her charcoal stub, leaving gray streaks across the back of her knuckles. Her grandmother—Queen Victoria, the most powerful monarch in all the world, except, perhaps, the Russian tsar—would have scolded Alix for her messy hands. But Grandmama and all her advice, not to mention her meddling, were far off in England.

Church bells clanged from the Stadtkirche just across the road. Alix always felt at ease here in Darmstadt, with its cobblestone streets and gabled roofs. Her family's "palace" was really just a spacious home, no more ostentatious than any of the massive residences in London's new fashionable neighborhood of Mayfair. But then, as grand duke of the minor German territory of Hesse, Alix's father wielded little political influence.

Ernie was staring at the row of linden trees along the far wall. He looked so much like Alix; they both had their mother's blond hair and sky-blue eyes. But their similarity was more than physical. It was a dreaminess in their expressions, the distracted way they both moved through the world, as if their interior dialogues were more interesting than what others had to say.

"Don't move," Alix commanded, crossing her legs beneath her dress in a distinctly unladylike manner.

Ernie gave a beleaguered sigh. "Must I be your model now?"

"I'm sorry, did you have other plans for the afternoon?" Alix had already pulled out a new sheet of paper.

"My plans involved napping." Ernie leaned back so that he was lying on the sun-warmed grass, folding his arms behind his head. "If you insist on drawing me, it will be like this. You can title it *Arthurian Knight in an Enchanted Sleep*."

Alix snorted. "Arthurian knight? More like, *Prince Ernest of Hesse, Sleeping Through the Sermon at Church*."

"I only did that once! And you must admit, Father Anton is excruciatingly dull."

"What does it matter if he's dull? It's church, not the music hall. You aren't there for entertainment."

Ernie huffed in drowsy protest and shut his eyes.

Silence fell as Alix's pencil darted over the paper. She had no burning artistic ambition; she'd learned the basics of drawing, like any other well-bred young woman. But she'd always found something soothing in the ritual of it: sitting, arranging the pencils in a neat row, quieting her mind. Looking at a person and reducing their face to a study in line and form and shadow, rather than fretting over their opinions of you.

Soon the paper was covered in swooping pencil marks that captured Ernie's eyelashes, the lock of hair falling onto his forehead. After a few moments he began to snore. A breeze rippled the surface of the water in a nearby fountain. Years ago the fountain had held live goldfish, which Alix and her siblings would scoop up with their hands, giggling at their sliminess. Their mother, Alice, would laugh, encouraging their daring.

They'd had such fun here: playing games of blind man's bluff, packing fresh-baked pies or bilberries and cream and picnicking out on the grass. Sometimes they would pile into a cart and ride out into the countryside, delivering baskets of bread or medicine to the sleepy little villages, where fields of poppies waved next to acres of golden corn.

Alix had lost her mother when she was six years old, yet some memories remained achingly fresh in her mind. She recalled how she used to slip into Alice's dressing room on the nights her parents went out. *Here, try it on*, Alice would urge, helping her daughter into oversized gowns and furs, threading jewels into her bright blond hair. *Look at you*, her mother would murmur, pressing a hand to the center of Alix's chest. *You are so beautiful on the outside, but most of all you are beautiful here. In your heart.*

"Miss?"

Alix put down her pencil and glanced up in surprise. A few feet away stood Johann, the new footman, holding a pile of envelopes in his gloved hand. His eyes flicked to Ernie before he flushed and addressed Alix.

"Pardon me, miss, but you requested that I bring the day's mail to you at once. It just arrived."

"Thank you." Alix nearly jumped to her feet, reaching for the mail so eagerly that she knocked Johann off-kilter.

"Anything from Russia?" Ernie lifted himself onto one elbow, rubbing sleepily at his eyes, but his question was serious.

Johann bowed and retreated. Alix fanned through the mail, but there was only a letter marked with Hélène's typical scribble. Not the handwriting she was looking for. "Nothing from Russia," she said meaningfully.

Alix didn't know how she and Nicholas would ever get his parents' permission to marry. It felt so impossible, and yet she couldn't bring herself to give up hope. Not entirely.

She hadn't *meant* to fall for the Tsarevich of Russia. Things would have been so much easier if she could have been happy with Eddy, the prince everyone expected her to marry. But the moment she'd seen Nicholas last year, standing outside the Winter Palace to greet her carriage, Alix had been a lost cause. It was like she'd been struck by some new illness—Alix was no stranger to ailments of the body—except that instead of making her weak, this one strengthened her. Loving Nicholas made Alix feel acutely alive, bright and wondrous and full of possibility.

When he'd proposed, Alix had said yes with hardly a moment's hesitation.

His parents, however, had been less than thrilled at the news. *You will never marry Nicholas, not while I have breath in my body*, the tsar had roared at Alix, at the wedding in Athens last fall.

Devastated, Alix had run outside, where she'd found Hélène in similar distress. It turned out they had the same problem, both unable to be with the man they loved. *We'll fight for them*, Alix had told Hélène that night. But . . . how? It seemed impossible.

Then Alix had returned to Darmstadt, and the letters had started to come.

Nicholas couldn't write regularly, but the notes he did manage to send were so utterly *him*—so intelligent, so thoughtful—that Alix felt like he was right there with her. Even if he was thousands of miles away. *We will change my parents' minds*, Nicholas repeated in each letter. *I know we will find a way forward, as long as your feelings for me haven't changed.*

Of course they hadn't changed. Alix cherished his letters, reread them so often that they tore at the creases. She loved Nicholas so much that it frightened her.

The possibility that she might lose him frightened her more.

"I'm sorry, Alicky," Ernie said quietly. "I know how hard it is."

"It's all right; I'm sure he'll write again soon." Alix paused as her brother's words registered. "Wait—what do you mean, you know how hard it is?" Was Ernie also in love with someone he couldn't be with?

"Just that all this pressure to marry is awful," Ernie said quickly, and smiled. "Really, Alix, I need you to find a way to marry Nicholas so that Grannie will stop pestering me. She and Papa keep demanding that I marry, insisting that the duchy needs an heir. Speaking of which . . ." He held out a letter in Alix's direction. "Grannie wrote."

Ernie and George were probably the only grandchildren who'd ever called Queen Victoria *Grannie*. Even Alix had always used *Grandmama*.

"I assume she wants to plan our summer trip?" Alix asked. The prospect of going to England again, as she and Ernie had done practically every year of their lives, felt suddenly wearying. There was no question of her marrying Eddy anymore; perhaps she could stay away for a year, let Hélène fight for Eddy as best she could.

"Grannie says that Uncle Bertie and Aunt Alexandra are having a party for their silver wedding anniversary. She wants us there." Ernie glanced over. "I think we should go, for your sake."

"For my sake?" Alix asked, confused.

"Grannie didn't exactly send me the guest list, but the tsar and tsarina will surely be invited."

The Tsarina of Russia and the Princess of Wales were sisters, the two princesses of Denmark who had married princes of the world's two greatest nations. Which meant that Eddy and George were Nicholas's first cousins.

"I doubt they'll make it," Alix pointed out. The tsar didn't leave Russia for anything less than a state occasion. A wedding, a coronation, perhaps even a funeral; but not an anniversary. No matter how much his beloved wife begged him to.

"Exactly my point. They won't be able to go, but someone needs to attend as the Romanov representative," Ernie pressed.

Alix's heart leapt. "You think Nicholas might be there?"

"Grannie didn't say as much in her letter, but then, she wouldn't." Ernie knew how much Queen Victoria disapproved of Alix's feelings for Nicholas. He gave Alix a nudge, nodding at Hélène's letter. "Now, what does mademoiselle have to say?"

"You're so nosy," Alix scolded, amused. She scanned the letter and looked up sharply. "Hélène says she is heading back to England!"

"Which means she'll probably be at the party, too," Ernie observed.

Alix stood, brushing off her long skirts. A smile stole over her features at the thought of seeing her friend—and the prospect, however slim, of being with Nicholas. "Very well, write to Grandmama and tell her yes. We're going back."

CHAPTER FOUR

Hélène

HÉLÈNE HAD BECOME ENOUGH OF AN ENGLISHWOMAN NOT TO mind a bit of rain. Not even a wild thunderstorm at sea.

"We should have gone from Calais," grumbled Antonia, the lady's maid whom Amélie had sent to chaperone Hélène back to England. Hélène didn't bother acknowledging that remark. They both knew that it was impossible for an Orléans to set foot in France. Hélène was forced to travel from Portugal to England through the rougher waters of the Atlantic, instead of the calmer winds of the English Channel.

Not that she minded. Hélène had always been tough of nerves—*a sailor's stomach*, her brother Philippe had said approvingly, that fateful day they were exiled from France. Hélène's mother and sister had spent the journey vomiting into a pair of buckets, but not Hélène. She'd stood at the window, staring out at the rain-lashed waves, wondering what their new life in England would hold.

When Hélène turned to leave their shared cabin, Antonia made an incredulous noise. "You're not going up in this weather?"

"I want to see England." Ignoring Antonia's muttered commentary, Hélène shut the door behind her.

Rain thrummed on the planks of the deck. Hélène lifted

one hand to shield her eyes, not caring that her green traveling dress was getting soaked through. She fixed her gaze determinedly on the horizon, willing the shore of England to appear.

When she finally saw it, a darker shadow against the blurred gray of the ocean, elation seized her chest.

She wiped the rain from her eyes, ignoring the curious glances of the sailors as they prepared the ship for landing. Eddy was standing on that very island. A large island, yes, and he was probably countless miles from her, but he was there all the same. For the first time in months, she would be within reach of him.

When they disembarked at Portsmouth, Hélène saw a waiting carriage emblazoned with her family crest. Thank goodness her parents had sent for her; Antonia would have complained at a hired hackney. Hélène hurried to throw open the carriage door—only to blink at the figure of her mother.

"Try not to track too much water inside." Marie Isabelle reached for a dry cloak that was folded on the opposite seat, as if she'd expected Hélène to show up bedraggled and rain-soaked. "We're headed to Farleigh, to stay with the earl. You've brought one of Amélie's maidservants with you, yes? She can go in the second carriage, with the luggage." Marie Isabelle gestured for her daughter to take the seat opposite her.

"I didn't know you were coming, Mother." As Hélène stepped inside, water dripped down the folds of her skirts, pooling on the carriage floor.

"I need to speak with you. I'm afraid it's a matter of some urgency."

Hélène's hands, which were fumbling to unwrap the dry cloak, fell still. "Is Father all right?"

"Your papa is fine. Though I must admit, he was devastated

to learn about you and Prince Eddy," her mother admonished. "Philippe had grown rather fond of the idea that his grandson would be King of England. I think he secretly hoped that child might unite England and France again, the way they were in the fifteenth century."

"As if that worked out the first time," Hélène muttered.

The carriage jolted forward, and her mother sighed. "Why didn't you tell us that you and Eddy had broken off the engagement? Philippe found out during a *card game*, when the Prince of Wales mentioned his regrets that you had ended things. I believe your father would have happily forced you to go through with it," her mother continued, "except that the Prince of Wales seemed to have abandoned the whole notion. Needless to say, Philippe lost a small fortune in that hand."

"I'm sorry," Hélène said curtly. She was grappling with too much heartache to worry about her parents' disappointment.

Marie Isabelle stared at her. "What happened, Hélène? And don't give me that nonsense about your religious change of heart. Your father might believe you don't want to convert, but I know better. I saw what you and Eddy were like together."

Hélène stared out the carriage's small window. The scene outside was blurry, rain still drumming on the uneven paving stones. Where was Eddy right now? What was he thinking?

"I can't explain what happened with Eddy," she said helplessly, though a part of her longed to. She had a sudden urge to lay her head on her mother's shoulder and sob like a child. To confess everything, as she had with Amélie.

Marie Isabelle's eyes narrowed. "Did he hurt you? If he

did, I'll head straight to London and rip him limb from limb, future king or no."

"Of course not! There were . . . obstacles," Hélène said at last.

"Obstacles," her mother repeated. When Hélène said nothing, she sighed. "And these obstacles were not religious in nature?"

"No." There was no use elaborating, not when she couldn't tell the whole story.

Her mother leaned back. "That's a relief, at least. I'm afraid you must abandon this insistence that you cannot convert."

Hélène looked up sharply. "I told you, I cannot announce an engagement to Eddy." At least not until she'd figured out how to handle May.

"I'm not talking about Eddy," her mother said levelly. "It's your father. He's already considering a new match for you."

Hélène's gown felt suddenly chilly, its damp fabric clinging to her rib cage. She wrapped her arms around her chest, angry that she hadn't seen this coming.

Her parents had happily agreed she could marry for love—when the man in question was a future King of England. And now that Eddy was no longer an option, they would still expect her to marry.

She was a princess, an arrow in the Orléans quiver. An item for trade that they would ship off to some other family, hoping to gain support in their never-ending quest to reclaim the throne.

"I won't do it," Hélène said stubbornly. "I'll scream all the way to the altar. This isn't the sixteenth century anymore, Mother. No priest will marry me against my will."

Her mother made a sound that was half exasperation, half amusement. "Nothing has been decided yet. I just wanted you to be aware that your father has begun discussing it."

Marie Isabelle was trying to help, Hélène realized. To warn her.

"Thank you," she said softly.

She spent the rest of the drive staring at the gleaming brass hinges of the carriage door, sorting through her mental family trees. Who might her father be in talks with? The Spanish prince was too young, just a baby, and what had her mother meant by *you must abandon this insistence that you cannot convert*? Was her father in discussions with one of the Protestant royal families? Prince Carl of Denmark and Prince Gustav of Sweden were both of the right age. Hélène highly doubted that her father would gravitate toward a German, though she supposed it was possible. Everyone always said wonderful things about that one German prince in particular . . . Maximilian of Baden, wasn't it?

No matter. Whomever he decided to match her with, Hélène would refuse to even consider it.

And then, as soon as she judged it safe—as soon as she was certain that her history with Laurent wouldn't explode into public knowledge—Hélène would find Eddy, and tell him that her heart was still his.

That it always had been.

CHAPTER FIVE

May

"LORD JESUS CHRIST, ALL OF CREATION IS FILLED WITH THE LIGHT of your grace." The archbishop held out his hands, causing the bell-shaped sleeves of his robe to flutter. "Dispel the darkness of our hearts, and forgive our sins and selfishness."

"Lord, forgive us." May recited the words along with the rest of the congregation, though she wasn't sure she agreed. Lately, she'd come to think that selfishness was an asset.

Sunshine filtered through the stained-glass windows behind the altar, making the waters of the baptismal font seem to glow with color. They were in the Chapel Royal at St. James's Palace, a gem of a space with its coffered ceiling, its massive tapestries and gold cornices. Half a century earlier, Queen Victoria had wed Prince Albert here.

This was where May would marry Eddy someday, if her plans succeeded.

Today the royal family was gathered for a baptism, not a wedding. Princess Louise—the older of Eddy and George's two sisters—stood next to her husband, the Duke of Fife, holding a bundle of lace and white silk.

"Your Grace, Your Royal Highness," the archbishop called out, gesturing to the parents. "Please present the candidate for baptism."

The couple stepped forward, exchanging the same adoring smiles that May had seen at their wedding. So much had happened to her since then. She'd set her sights on Prince Eddy, fallen for his brother George, realized that those feelings for George were hopeless. And now here she was, right back where she'd started. Living under her parents' roof and desperate to get out.

May stole a glance across the chapel. Apparently, Uncle Alfred—Queen Victoria's second son—was here, along with his wife, Marie, and their two daughters, Missy and Victoria Melita, known in the family as Ducky. May craned her neck, but she couldn't see much of Missy except a few dark curls. She was hidden behind her taller, ganglier sister.

May and her mother would have gotten better seats if they'd arrived on time, but of course, Mary Adelaide had been running late. If only May could have come alone. Her mother was so gauche and loud, always singing the hymns woefully off-key. But May needed a chaperone, and Mary Adelaide, at least, wasn't cruel.

May tugged her sleeve farther down her arm, hiding the spot where her father had grabbed her the other day. A nasty little bruise was blossoming there. Francis had always been vicious with his words, but now his anger had grown physical: he might hold her wrist harder than was necessary, or press fingers sharply into her flesh. He hadn't actually *hit* her yet, but May figured it was only a matter of time.

She had to get out of his house, and fast.

At the baptismal font, the godparents—the Prince and Princess of Wales and the queen herself—stepped forward. Queen Victoria held out her hands, and Louise obediently passed the baby girl to her great-grandmother. In her beribboned white gown frothing with lace, a cap tied over her head, the infant looked more like a parcel than a person.

Lucky girl, getting the queen herself for a godmother.

The archbishop reached for a ceremonial silver ladle. "I baptize you, Alexandra, in the name of the Father, and of the Son, and of the Holy Spirit."

The girl had been named after her grandmother, Alexandra, the Princess of Wales. May couldn't help thinking that Louise had made a mistake, not calling the baby Victoria.

Though technically speaking, May's parents had named *her* Victoria—she was Victoria Mary, even if she'd always gone by May. And look what good it had done her.

Queen Victoria held the infant with a steady grip as the archbishop drizzled water atop the baby's head. Alexandra blinked in wide-eyed shock, then screwed up her little face and screamed.

The archbishop hurriedly made the sign of the cross over her and bowed to the queen. Victoria passed the baby back to Louise, but little Alexandra just howled all the louder. May saw a few family members exchanging judgmental glances. *That girl is headstrong,* they would whisper later; *like her mother, she'll be trouble.* Whereas if a baby boy had screamed like that, they would have laughed and complimented his healthy set of lungs.

Even as newborns, girls should know how to moderate their voices.

Once the service had ended, everyone streamed outside, flocking around the Wales family. Alexandra looked as quietly beautiful as ever; Bertie grinned proudly next to her, the buttons of his waistcoat straining against his expanding girth. Last winter, he'd actually stopped bothering to fasten the final button. If anyone else had done so, it would have been an embarrassment, but instead the men of London had all followed Bertie's lead. Now tailors were cutting waistcoats to accommodate that final, unhooked button.

"Look, it's Helena!" Mary Adelaide waved to someone. "Should we go say hello?"

"I was hoping to greet the Coburg sisters," May replied. She had a sudden, intense urge to speak with Missy herself. Perhaps she would see why Missy had succeeded where she had failed, and captured George's interest.

Not that May cared anymore. Her feelings for George had been extinguished, as firmly and definitively as snuffing a candle. She'd hardly even seen him in the past few months; soon after Sophie and Tino's wedding he had left on another naval tour.

When she reached the sisters, May smiled through the sour feeling in her chest. Missy was so unfairly pretty, her blue eyes darting around the gathering with avid curiosity. At least May had on a nice dress today: an old one of Agnes's, made of lilac silk with graduated tucks that emphasized her narrow waist.

"Welcome back to England," she said in greeting. "How was your journey?"

"Loud," Missy said cheerfully, nudging her sister's shoulder. "Mama and Ducky fought the whole time."

May glanced at Ducky for an explanation, startled by such bluntness, but Ducky just crossed her arms and glared out the garden gates.

"What are your plans while in London?" May asked after a beat. "Aside from next week's anniversary party, of course."

"I shall go riding," Missy said eagerly. "There's no way Mama can forbid it, not after I spent the winter riding in St. Petersburg with Ducky and Kiril. We got lost in the snow once, and had to—"

"Come now, Missy. May has no desire to hear about our misadventures," Ducky cut in, too quickly. She turned back to May. "I'm sure we'll view some picture galleries while here. Do you have any recommendations?"

"The Earl of Stafford has a lovely collection; he opens his home to friends on Thursday afternoons. How long will you be in town?" May asked.

Missy grinned mischievously. "That depends on Ducky."

Ducky ignored the statement, though something flashed behind her eyes. "A few weeks, most likely."

There was a secret here; May could sense it. Before she could ask more, the two sisters looked at something over May's shoulder, then swept into curtsies.

May curtsied on instinct. She stayed low, her knees bent, until she was staring at the hem of a long black gown.

"Good morning, Missy, Ducky." The queen paused for a fraction of an instant before adding, "And May."

The Coburg girls dutifully replied with "Hello, Grandmother." May waited until they were finished before daring her own greeting. "Good morning, Your Majesty. Congratulations on your new goddaughter." As if Queen Victoria didn't have two dozen godchildren already. "It was a lovely service."

"I'm afraid little Alexandra disagreed. She certainly made her displeasure known." Victoria chuckled indulgently. At moments like this, in her plain black gown and bonnet, she resembled a grandmother more than a queen. But May knew it would be a grave mistake to forget, even for a moment, whom she was speaking with.

Which was why she decided to risk saying, "A healthy baby is such a blessing. It makes one long for a child of one's own."

Missy and Ducky were staring at her with confusion, or perhaps alarm, but May didn't care. She had to do *something* to make Victoria pay attention to her. And waxing eloquent about motherhood seemed a safe bet with a woman who'd done it nine times.

Not that May actually meant what she'd said. She'd never played with baby dolls; she felt no emotional yearning to become a mother. But, of course, a baby was highly useful for one's own security.

A man could get rid of a wife far too easily, by divorcing her, or simply shuffling her off to be "cured" at an asylum, like Lord Mordaunt had recently done to his wife. If you were the mother of an heir, you were a bit safer.

The queen looked at May thoughtfully. "May, Bertie was just telling me about how you and Eddy went into one of those elevator contraptions. Lord Salisbury keeps urging me to install one at Buckingham Palace. He says I'll like the ease of moving from floor to floor without having to walk. Or be carried," Victoria added ruefully. "What do you think? Should I add an elevator?"

May nodded. This was a test, and she hoped she was giving the right answer. "I believe so, Your Majesty."

"Why?"

"Aside from the financial cost, I do not see any drawbacks. Your Majesty is quite implacable; I doubt that an elevator would frighten you. And there are a number of benefits to installing an elevator now. If it is true that this technology will eventually be in all buildings, then the palace should be one of the first to include one. The duty of the Crown is to set an example that the rest of society will follow."

The queen looked at May as if seeing her for the first time. "I quite agree."

For a fleeting instant May thought she had done the impossible, and made a lasting impression on Victoria—but then Victoria dismissed her, turning to the Coburg girls.

"Ducky, would you walk with me?"

Though it was phrased as a question, the words were unmistakably a command. Ducky nodded, letting her grandmother steer her aside.

Directly to Prince Eddy.

May thought of what Missy had said mere minutes ago, when asked how long the sisters would be in town. *That depends on Ducky.*

She tried to sound nonchalant as she asked Missy, "I take it Her Majesty is matchmaking?"

"I know! Poor Ducky," Missy agreed.

"*Poor Ducky?*" May couldn't help it; the words shot out of her like gunfire.

Missy didn't seem to register the sharpness of May's tone. "It would be awful, being told you must marry someone you don't love. Just look how miserable they both are."

Neither young woman made a pretense of subtlety. They both stared at Eddy and Ducky, who were now talking in a forced, polite way.

"He clearly has feelings for someone else," Missy went on. "Do you think it's Alix? I always assumed he would marry her."

"I heard that they were never truly engaged. Or if they were, it didn't work out." May's voice came out admirably calm, given that she wanted to shout in frustration.

What a fool she'd been, thinking that it was enough to eliminate Alix and Hélène. She should have known that another contender would rise up, another match in the endless line of princesses who could be queen.

Missy shrugged. "Perhaps I'm overreacting. It's just that Eddy doesn't seem . . ." She struggled for the right word, then settled on, "Faithful. Not like George."

As she watched Missy glance fondly at George, May felt anger bubbling up within her. It was just so unfair. Missy and Ducky would have a perfect life handed to them, without any effort on their part! One of them was marrying a future king, the other marrying for something as frivolous as *love.* A pair of sisters marrying a pair of brothers? It was like something from a fairy tale.

May wasn't like them, some enchanted princess out of a story. She was less wealthy, less well connected, less *everything* than Missy and Ducky.

But she was here. And she wanted to marry Eddy, more than Ducky seemed to.

Fine, then. She would have to get rid of Ducky, the same way she'd gotten rid of Alix and Hélène. No matter what it took, May would find a way.

She had to keep eliminating her competition, one by one, until she was the last princess standing in this endless, relentless quest to become queen.

CHAPTER SIX

Hélène

THE ORLÉANS CARRIAGE WAS STILL BEHIND AT LEAST FOUR OTHers, part of the long line that wound up to Marlborough House. Ordinarily, Hélène would have been impatient at the delay: tapping her foot, perhaps even slipping out of the carriage to run up the drive herself, skirts in hand. Tonight she was subdued.

Her mother must have noticed, because she leaned over and murmured, "You can turn right around and head back to Sheen House. No one even knows you're in town."

That was precisely the point. Since Hélène had only just arrived back in London, she would catch everyone by surprise. Particularly May of Teck.

When their carriage finally made it to the front, Hélène stepped out quickly, forcing a smile in her parents' direction. "I'll catch up with you both later?"

"Hélène, wait," her father began. She pretended not to hear, hurrying through the grand hallways and onto the back terrace.

It was a glorious party. Colored lanterns hung every few feet, casting the guests in a jewel-toned glow, making them resemble a flock of tropical birds in their silk gowns and gleaming dinner jackets. Star-shaped flowers twined around the iron railing. In the center of the garden stood a marquee tent, where servers carried trays of honey-colored champagne.

"Hélène."

She turned slowly, heart pounding. "Eddy," she managed, though it came out as a whisper. Why had he been waiting near these double doors? Had he been looking for her—or for someone else?

"I hoped you would come," he said, answering her unspoken question. "I told the footmen to let me know if they saw a carriage emblazoned with a fleur-de-lis. When they did, well . . ."

He ventured a step closer, lifting his hand, then lowered it again. That gesture nearly broke Hélène—that after so many nights together, their breaths and bodies intertwined, Eddy now hesitated to touch her.

"Can we talk?" he asked, voice rough.

Hélène darted a glance in each direction. They might feel alone, standing together on the terrace in relative privacy, but at a party this crowded, you never knew who might be watching.

"Not now," Hélène said helplessly. "There are so many things I need to—"

"Hélène!"

At the sound of her father's voice, she and Eddy both stood up a little straighter. Hélène hadn't even realized they were leaning toward each other, drawn together like plants desperate for sunlight.

"Your Royal Highness," Philippe said stiffly, in Eddy's direction. "You'll forgive me, but I require my daughter's presence."

Eddy cast Hélène a beseeching glance. If only she could give him a nod, a whispered *I love you.* But Hélène didn't dare, not when May was probably nearby.

Not when the secret that could ruin everything was still in her enemy's possession.

She and her father didn't speak until they were halfway down the steps, heading toward the lawn. "You didn't need to interrupt," Hélène muttered resentfully.

Philippe smiled for the benefit of the guests who drifted past, but his reply was tense. "You looked miserable! What was I supposed to do, let you keep talking to the young man who broke your heart?"

"That isn't what happened!"

"Then what *did?*" he demanded. When Hélène said nothing, Philippe sighed. "No matter. Please just try to be cordial, all right? There's someone I'd like you to speak with."

Hélène stopped right there in the middle of the lawn, her cheeks hot. Did her father honestly think he could push her toward a new suitor tonight? When they were at the home of her former fiancé's family, celebrating his parents' *anniversary?*

"I think I feel indisposed."

"I'm not asking you to get engaged tonight! Please, just talk to him. He's a nice young man." Her father put a hand awkwardly on her shoulder, evidently trying to console her. "At the very least, he won't make you cry."

"I wasn't crying," Hélène retorted, though perhaps her eyes had been a *little* misty. If so, it was May's fault—not Eddy's. Though her father could have no way of knowing that.

"Your Imperial Highness!" her father exclaimed, tightening

the hand on Hélène's shoulder. "It's good to see you, I trust you had a safe journey, have you met my daughter Hélène?" The sentences came out in a single breath, rushed and frantic.

Hélène turned slowly, coming face-to-face with a young man in a dark jacket. Her eyes widened.

Though she had never met Nicholas, she knew him at once. He looked so much like his cousin George that they could have been brothers.

"It's a pleasure," the tsarevich murmured, reaching for her gloved hand. Hélène was so shocked that she let him press a polite, utterly chaste kiss to her wrist.

Her father wanted her to marry the future *Tsar of Russia*?

Well, now Hélène understood her mother's remark about converting. She had assumed that her father was considering a Protestant prince. Why hadn't she thought of the Russian Orthodox Church?

"Your Imperial Highness, Hélène and I were just discussing the stars. Aren't they lovely tonight?" Philippe prompted.

"They are," Nicholas agreed, sounding a bit puzzled.

"Perhaps you and Hélène might look at them together? I find it's easier to see the heavens deeper in the gardens, away from all the noise and the light."

In other circumstances, Hélène might have laughed at how flagrantly her father was disregarding chaperonage requirements.

Nicholas hesitated, then held out an arm to escort Hélène. "I would be honored."

Hélène's body screamed at the wrongness of this; yet she forced herself to put a hand on Nicholas's forearm, following him to the hedges that marked the Marlborough House gardens.

It was hard not to think of when she'd been out here with Eddy last year, the night of his investiture. The two of them had slipped into these gardens and run around like children, chasing each other with suppressed laughter until they'd become tangled up together, and their giddy laughs had turned into something else entirely.

Realizing how long she'd been silent, Hélène cleared her throat. "The stars are indeed beautiful."

They weren't, actually. They were obscured beneath the hazy lights of London, a city now illuminated by so much electricity that it dimmed the heavens.

Nicholas drew to a halt near a rosebush. He stared out into the distance, his only reply a noncommittal *mmm*.

"It's a beautiful party," she added awkwardly. "How thoughtful of you, to come all the way from Russia."

Again Nicholas huffed out a nonverbal response. He really was quite sullen, Hélène thought with sudden irritation. She didn't want to be here either.

"Really, Your Imperial Highness." Her tone was slightly teasing, though her annoyance crept through. "I have made two attempts at conversation; now it is your turn to remark upon something. You might say how happy you are for your aunt and uncle that they have been married for twenty-five years."

"Nicholas," he muttered, finally turning to look at her.

"Excuse me?"

"Please don't use my title. Call me Nicholas."

"Very well, *Nicholas*. Since you are clearly so undesirous of my company, perhaps we might both return to the party?"

"Wait, please." His hand clenched into a fist, then unclenched. "I owe you an apology. Whatever our parents have decided among themselves, I need to . . . I cannot marry you."

Hélène blinked at the turn this conversation had taken.

"I'm sorry to disappoint," Nicholas continued awkwardly. "You seem like a charming young woman."

He clearly didn't know her at all, if he thought she was *charming.* "I assure you, I'm not at all disappointed. I do not wish to marry you, either."

Nicholas stared at her for a moment. "You aren't angry?"

"Would you prefer that I swooned at your rejection?"

That, at least, coaxed a half smile from him. "I'd rather you didn't, actually."

"What a relief. I've never swooned before, and fear I don't even know how."

Now he was definitely smiling. "I just wanted you to know that my decision isn't a reflection on your . . . person," Nicholas explained, with a vague gesture that encompassed her body and face. "My heart is promised elsewhere."

What a funny, old-fashioned phrase. It struck her as the sort of thing Alix would say.

"If it makes you feel better, my heart is promised elsewhere, too," Hélène assured him.

"Very well, I'll inform my father. He'll be livid," Nicholas added under his breath. "He really was excited at the prospect of a French alliance."

"You *do* know that my father has no throne, right?" Hélène arched an eyebrow. "There was a revolution, and we got sent away. A terrible inconvenience, really."

"My parents don't recognize the French Revolution." Nicholas spoke as if this were a reasonable announcement to make, like deciding to sleep late one morning, or wearing a jacket without a cravat. "They refuse to treat with your nation's republican government. My father calls them a bunch of peasants, says that your father is the undisputed King of France."

Well, hadn't the Romanovs stamped out all anarchy and rebellion in their own territories? It stood to reason that they would willfully ignore it elsewhere.

A sudden prickle of awareness traced down Hélène's spine. She turned around to see May of Teck standing on the balcony above them.

Irritatingly, May looked better than Hélène had ever seen. She'd twisted her hair up into a knot, leaving a few pieces to fall around her face, and the soft blue-gray color of her gown echoed her eyes. Eyes that currently narrowed on Hélène.

Fine, then. If May wanted to lurk in corners and spy on her, then Hélène would give her something to spy on. Something that suited her own purposes.

"Would you mind if we waited to share this with our parents? If we let everyone think that we really are courting, just for a little while?" Hélène dared another glance at the terrace, but May had vanished.

Nicholas followed her gaze. "You want to make him jealous, don't you? The man you love."

"It's more complicated than that."

"I see," the tsarevich added, though he clearly didn't. Then he shrugged. "As it happens, I think your proposal might help me, too."

"Because you want to make *your* secret lover jealous?"

He winced at her phrasing. "No, because I want my parents to think I've forgotten her. They don't approve."

Probably a ballerina, Hélène thought. Or a married woman.

"She should be arriving in London soon," Nicholas went on softly. "If my father thinks I'm here to court you, then I can stay longer. See the woman I love without consequence. Otherwise he'll drag me back to Russia."

Drag him back? "Doesn't your father allow you more freedom than that?"

"He is my tsar much more than my father," Nicholas said flatly.

Hélène played with the skirts of her gown, folding the crimson fabric over itself. "It seems we are equal in that, then. Both of us subject to the commands of our fathers. Both unable to be with the person we love."

"For now," Nicholas pointed out, and those two words heartened her.

A silence fell between them, but it was an easy, amiable silence. Nicholas wasn't surly at all, Hélène realized. She was just so accustomed to Eddy, whose attention spilled outward, eager and excitable. Nicholas had a stillness that reminded her more of George. His introspection seemed to invite her to join in, to be silent *with* him, rather than shutting her out.

Hélène shifted; though May had disappeared, she couldn't shake the feeling that they were being watched. "If we're going to do this, we might as well put on a good show."

A bark of startled laughter escaped Nicholas's chest. She recalled, belatedly, that young women weren't supposed to speak so bluntly.

"I suppose we should," he agreed. "I don't make a habit of doing things by half measure."

"No, it hardly seems the Romanov way."

Hélène saw that a few of the guests had noticed them

together. After all, it wasn't every day that the princess of an exiled royal house flirted with the man who would someday rule Russia.

Nicholas came to stand behind her, tucking his head over the top of hers—he really was quite tall, taller even than Eddy. Then he ran his hand down her arm to lace their fingers, lifting Hélène's gloved hand to point into the air.

"What are you doing?" Hélène hissed. She felt rather than saw Nicholas smile in response.

"I'm doing what I told your father I would do. Showing you the stars." He adjusted the position of her hand. "See that grouping of stars just over your finger? That's the evil bear."

"The evil bear?"

"I suppose I could translate the Russian as 'the merciless bear,'" Nicholas amended. "The cruel bear? In any case, he kills the peasant who tries to trick him into eating a turnip."

Hélène stepped back and turned, breaking their physical contact. "The Russian bear sounds quite violent."

"Let me guess, in French stories the bear is sweet and gentle?"

"He's just a simpleton who gets outwitted by the fox." At Nicholas's questioning look, Hélène recounted the fable her childhood nurse had told her. "The fox persuades the bear to go fishing during the winter, by sticking his tail in the lake as bait. When the lake freezes around the bear's tail, he has to rip it out, leaving half behind. That's why bears' tails are so short."

"Ah. The fox is the hero in French stories, since the French value wit and cleverness."

He didn't mean anything by the statement, but it still made Hélène pause. Maybe life was more like that fable than she'd realized. Maybe the people who came out on top were those who used subterfuge, who manipulated others, who were clever and sly and self-centered.

Maybe Hélène needed to be a little more foxlike, if she was going to beat May at the game that May had been playing all along.

She would do it. She would go to every party and social gathering, and smile up at Nicholas as if he'd hung the stars, and let May think she had completely moved on from Eddy.

Footsteps sounded behind them.

Hélène whirled around, and saw the figure standing there—and then she saw the look on Nicholas's face.

The truth hit her all at once.

She should have figured it out months ago, when she and Alix were at the wedding in Athens, exchanging secrets. *His parents won't let us marry. They hate me,* Alix had murmured. Hélène had wondered who could possibly disapprove of Alix as a daughter-in-law.

The Romanovs, of course. The most excruciatingly stuck-up family of them all.

Alix was in love with Nicholas—and now she had walked in on him, alone with Hélène.

CHAPTER SEVEN

Alix

ALIX HAD BEEN LOOKING FOR NICHOLAS FOR THE PAST HALF hour, but she hadn't expected to find him here. In the gardens, leaning close to Hélène, murmuring in her ear.

When she'd arrived in London several days ago, Alix had tried to ask Grandmama about this evening's guest list, but the queen had brushed off her question. *It's not my party, it's Bertie's,* Grandmama had sniffed. So Alix hadn't known for sure whether Nicholas was coming. Not until she arrived tonight and found Aunt Vicky, always the most loose-lipped of the family. Vicky had been too distracted to notice how pointed Alix's questions were. She had merely shrugged and said, yes, the tsarevich was attending on his parents' behalf.

Seeing her, Nicholas and Hélène stumbled apart, both hurrying to explain themselves.

"Alix! I'm so glad you're here, I didn't know you were in town—"

"Please don't think this means anything. We hadn't realized our parents were in talks, but of course, we will tell them no—"

At Hélène's words, Alix's stomach twisted with dread. Hélène's parents and Nicholas's parents being *in talks* could only mean one thing. They were arranging a marriage.

Alix remembered hearing how, two hundred years earlier, Peter the Great had repeatedly tried to marry his daughter to the child king Louis XV. The French Regent, Louis's uncle, had been perfectly content for Peter to send over a wealth of presents—furs, necklaces, slippers stiff with embroidery and jewels—only to laugh and reject the Romanov princess. Perhaps the Russian royal family had never lost this obsession with France, if they still sought a French alliance.

It wouldn't matter to them that Hélène's father didn't have a fortune to bestow on her as a dowry, that he didn't even have a *throne.* They already had plenty of money and territory to rule.

The things they sought in Hélène were her unparalleled pedigree, her centuries of royal blood that went back to Charlemagne.

Other guests were streaming from the lawn toward the main house, where gossip and music drifted from the windows. Alix suspected that Uncle Bertie was about to make a speech.

None of their trio moved.

"Alix, I had no idea Nicholas was the man you loved," Hélène said urgently. "I wish you had told me."

"You must know that Hélène and I have no intention of doing as our parents ask," Nicholas added.

"Are you going to tell them, then?" It hurt, asking this; Alix swallowed and tried again. "You're going to let your parents know that the courtship is off?"

She saw Hélène and Nicholas exchange a glance. Then the tsarevich turned to her, his blue eyes beseeching. "It might help if we let everyone think that Hélène and I truly *are* courting. Just for a little while."

"Why?" Alix's question was sharp.

"It was my idea, Alix," Hélène cut in. "I thought it might give me some time, while I figure out how to deal with . . ." *With May*, she didn't need to say.

Alix understood at once. If May thought that Hélène had moved on, that she no longer cared about Eddy, then May might relax her guard. And Hélène could try to find her weak spot.

Hélène looked like she wanted to say more, but seemed to think better of it. "I should rejoin my parents," she said tactfully, leaving Alix and Nicholas alone.

Alix waited until Hélène's footsteps had receded before turning to Nicholas. "Why would you agree to such a thing? To let everyone think you and Hélène are truly courting, when none of it is real?"

"Because it would allow me to stay in London longer. Finally, we would be in the same place." Nicholas reached for Alix's hand, closing it in both of his. "I miss you so much, Alix. I just want to be near you."

"Except that you won't be with *me*; you'll be with her."

"Only in public. I'll spend every moment that I can with you."

Before Alix could reply, there was a roar of applause from the ballroom. Everyone was clearly in there, lifting their champagne glasses as Bertie praised his long-suffering wife. Alix could picture it: guests stepping on the hems of each other's gowns, craning their necks as they glanced from the hosts to each other. Her absence—and Nicholas's—would soon be noticed.

"We should get back." Nicholas held out a hand to Alix. "Come with me?"

She stared at him, brow furrowed. "I thought you just said you need to publicly court Hélène."

"I think we can get away with a single dance," he said softly.

It was true that no one would remark upon a single dance. A young lady who danced more than three times with the same man would be considered fast, unless the couple were engaged; but a single dance was hardly anything, a handful of minutes in one of these long evenings. There were plenty of women who would get a single dance from Nicholas tonight: his aunt Alexandra, his cousins, various noblewomen who threw themselves in his path.

For these few minutes, Alix could hold him with absolute impunity. Could rest her hands on his shoulders, look up into his deep blue eyes.

"Of course I'll dance with you," Alix agreed. As if she had ever been in danger of refusing.

They didn't dare walk together into the ballroom; Alix followed a few beats behind. Some of the flowers that had been wound around the terrace's iron railing were already wilting; a few petals had been crushed underfoot. Alix stepped over them and into the crowded ballroom.

Sure enough, Bertie's booming laugh echoed around the room, which erupted in more applause. The Princess of Wales stood next to him, as thin and impeccably dressed as ever, her smile fixed and immobile. The toast was evidently concluding, servers moving through the room with empty flutes of champagne.

When the orchestra played the opening strands of a waltz, Nicholas greeted Alix as if seeing her for the first time. "Alix. May I trouble you for a dance?"

He stepped closer and set a hand on her waist. Even that slight sensation made her heart skip.

"I have missed you," he murmured.

"And I you. So much." She left it there, because she didn't want to pester him when they were only just reunited, but Nicholas clearly sensed her unease.

"What is it?"

"I don't . . ." *I don't know what we are doing,* Alix wanted to say. *I don't know how long we can keep doing it, waiting for a resolution that seems hopeless.* Instead she said, "When did you arrive in London?"

"A few days ago. You didn't get my letter?"

"Your letter?" Alix repeated.

"I wrote to tell you that I was coming to London." At the look on her face, Nicholas sighed. "So, they're going through Misha's mail. My parents knew that I was writing you, and told me to stop, so I asked Misha to post the letters."

"We have a long road ahead if your parents are intercepting your brother's mail to keep us apart." Alix's words were tight.

Nicholas spun her gently, and Alix's gown, a cerulean blue shot through with threads of silver, fanned out around her. "I promise, we will find a way," he murmured softly. "I love you."

Alix settled back from the turn and Nicholas tucked her closer, moving his hand daringly low on her back. "I love you too," she risked saying.

It was bold of them, whispering such things in a ballroom full of people, but Alix couldn't bring herself to worry about that. Nicholas was *here*—not in Russia, or on a ship halfway around the world, but in her arms. It was delicious and wondrous and at the same time, nowhere near enough. Nicholas's left hand was still in Alix's, his right curled around her back. She felt the air filling his rib cage with each breath, the warmth of his body, the tension of his muscles through the layers of fabric that separated them.

She was slightly alarmed to find that she wanted more of it, wanted to press away every last bit of space until there was nothing between them.

"I will try to call on you at Buckingham Palace," Nicholas promised. Alix realized dazedly that the song was ending, the final chords of the waltz echoing through the ballroom.

With every ounce of will, she forced herself to step away.

"Hélène. How lovely to see you. Shall we dance?" Nicholas was looking behind Alix's shoulder.

As she brushed past, Hélène leaned toward Alix's ear. "I'll bring him back to you. Once the baccarat games begin, try to linger near the coatroom."

Near the coatroom. Alix felt herself flush as she realized what Hélène meant. It was hardly surprising; given how long Hélène and Eddy had kept up an illicit romance, she was clearly an expert in sneaking around. But Alix wasn't brave enough for such wanton behavior.

Or was she?

Alix turned aside, fighting to suppress a smile. Maybe she was braver than she'd realized, because meeting with Nicholas in the coatroom didn't sound frightening or wanton at all. It sounded wonderful.

After all this time, she and Nicholas were finally in the same place, and Alix was determined to make every moment count.

CHAPTER EIGHT

May

MAY DIDN'T NORMALLY PARTAKE OF THE LATE-NIGHT MEAL AT these events. Aside from the fact that it was too chaotic—drunk guests swaying down a buffet line while footmen ladled food from silver chafing dishes onto their plates—the food was far too heavy. Who wanted lobster in cream sauce at midnight?

Tonight, however, May had ventured into the loud hubbub of the dining room. Missy was in there somewhere. And May suspected that Missy was her best chance at getting close to the situation with Ducky and Eddy.

"Plotting how to eliminate your competition?" asked an unexpected voice. May turned, startled, to see Agnes Endicott.

As always, the American wore a gown that was excruciatingly, obviously new: an ivory broché satin with countless tiny pleats and ruchings. A diamond necklace settled over her collarbone, its stones refracting the light.

Following May's gaze, Agnes gave a self-deprecating smile. "I know, the necklace is a bit much; but Papa bought it for me, and I didn't have the heart to tell him I can't wear it. At least it's not a tiara," she added. "You should have seen the ones the Vanderbilts are wearing in New York. Tiaras in a box, from Tiffany's!"

Those were May's words, from the time Agnes had asked if she could purchase a tiara at a jewelry store. *A true lady would never wear a tiara in a box*, May had warned. *If you don't have a family tiara, better not to wear one at all.*

It hurt, thinking of all the afternoons they had spent together in Agnes's sitting room. Back when May was teaching Agnes the rules of society—when she'd thought they were friends.

"Is that where you've been all this time? New York?" May heard herself ask.

Agnes shrugged. "Chicago, and then New York. My grandfather died. We had to go back to settle his affairs."

"I'm sorry to hear that," May said automatically, then drew back, recollecting herself. "Agnes, what are you doing here?"

"The Prince of Wales lost some money to Papa at baccarat, which Papa conveniently forgot to collect." Before May could reply to that, Agnes reached for her hand and squeezed tight. "Don't look, but *she* is here."

Of course May looked. Striding into the dining room, arm in arm with the Tsarevich Nicholas, was Princess Hélène.

"She's certainly trying to make a statement in that gown," Agnes added disdainfully.

May tugged free of Agnes's grip, though she couldn't help but agree with her remark. "That *is* a rather bright shade of crimson. It almost reminds me of a military jacket."

Agnes snorted. "If she's trying to make us all stare, she's succeeded. And she's been with His Imperial Highness all night."

May had noticed it, too: all the shameless dancing and flirting between Hélène and Nicholas. Even now Hélène was beaming up at the tsarevich as if she'd never heard Eddy's name. It made May feel oddly relieved; she'd always felt slightly guilty about the blackmail Agnes had set in motion. But Hélène clearly hadn't loved Eddy the way she'd claimed to, if she had moved on to another prince—admittedly, the only prince in the world who was richer and more powerful than the Prince of England.

"What a hypocrite," May couldn't help muttering.

"Exactly."

Agnes and May shared a look of understanding, almost amusement. Then Agnes said softly, "I miss you, May."

Instantly May stiffened. "How can you miss me when our friendship wasn't real? When you were using me the entire time?"

"I don't see why both things can't be true at once! I had my own goals, but I also really was your friend, and trying to help."

May realized, with a sinking feeling, that it didn't matter whether Agnes had really been her friend. All that mattered was that Agnes stayed silent. She knew what May had done, and that made her a liability. One that May needed to control.

"Perhaps I can help you someday," May said slowly. "If my plans succeed, as you hoped, then I'll be well positioned to introduce you to all manner of titled men."

Agnes smiled. "I know! I can be useful to you, too; just let me know what you're planning."

"No, Agnes," May said heavily. "Not after you violated my trust."

Agnes's eyes flashed with what might have been hurt, but then she shook out the flounces of her dress. "Very well. If you need me, you know where to find me."

When her old friend had disappeared into the crowd, May scanned the room once more. She saw Missy on a fringed ottoman near the fireplace.

Fixing a smile on her face, May started toward her. On her way she lifted two flutes of champagne from a passing tray.

"Cheers," she said brightly, and handed Missy one of the glasses.

Missy's eyes lit up with excitement, though she hesitated. "Are you sure we're allowed? Mama never lets me have any."

"I promise that if your mother catches us, I will take the blame."

To May's relief, Missy propped one hand behind her on the ottoman, leaning back to take a long sip of the champagne. She lowered the glass with a pleased sigh. "Hopefully, Mama will be too distracted by all the eligible men to notice. You know how mothers can be when they want to marry you off. It's exhausting, isn't it?" Missy rolled her eyes.

May fought to hide her irritation at Missy's cluelessness. Didn't she see that May was older, and far less eligible, and in possession of a mother who hadn't helped her in the slightest?

"I know what you mean," she forced herself to say. "Is there a gentleman in particular that we should name to your mother? Perhaps His Royal Highness Prince George?"

Missy was silent for a moment. May feared she'd overstepped, but then Missy drained the last of the glass and smiled. "George is wonderful. You know we used to see each other every year, when my family summered in Malta?"

If May hadn't hated Missy already, she would have begun hating her now, for speaking with such casual affection about

George. About their shared enchanted childhoods and how they'd *summered* on the Mediterranean.

She waved over a passing footman, who quickly refilled Missy's champagne flute. "Do you and George have an understanding?"

"Oh, no! George is very private about his feelings." Missy took a hearty sip from her newly full glass, then grinned wickedly. "Unlike some princes I know."

"Really? Who?"

May winced; she'd sounded so eager she was almost shrill, but to her relief, Missy didn't seem to notice. The other young woman's cheeks were growing flushed. "You wouldn't *believe* how obvious Ferdinand of Romania was. The last time my sister and I visited Munich, he was quite forward."

"Really? What did he do?"

"Just followed me around all week like a puppy, talking about his hunting. He's all brawn and brute force," Missy added with a giggle.

"And you and your sister want to marry someone more . . . intellectual?" May was trying, in a roundabout way, to steer the conversation toward the point of interest—toward Ducky.

Missy tittered again. "I'm not sure Ducky would mind brawn and brute force. You should *see* Kiril's muscles. He's so broad-shouldered; I imagine that he could rip a tree from its roots. With his bare hands."

Kiril. The name was familiar. . . . Hadn't Missy mentioned him at the baptism, in connection with Ducky? Little alarm bells went off in May's mind.

"Missy!"

Before May could ask anything more, Ducky swept forward,

plucking the champagne from her sister's grasp. "That's enough for you, I think."

Missy shook her head, a bit too emphatically. The pearl droplets in her ears swayed with the movement. "As if you have any right to talk, Ducky! I saw you sneaking cigarettes in St. Petersburg, not to mention that I never told Mother you were alone with—"

"That's *enough*," Ducky snapped.

It didn't matter; May could have finished the sentence on her own. *With Kiril.*

An idea began to coalesce in her mind: an outrageous, far-fetched, completely absurd idea.

"Why don't we go get some air," May suggested.

Ducky shot her a grateful look, and each of them took one of Missy's arms, leading her forcibly through the room and onto the terrace.

May waited until they were near the iron railing, far enough from any other guests to be overheard. Then she looked at Ducky. "Missy told me about you and Kiril."

Ducky's eyes widened, and she whirled angrily on her sister. "How *could* you?"

Missy winced. "I only remarked upon his muscles. I never said that you two—"

"I promise, your secret is safe with me. I want to help," May assured Ducky, before Missy could say something worse. Really, that girl needed to learn how to hold her tongue, even after a glass of champagne or two.

"Help?" Ducky barked out a humorless laugh. "Are you visiting Russia soon, and offering to slip Kiril a note?"

"I can help *here.* With your situation regarding Prince Eddy," May explained.

"Good luck with that. Grandmama has decided that Eddy and I will marry, and so we shall. How in the world can I get out of it?" Ducky asked bitterly.

"Alix of Hesse got out of the very same engagement. She didn't want to marry Eddy, either."

Ducky gave May a long, searching look. "I see," she said at last. "You want to be in contention for Eddy yourself."

May didn't correct her. Out on the lawn, guests still drifted in and out of the white tent, which seemed to emit a ghostly glow in the moonlight.

Ducky's hands fell to her sides. "I appreciate your help, truly, but I don't see how I can avoid this engagement. There's no telling Grandmama no."

May nodded. "*You* cannot tell her no, but Eddy can. He needs to call it off."

"And how am I to accomplish that?" Ducky demanded. "Just walk up to him and politely say I don't wish to marry him? Even if he felt the same way, well . . . word would get around. It would destroy me," Ducky added helplessly.

Of course it would. A single woman could never admit to not wanting to marry a man, let alone a future king.

"You'll have to be more circumspect," May agreed. "You'll pretend to go along with the engagement, but when you are with Eddy, you will undermine your own cause. Make yourself unattractive in his eyes."

To her immense relief, Ducky seemed to be considering this unprecedented suggestion. "You mean that I should sabotage the engagement?"

"I suppose so, yes."

"And how exactly would I do that?"

May started to reply, but Ducky and Missy's mother stepped

out onto the terrace. "Girls! There you are! I've been looking all over for you."

"We'll talk soon," May promised, as the Coburg sisters followed their mother back inside.

May leaned against the railing, lost in thought. Agnes would be amused by this plan, but of course May couldn't tell Agnes. She couldn't tell *anyone*, could keep no counsel but her own. The stakes were simply too high.

From now on, May worked alone. Which was just fine with her.

Other people had always proven a disappointment, anyway.

CHAPTER NINE

Alix

"TELL ME, WHAT DID YOU THINK OF LAST NIGHT?" QUEEN VICTORIA cracked a spoon against her soft-boiled egg, placed before her in a golden egg cup. "It was a bit *crowded* for my taste, but then, Bertie is *quite* social. And he made such a fuss about guests coming from all over! I don't mean you two," she clarified, nodding at Alix and Ernie. "It just felt excessive, having the Saxe-Meiningens *and* the Oldenburgs. Not to mention that the King and Queen of Denmark come all the way from Copenhagen!"

Sunlight streamed through the windows, illuminating the paneled oak walls, the rose-colored carpet. The table was piled with far too much food for three people: sausages and kedgeree and sweet rolls stuffed with raisins. Alix picked up a blue-and-white Sèvres mug and filled it with coffee, only to pause and study the mug's motif, a bucolic pattern of frolicking sheep. It made her think of home, though Darmstadt was more a place of forests and wolves than of shepherds. She felt a sudden longing to bring Nicholas there, and show him all the places that mattered to her. The ponds where she used to catch tadpoles, the church where her mother was buried. The small, familiar corners of the house where she used to hide, and read, and daydream.

"It was quite unnecessary for the tsarina to send Nicholas

in her stead," the queen went on with a huff. "And really, the way he was carrying on with that French girl! She certainly made a spectacle of herself, dancing so many times with him."

Alix realized that their grandmother was *angry* on Eddy's behalf. She felt protective of her grandson, resentful that Hélène had, to all appearances, deserted Eddy and begun flirting shamelessly with Nicholas. Alix found it surprising, and also endearing.

Ernie shot her a look across the table, but Alix merely said "Oh, really?" and took a sip of coffee, as if Nicholas's name meant nothing to her.

Alix had managed to find Nicholas again later in the evening. They'd waited until the rest of the guests had started to filter home or were gathered around the baccarat tables, gambling dizzying sums of money. No one had noticed them slipping into the coatroom for a few precious moments. They had managed a hurried kiss and several quick *I love you*s before Alix had reemerged into the party, heart pounding.

"I must say, I'm disappointed in the Orléans girl," Victoria went on. She seemed determined to punish Hélène by not using her name. "As her behavior last night made evident, it is all over between her and Eddy! They were secretly engaged, and then the next thing I knew she had changed her mind—she said that, upon reflection, she couldn't convert to the Church of England as she'd promised." Victoria's voice shook with anger as she added, "If she thinks the Romanovs will let her remain Catholic, she is *quite* mistaken!"

"Poor Eddy," Alix murmured in reply. She'd seen him on the dance floor last night, watching Hélène and Nicholas with a wounded, bewildered expression. Alix wished she could tell him that it was all just a show, but it wasn't her place.

And really, Hélène was right to keep him in the dark. Tact was not exactly one of Eddy's best qualities. In his hands, the situation might detonate, letting Hélène's secret explode into the world. Then he would never get permission to marry her.

"Well, I have made other plans for Eddy," Victoria went on, in a brisk tone. "No more of this nonsense about foreign princesses. I've found him someone much better, someone in our own family—a nice young woman who will do as she's told."

For a terrifying instant, Alix thought *she* was the young woman in question, that she would have to fight off an engagement with Eddy again, the way she had once before. But then the queen smiled.

"I've also started making plans for you two. It's high time you were both engaged."

Ernie's fork clattered noisily to his plate. Alix and her grandmother turned to look at him, and he flushed. "Thank you, but I'm in no rush to be wed."

"What nonsense. You're the future Duke of Hesse, not to mention my grandson; you can hardly expect to continue as a bachelor indefinitely. When we head to Osborne House for Cowes next month, I expect you to pay court to your cousin Maud."

"Maud?" Ernie repeated faintly.

"Yes, Maud! You can hardly expect to do better than a daughter of the Prince of Wales. As for you, Alix," her grandmother continued, "I have a special guest arriving soon. If all goes well, I will invite him to join us at Cowes."

This was a complication Alix hadn't foreseen. "Who is it?"

"A German prince I've been corresponding with. His rank, of course, is nowhere near as illustrious as Eddy's. He's not even set to inherit. But he's a wonderful man, quite intelligent and educated in the law." The queen paused before adding, "I see now that you and Eddy would never have worked. You belong with a German prince of steady position, a good-hearted man who will keep you close to home."

Alix opened her mouth to protest, then shut it again.

"And really, Germany is an excellent place to find a husband. My own dear Albert was from Germany, of course," Victoria went on. "It is Britain's natural ally, a country whose roots have been intertwined with ours since King George I came to England from Hanover."

"Grannie," Ernie cut in. "As always, you are impossibly generous to Alix and me, but I'm afraid we cannot stay. Our father needs us at home in Darmstadt."

"Nonsense! I've already written to Louis, and he agreed that you two could remain with me all summer. So I'm afraid we must consider the question as utterly settled." Their grandmother leaned back in her chair. "It's been some time since I attended the Cowes Regatta. It will be quite a treat for me to watch the races."

By *the races*, she meant their romantic progress as much as the sailing. If Alix weren't so irritated, she might almost have laughed. There was nothing her grandmother enjoyed more than a good matchmaking.

THAT AFTERNOON, ALIX AND ERNIE ESCAPED FOR A GAME OF croquet on the back lawn so that they could discuss their grandmother's plans in private.

"I can't believe they are *pretending* to court," Ernie

exclaimed, after Alix had explained what Hélène and Nicholas were doing. "It's brilliant, honestly. Perhaps I should do it with Maud."

"Why?" Alix asked, and Ernie shrugged.

"To buy myself some time. If Grannie thinks I'm going along with her plans, she'll ease up on me, and then I can . . ." He trailed off, flipping the croquet mallet around.

Alix watched him thoughtfully. "Do you think I should do the same?"

"You mean, feign interest in this match she's made for you?" Ernie nodded. "If nothing else, it will make things easier for you and Nicholas. You can slip away with him, and Grannie will assume you're with her German man."

"Alix, darling!" As if on cue, the queen stepped onto the back terrace of Buckingham Palace. "I'd like you to meet someone."

"She came outside to introduce him personally," Ernie breathed, with a sidelong glance at Alix. "Be careful. That means she's serious."

Forcing a smile, Alix set down her croquet mallet. She could do this. She'd survived a year of being pushed toward Eddy, after all.

Her grandmother swept down the stairs, black lace skirts swishing behind her. She was accompanied by a man who looked a few years older than Alix. He wasn't handsome in the traditional sense; his nose was too prominent, though it was somewhat balanced by a full, dark beard. And he was exceedingly tall: not as broad-shouldered as Nicholas and his cousin George, but lithe and lean, in a way that reminded Alix of Eddy.

"Alix, I'd like you to meet my dear friend, Maximilian of Baden," Victoria explained. "Maximilian, my granddaughter Alix of Hesse, and her brother Ernest of Hesse." Ernie's introduction came as something of an afterthought.

"Alix, it's a pleasure to meet you. I was wondering if you'd like to stroll in the gardens?" Maximilian suggested.

Ernie murmured something about accompanying Her Majesty inside, looping an arm chivalrously through their grandmother's. As he retreated, he shot Alix a look that seemed to say *good luck*.

"Thank you for walking with me." Maximilian waited for Alix before he started into the gardens. "I fear that I've gone bowlegged from so long in the saddle."

Alix almost remarked upon the fact that he had ridden here—surely not all the way from Dover? Wherever he'd come from, he must either have been in a hurry, or be a man accustomed to the outdoors. But she simply said, "It's my pleasure."

For a while, the only sound was their footsteps crunching over the gravel path. The gardens stretched out before them, camellias and roses spilling out of flower beds.

"You and I have met before, though you probably don't remember," Maximilian told her. "At your cousin Wilhelm's wedding."

"Oh, really?" Alix didn't remember much about that wedding; she'd only been ten years old.

"I remember being downstairs when I heard the Crown Princess Victoria raise her voice. I snuck closer to listen." Maximilian looked amused as he added, "She had caught you and your brother stealing something from the library."

"I remember! Ernie and I had broken into Aunt Vicky's glass-fronted cabinets. We were searching for pirate treasure for our game, but I got distracted by a butterfly."

"A butterfly?" Maximilian asked. "As I seem to recall, your uncle has a wonderful collection of Japanese samurai swords."

"No, it was a butterfly. I remember thinking that it couldn't be real, that such a vibrant shade of blue must have been created by a paintbrush. It reminded me of my mother," Alix breathed, caught in the strands of memory. "My father used to call her his butterfly. He didn't mean it the way most people do; he wasn't saying that Mother was flighty or social: more that she was delicate, and beautiful, and tirelessly working. We forget that butterflies aren't just ornamental," Alix added, with a glance at Maximilian. "They are forever on the move, pollinating flowers for us."

"That's lovely," Maximilian said quietly.

"I think of that nickname my father had for her, and I can't help wondering if he knew that she was ephemeral. That she was too good to be always with us." Alix paused. "I'm sorry. I didn't mean to speak of such sad things when we've only just met—"

"Please don't apologize."

Alix was startled when Maximilian reached for her arm. He quickly released her and retreated a step, running a hand through his hair.

"I wish more people shared the truth of their feelings, as you just did. Sadness is not something to hide or be ashamed of," Maximilian insisted. "As you say, we have only just met, but I can tell that you're not artificial. I am weary of dealing with false people, the sorts who turn on their smiles the way one switches on an electric light."

It was shockingly similar to what Alix had thought on countless occasions. "I know the people you mean. They are always at crowded parties, asking shallow questions and digging for gossip."

"Exactly! That's why I avoid large parties at all costs."

Alix looked at him in surprise. "Surely you must throw parties at Karlsruhe?"

"Our parties are quite provincial compared to those in London." Maximilian smiled shyly. "I'm sure Her Majesty would be horrified to learn that my family decorates our own Christmas tree, instead of having servants do it for us."

"My father used to take us out into the woods to select our tree," Alix recalled. That was long ago, before her mother died.

"All Christmas trees should be proper German firs, selected from the forest. I hope you hang it with candles and not those odd little ribbons everyone uses here."

"Oh, yes," Alix agreed. "We will hang it with candles until the year that we knock one over and burn the whole place down."

"My thoughts exactly," Maximilian replied, swallowing back a smile. It made Alix feel guilty. He had been nothing but honest with her; didn't she owe him the same courtesy?

"Maximilian," she began awkwardly, "I don't know what Grandmama said about me. . . ."

Hearing her distress, he slowed his steps. "You do not wish to be courting, do you?"

"I just—I don't want you to have false hopes when it

comes to me. My grandmother keeps trying to interfere in my affairs. She doesn't understand that I want to marry for love, or not marry at all. Some people might think that's foolish," Alix added, a touch defensively. "But it's how I feel."

"I don't think it's foolish," Maximilian assured her. "On the contrary, knowing what you want from life is the height of wisdom. If only more people knew what they wanted, the world would be a far better place."

Alix had no idea what to say to that. No one had ever complimented that part of her—her dreaminess, her romantic nature.

"Rest assured, I won't court you if you don't wish it. I'm only here because your grandmother asked me to come. I'm a Prince of Baden, and from the younger branch of the family." He gave a self-deprecating smile. "I am hardly in a position to refuse a personal invitation from the Queen of England."

"I understand, but I'm not ready to be courted by anyone." Meeting his gaze, Alix added, "Would you mind terribly if we were just friends?"

"Friends," he repeated. "Of course I wouldn't mind. I would be honored."

They kept walking, talking occasionally, lapsing into silence when neither of them felt like speaking. But it wasn't an uncomfortable silence. As they strolled through the verdant gardens, the wind sending little ripples over the surface of the pond, Alix decided that this was not nearly so painful as her and Eddy's awkward forced courtship. Things went so much smoother when you were honest with men, instead of hiding your thoughts as society dictated. And perhaps, Alix admitted to herself, she was more similar to Maximilian than she had ever been to Eddy.

He shared her love of quiet, gave her the space to be herself. And most of all, he had listened, and agreed to be simply a friend.

CHAPTER TEN

May

THE EARL OF STAFFORD WAS NEARLY APOPLECTIC WITH DELIGHT at having so many royal guests attend his gallery tour. He bent in a horribly exaggerated bow, glancing nervously from Princes Eddy, George, and Nicholas to the two Coburg sisters. "Your Royal Highnesses, Your Imperial Highness, I'm so honored that you're here." He practically tripped over his own feet as he led the group into the two-story entrance hall, where several other members of society already waited, casting curious glances at the royal party. May knew most everyone there, of course—elderly dukes, society matrons and their beribboned daughters, and even a deacon.

Unfortunately, Hélène d'Orléans had come, too.

May had thought Hélène would flinch at the sight of her: because as far as Hélène knew, May really was the author of the blackmail note, threatening Hélène with all her sordid secrets. But Hélène had hardly spared May a glance. She'd just walked right past May—and Eddy—to stand near Nicholas, giggling flirtatiously at something he'd said.

Perhaps Nicholas was the one who'd alerted Hélène to this little outing. May was not such a fool as to think it was coincidence.

The Earl of Stafford cleared his throat. "Thank you all for

coming! This is a much larger group than normally attends my little tours. Please, if you'll join me in the conservatory . . ."

May followed the group into a massive room with a domed glass ceiling. Sunlight glinted on classical statues in various attitudes: heroes brandishing swords, satyrs, at least three sleeping nymphs.

"One of my greatest acquisitions is this fragment of a Roman temple from Pompeii. Please, if you'll note the bas-relief along the bottom . . ." the earl began, but May stopped listening. She was looking at Ducky, who must have felt May's gaze, because she glanced up and nodded.

When the group moved on, the two of them lingered, ducking behind a marble statue of a reclining young man. The sculpture was nude, May noted, and not at all covered in the usual carved loincloth or bunch of grapes.

"It was a good suggestion, trying to bring us all here," Ducky whispered. "What do I do now?"

May had been pondering the best way for Ducky to cultivate Eddy's disinterest. Based on what she knew from Eddy after a lifetime of family events—and what she knew about Hélène, the one woman Eddy *had* fallen in love with—May had put together a plan.

"He should think of you as delicate, sensitive, the sort of woman who wants a man to hover over her. Act as though you'll demand all his time. Talk as much as you can about the wedding."

"Anything I should avoid?"

"Perhaps don't talk about all your recent travel," May added, thinking of Eddy's instinctive restlessness. "Or remind him what an inconvenience it is."

There was a sound nearby, almost like a sharp intake of breath. May whirled about, but no one was there.

Ducky smiled nervously. "All right, then. Wish me luck."

They rejoined the group just as Lord Stafford was leading everyone into a picture gallery, its walls nearly obscured by heavy gilt frames. At the far end of the room, a pair of double doors had been thrown open to the sunshine-drenched lawn.

"My collection of oil paintings," the earl explained, lifting his arm. "Please enjoy yourselves. I am available to answer any questions."

The group quickly dissolved, everyone drifting off alone or in pairs to examine a favorite work. May pretended to be studying the paintings alone, lost in thought, though she was really following several paces behind Ducky.

Ducky came to stand near Prince Eddy, who slowed with visible reluctance. He had clearly also been told that they were courting.

"What do you think of Lord Stafford's collection?" Eddy asked politely.

May watched Ducky transform before her eyes. She tipped her face up, looking at Eddy through her lashes, an expression of silly infatuation on her face. "It's so romantic, don't you think? It makes me want to paint something! Why, perhaps I could paint you," she added breathlessly. "Would you sit for me?"

"I didn't realize you painted," Eddy replied. May noted that he had ignored Ducky's request. "You're more of a rider, aren't you? We could go out in Hyde Park tomorrow, as long as it doesn't rain."

"You must be thinking of Missy. She is the rider," Ducky simpered. "It's far too active for me—not to mention how dirty one gets! But of course, I *adore* painting."

Eddy frowned. "Really? We raced through the grounds of Sandringham just a few years ago at Christmas. And didn't you pick the winner at Ascot two summers ago?"

Fear flickered through May. She hadn't considered that Eddy and Ducky might actually be a good match. Perhaps Queen Victoria had been onto something, pushing them together. Ducky was nearly as horse-mad as Hélène.

There was a flash of emotion from Ducky; then the vapid mask settled back over her features. She turned aside, and gave a dramatic, horrified gasp.

"Oh my!" Ducky lifted both hands to cover her eyes. "That painting is far too salacious for my taste!"

Eddy turned to look at it with evident confusion. May—who was standing at a distance, pretending to study a rather grim-looking Perseus and Medusa—did the same. It was a landscape, a forest scene with a river twining through it.

"This painting? The one of trees, and—" Eddy floundered, clearly as confused as May. "And oxen?"

"Near the cart, look! That man!"

May stole another furtive glance. She could just about make out the small human figure near the stream, alongside the cart and oxen. The man had been painted wearing pants, but his bare chest gleamed in the sunlight.

"Let's go examine something in better taste," Ducky sniffed, leading Eddy forward.

Ducky, who'd just been whispering near a statue's carved genitalia, pretending to be shocked by a *bare chest*? May was impressed.

"Here, this one is far more appropriate." Ducky led Eddy in May's direction, pausing at a Dutch still life of a gourd surrounded by fruit, arguably the most boring painting in the room.

"This is utterly brilliant," Ducky said reverently.

Eddy looked as though he wanted to laugh, but then he glanced at Ducky's face. "Brilliant? A painting of . . . carrots and apples?"

"But they're not just apples! They are *symbols,*" Ducky insisted. "Of humanity's fallibility, of course, and original sin. Of life's transience and our moral obligations. And since you buy apples at the market, there are connotations of commercialism and expansion, and the commoditization of everyday items in the rise of international trade. . . ."

May wondered if Ducky's governess had taught her this nonsense, or if Ducky had adopted the decidedly unladylike habit of reading newspapers. This sounded suspiciously like what might be written in the arts and culture section.

"Indeed." Eddy looked half-ready to turn and flee, but Ducky didn't seem to be done with him yet.

She flung a hand up, indicating the painting. "Seeing this beautiful image reminds me to ask, what is your favorite food?"

Eddy seemed confused. "Venison, probably, with baked potatoes. Why?"

"I need to start learning your preferences if I'm to manage your household someday. Actually, is your valet here?" Ducky made a show of looking around. "I'd like to speak with him."

Eddy looked bewildered. "I really don't see what business you can have with my valet?"

"I need one of your shirts," Ducky replied, her voice

painfully sweet. "I shall have to cut it apart to learn the pattern, but never fear, I promise to sew it back."

May turned aside so they couldn't see her fighting not to laugh. Ducky really was outdoing herself.

"Ducky, while I appreciate the gesture, you don't need to be cutting apart my shirts," Eddy insisted.

"Of course I do! A wife's primary duty, aside from having children, is to care for her husband. Mama *always* stitches Papa's shirts herself," Ducky added piously. "I hope you don't imagine she entrusts that sort of thing to a maidservant!"

Eddy's reply was so quiet that May could only just hear it. "Thank you, but I assure you that my valet is perfectly capable of handling all aspects of my wardrobe."

"Very well," Ducky said in a placating tone. "I suppose that means I shall have to focus all my energies on our children. I assume that if we have a girl first, she will be named Victoria. But for a son, would you prefer Albert or Edward? Or perhaps George?"

There was a beat of silence. May desperately longed to look behind her at Eddy's expression, but she didn't dare.

"Are you pleased?"

May whirled around, her throat dry. She'd been so focused on Ducky and Eddy that she hadn't noticed Prince George coming to stand near her.

Are you pleased? he'd asked. Surely he didn't mean, *Are you proud of what you've done?*

"The gallery tour," he went on. "Are you pleased with it?"

"Oh—yes," May replied swiftly. "I so rarely get the chance to look at art." It was true; May never went to picture galleries unless it was for a social occasion.

George tucked his hands into his pockets. "Which painting is your favorite?"

May's eyes drifted to a portrait she'd noticed earlier, of a man in a sixteenth-century ruff with a slashed doublet. "Him," she declared. "He reminds me of what you wore to the Cadogans' fancy-dress party."

"You remember that?"

May must not have been thinking clearly, because she blurted out, "Of course I remember. We danced that night."

The Cadogans' party had been the first time she'd felt this pulse of affection, or attraction, or whatever it was, between her and George. May instantly feared she'd said too much, but George's eyes were warm.

"I don't think I've danced since that night. Not a lot of dancing on board the ships of Her Majesty's Navy."

The two of them drifted toward a far corner of the room, where a wistful-looking water nymph stared at them from a canvas.

"I haven't heard much about your tour," May admitted. "Where did you go this time?"

"To Australia."

"A nation of thieves!" she exclaimed, and George laughed.

"Perhaps it was that way once upon a time, but not anymore. And besides, we're a nation of thieves too. Constantly stealing things that aren't ours."

May looked at him in surprise. He sounded positively socialist. "Don't let Her Majesty hear you say such things."

"Oh, she knows my opinions." George shrugged. "Speaking of places we've stolen from, I've been thinking I'd like to go to India next. Perhaps I could serve as viceroy someday.

Might as well find a way to be useful to the Crown," he added, his tone self-deprecating.

"You are useful to the Crown right here in England," May said firmly. "And really, India is too far. Everyone would miss you."

"Would you? Miss me, I mean?"

He was turning her words on themselves, and yet May was about to agree, to say that of course she would miss him—

The moment was cut off by a scream out on the lawn. An instant later Missy was stumbling inside, grabbing at her arm, where a red welt was already forming.

"I was stung by a wasp!" she cried out, voice shaky with tears.

George mumbled something about needing to help, then sprinted toward his cousin. He shrugged quickly out of his jacket and wrapped it over her shoulders. As if feeling *warmer* would cure a wasp sting.

May stood there, watching him handle Missy with infinite tenderness, and felt the tiny hope that had bubbled in her chest quietly deflate.

What a fool she'd been, thinking George saw her as anything but a friend. It wasn't like May to make the same mistake twice. She must have some kind of willful blindness when it came to George.

She wasn't Hélène or Alix, to dream of marrying for love; she was May of Teck, and could only afford to be brutally practical. She didn't chase childish fantasies. She would marry for the only reasons that mattered: security, practicality. Position.

And if her plan worked, she reminded herself, she would have them all.

CHAPTER ELEVEN

Hélène

HÉLÈNE WAS GRATEFUL THAT NICHOLAS HAD ALERTED HER TO this gallery tour at the Earl of Stafford's house. Earlier, when she'd come downstairs and seen the waiting letter, she had hoped—for a fleeting, foolish moment—that it was from Eddy.

"It's from the tsarevich, isn't it?" Hélène's father had demanded, watching her rip open the envelope. Hélène had nodded, her heart sinking. Of course Eddy hadn't written. Why would he, when she'd given him no reason to hope?

"Yes, it's from Nicholas," Hélène said distractedly.

Her father beamed. "Already you're calling him by his Christian name! Ah, the number of ships the Romanovs could muster in a war, not to mention the number of troops . . ."

Ignoring her father, Hélène had scanned Nicholas's message. It was only a single line of text.

If you'd like to continue furthering our mutual goals, I shall be at the Earl of Stafford's gallery tour this afternoon with my cousins. Three o'clock.

So Hélène had come, just in time to see May sneaking off with one of Eddy's cousins. What was the girl's name—Daisy? Dona? Whoever she was, May had fed her a bunch of nonsense, effectively telling the girl to act like a clinging vine, to make Eddy feel suffocated and stifled. As if any man would want that.

Clearly, Queen Victoria was trying to push Eddy toward the cousin, and May was sabotaging the engagement.

Disgusted, Hélène had retreated, not wanting May to catch her eavesdropping. She'd hurried to rejoin the group in a gallery full of oil paintings.

Hélène was too distraught to even pretend to study the collection. She needed to clear her head, needed to *think*. Lifting a hand to shade her eyes, she headed through the double doors that led to the earl's back lawn.

There were more statues out here, arranged along a wandering path lined by trimmed hedges. Hélène lingered near a stone Cupid, relishing the sensation of the sunlight on her face.

"Hélène."

She had known this would happen, hadn't she? Perhaps her subconscious had drawn her outside for that very purpose, because she knew Eddy would also choose the outdoors over the art.

"Your Royal Highness," she said, dipping into a curtsy. They were alone out here, but she suspected that May was still watching.

Eddy cursed softly. "Please don't act like that."

They stared at each other, both holding their breath. Hélène longed to reach for his hand, pull him close, lower his mouth to hers.

She realized she was staring at his lips and tore her gaze away.

"You never replied to my letters," Eddy said hoarsely.

"I'm sorry." It was all she could give him.

Eddy ran a hand through his hair, frustrated. "My grandmother is pushing me to marry Ducky. She says that if I don't announce an engagement soon, she'll send me on a three-year world tour."

"Three years?" Hélène blurted out.

He nodded, watching her closely. "I would stay in each location for several months—Canada, the West Indies, Bombay, Africa. The only way out is to get married. I'll put Grandmother off as long as I can," Eddy insisted. "I'll *go* on the tour if that's what it takes, as long as I know you're waiting for me. As long as I know there's hope."

"Eddy," Hélène began helplessly, "you know that—"

She broke off before saying, *You know that I love you.* Because of course she did; her love for him suffused every fiber of her being. How could he doubt that?

She dared a glance toward the house, and her heart sank. May stood there, arms crossed over her thin chest. Staring at them.

It took every ounce of Hélène's willpower not to march up there and slap May across her lying face. God, how she itched to fight this battle out in the open, the way Eddy would do if he knew.

But that road led to certain defeat. At least if she tried to outsmart May, Hélène had a chance—however slight—of still marrying Eddy.

So she forced herself to do the hardest thing of all, and walk away from him.

"I'm sorry, Eddy. Truly, I am," she told him, and turned back to the house.

She was moving so blindly, fighting back tears, that she nearly walked straight into a man's chest.

"Your Royal Highness, there you are." Nicholas caught her arms, steadying her. "I was hoping I could show you the Rembrandt in Lord Stafford's collection."

Clearly, Nicholas had seen her distress, and was covering for her; in a firm voice that warned everyone else to mind their own business. Hélène couldn't help noticing that he'd called her by her royal title, unlike everyone in England who referred to her as *Miss d'Orléans.*

"I hate Rembrandt," Hélène muttered, her words shaky. She was still on the verge of tears.

"Let me guess, his works are too dark for you." Nicholas almost sounded like he was teasing. "You'd rather look at something bright and colorful—Monet's water lilies, perhaps—than a shadowy Rembrandt."

"It's not my fault that France has produced the world's greatest artists." Hélène let Nicholas put a hand on the small of her back.

He steered her gently toward the wall until they stood before an Impressionist scene of a beach at sunset, all golds and blues and shining amber. "Will this do?" Nicholas asked, an eyebrow lifted.

"Exceedingly. Thank you."

"If you truly hate darkness, you should avoid Russia in the winter. There are months when we only get a few hours of sunlight a day."

"In that case, it's a good thing our courtship is a farce."

He coughed. Hélène realized he was hiding his laughter. It almost made her want to smile.

Nicholas must have sensed her sadness, because his laughter died. "I saw you talking to my cousin. Dare I ask . . . is he the one you . . ."

"Yes," Hélène confessed, because there was no point in hiding it. She and Nicholas were in this together now.

"And you've quarreled?" Nicholas guessed.

"It's more complicated than a quarrel."

He didn't ask what she meant. Instead he simply said, "How can I help?"

"If only you could."

"Nothing? Please, Hélène, ask me for a favor, because I'm about to ask a very big one of you." Nicholas was still speaking in low tones, as if they truly were courting, and were whispering sweet nothings. "I was hoping you would accompany me to the Isle of Wight, to see the Cowes Regatta."

"The Isle of Wight," Hélène repeated.

"The Waleses are all going. Whatever has happened between you and Eddy, you would be near him. . . ." Nicholas trailed off as if uncertain.

Hélène saw at once why he had invited her. "I take it Alix and Ernie are going as well? And you need me to cover for you while you see her in secret?"

"I'm sorry, I shouldn't have asked. It was thoughtless of me—you might not want to go anywhere, not when you and Eddy . . ." He floundered uncomfortably.

Hélène forced a pale imitation of a smile. "Of course I'll help. We promised to aid each other, didn't we? And Alix is my friend."

Nicholas looked visibly relieved. "I'll ask my parents if we can borrow one of the yachts. The *Polar Star* is smaller than the others, but it's already anchored in the Baltic, and we're not a large party. I'll invite your parents, unless you have a dowager aunt who could chaperone instead?" Because, of course, it wasn't as if she and Nicholas could travel alone.

Hélène was too distracted to even marvel at the fact that the Romanovs had multiple yachts to choose from. She merely said, "My parents will be delighted."

"I'm sure my own parents can't get away, but I'll ask Uncle Vladimir to join."

Hélène nodded, making a silent plan of her own. Because she didn't doubt that May would be at this regatta, too.

Things were moving too fast for her to play it safe any longer. Eddy was being threatened with a world tour, being pushed toward his cousin, losing hope.

Hélène had no other choice. She would have to steal the letter back from May.

CHAPTER TWELVE

May

MAY COULDN'T BELIEVE SHE WAS REALLY HERE, ON A PADDLE wheel steamer headed for the Isle of Wight. Spray misted up from the waves, dampening the hem of her traveling gown. The ferry was nearly full; Cowes was a popular regatta, even more so this year, since the queen herself had announced her attendance. Surrounding Victoria, all wearing sashes and wide-brimmed hats, were a few ladies-in-waiting and various children. The Coburgs had come, and the Waleses, and Alix and Ernie—plus a rather plain and serious-looking German prince, who seemed to be included for Alix's sake.

Everything had happened quickly once May had helped Ducky at the gallery tour. The note had come on Queen Victoria's stationery the following week, just like the previous year's invitation to Balmoral—a request that "sweet May please join us for a family weekend at Cowes." When May's father had seen the message, a vein had pulsed on his forehead in silent rage, but he'd let her go. No one turned down an invitation from the queen. Especially not to Osborne House. Balmoral was a private residence, too, but the queen was forever hosting people there: inviting ambassadors or prime ministers to visit, letting them borrow her plaids and traipse through the highlands.

Osborne House was her refuge, the closest thing to a break Queen Victoria ever took. No statesman ever received an invitation there.

May edged closer to the ferry's railing, where Ducky stood alone, a solitary figure gilded in the afternoon light. "Thank you for making sure I was included," she murmured, so softly that only Ducky could hear.

Ducky glanced over with a smile. "Thank *you* for getting me out of that engagement. Apparently, Eddy has already told the queen that he refuses to marry me."

"Now that you're free of Eddy, how will you get permission to marry Kiril?" It was a forward question, but May assumed Ducky wouldn't mind.

"There's no way I can marry Kiril." Ducky blew out a breath, staring at the horizon. "Mother says he's too wild and unpredictable, but it's really about his fortune. For a Romanov, he's not very wealthy. He gambles a lot."

"Oh," May replied, because she couldn't think of a proper response to this statement.

"Perhaps I'll never marry," Ducky replied, clearly trying for a careless tone. "I can live in Coburg forever, have all the horses I want, sneak off to see Kiril whenever possible. There are worse things."

At the sound of a nearby commotion, May looked over. It was Prince Eddy. He had lowered himself into a small sailboat, accompanied by another man in sailor's uniform.

"Grandmother, may I go ahead to raise your standard?" he called out.

Queen Victoria stood on deck, frowning down at her

grandson. "Why don't you take Ducky with you. I'm sure she'd love to see Osborne House from the water."

No one dared point out that the ferry also offered views from the water.

Ducky made a show of clutching her belly. "Of course, Grandmother, but I would hate to get seasick. You know how weak my stomach is." She glanced meaningfully at May, who decided she might as well seize the moment.

"If Ducky is indisposed, Your Royal Highness, perhaps I could sail with you?" May called out to Eddy, her blood humming at her own daring.

Eddy seemed relieved at her offer. "Of course."

One of the sailors helped May down the ladder. The wind tugged the skirts of her gown, trying to rip her hat from her head. May held it in place, then reached for Eddy's hand, letting him help vault her into the smaller sailboat.

"George?" Eddy called out. "Come with us?"

George met May's gaze for a fraction of an instant, then shook his head. "I'll stay on board, thanks."

He probably wanted the chance to be alone with Missy, May thought. Not that she cared.

There was a little jolt as their sailboat pulled away from the hulking mass of the ferry, its wake churning white around them. The sailor who accompanied them began untying a rope, but Eddy waved him away.

"Please, Lucas, let me. I never get to sail anymore."

"Of course, sir. I shall be up front." Lucas smiled in May's direction, revealing a gap between his two front teeth, and disappeared.

Eddy looked at May with a slightly sheepish expression.

"Welcome aboard the *Minnow.* I just need a moment to set everything aright."

"I shall make myself as unobtrusive as possible," May promised, and perched on the side of the sailboat.

Eddy shrugged out of his jacket and rolled up his shirt-sleeves. May was a bit startled at the sight of his bare forearms. He was wiry but strong, his skin covered in light brown hair that glinted in the sun.

She watched as he launched into movement, untying ropes before retying them other places, letting a great canvas sail unfurl behind them with a resounding snap. It filled with wind, and their boat leapt forward like a living thing. Eddy's motions were precise, automatic—the way you do something you have mastered, something you've done a thousand times before.

When Eddy finally came to stand behind the tiller, May ventured to speak. "I'm surprised Her Majesty lets you sail alone. Isn't it a safety hazard, having the future king on his own boat? The tides are strong here."

She'd overheard one of the boatmen on the ferry say that, but Eddy looked at her with unmistakable approval. He clearly thought May had reached that conclusion about the tides on her own.

"You're right. The sailing is trickiest around Egypt Point, where back eddies from shore meet the English Channel. But I know my way through it." Eddy shrugged. "Plus, if I die, there's always George."

"Don't say that!"

"I was joking, May."

She looked over and saw that he was grinning, the relaxed grin of someone who feels truly at ease. She'd known Eddy for years, but May realized that she'd never seen this side of him. Probably because most of the time she saw him, they were in a ballroom.

"Why is your boat called the *Minnow?*" she asked.

"Father named it when he gave it to me. I think he was mocking me, but I actually like the name. Minnows are quick and agile."

"I see that," May replied. The boat tipped slightly to the right, causing her to slip. Eddy reached out a hand to catch her.

May startled at the contact, but Eddy stepped back, hardly seeming to have noticed.

"Sorry, I know this is not the sort of comfort you're used to. Grandmother should never have suggested I bring Ducky," he added, "but once she did, I'm glad you offered to come instead."

Here was May's chance. "Are you and Ducky . . . ?"

"Grandmother wants us to marry, but I won't do it," Eddy said quickly.

"I'm sure Her Majesty is disappointed."

"Oh, she's furious." Eddy's fingers drummed nervously over the tiller. "You know, Ducky has changed quite a lot. I thought I knew her, but I was mistaken."

Because the Ducky you saw was nothing like the real Ducky. "I think we've all changed since we were children," May said neutrally.

"I suppose so. *You* have certainly changed," Eddy added with a sidelong glance. "I don't remember you being the sort to climb into an elevator, or venture out onto a two-person sailboat."

"I believe there are three of us on this sailboat."

"Ah, yes. Lucas, our trusty chaperone."

It was a good sign that he'd used the word *chaperone,* wasn't it? That word was usually employed in a romantic context, by couples who were courting. "It's nice, seeing you like this," she said softly. "You are so at home on the water."

Eddy frowned into the distance. They were getting closer to the Isle of Wight, its rocky outcroppings stretching toward the sparkling blue waters of the Solent. Osborne House rose above it all, punctuated by a clock tower.

"I like it out here. No one is judging me, or trying to make me into something I'm not," he said at last.

"I would never try to make you into something you're not." May's heart thudded, her words coming out in nearly a whisper.

"Um—thanks." Eddy sounded confused, so she tried again.

"Now that things are over with Ducky, are you . . . what will you . . . ?" May was usually so articulate, but to her surprise, her words were slipping over each other.

"Grandmother has given up on Ducky, but that won't be the end of it. Thora is coming next week," Eddy said darkly, naming yet another of his cousins, Helena Victoria. "If I don't propose to her soon, Grandmother is sending me on a three-year tour of the colonies."

May had a wild urge to scream into the wind. Of course Her Majesty had another well-bred granddaughter lined up in case things didn't work out with Ducky. *Another* young woman named Victoria, who went by an absurd nickname. Another princess to scheme against.

She felt so weary, suddenly, of all the subterfuge and manipulation. All the endless, relentless climbing.

"You don't have to marry Thora," she heard herself say.

Eddy shifted uncomfortably. "Remember what I told you in the elevator, that I'm in love with someone else? I just . . . I don't know where things stand with her."

He was still holding out hope for Hélène.

May knew she was venturing into dangerous territory, but she had to ask. "Forgive me if I'm intruding, but the woman you love: What is the problem? Does Her Majesty not approve?"

For a long moment Eddy said nothing. His hand tightened on the tiller as he guided them around the curve of the island.

"Grandmother approved," Eddy said at last. "But the woman I love changed her mind."

May waited, sensing that silence would draw him out. Sure enough, he sighed.

"I don't know what to do. I still love her, but she's seeing someone else now. I can go on the tour, of course, but what if I come back and she's married him—and then I've lost my chance to win her back?"

May decided to risk it. She couldn't keep competing with Eddy's cousins, trying to eliminate them one at a time. She would put all her cards on the table, come what may.

"Eddy," she said, using his Christian name for the first time. But really, one couldn't begin a proposal of marriage with *Your Royal Highness.*

"I know this is unconventional and perhaps a bit shocking, but . . . this woman you love. If you cannot marry her, if she ends up married to someone else . . ." May let that trail off for a meaningful moment. "Well then, you should do the next best thing. You should marry someone who will make your life easy, who will let you be yourself."

"What do you mean?"

"I mean that you could marry me."

Eddy stared at May, dumbfounded. Clearly, he hadn't considered this possibility.

"I know you thought about marriage as something based on love, but what if it was more of a partnership? I don't expect you to love me," she added hastily, "but I've always felt that we understood each other. We could be friends, you and I."

"May . . ."

"Don't say anything yet. Just hear me out," she pleaded. "If you married me, you would escape Her Majesty's incessant pressure to find a wife. Not to mention that you would be granted houses and a much larger income. As for the two of us—I would be as unobtrusive in your life as I have been on this boat. I will make no demands of you. I will manage your household and your public appearances and your children, and let you do as you please."

Eddy went slightly pale at the mention of children, but May forged ahead.

"I have no issue with you continuing to live your life as you do currently. The woman you love—I would never make you feel guilty," she said clumsily. "I mean, if you wanted to keep seeing her."

Well, she had done it. She had offered him everything she could think of, including a carte blanche for all future infidelities. There was nothing else to say.

"You're suggesting a loveless marriage," Eddy said at last.

"I'm suggesting an arrangement that will benefit us both. I think, in our own way, we could find happiness together. Even if it is not the sort of happiness you expected," May concluded.

Eddy stared at her for a moment, his expression unreadable. Then he looked away. "I'm sorry if I gave you the wrong impression, May. But I meant what I said. I am in love with someone else, and as long as there's a chance I can win her back, I have to keep hoping."

May swallowed and nodded. She felt the sea air cutting through the fabric of her gown, chilling her all the way to the bone.

"Your Royal Highness! Welcome back!" called out a sailor on the beach.

Atop the hill, a blue, yellow, and red flag began to snake up the flagpole: the royal standard rising over Osborne House.

"May, I trust that everything we spoke of will stay between us." Eddy's words were soft, but for the first time, May heard a blade of command in his voice. He sounded . . . well, he sounded like a king.

She hurried to nod. "Of course. I won't speak of it again."

What had she done? She was as bad as her father, staking his entire fortune on a single hand of whist. May had gambled everything on this conversation with Eddy, and she had lost.

CHAPTER THIRTEEN

Alix

HÉLÈNE WAS UNDOUBTEDLY A BAD INFLUENCE, ALIX THOUGHT, her entire body flushed with anxious heat. Just look at what Alix was doing now, leaving a party to wait at the top of the servants' staircase at Osborne House. Waiting for Nicholas.

Hélène had suggested it earlier in the evening, after she and Nicholas had danced together very publicly, multiple times. Alix understood that it was all for show, and yet—it was hard to watch, knowing that everyone assumed Hélène and Nicholas really *were* on the brink of an engagement.

When Hélène had looped an arm through Alix's and suggested they walk along the gallery, Alix had readily agreed. At least it would separate Hélène from Nicholas.

Behind them, the party had been in full swing. Uncle Bertie always hosted a gathering at Osborne House for the opening night of the Cowes Regatta; but this year Grandmama was present, so the event was less raucous than usual. Guests in their evening finery drifted through the Royal Pavilion, spilling from the billiards room to the reception hall to the dining room.

"I finally understand how awful you felt last year, when Grandmama was trying to match me with Eddy," Alix said softly. And it must have been worse for Hélène. At least Alix knew that this courtship between Hélène and Nicholas was all a sham.

"I know you hate it—seeing me and Nicholas together." Hélène's voice darkened as she added, "I hate it, too. I keep thinking about Eddy. What must he think of me right now?"

They were walking the marble corridor, its walls lined in great windows that reflected the light of the chandeliers. Alix glanced outside. Osborne House looked out over the Isle of Wight, its dark slope dotted with houses, all currently rented out for the regatta. In the distance, moonlight glittered on the waters of the Solent.

"I'm so sorry," Alix murmured, because what else could she say?

"It's all right. I have a plan." Hélène's reply was bright, but Alix heard a quiver of fear underneath.

"How can I help?"

"You can't. If things end in disaster, I don't want you suffering for my mistakes."

Alix drew to a halt. "That sounds dangerous."

"Don't worry! Come on, let's rejoin the party. I should get back to Nicholas," Hélène declared. "And you need to rejoin that nice German man your grandmother found for you."

Alix felt a stab of guilt at the thought of Maximilian. Yesterday on the ferry, when he'd seen her shivering and damp with sea spray, he had wordlessly shrugged out of his jacket and draped it over her shoulders. Not in a romantic way, but with tenderness, the way he might care for a younger sister.

He had offered to be a friend, and here she was, using him

to distract Grandmama from the truth of who she was *really* occupied with.

"Maximilian is sweet," she told Hélène, wondering why she was defending him. "It's just that he's not . . ."

"Not Nicholas, I know," Hélène finished for her. "Good thing you and Nicholas are meeting up later."

"What?"

"At least *one* of us should be getting some time alone with our beloved." Hélène's voice was still determinedly bright. "I need to deal with May before I can find Eddy again. But there's no reason you and Nicholas shouldn't be together."

Alix had flushed at what she'd thought Hélène meant. "How would we do that without getting caught?"

"You won't get caught." Hélène had smiled, and there was a touch of mischief in it. "Don't worry, I'm an expert in sneaking around at crowded parties. I know all the tricks."

Which was how Alix had wound up here, waiting for Nicholas at the servants' staircase.

He and Hélène had made a very public exit just half an hour earlier. Hélène had complained of a stomachache, but assured her parents and Vladimir—who were all enjoying the party, most especially the drinks—that they should stay. She would return to the yacht with Nicholas and her lady's maid, Violette.

Once they had entered the long drive that snaked toward Osborne's main gates, Nicholas would slip out of the carriage—an easy feat on a road lined with such thick foliage. He would head back uphill to the main house, where Hélène had opened one of the ground-floor windows earlier in the evening.

Alix had waited a few minutes after their departure, then

complained of a similar stomach pain. Perhaps it had been the prawns, she said, to enough people that no one would check on her.

From downstairs she heard the roar of the party, the gossip and music and clinking of glassware.

"Alix?" a voice whispered from the bottom of the staircase.

"Nicholas!" She hurried down a few steps, hardly believing that Hélène had arranged this for them. "You came."

"You didn't think I would? I'm quite sneaky," Nicholas said softly.

"You? Sneaky?" He was the most painfully forthright person she knew.

He gave a nervous smile. "You're right, I'm not. But I try to do the things that matter; and you matter a great deal to me, Alix."

They needed to get off this staircase before someone appeared. "Will you come up?" Alix asked.

Still, Nicholas hesitated. "I didn't realize—I mean, I thought we could go to a sitting room, or—"

"Please, Nicholas. There's nowhere else in this house that we can be alone." Feeling shockingly bold, she padded down the stairs to where Nicholas stood, then led him up to the hallway.

Each door was mounted with a small brass frame that contained a card—a card that was lined, as all Her Majesty's paper goods were, in an inch-wide band of black. Nearly thirty years since Albert's death, and the queen still observed his mourning.

Princess Alix of Hesse, read the card on her door.

Alix pulled Nicholas inside, then turned the lock behind

him. The sound of the bolt falling into place felt oddly final. As if she'd turned some corner, reached some decision within herself, that would forever change things.

Nicholas wandered over to the window, which looked out over the eaves of the roof. He released the latch and lifted the windowpane, letting in the cool night air. They both stared out at the wine-dark sky.

"Misha and I used to climb on the roof of the Winter Palace," he mused aloud.

"Really? Ernie used to do the same, but I was never so brave. Not after Frittie." Her younger brother who'd fallen out of a window. A ground-floor window, but a window just the same.

Nicholas instantly started tugging the window shut. "I'm sorry, I didn't think."

"It's all right." Alix was tired of being afraid, of living with regrets. She ducked her head out the open window.

Then, before she could think twice about it, she lifted the skirts of her gown and clambered outside.

"Alix! What are you doing?" Nicholas tried to pull her back, but her feet were already on the slate tiles.

"Come on!" she insisted. Nicholas smiled softly and joined her outside, sliding down to a flat section of roof that was several yards square. They settled next to each other, staring at the moonlit harbor, their hands clasped.

"What did you and Misha do on the roof of the Winter Palace?" Alix asked. "Were you hiding from your tutor, or did you play pranks, as Ernie did? He loved to throw stockings full of water on unsuspecting people."

"Misha had his fair share of pranks, but I spent most of our time on the roof trying to plot how to leave."

"What?" Alix looked over at Nicholas, startled.

"My tutor taught me the basics of navigation: how to calculate one's location by triangulating the distance between two points, how to use the sun, that sort of thing. I had told him I wanted to be an explorer." Nicholas's voice was rough. "My tutor used to take me down to the shipyards. I peppered the workers with questions—how did they hammer the metal plates of the hull together, how did the propellers work? When the ship increased in speed, could you feel it? That's part of why I find it so perplexing, staying on a yacht that's anchored in a harbor," he added with a humorless laugh. "I prefer to be on a boat with a destination."

"Why didn't you serve in the navy instead of the army?" Alix asked.

Nicholas turned to her then, his expression resigned. "My father, of course. When he learned what was going on, he fired my tutor. Said it was unseemly for a future tsar to be out mixing with commoners, asking them questions, as if I was not God's appointed ruler and above them all."

"I'm so sorry, Nicholas."

"Father told me it was a foolish wish, wanting to be an explorer. That there was nothing left to explore, because we know every last corner of the world now, anyway."

" 'And Alexander wept, for there were no lands left to conquer,' " Alix murmured.

Nicholas let out an amused breath. "That's not what Plutarch wrote, actually. It was misquoted."

"In an English translation, I know." Alix smiled. "I prefer the misquote, though. It sounds rather poetic. The English are good at that."

"At getting things wrong or sounding poetic?"

"Both, probably."

Alix looked at Nicholas's hand, still clasped in hers. She felt as if he'd reached that hand up into the twist of her blond curls, pulling them loose from their pins, and then she would tip her head back and bring her mouth to his—

She blinked. Her imagination was playing tricks on her.

Or perhaps her mind was skipping ahead of her body, which had every intention of actually doing all those things.

Suddenly she understood why Hélène had risked everything to sneak around with Eddy.

"I think we should go inside," she declared.

Nicholas rose to his feet, then held out a hand to help her up. "Of course. It's getting cold, isn't it?"

"I meant, let's go into my bedchamber. Together," she said clearly.

When he understood her meaning, Nicholas's eyes widened. "Alix, no, we can't—"

Before he could talk her out of it, she lifted a hand and put it on his lips. This was all new and exhilarating and terrifying and wondrous. But whatever it was, Alix wanted to feel it in all its intensity. She wanted as much of Nicholas as she could get, for whatever time they had before he needed to leave.

"I am very certain of this," she replied. "Please, Nicholas, don't tell me no."

And then she brushed a kiss lightly over his lips.

When they pulled apart, Nicholas's voice was ragged. "I have no intention of ever telling you no. I will tell you yes, as much as I can, for the rest of our lives. But if at any point you change your mind—"

"I won't."

Still, once they were inside, Nicholas gave her so many chances to pull away. He started with her hair, pulling out its pins one by one, just as she'd daydreamed. When it fell in a cascade over one shoulder, he reached out to cradle her face with his palm. His lips were so close to hers.

"I love you," he said.

"I love you," Alix echoed.

They fell together onto her bed, not bothering to close the window, letting the night air kiss their bare skin.

CHAPTER FOURTEEN

Hélène

THANK HEAVENS ALL ROYAL RESIDENCES WERE EFFECTIVELY THE same, Hélène thought as she padded through the upstairs of Osborne House. She'd never set foot here, but it was easy enough to find her way around; she'd located the hallway where all the younger guests were housed, scanning the placards on each door. *Princess Victoria Melita of Saxe-Coburg*—that was Ducky, the cousin May had tricked into acting like a fool around Eddy; *Princess Maud of Wales; Prince Ernest of Hesse*; and, ah, here was *Princess Alix of Hesse.*

Hélène moved past that door quickly, not wanting to overhear anything. She hoped Nicholas and Alix were enjoying their time alone. It was nice, thinking she'd helped them, since she didn't seem able to help herself.

At least, until now.

Around the corner she found the room she was looking for, labeled *Princess May of Teck*. Hélène stepped inside, shutting the door behind her with a silent click.

She started with the most obvious places—the traveling chest at the foot of the bed, the space beneath the mattress—even running her hand around the lining of the trunk to check for hidden compartments or secret latches. Nothing.

Hélène moved to the wardrobe, systematically sorting through the dresses, the hatboxes, the shoes. May's clothes seemed much nicer than Hélène remembered. Perhaps her parents had realized that May couldn't catch a prince in her shabby, twice-turned dresses and had borrowed the funds for her new things.

Or perhaps May had gotten the money herself. She'd already blackmailed Hélène, after all. What if she'd gotten her hands on someone else's secret, and was holding it over their head in exchange for cash?

Hélène wouldn't put it past her. There seemed to be no line May wouldn't cross in her quest to become queen.

When Hélène had exhausted every corner of the room, she sat back on her heels, the skirts of her violet gown rippling around her. She could still hear the noises of the party downstairs; the music was softer now, reflecting the lateness of the hour. She was running out of time.

Laurent's letter had to be here. It was May's greatest weapon against Hélène; why would she leave it in London, and risk losing it? May was far too clever to let it out of her sight. She would have brought the letter with her, wouldn't she?

"Most people consider it rude to go through someone else's belongings."

Hélène stumbled to her feet and whipped around. May stood in the doorway, surveying the scene with pursed lips.

"Most people consider it rude to spread vicious rumors about someone," Hélène countered.

May seemed to decide that this conversation had best not be overheard, because she walked into the room and shut the door behind her. "I'm not sure what you mean."

"Do you deny that you ruined Alix's chances with Eddy by telling everyone she suffered from fainting spells?"

Something flickered behind May's eyes, but her mask of polite behavior didn't slip. "If Alix has an affliction, I'm sorry to hear it."

"What about Ducky?" Hélène exclaimed. "I heard you at the Earl of Stafford's house, giving her terrible advice about Eddy. If that poor girl did a fraction of what you suggested, I'm sure Eddy went running in the other direction."

May's expression darkened. "You eavesdropped on me?"

"*You* blackmailed *me*!"

There was a heated pause. Hélène stared at May, who was breathing heavily, hands clenched into tight fists.

At least now they were fighting the way Hélène had always wanted to—in the open, with weapons drawn.

"I don't like that word, *blackmail*," May said at last, her voice tense. "You're the one who slept with your family's coachman. All I did was remind you of that fact. I could ruin you, yet I have shown great restraint in keeping your tawdry behavior a secret."

Hélène drew herself up to her full height, grateful that she was tall, and stared down at May. "Give it to me."

"Excuse me?" May spluttered.

Hélène strove for her most commanding, princess-like tone. "Give me the letter. After everything you've done, you owe me that much."

"I don't owe you anything!"

"I am going to marry Nicholas. Do you really want to get on my bad side? Or do you want to *help* me, and know that you have an ally in the next Tsarina of Russia?"

It hurt something deep inside Hélène, acting like Eddy

meant nothing to her. Especially to May. But she needed to get Laurent's letter back, and May would never surrender it if she harbored any suspicions about Hélène and Eddy.

May gave an incredulous little laugh. "You're the worst sort of hypocrite! All your claims of loving Eddy, and now that you've lost him—through your own foolishness, I might add—you've moved on to his *cousin*!"

Hélène shrugged. "As if you wouldn't go after Nicholas yourself if you thought you had a chance."

"I would have more chance than you if he knew how promiscuous you've been!"

"That's why I need the letter," Hélène said evenly. "You're right, of course; you could show it to Nicholas's family, and our negotiations would fall apart. But if you do that, I swear that I'll bring you down with me." She met May's gaze. "I highly doubt that Her Majesty would be pleased to hear how cruelly you treated Alix and Ducky, two of her favorite granddaughters. Or how you bullied and intimidated me."

Beneath her cool exterior, May flinched—slightly, but Hélène caught it. Good. She'd touched a nerve.

"You can't prove anything," May replied, but she sounded uncertain.

"I don't need to. Don't you know by now that the higher you climb, the more perilous it becomes? A mere hint of scandal would knock you forever out of reach of Eddy. As you helpfully reminded me in your note about Laurent, a future queen must be above reproach."

May stared at Hélène for a long moment, then let out a breath. "Even if I had the letter, I wouldn't give it to you."

Footsteps sounded out in the hall, but neither young woman

moved. If someone walked in on them, Hélène would pretend that they were best friends, exchanging hair ribbons and gossip. The thought was laughable.

"What do you mean, you don't have the letter?" she asked quietly.

"It's in safekeeping with someone else. And as long as you stay out of my way regarding Prince Eddy, it will stay hidden with her. The Romanovs will never hear of your indiscretions—at least not from me."

Her, May had said. The letter was guarded by a woman. May's mother, perhaps; but if it was with her mother, wouldn't May have access to it?

"I know you won't believe me, but I wish you good luck in your pursuit of Nicholas," May went on. "You are right: I would rather have a future tsarina as an ally than an enemy. Which is why you can trust that I won't reveal your secret." She gave a venomous smile. "I'm sure I'll call in that debt at some point. When I do, I'll expect you to pay up."

This whole plan had failed miserably. Even after searching through May's things, even after a direct confrontation, all Hélène had learned was that the letter was elsewhere.

At least May believed she'd moved on to Nicholas. Hélène knew that if May suspected the truth, she would have circulated the letter at the party and let Hélène live with the cataclysmic fallout.

Still, time was running out. Hélène needed to get that letter back in her possession before Eddy started to believe this nonsense about her and Nicholas.

If he gave up on her and agreed to the world tour—or worse, began to entertain the idea of marrying someone else—

No, Hélène refused to think of that. She would find a way. Somehow.

THE NEXT MORNING, THE FIRST DAY OF THE RACES, HÉLÈNE emerged onto the *Polar Star*'s main deck and saw that Nicholas was already dressed.

Hélène's parents were still below, probably drinking coffee and nursing their hangovers; they had returned with Vladimir in the early hours, all raucously singing what sounded like a Russian drinking song.

Nicholas nodded in greeting. "Hélène. I hope you slept well." He paused, seeming awkward. "I wanted to . . . thank you, I mean. For helping last night."

Hélène came to join him at the iron railing. "I'm glad at least one of us had a good night." Normally, she might have attempted a shocking joke, like *I trust you* didn't *sleep well*, but she didn't have the heart.

Nicholas clearly saw her distress. "Are you all right?"

"It's Eddy." She stared down at the water below, the wind sending little ripples over its choppy surface. "Her Majesty told him that if he doesn't announce an engagement soon, he will be sent on a three-year world tour."

"She's probably been talking to my father. That's exactly the type of threat he would come up with," Nicholas said. Hélène could tell that it wasn't a joke.

She fought to keep her voice steady. "I just . . . I wish I knew what to do."

Nicholas nodded slowly. "You said that it was more

complicated than a quarrel. Did the queen refuse you permission to marry?"

"She gave us permission, actually. Last year, before I . . ." *Before I ruined everything.*

"Then what's the problem?"

"I can't explain." Hélène's voice caught. "All I can say is that there's an obstacle, and I'm trying to solve it without telling Eddy because he would only make things worse. If he got involved, everything would fall apart, and then he and I would *never* be able to get married. . . ."

Hélène was rambling. She realized, to her mortification, that tears were streaming down her cheeks.

"I'm sorry. I'm not usually this distraught," she managed, sniffling.

"Of course you're distraught. You're hurting, and you can't even be comforted by the person you love." Nicholas hesitated. "I know I'm not Eddy, but you can always talk about these things with me."

"Thank you," Hélène replied, but for some reason she was crying harder.

Then Nicholas did something completely unexpected. He stepped forward and pulled her into a hug.

"It's all right," he murmured, cradling his arms around Hélène's upper back, her hair. "Everything is going to be all right. Please, don't cry."

After a moment of shock, Hélène found herself relaxing into the hug. There was something so reassuring about Nicholas. His body felt so warm and steady against hers, so resolute. Hélène guessed that he'd done this many times with his mother, or his sister Xenia, or perhaps even with Alix, though this embrace didn't feel romantic in nature. It felt calming. She sensed that she could offload all her problems on him and he wouldn't be fazed; he would just help her think through them all, with logic and reason. As a friend.

Hélène's head tipped onto Nicholas's shoulder, and she let herself listen to his heartbeat. It was nice, simply being held like this. No one had wrapped their arms around her in weeks, not since she'd seen Amélie in Portugal.

"Sasha will be pleased to hear how *close* you two have become," purred a voice to her left.

Hélène opened her eyes and stepped back, wiping at her cheeks in case they were still wet with tears. Nicholas's uncle Vladimir stood near the entrance to the yacht's salon, leaning against the doorframe.

"Uncle," Nicholas said warningly.

Vladimir chuckled, waving away Nicholas's concern. "Don't worry, I doubt anyone saw you two together. And even if they did, what does it matter? You and Her Royal Highness are practically engaged," he added, with a deferential nod in Hélène's direction.

She realized with a bolt of surprise that Vladimir had drawn his own conclusions about her and Nicholas. He assumed their easy manner meant that they had held each other before, in a far more intimate setting.

For some people—people who weren't as demonstrative with their emotions—that might be the case. Well, Vladimir didn't know Hélène.

"Speaking of the engagement," Hélène's father cut in, "you must ask His Imperial Highness to reply to my last letter."

Hélène whirled about to see her parents standing at the top of the staircase, watching the scene that had just transpired. Philippe seemed to be bursting with glee, while Marie Isabelle was quietly studying Hélène. She alone seemed to sense that her daughter was upset, that this was not the embrace of two lovers, but something else.

Hélène didn't care what her father or Vladimir thought. What did it matter, when this farce of an engagement with Nicholas would be over soon anyway?

She had bigger problems. Like what she was going to do about Laurent's letter.

As strange as it was to believe anything May claimed, Hélène sensed that May hadn't been lying about the letter's location. She really had given it to someone else. But whom?

Hélène needed to figure it out, and fast. Because if she didn't get the letter back soon, she risked losing Eddy for good.

CHAPTER FIFTEEN

Alix

ALIX GRIPPED TIGHT TO THE SIDE OF THE SMALL BOAT, TRYING TO ignore the choppy sensation as they skimmed over the waves. Why had she agreed to go out into the harbor with Eddy and May?

Of course, she knew precisely why. She was hoping for a glimpse of Nicholas, however brief.

That morning at breakfast, Uncle Bertie had asked Eddy if he wouldn't mind picking up a few guests from the royal yacht. Alix had immediately offered to join him. Seeing her grandmother's curious glance—the queen probably thought Alix was romantically inclined toward Eddy again, though she had never actually felt that way in the first place—Alix had mumbled something about wanting to see the yacht club from the water. As if she cared about that.

"I'd love to come, too, if that's all right," May had ventured, glancing tentatively at Eddy. Alix had nearly rolled her eyes at May's painfully obvious flirtation. She'd looked over at George, wondering if he would offer to join, too, but he had just stared down at his plate.

Now, the wind tore at Alix's hat, making its blue ribbon snap out behind her. Eddy was navigating their little motorboat through the harbor, assisted by a sailor in a crisp white uniform, while the two young women perched on wooden seats at the front.

Alix had expected May to keep up a steady stream of chatter, but she was silent, as if reluctant to bother Eddy. The yachts rose up around them like sleeping beasts. Alix recognized Leopold of Belgium's, and her cousin Wilhelm's, and a few gleaming white hulls of new American yachts. Farthest from shore was the *Victoria and Albert II*, where Uncle Bertie was currently hosting a number of guests.

"Oh, look, the Romanov boat!" May pointed to a yacht marked with Cyrillic writing.

Alix reached up to adjust her hat, trying to hide the sudden, obvious joy she felt at simply being near Nicholas. She felt Eddy glancing at her; he knew about Alix and Nicholas, since she had told him last year.

When Nicholas stepped out onto the deck, Alix's smile broadened. He didn't see their boat, and she was loath to cause a scene by shouting hello. So she allowed herself a decadent moment of simply watching him: drinking in the strong lines of his body, the impatient, eager way he moved. In just a moment he would catch sight of them, and then he would insist that they all come aboard for a cup of coffee. Inevitably, someone would ask for a tour—and then he and Alix might find a chance to slip away, down to his room, where he would tug at the strings of her gown, his lips on hers. . . .

She flushed and looked down, though she was unable to stop smiling. Hopefully, no one had guessed the content of her daydreams. Oh, she was wanton, and she couldn't even bring herself to care. Her whole body still tingled with joy from the previous night. Alix knew that after what they had done, she was supposed to feel guilty, but she simply didn't regret it.

Even more shocking, she knew that she would be with Nicholas again the next chance she got.

"Look how happy those two are together!" May leaned toward Alix as if exchanging girlish gossip, but she spoke loud enough for Eddy to hear. "From what I've heard, we can expect an engagement announcement any day now!"

Alix looked back up at the *Polar Star.* Hélène had emerged and was talking to Nicholas. Hélène was turned away from their little boat, so Alix couldn't see her face; but even from this distance she could tell that Nicholas was looking at Hélène with concern.

"I think the news of an engagement is just a rumor," Alix replied, as calmly as she could.

Eddy had not spoken, but his eyes were fixed on the two figures.

And then, as everyone in the motorboat watched, Nicholas stepped forward and pulled Hélène into a hug.

Next to her, May let out a false laugh. "I see now why Hélène claimed a stomachache and left the party early last night!"

No, Alix wanted to cry out. Hélène and Nicholas had left the party early so that Nicholas could be alone with *her,* not with Hélène. But of course, she couldn't very well correct May's rather presumptuous statement—not without admitting her own lack of virtue.

As Alix watched, Nicholas's uncle emerged onto the deck,

smiling in unmistakable approval. And there were Hélène's parents, seeming equally delighted by this turn of events.

Eddy was completely still. Finally, his voice gravelly, he said, "We need to get back to shore."

May tilted her head. "But the guests on the *Victoria and Albert II*—"

"They can find their own damned boat. We're going back," Eddy snapped, and May didn't argue again.

No one seemed to notice that Alix hadn't spoken.

It's just a charade, she kept telling herself. Hélène had probably been upset over Eddy, and Nicholas had stepped forward to comfort her, and it meant nothing more than that. And yet . . . it was impossible not to see how well he and Hélène fit together, how totally at ease they were with each other.

Or how supportive their families were.

Alix's eyes were still fixed on Nicholas and Hélène even as Eddy sped their boat toward the yacht club. They were a striking pair, she had to admit: both tall and dark-haired, with aristocratic good looks. They even *moved* the same. It was something in the tilt of their heads, the absolute command of their gazes. You could see centuries of dynasty reflected in their every gesture. It wasn't something that could be taught; it had to be bred into you, absorbed from your parents the moment you drew your first breath.

Hélène's family had been rulers since before the Crusades, even if they no longer sat on a throne. Alix felt provincial and quaint by comparison.

But that wasn't what hurt the most.

Watching them, Alix realized that she would never get to behave with Nicholas as Hélène was: to walk with him arm in arm, share all his dances, hold him close while his family beamed in approval. All she would ever get was what she had now. Stolen moments when he snuck away from a party, illicit whispers on the dance floor for a single, precious dance.

Since the moment he'd arrived in London, Alix had been too swept up in the joy of seeing him to question what they were doing. But now, the reality of their situation hit her as it hadn't before.

She would never get permission to marry Nicholas. His parents would never look at her the way Vladimir had looked at Hélène.

Alix blinked as they pulled up to the yacht club. Sailors bounded toward their boat, tethering it to the dock, holding out a hand to help her and May ashore.

Eddy leapt out of the boat without a goodbye and marched with bold, angry strides up the lawn. Every line of his body screamed outrage and hurt.

Oh no. Alix wasn't sure what he thought, exactly—did he assume that Hélène had left him for Nicholas? That she had seen a greater opportunity than Queen of England and leapt at it? Whatever conclusions he'd drawn, they were based on a misunderstanding.

Alix wasn't sure what he was about to do, but she knew that she needed to stop him. Forget Hélène's admonitions about keeping him in the dark; she would race after him, grab his shoulders, and tell him not to worry, that Hélène and Nicholas were just playacting.

That he and Hélène still had a shot, even if Alix was no longer sure that was true for her and Nicholas.

"Eddy!" Alix grabbed her white linen skirts in both hands

and stumbled after him, ignoring the glances of fellow guests. "Eddy, wait!"

He paused, but not for Alix's sake. He had reached their grandmother.

Queen Victoria was the most visible person on the whole shore, dressed as always in black, which was glaring amid the sea of festive summer whites. Guests spilled out of the clubhouse's deck toward the water, clutching flutes of champagne or tumblers of whiskey despite the morning hour. Everyone wore airy blouses or cream-colored dresses, spotless white suits with matching top hats.

Alix watched as Eddy leaned over and murmured something in their grandmother's ear. The queen looked at him in surprise and asked a question Alix couldn't make out. Eddy nodded once, fiercely, then bowed a curt goodbye and started up the hill. He disappeared through one of the doors of the clubhouse, a clapboard structure with a gabled roof.

Alix hurried to follow. She couldn't say why, but she felt like she needed to stop whatever action he'd just set in motion.

The clubhouse was empty; everyone had gone outside to watch the races. Alix wandered past a room with leather furniture and nautical flags on the walls. In one corner was an old wooden steering wheel, so big it looked like it had come from a pirate ship.

She found a corridor and turned, heading toward the telltale clatter of pots that signified a kitchen. The servers would know where to look, she thought; at the very least they could direct her to the bar. That's where Eddy was headed, right? To get a drink?

Alix paused halfway down the hall. There was a single

door to her right. At first glance she'd thought it was a closet, but she heard noises inside, so maybe it wasn't a closet at all.

Alix threw open the door. It took a few moments for her eyes to adjust to the dimness and register what she was seeing.

It was indeed a closet, and her brother Ernie was inside—with their footman, Johann.

They were kissing.

CHAPTER SIXTEEN

May

THAT AFTERNOON, AFTER THEY HAD RETURNED FROM THE REGATTA—a regatta where Eddy had been conspicuously absent—a footman knocked at May's bedchamber and asked if May would please join Her Majesty for tea. May hurried after him, grateful that her white dress was still as spotless as when she had put it on that morning.

"You can wait for Her Majesty here," the footman announced, leading her into Victoria's second-floor sitting room.

May took a seat on a floral-printed sofa, then nervously stood again. What if Hélène had made good on her threats, and told the queen everything May had done? Surely she wouldn't dare while May still had the power to ruin her?

In the corner sat Victoria's writing desk, a half-finished letter on its surface. Framed pictures hung on the butter-yellow walls. A console table behind the sofa was covered in dozens of personal knickknacks. May stepped closer to examine them. There were little statuettes and a miniature of Prince Albert, and was that a brass paperweight shaped like a baby's foot?

"That was Alfred's. I had a sculptor cast it on his first birthday." Victoria's voice cut into May's thoughts.

"Oh! Your Majesty." May sank into the lowest possible

curtsy, embarrassed to have been caught snooping. She was as bad as Hélène.

"It's quite all right, May. I must admit, I'm glad you gravitated toward the baby's foot. When I brought Alexandra here twenty-five years ago, she just sat on the sofa and stared out the window. Didn't pick up a single thing, and this room is full of them." Victoria sniffed disapprovingly.

"I'm sorry," May said again. Had she heard correctly? It sounded like Victoria was suggesting that she'd brought Alexandra to this very room before Bertie proposed—and that May might be in a similar position.

Maybe she wasn't here to be reprimanded after all.

"A small amount of curiosity is an admirable quality." Queen Victoria gestured toward the French doors that led to a balcony. "Please, do come outside."

Striped curtains lifted in the breeze, revealing that a table had been set for tea, with solid-gold flatware and monogrammed napkins. May waited until the queen was seated before tentatively taking the other chair.

"Are you enjoying Cowes thus far?" Queen Victoria asked, immediately reaching for a scone and the clotted cream.

"Very much so, Your Majesty. What a joy it is, falling asleep to the scent of roses and magnolia, listening to the sounds of the ocean."

"Osborne is at its best in the summer. The colors are so vibrant," Victoria said, as if she didn't live her own life wearing nothing but black. "You know, Albert and I built this house together. He called it our little Naples on the English Channel."

May had been to Naples, and didn't see the resemblance, though she wisely refrained from saying so.

"You and His Royal Highness built a beautiful home," she replied instead.

"The children always loved it here," Victoria mused. "I have such fond memories of watching George learning to ride on the lawn—a sweet little cream-colored pony that I gave him one summer. I wanted George to have something of his own, since Eddy always overshadows him."

Victoria was watching May as she said this. Did she have a purpose in bringing up George, the brother whose heart May once thought she knew? Bewildered, May simply said, "How lovely."

The queen's eyes were still fixed on May, inquisitive and sharp as an owl's. "George has always been the steadier of the two Wales brothers. Unlike flighty and impulsive Eddy. Which is why it came as such a surprise this morning, when Eddy asked to speak with me about his future."

May knew she should say something, but all she could manage was "Oh?"

Victoria seemed to think this was sufficient, and continued. "You have known Eddy his whole life, so you are aware how stubborn and willful he can be. It might not surprise you to learn that he recently asked my permission to marry a young woman—a foreign princess, as it happens. I granted it, to my own regret." She meant Hélène, of course.

"I congratulate His Royal Highness," May began, but Victoria waved away her words.

"That young woman was a complete disappointment. Promised to convert and then went back on her word. Eddy was devastated!" Victoria seemed surprisingly protective of her grandson. "He persisted in thinking she might change her mind a second time, but I don't share his confidence. So I told him that he has two choices," the queen said crisply. "He can leave for an extended tour of the colonies, a grueling round-the-world trip through all our dominions overseas. To India, Burma, Australia, New Zealand, and Canada. It would be a tour full of public events, with little opportunity for adventure. No hunting tigers or climbing temples."

May poured tea into her cup simply to have something to do with her hands. She was far too nervous to take a sip.

"Or he can be married next spring."

May sensed that it was in her best interest to remain silent, so she merely nodded. Below in the grounds, a gardener was cutting one of the hedges. His shears made a slicing sound in the warm afternoon air.

"I had several young women selected as prospective brides, but Eddy informed me that he is not interested in any of them. He kept insisting that he would wait for the princess he loved, however long it took." Victoria set down her spoon with a definitive clang and looked across the table. "Until this morning, when he declared that he wanted to marry you."

So it had worked.

May hadn't formulated a specific plan when she invited herself on Eddy's excursion this morning. She wouldn't have dared to do it if Alix wasn't already joining—May knew better than to be alone again with Eddy, after she'd asked him to marry her and he'd said no—but a group outing felt safe enough. May hadn't even known they would see Hélène. She'd merely wanted to stay close to Eddy in case something transpired.

And how it had.

It had been an unexpected stroke of luck, catching Hélène and Nicholas in that embrace. All May had done was gently point out that those two had left together the previous evening, and remark that they would probably get engaged. Now Eddy finally realized that Hélène had left him for good.

It was really happening, May thought, twisting her napkin in her lap. After all her scheming, after wounding Alix and negotiating with Ducky, after her endless feud with Hélène, she had finally made it.

"I am humbled," May said softly, "and fully sensible of the honor that Eddy does me."

"You speak of the position. Not of the man," Victoria noted.

May went still. She was not at the finish line, not yet. "I didn't mean—"

"Eddy does not claim to love you," the queen cut in. "But he prefers you to the other options, and claims that you are well suited to the role of queen. Do you agree?"

Prefers you to the other options. May wondered how much Victoria knew about the morning's events, whether she guessed that Eddy was proposing to May out of spite. She weighed her reply with excruciating care. "His Royal Highness pays me a high compliment. I hope to live up to his expectations."

"So you do not love him?"

Would Victoria believe her if May pretended that she had shyly loved Eddy all these years, afraid to admit the truth of her feelings out of fear of rejection? Was that the right answer?

May suspected not.

"I consider Eddy a friend. Of course, I have the utmost

respect for him and for our entire family. And I believe that over time, Eddy and I can develop love between us, based on our shared duties, and children."

There was a long silence. Victoria stirred her spoon in her cup of tea, then lifted it for a slow sip. May hardly dared to breathe.

Finally, the queen lowered her cup and stared at May. "I was prepared to let Eddy marry for love once before, and I will not make that mistake again. Our future queen must not be chosen based on emotions and impulse, but on her fortitude. Her poise," Victoria declared.

May liked to think she had those things in spades, thanks to her father.

"Eddy is not perfect, as you know," Victoria went on. "He is impetuous, and not nearly intellectual enough. Try as I might, I never could get him to learn a single foreign language. Do you speak any languages, May?"

"German and French. And a bit of Italian, though it's largely conversational."

"I'm pleased to hear it," the queen said soundly. "Eddy needs a wife with a good head on her shoulders. One who is mature, free from impulsiveness or reckless actions. One who will remain constant."

Clearly, the queen had taken Hélène's refusal to convert as a sign that she was headstrong and willful, and careless with Eddy's feelings. May hoped it made her seem more reliable, more responsible, by comparison.

The queen leaned back in her chair. "There is, however, the issue of your family. You know some people will say you are insufficiently royal."

"I am a great-granddaughter of King George III and Queen Charlotte," May hurried to remind her.

"But your father is merely the son of a grand duke, and an inconsequential one at that. Not to mention that he and your mother squander any income I grant them."

Well, no one could accuse the queen of mincing words.

"The manner in which my parents conduct their financial affairs grieves me deeply." May lowered her eyes.

"Bertie says he will not have it," the queen added, with brutal frankness. "He cannot stand the thought of your parents at Marlborough House. He finds them too . . ." The queen trailed off, but May could finish the sentence. *Too tacky, too gauche.*

If only the Prince of Wales, or the queen, understood the truth—that the Tecks' greatest problem wasn't their social standing; it was Francis's temper. His unadulterated cruelty.

But then, no one ever saw what went on behind closed doors.

"I understand the Prince of Wales's opinion, though it saddens me," May said gravely. "Still, the opinion that primarily concerns me is yours. If you'll forgive me for saying it, you were about to let Eddy marry a young woman who was not raised in the Church of England. Would you weigh the sins of my parents as greater than the sin of not sharing our faith?"

There was another drawn-out silence, heavy with significance.

"May, you are not who I would have picked for Eddy, but I am beginning to think that he made a sound choice for himself. You are clearly a woman of good sense. And that is what Eddy needs more than anything. Far be it from me to hold your parents against you," she added, almost as an afterthought. "My mother caused her fair share of problems for me, when I was a young woman."

"Thank you, Your Majesty." May felt a hollow shock ringing through her, making her almost dizzy. It was, she realized, the feeling of victory. Of no longer having to struggle.

It was *relief.*

Victoria studied her for a long moment, head tilted. Then she remarked, "I doubt any of my tiaras would suit you."

"Your Majesty?" May asked, with some alarm.

"No matter. We shall make you a new one."

THAT EVENING, THE PRINCE OF WALES HAD BEEN SCHEDULED TO hold a reception aboard the *Victoria and Albert II.* Now that reception had been commandeered by the queen.

May couldn't be certain, but she had the sense that the yacht had been rapidly cleared of guests, Bertie's mistress and the baccarat tables shuffled onto another boat, replaced by flowers and a sense of decorum.

Now May was here, standing on the middle of the yacht's three decks. There was a chill in the air off the Channel. In the distance, the sun was setting over the slate-gray waters, which were still punctuated by colorful sails as a few competitors—mainly the victors of various races—returned their boats to the harbor. May felt an odd sort of kinship with them. *I won today, too,* she wanted to cry out. *I started the race at a disadvantage, and yet here I am, about to win the greatest prize.*

Guests spilled out of the yacht's main salon, which was

essentially a floating stateroom, its walls paneled with green silk and its furniture gilded. Brocade curtains hung around the great glass windows overlooking the harbor. From deeper in the ship, uniformed staff emerged with drinks; a pair of violinists played in the corner of the deck. Since this was the queen's party, everyone wore evening dress—frothy gowns and diamond necklaces, the men in dark tailcoats or military uniforms with sashes. May reached down to finger her broché satin gown, the nicest one she owned. If only she had some decent jewelry. Well, that would soon be fixed.

She noted with pleasure that everyone was here to see her triumph. Alix stood along the railing, seeming lost in thought; the Coburg sisters were talking with their Prussian cousins, who'd come over from their yacht, the *Hohenzollern*. And the tsarevich was in attendance with his uncle, accompanied by Hélène and her parents.

Studiously *not* looking at Hélène, his arms crossed, was Eddy.

May hadn't seen him all day, not since he'd gotten off their motorboat and marched up the slope of the yacht club toward his grandmother. When he was still missing an hour before his supposed engagement announcement, she had started to panic—but then George had arrived, dragging Eddy in his wake, as well as their cousin Ernest of Hesse.

Both Eddy and Ernie were in distinctly rough shape. Their cheeks were sunburned, their movements slow; though somehow, probably with the help of very competent valets, George seemed to have gotten both young men into evening attire.

It would seem that Eddy had gotten off the boat that morning, declared to Queen Victoria that he would marry May, and then spent the day with Ernie, getting drunk. Probably at a dockside bar that catered to common sailors.

As if he wanted to get drunk enough to forget this engagement altogether.

"What a divine view," Mrs. de Falbe remarked. May smiled and murmured a reply; Mrs. de Falbe was one of the few guests who paid her any mind, and she suspected that the woman only did so because Mr. de Falbe was the Danish ambassador, and had never explained to his wife just how unimportant May was. Earlier, May had tried to start up a conversation with a few of the married ladies her own age, who had all come with their husbands from London—Lady Clementine Walsh, Lady Leigh Arlington. They had turned up their noses at her. If they only knew.

"Good evening, everyone."

Though the queen did not shout, her voice projected through the space like an actor's. She stepped up near the railing of the yacht, diminutive and yet unmistakably the most powerful force present.

One by one, everyone fell silent and turned expectantly toward Victoria. She held out her hands. "Bertie and I are so pleased to welcome you on our family's boat this evening. I do hope you all enjoyed the races. I had my money on the *Jasper*, so I'm afraid I lost a few bets. Apparently, I know horses better than I know yachts." There was polite laughter at the queen's words.

May tried to catch Eddy's gaze, but he didn't see her. His expression was glassy and vacant, almost haunted.

"I have an exciting announcement," the queen went on. "My dear grandson and heir, Eddy, recently came to me with momentous news. *Grandmother,* he said, *I have fallen in love and asked a young woman for her hand in marriage. Now I come to you for your blessing.*"

Victoria was taking a rather liberal approach to the truth, but this was the sort of story people wanted to hear, wasn't it?

May tried to arrange her features into a simpering sort of smile, the way a young woman in love would look.

"Luckily for us," Queen Victoria went on, "the young woman in question is far from a stranger. Why, she's a member of our own dear family!"

All over the yacht, eyes cut to Ducky, though a few people glanced at Alix, too. Not a single person was looking at May.

So there was a moment of uncertain shock when the queen said, "I am delighted to congratulate my darling Eddy for his engagement to Princess May of Teck!"

There was a heartbeat of flat, disbelieving silence. Then the guests all came to their senses and began to applaud, even if they looked at May in bewilderment.

Uncle Bertie stepped forward, gesturing to May. When she placed her palm in his, he held out his other hand to Eddy, as if he meant to clasp their two hands together.

Eddy stumbled as he came to join her. May forced herself not to wince, though her eyes cut to George. Wasn't it his job to keep track of Eddy, to keep him from getting so roaring drunk?

When she met George's gaze, though, there was something in it she couldn't decipher. May's heart skipped.

Eddy had regained his balance, reaching a hand obediently to May. He wasn't smiling. It didn't matter, she told herself, and smiled broadly enough for both of them.

None of the rest of it mattered now May was going to marry Eddy. Finally, after all her striving, she had won.

Finally, she was safe.

CHAPTER SEVENTEEN

Hélène

EDDY WAS ENGAGED TO MAY OF TECK.

Listening to Queen Victoria congratulate the happy couple, Hélène felt frozen in place, as if she'd transformed into one of those marble statues at the Earl of Stafford's house. Unable to even lift a hand toward the man she loved. Unable to breathe.

How many times had she imagined the queen making this very same announcement about her? Not that Hélène cared about the social status such an engagement would convey. She wasn't like May, staring around the party with that smug little smile on her face. Hélène only wanted a public engagement because she wanted to proclaim her love for Eddy to the world. She longed to stake her claim on him, to shout from the rooftops that he was hers and no one else's.

Instead she had to stand here, the world spinning around her, while he got engaged to *May*. And no one knew how much it hurt her.

Except Nicholas, she realized, as he reached a steadying hand beneath her elbow. Nicholas knew.

"Hélène." Nicholas's breath was warm in her ear. "Should we leave?"

Yes, she wanted to leave. She wanted to sprint to the side of the yacht and jump out into the ocean, swim all the way to Portugal and cry on her sister's shoulder.

The deck had become chaotic as guests crushed eagerly toward May. They all exclaimed that they'd had no idea about her and Eddy, none at all! Had he started courting here at Osborne House? When did it happen?

Hélène heard the subtext in their questions. They were trying to puzzle out how this shocking, inexplicable engagement had come about. *By sabotage,* Hélène wanted to tell them. *And cruelty and blackmail.*

May wasn't wearing a ring, Hélène noticed with a stab of relief. Still, this all felt unbearably official—announced by the queen herself, at a reception full of gossipy nobles and foreign royals, who would go home and write to their friends of the news. By tomorrow, half of England would know about Eddy and May.

It was far more official than Eddy's so-called "understanding" with Alix, an arrangement that had never been formalized.

Or Eddy's engagement to Hélène, which had been known only to their respective families. An engagement like that, made in secret, was easy to break off.

Hélène stared at Eddy, noting how stiff and resentful he seemed. Actually, she realized, he might be drunk. Feeling her gaze, Eddy looked up.

His eyes slid from her to Nicholas, anger radiating from him in waves that were practically visible. *No,* Hélène mouthed, when she understood. No, no, surely he didn't believe she and Nicholas were really together?

But it seemed that he did. Hélène's heart broke at what an earth-shattering mistake she'd made.

"That's it. We're getting you out of here," Nicholas said, a bit protectively.

His hand still on her elbow, he guided her through the crowds, saying something about her seasickness; Hélène didn't know and didn't especially care. She felt hot and dizzy and weak all at once. A few people glanced their way, because he was Nicholas, after all, the future tsar. But they quickly looked back to the greater drama of the evening—May, who was at the center of a sea of admirers, smiling more broadly than Hélène had ever seen.

May, a princess so far down the pecking order that most of them had forgotten her, who would now become queen.

Hélène was only dimly aware of Nicholas helping her into a rowboat, where a sailor in a uniform asked where he could take them. Hélène felt numb. She leaned over, trailing her fingers in the choppy water, relishing the cold.

"I'm so sorry," Nicholas said, quietly enough that the sailor couldn't hear. "This is my fault. I'm the one who asked you here, out of selfish reasons, because I wanted the chance to be with Alix. But now Eddy thinks—I mean, he assumes—"

"You're not to blame, Nicholas," Hélène heard herself say. "It was my idea that we pretend to court, remember?"

She had trusted that Eddy would wait for her: that somehow he would see through the performance she and Nicholas were playing out before the world. Even if he hadn't, even if he truly thought he'd lost her to his cousin, why had he gotten engaged so quickly? And to such a venomous, heartless person as May, someone who only viewed him as a title, not a person.

Hélène should have told Eddy everything. She should have let him in on all her plans, explained that she was playing a dangerous game against May and that he needed to be careful. It would have been risky, certainly, but at least she wouldn't have risked *this.*

When they were back aboard the *Polar Star,* Nicholas handed Hélène to a concerned-looking Violette. He hesitated. "Are you sure you're all right? I mean, of course you're not all right, but—should I—"

"Go back to the party," Hélène forced herself to say over the roar in her ears. "Everyone will be focused on Eddy and May. This is a great opportunity for you and Alix. I want to be alone, anyway."

Nicholas's deep blue eyes were dark with sympathy. "I'm so sorry."

Hélène allowed Violette to shepherd her belowdecks. Her room aboard the yacht was lavish, its bed piled high with embroidered coverlets, the paneled wood walls inlaid with brass. It felt like they were in a palace, except for the small round window set into the wall, looking out over the water.

Violette said nothing as she helped Hélène out of her gown and into a chemise, then brushed her long dark hair until it rippled over her back.

"I'd like to rest," Hélène said woodenly.

Violette nodded and retreated, shutting the door behind her with a click.

Through the window, Hélène could just see the *Victoria and Albert II,* anchored only a hundred yards away and yet at an impossible distance from her. Its staterooms were aglow, the windows golden squares against the dimness. May and Eddy's impromptu engagement party was in full swing.

"I'm sorry, Eddy. I ruined everything," Hélène whispered into the silence.

Then she laid her head on the Romanovs' priceless silk pillow and cried.

CHAPTER EIGHTEEN

Alix

ALIX STOOD WITH MAXIMILIAN ON THE DECK, GLANCING FROM Eddy's glum expression to May's hard, polished smile. This was a disaster. Eddy had clearly gotten engaged to May out of hurt, after he'd seen Nicholas and Hélène together on the deck that morning. He'd done something drastic, as Alix had known he would.

If only she'd caught up with Eddy and explained that Nicholas and Hélène's courtship was just for show. She had tried to chase after him—but then she'd found Ernie and Johann, who had both promptly run off. Alix hadn't seen any of them for the rest of the day.

When Ernie and Eddy had shown up at this engagement party, dragged here by George, it was too late. The engagement was announced, and the damage was done.

Alix supposed she could tell Eddy the truth now . . . but what if it only made things worse?

"You seem surprised by this engagement," Maximilian observed, in a low tone. "Are you all right?"

Alix turned to look at Maximilian then. He didn't resemble the other guests, all painfully glamorous in their petal-soft dresses and glittering jewels. His clothes felt somewhat dated, his jacket cut too wide, the colors from at least five years ago. And, of course, he had that distinctly German beard.

Alix found it endearing, almost commendable, that he hadn't bought new clothes for the regatta—or shaved—in an effort to look like everyone else.

Maximilian colored, sensing her scrutiny. "Sorry if I overstepped. But I'm here, if you'd like to talk about it. As friends."

He thought that Alix was upset by Eddy and May's engagement. Come to think of it, many other guests had been shooting her curious glances. They must have all heard her name linked with Eddy's, back when Grandmama was trying to push the two of them together.

"Thank you," Alix told Maximilian. "I am surprised, yes. But not for the reasons you think. I do not love Eddy, and I never did."

He studied her, puzzled. "Her Majesty had told me that you were previously engaged to Eddy. When you told me that you didn't wish to be courted, I thought— That is, I assumed he had broken your heart."

"I didn't wish to be courted because I love someone else," Alix confessed.

If Maximilian was shocked by her honesty, he didn't show it. "I see" was all he said, with a solemn nod.

Alix hurried to change the subject. "Do you know where Ernie is? I'm concerned for him." Maximilian would assume she was worried about Ernie's drunkenness, but of course it was much bigger.

She wanted to talk to her brother about Johann, to make sure he was all right.

It had startled her, seeing the two of them together. Alix was not so sheltered as to be completely unaware that there could be romance between two men or two women. She had read novels, after all, many of which were written in France. It was just that in books, such men were always ridiculous and foppish, painting their faces with rouge or wearing earrings. Ernie loved to hunt and ride and drink liquor as much as any other man.

But then, Alix had already learned the hard way that life rarely resembled the world depicted in novels.

"There are some gentlemen on the upper deck smoking cigars. I'll look for your brother there," Maximilian promised, seeming grateful to have been given a task.

As he walked off, Alix caught sight of Nicholas. He must have just rejoined the party; he was approaching from the back of the yacht, where rowboats ferried guests to other boats or to shore.

Alix didn't hesitate. She wove through the crowds, ducking past servers with champagne on silver trays.

"Your Imperial Highness." She curtsied before him, because they were still in public and she knew enough to be careful.

"I was just escorting the Princess Hélène back to the *Polar Star.* She felt unwell," Nicholas explained.

Before Alix could reply, he waved his wrist in the direction of the yacht's interior. "I'm sorry. I seem to have lost a cuff link inside. Would you help me find it?" He spoke loudly, in case anyone was eavesdropping.

Alix followed him to the yacht's interior and down a narrow hallway that was clearly meant for staff. Nicholas tried a door, revealing a closet filled with wineglasses and folded cloth napkins. He pulled her inside and quickly shut the door behind them.

The only illumination was a thin golden light that crept in from the hallway. It gleamed on Nicholas's dark hair, casting a shadow along his jawline.

"I'm glad you're here," Alix began, but couldn't say more because Nicholas's mouth was on hers.

Her heart thudded wildly as he reached his arms around her. Within moments they were chest to chest, Alix's back colliding with the shelves as Nicholas lifted her, his thigh pressing into her skirts. His hands seemed to be everywhere at once: on the back of her neck, in her hair, around her waist. It was intoxicating and, at the same time, not nearly enough. She wanted all of him, right now—

Alix pulled back with a start, turning her face aside so that Nicholas's kiss fell on her hairline instead of her mouth.

Slowly, he lowered her and took a step back, running a hand through his hair. They were both breathing heavily.

"I am sorry," Nicholas said quickly. "I got carried away. It is just that I have thought of you every minute since we were apart."

"So have I," Alix whispered.

As her heartbeat slowed, the reality of her situation began to sink in. She was alone, in a closet, with a man. Just as Ernie had been earlier today.

"What are we doing, Nicholas?"

He winced apologetically. "We won't do this at a crowded event again. I will come back to Osborne House, or we can sneak you onto—"

"No," she interrupted. "I mean, what are we *doing*?"

Hélène and Eddy had spent a year in exactly this manner: meeting for flustered, frantic kisses at parties, stealing hours together whenever they could. Living separate lives in public and falling in love in secret, in the middle of the night.

Look where it had gotten them. Eddy was engaged to a woman who only wanted him for his title, and Hélène was heartbroken over it.

"I don't understand." Nicholas reached for her hands, and Alix, knowing she shouldn't, let him take them.

"We need to talk," she explained.

"If you're upset about last night, I take full responsibility. We do not have to—I mean, we can go back to the way things were—"

"Please do not think I have any regrets about last night," Alix whispered fiercely.

"Then what is it?"

"We will never get your parents' permission to marry, will we." She didn't phrase it as a question.

Nicholas's brow furrowed. "I promise, I will talk with them upon my return."

"And their opinion will be the same as it has always been! They have only allowed you at the regatta because they think you're here to court Hélène!" Alix's voice quavered as she thought of what she'd seen this morning—that moment between him and Hélène, which both of their families had watched with eager smiles. Her realization that she would never be the type of princess that Hélène was.

"I intend to tell my parents that Hélène and I are just friends," Nicholas began, but Alix tore her hands from his grip.

"And they'll insist you marry her anyway! They'll probably be grateful that you consider her a friend, unlike every other princess they have thrown your way!" Alix tried to step back, though there wasn't much space. "Your parents will win in the end. Our mistake was thinking we could change their minds."

When she'd tugged him into her bed the night before, her heart aching with love, Alix had thought of nothing except Nicholas, that she wanted to be as intensely close to him as possible.

She hadn't realized that she was making herself into his mistress.

"I don't know why you're saying this," Nicholas argued. "You got out of an engagement to Eddy. Why don't you think I can do the same with my engagement to Hélène? It's not even official!"

"Because the only person I had to convince was my grandmother! The Romanov dynastic machine is something else entirely."

Nicholas's voice caught on his reply. "What are you saying, Alix?"

"I'm saying that we need to stop seeing each other."

"No!" he cried out. When she flinched, he lowered his voice. "No, Alix, I refuse to accept this. You said you loved me, and you know I love you."

"Of course I love you. I'm just no longer convinced that it's enough. Look at us," she hissed, gesturing to the shadowed closet. "This is all we're ever going to be able to do together. If we can't marry, then—I can't go on. Not like this."

Alix was not Hélène, bold and brave and impetuous. She

could not live on stolen moments and slivers of time, hoping that somehow, someday, she could be with the man she loved despite the odds.

If she and Nicholas continued down this path, it could ruin her reputation—and it would certainly break her heart.

She had given her whole self to Nicholas, heart and body, and if she kept on doing so, over and over, what would be left when he walked away? He might not marry Hélène, but it was abundantly clear that he would never be able to marry Alix. Eventually he would choose someone else as a wife, and it would destroy her.

Alix had to walk away now, out of self-preservation. While there was still enough of her left to save.

She allowed herself one last moment to relish it all: the feel of Nicholas's breath on her cheek, the murmur of his voice as he begged her not to do this. The way his deep blue eyes fixed on hers, the tears streaking down her own cheeks.

Quietly, deep inside herself, she was letting him go.

"I am leaving," she declared, and this time Nicholas didn't try to change her mind.

As she stumbled out into the hallway, wiping at her face, Alix hurt so acutely that she felt like she would die. But of course she knew better. You couldn't actually die from a broken heart.

You just had to live with the pain of it.

LATER THAT NIGHT, WHEN SHE WAS FINALLY BACK IN HER ROOM at Osborne House, Alix stared up at the green canopy over her bed. She couldn't sleep. She had cried so hard her pillow seemed to be drowning in tears—knowing that on a yacht in the harbor, bobbing on the waves, Hélène was doing the very same thing. If only she could go see Hélène, find some comfort in their shared pain.

Instead Alix slipped out of bed, pulled on a silk dressing gown, and padded into the hallway.

Prince Ernest of Hesse, read the card a few doors down. She knocked.

An instant later the door swung open, revealing her brother, his own dressing gown tied at the waist. "Alix," he breathed, lowering the gas lamp he held. "It's you."

"You were expecting Johann?"

Ernie flinched and tried to shut the door in her face, but Alix held out a hand to prop it open.

"I've been trying to talk to you all day, Ernie!"

He let out a breath. "Whatever you thought you saw, you were mistaken."

"Please, don't shut me out! We have already been through so much together." Losing their mother. Losing Frittie. "Whatever is happening, let me be part of it."

Ernie hesitated, his eyes traveling over her face. "Have you been crying?"

"Only as much as you've been drinking."

Her brother let out a strangled laugh at that. "Please, I got enough judgment from Grannie and Aunt Alexandra today, and I'm dealing with an awful headache."

"You didn't need to run from me, you know," Alix said softly.

"Who said anything about running?" Ernie asked, in a flippant tone that didn't fool her. "I found Eddy outside the yacht club, getting into a carriage. He said he was going to get beers, and I asked to join."

Alix pushed past her brother into his room, a mirror image of hers but with darker, more masculine fabrics. He sighed and followed her, setting down the lamp before climbing up into his four-poster bed. Alix scooted up to sit next to him, the way she used to when they were children: when their mother tucked them in bed, telling stories of castles and knights, of sorcerers and enchantments.

Everything had felt so simple then, Alix recalled. So abundantly clear. Now she felt certain of nothing at all.

"Did Eddy tell you what he was upset about?"

"No," Ernie said simply.

"And you didn't *ask?*"

Ernie shook his head. "No, we just talked about the usual things. You know, the regatta. Horses. Gossip about other princes who are less wonderful than ourselves."

Of course that was all they'd talked about. Alix wondered why she'd expected otherwise. Even among family, society dictated that conversation avoid anything problematic—or anything that actually mattered.

"I'm sorry about my reaction. I mean—when I found you," Alix said haltingly. "I was just surprised."

Ernie turned to look her in the eyes. "You aren't ashamed of me?"

"Of course not!"

"But such desires are counter to God's will. Everyone knows that."

"Don't you remember what Mother always used to say? *God made you, and you are wondrous in His eyes.*"

"Yes, but—"

"Do you think that there is anything in all of creation that God doesn't touch?" Alix demanded. "Are you somehow the one single thing that exists outside His power?"

"No, of course not," Ernie mumbled.

"Well then, God made you this way. *He* gave you these feelings. Therefore, they cannot be wrong," Alix said firmly.

Her hand lay atop the scalloped edge of the coverlet; Ernie reached for it, giving her a fierce squeeze. "Thank you."

Alix saw that he was close to tears, and looked away so that she wouldn't start crying, too. She couldn't bear to weep any more today.

"Can I ask . . . you and Johann . . . ?"

"I love him." Ernie's reply was almost a whisper.

"When did it begin?"

"Last winter."

"Was he the first . . . ?"

"There was a groom once." Ernie let go of her hand, pulling a pillow into his lap to play with the fringe. "Alix, I have always known that I am different. Standing in the gentlemen's lounge at the opera or the races, hearing the way the other men talk about women . . . I think I was twelve when I realized that I was not like them."

She thought of what Ernie had said all those months ago in Darmstadt, when she was upset about Nicholas: *I know how hard it is.* He did know what it meant to love someone you couldn't be with.

"I'm so sorry," she whispered. "Thank you for sharing this with me."

Ernie stared out the window. "I promise that I have been discreet. I know what damage it would cause our family, you in particular, if this came out. It would ruin your marriage prospects."

"You think I care about that?" Alix asked. "All I care about is *you*, Ernie. I want you to be happy. And it's not as if you can go ask Grandmother for her blessing in marrying Johann."

"Unfortunately not." Ernie hesitated, then added, "Johann is nowhere near noble enough. Not even a baron, and Grannie would insist upon a duke at the very least."

He had *joked* about it. Alix was startled into a smile, but it quickly faded. "What will you do, since you cannot have Johann? Will you marry Maud?"

"It doesn't seem fair to marry Maud, or any woman, really. It feels deceptive, don't you think?" Ernie sat back with a sigh. "I suppose I'll just keep putting Grannie off for as long as possible. Maybe now that Eddy and May are engaged, she'll ease off on the rest of us for a bit."

Alix was silent at that. Ernie noticed and shifted, glancing over. "You're clearly upset about more than just Eddy's engagement. Did something happen with Nicholas?"

She decided to tell him. She skated over the details of the previous night, but she didn't hide that Nicholas had visited her in secret; she imagined Ernie could fill in the blanks just fine. Then Alix told him about the moment between Hélène and Nicholas on the yacht, how she had seen it and realized the hopelessness of her own situation with Nicholas.

"Alix. Are you sure?" Ernie asked slowly.

"I can't keep doing this, hiding my love, turning it into an awful, shameful secret—" Alix broke off, cringing. "I'm sorry. That was heartless of me, given what you and Johann are going through. It's far worse for you."

"I know what you meant," he assured her. "It is indeed awful—all the sneaking around, the lies, the stolen moments. Johann and I have kept our love a secret, but only because we have no other choice. You do."

"Are you saying I should fight for Nicholas?" she asked. "Because we've tried that, and his parents never budged."

"I meant that you can give him up, as you already did." Ernie's voice was infinitely gentle as he added, "I know it feels impossible, but you might love someone else someday, and marry that person. And it wouldn't be a lie. Unlike my marriage to any woman on this earth."

"I'm sorry. I didn't mean to say that Nicholas and I are as hopeless as you and Johann," Alix murmured. Because, of course, Ernie's situation was far worse. At least she could tell people that she loved Nicholas without them calling her a sinner.

Ernie tossed a pillow at her. "It's not a contest in suffering, Alix. We both love men who are forbidden to us, for one reason or another."

A clock chimed in the hallway. The wind was still howling outside, whistling down the grate of Ernie's fireplace. Alix tipped her head onto her brother's shoulder. She still felt the pain of losing Nicholas, like a shard of ice wedged in her chest, freezing her and slicing her all at once. But talking to Ernie had melted the ice, just a little.

After a while, Alix blurted out, "Which groom?"

"Hmm?" Ernie asked drowsily.

"You said you were"—she struggled to find the right word—"involved. With a groom, before Johann. Who was it?"

"Christoph, of course! Who did you think it was?" Ernie

asked with a strangled laugh. "Anselm and Leopold are both as old as the hills!"

For the second time that night, Alix surprised herself by laughing. It was a ragged sort of laugh, torn unwillingly from her chest—the kind of laugh that verged on tears.

"It's all right, Alix," her brother murmured, rubbing her shoulder. "Everything will be all right."

They both knew that Ernie was lying, that he had no way of knowing that anything would be right again. But he kept saying it anyway, and Alix pretended to believe him.

CHAPTER NINETEEN

May

THE FINAL MORNING OF THE REGATTA, MAY STOOD IN THE ENtrance hall of Osborne House. A row of carriages waited outside, ready to take the guests to the closing races.

May resisted the urge to remove her ivory gloves and steal another glance at her new engagement ring. Eddy clearly hadn't had time to visit the Crown Jewels vault or even a jewelry shop; May suspected that Her Majesty had been holding on to this ring, saving it for whenever he finally proposed. It had probably been meant for Alix, given how perfectly the turquoise stone matched Alix's bright blue eyes. At least the queen had managed to have the inside of the gold band engraved with May's and Eddy's full names—*Albert Victor and Victoria Mary, 1891*.

Eddy had given the ring to May a few nights earlier, amid much toasting and champagne and a profusion of speeches. Not that Eddy himself had said much. The only words he'd exchanged with May all week were *Shall I escort you in?* when the dinner bell rang. May had just nodded and kept on smiling until her cheeks hurt.

He had chosen May because he wanted to get engaged to *someone*, to prove to Hélène that he was as finished with her as she was with him. May had promised to be the easiest option.

Now she needed to keep her word, and ask him for nothing at all.

That was just fine with May. This engagement was a transaction, clean and devoid of emotion, and for her part, May was pleased with how the arrangement had gone thus far.

The news of their engagement hadn't yet been printed in the papers; Her Majesty would have to announce it before Parliament, and technically Parliament would need to approve. But May already felt like a future queen. The other ladies at the regatta were all swarming around her now, when just days ago they had stared blankly through her.

The only people absent from the weeklong engagement festivities had been Hélène and Nicholas. The *Polar Star* had weighed anchor the morning after Eddy and May's announcement; Nicholas had sent the queen a note, claiming "pressing business" back in Russia and thanking her for the lovely parties. May couldn't help feeling slightly curious about the timing. Had Hélène told Nicholas about her confrontation with May . . . pointedly leaving out the reason for their conflict? Surely Hélène wouldn't have admitted her previous liaisons to her new fiancé—unless she was sleeping with Nicholas now, too? But even if Nicholas didn't care about Hélène's lack of innocence, May knew that his parents most assuredly would. She still had Hélène under her thumb.

And in the meantime, news of May's engagement was spreading to London. Yesterday she had come downstairs to a pair of telegrams from her parents.

Her mother's message was predictably joyful.

Oh, May! I was speechless, utterly flabbergasted! What wondrous news! Only somehow word has got out in

London. Please do come back soon, people have been dropping by the house to congratulate you & we have not got a moment's peace & of course your Papa does get much annoyed. . . .

May could read between the lines. By *much annoyed*, Mary Adelaide meant that Francis had shouted at her. Perhaps even thrown a vase or a candlestick at her head. Only her father, May thought darkly, would be enraged over his daughter's engagement to a future king.

She had opened her father's telegram with shaking fingers.

May, we heard the news. I hope the queen will apologize for making such an announcement when your mother and I were not present. A deliberate insult, I think. Well, we are all quite surprised. A great position has been handed to you. Let us see whether you are up to the task.

Even now, after a lifetime of her father's slights—his neglect, his careless cruelty—May still felt wounded. His daughter would be queen someday, and he hadn't even congratulated her! *A great position has been handed to you!* As if May hadn't plotted and schemed and worked for years to bring this to fruition.

Her thoughts were interrupted by the rest of the houseguests, who descended the stairs in a whirl of muslin skirts and white linen jackets, their voices raised irreverently high.

"Grandmama!" Missy called out, hurrying to the queen. May noted with irritation that the girl didn't even curtsy.

"Ducky and I were wondering if we might be excused from the races today? I haven't gotten to visit town yet, and we leave tomorrow!"

May watched Victoria take in her granddaughter's eager smile. Missy's cheeks were flushed, her eyes bright with excitement.

"Very well," the queen relented. "George, you will accompany Missy and Ducky."

May's eyes cut to George, who was standing near the railing of the great staircase. Surely he would be thrilled at the prospect of some time alone with Missy.

Yet he wasn't smiling. He just nodded, his expression unreadable.

May wasn't sure what impulse caused her to blurt out, "Your Majesty. May I join the outing?"

"You don't want to come to the regatta?" Victoria asked; then she sighed and answered her own question. "You young people and your energy! Albert and I used to be the same when we visited new places. He always stopped at the local church to say a prayer, and at the confectionery for squares of dark chocolate. Yes, you may go."

"Thank you." Unlike Missy, May made a point of curtsying.

"Why don't you make it a group outing?" the queen suggested. "Eddy, you shall accompany your fiancée. Ernie and Maud, Alix and Maximilian, you must go as well."

The queen's matchmaking was comically obvious. Apparently, now that Eddy's future was resolved, she had decided to move on to the next few couples among her grandchildren. May stole a glance at the Hesse siblings, who were so alike, with the same blue eyes and tawny blond hair, keeping their own counsel as always. Even now they were exchanging murmured secrets.

May turned her back on them, fighting off a strange jealousy. Her brother, Dolly, had left home years ago to attend the military academy at Sandhurst, and rarely came back for visits. May didn't blame him. But sometimes she wondered how it would feel to have a sibling to confide in: someone she trusted implicitly, the way Alix did Ernie or Ducky did Missy.

It was never wise to trust people, she reminded herself. Just look at what had happened the previous year, when she'd thought she and Agnes were friends.

From now on, May relied on no one but herself.

The town of Cowes was picturesque, its cobblestone streets hung with paper flags for the regatta. Their group of nine was too unwieldy to stay together; they broke into clusters, exploring shops where bells tinkled overhead as the door swung open, buying chocolate for Her Majesty from the store on High Street.

They regrouped at a flower market a few blocks away, to Missy's evident delight. She whirled through the stalls like a princess from a storybook, fresh-faced and buoyant. Within minutes her arms overflowed with lilacs, violets, bluebells. "Can someone please open the carriage door?" she cried out, laughing.

May waited for George to run to Missy's aid. But he didn't move. He lingered at the back of the group, letting Maximilian and Eddy help her.

Curious, her heart skipping a little, May watched George. He wandered close to one of the carts, where rows of white flowers were arrayed on a shelf.

She followed.

He didn't look up at her approach, but he said, very softly, "It's your flower, May."

"I'm sorry?"

George handed a few coins to the man behind the cart, then withdrew a single white blossom from a cluster. It was small but perfectly symmetrical, with pointed petals and a golden center. "A mayflower. Your namesake. May I?"

There was something old-fashioned and courtly about the way he had asked her permission. May nodded, suddenly unsure of herself.

"Yes, of course."

George stepped forward and tucked the mayflower behind her ear.

There was nothing inappropriate about the gesture; it was polite, chivalrous even, a lovely gift from a future brother-in-law to his brother's fiancée. Yet somehow it didn't feel that way.

May was acutely aware of the warmth of George's fingers against her hair, the tenderness of his touch. His expression was gentle as always, but May caught a spark of something in his deep blue eyes.

A wild impulse crackled through her. May wanted to reach for George's hand and catch it in her own, to guide his fingers to her face.

She imagined him running a thumb over her lower lip, then settling his hand on the back of her neck, behind the knot of her ash-blond hair. She imagined him lowering his mouth to hers.

What was wrong with her? She couldn't be having such

daydreams about George; she was engaged to his brother, and besides, everyone knew George was going to marry Missy.

Yet he wasn't up there with Missy, gallantly loading flowers into the carriage for her.

He had walked slowly on purpose, to stay back with May and put a blossom in her hair.

"May . . . forgive me if I'm overstepping, but I have to ask," George said hesitantly. "Are you happy?"

"Happy?" May repeated, startled.

"I just— You and Eddy. It took me by surprise." George glanced down at his shoes, as if they might somehow help him navigate this awkward moment. "I had no idea that either of you was considering— That is, I thought Eddy . . ."

The others were half a block ahead by now. Ducky and Missy were at the center of the group, laughing, weaving flowers into necklaces and bracelets. Maximilian kept following Alix around; it was so clear to anyone watching that he was infatuated with her. Yet Alix seemed oblivious, treating him as nothing but a friend.

"Eddy says that you will make a wonderful queen. Of course, he's right," George fumbled to add. "I just want to make sure that Grandmother didn't force you into it. You are happy, aren't you?"

May couldn't remember when anyone had asked whether she was *happy*. She was used to being asked many things—for her time, for her patience. For forbearance and duty and silence. But no one had ever inquired about something as frivolous as her happiness.

She recalled what she'd said to Agnes last year: *I don't think women* can *be happy.* At the time, she had meant it.

"George, I . . ." *I am happy,* May needed to say. That was the correct response to George's question: that she would marry his brother and was delighted about it. That she had *chosen* this.

For some reason, her mouth didn't form the words.

"You can still change your mind if you're having second thoughts." George spoke so quietly that she had to lean closer to hear him. "It's not even in the papers yet, which means it's not really official. If you need help getting out of it . . ."

May felt dizzy. The rest of the world—the sun beating down on her through the fabric of her lace sleeves, the clamor of haggling and laughter and the jingling of harnesses—all of it receded, as if she were in a dream.

What are you saying? she longed to ask George. *Are you not engaged to Missy after all?*

A sliver of doubt worked its way into her mind. What if she had misread all his interactions with Missy, seeing romance where there was nothing but friendship? Queen Victoria clearly wanted to push them together, but perhaps that didn't matter. Victoria was always shuffling and reshuffling her grandchildren into various royal families, playing a generations-long game of dynastic chess across the thrones of Europe.

Perhaps May had heard all the gossip about George and Missy and had made the mistake of believing it.

"I don't . . ." she began.

"May! Look what I have for you!"

May was prevented from elaborating by the arrival of Missy, who brandished a crown of vivid pink flowers. She placed it triumphantly on May's head. "It fits you perfectly!

All hail our future queen!" Missy proclaimed, folding forward into an elaborate bow.

How typically Missy, May thought, with an uncharitable flare of anger. Always causing a scene, always making everything about *her.*

People were beginning to stare. Missy's words were repeated in murmurs, then again, louder—*our future queen! She's the one engaged to Prince Eddy! Who is she?*

May was on display now. This scene would be reported, repeated. The private drama playing out between her and George, whatever it was, had ended. She felt a pang of frustration, but what could she do?

She had agreed to this: to a life of unending public performance.

"I'm sorry, did I miss something?" Missy asked blithely, looking from May to George. "May, you look pale."

"Of course. Let's get our future queen out of the sun," George said gruffly. Eddy had walked up, clearly curious about the commotion, and George nodded to him. "I was just congratulating May on your engagement."

"Thank you," Eddy told his brother, and held out an arm for May.

She forced a smile in Missy's direction. "The crown is lovely. You shouldn't have."

It wasn't until she reached the carriage at the end of the street that May saw something white drift by in her peripheral vision, only to be stomped on the cobblestones by someone's boot.

It was the mayflower George had given her.

CHAPTER TWENTY

Hélène

ANOTHER NIGHT, ANOTHER ROOM IN AN UNFAMILIAR HOUSE.

At least the Quirinal Palace had wonderful bedcovers, so soft that Hélène felt like she was drifting on a cloud. The Italians had always been good at creature comforts—food, fine linens, wine—perhaps as a counterweight to the constant spirituality of living so near the pope.

Not that Hélène was currently able to enjoy any of those creature comforts.

She kept alternating between anguish, and self-recrimination, and anger: at herself, and at Eddy. Clearly, she should have risked the consequences and let him in on her plans. But what had Eddy been thinking, getting engaged to May? The queen was threatening him with a three-year tour, yes, but he was hardly about to be shipped off in the middle of the regatta. What had prompted him to make that announcement?

The morning after that party, Nicholas had come to breakfast and announced that he and Vladimir were returning to Russia. "I'm so sorry, but we need to leave the regatta straightaway," he'd told Hélène's parents. "The *Polar Star* will be going to Calais, to let us disembark so we can travel overland. Please feel free to stay aboard; the yacht is heading to the Black Sea, if you'd like to make some stops along the way."

Hélène's parents had been so delighted at the prospect of a Mediterranean cruise that they weren't even upset about anchoring in Calais, where they would have to stare mournfully at the forbidden shores of France.

"What happened?" Hélène had whispered the moment she was alone with Nicholas.

He looked utterly heartbroken as he replied, "Alix ended things."

"But *why?*"

"She worried that my parents would never let us marry." He sighed. "I don't think I realized how hard it was on her—meeting up in secret, hiding how we really felt. And the longer it went on, the more it seemed to crush her."

It hadn't gone on *that* long, Hélène thought. She and Eddy had been sneaking around far longer. But then, that sort of behavior would weigh on a girl like Alix.

"I'm so sorry, Nicholas," she told him.

"I just . . . I need to get off this boat," he said morosely. Well, that explained why he was taking the train to St. Petersburg instead of going by yacht. "I'm sorry, too, for what it's worth. About Eddy," he added.

"What a sad pair we are. Leaving the regatta early, wallowing in our sorrow while everyone else is celebrating." Hélène had meant to be flippant, but the words didn't quite come out right.

"We deserve each other, I suppose." There was a beat of silence, and then Nicholas said, "Perhaps we should just get married after all."

His words hung in the air between them. Hélène waited for Nicholas to take it back, but he was staring out at the horizon, his jaw clenched.

"I don't think you're serious," she said at last.

"We both have to marry eventually. If I can't have Alix . . . Believe me when I say that of all the princesses I've met, you are by far the most preferable."

"Of course I am," Hélène couldn't help saying. "But Nicholas, you aren't thinking clearly. You don't want to do this to Alix."

Nicholas hung his head in his hands. "You're right. When I get back to St. Petersburg, I'll tell my parents that you and I cannot get engaged."

"Thank you." Such an announcement could never come from Hélène. In this circumstance, only the man could end things.

"Hélène—know that you will always have a friend in Russia, should you need one."

She had reached for his hand then, to give it one last squeeze. "You will always have a friend in me, too."

Hélène's parents had been blissfully unaware that the two were ending their supposed courtship. They'd clearly assumed that Nicholas had granted them use of the yacht as a gift to his future wife, and Hélène hadn't disabused them of the notion.

So for the past week, Hélène and her parents had been on a pleasure cruise through the Mediterranean. At every port they pulled into, they stopped for dinner—and often stayed overnight—with whatever royal relatives or friends lived nearby. So far they had seen Hélène's sister in Lisbon and her mother's family in Malaga, and skirted around the French Riviera to visit Livorno before arriving in Rome. Now they were at the Quirinal Palace with King Umberto and Queen Margherita.

Hélène slid out of bed and began searching the room for a dressing gown and slippers. She needed some tea. Look how English she'd become, craving tea when upset. Eddy would have teased her for it.

The palace was quiet, with the rustling stillness of a building where dozens of people currently slept. Hélène's hand skimmed over the iron railing as she descended the staircase. Moonlight fell through the arched windows overhead, pooling on the parquet floors. At the bottom she hesitated, uncertain in which direction lay the kitchens.

"You seem lost."

Hélène whirled about, heart racing. It was too dark to fully make out the young man behind her; though he'd spoken in French, which implied that he knew who she was.

"I was looking for the kitchens. Could you direct me there . . . ?" Hélène trailed off, waiting for him to provide his name.

"Emanuele. You don't remember me, Your Royal Highness? I'm hurt," he teased, putting a hand on his chest in mock sorrow.

He'd used her formal title instead of calling her *Miss d'Orléans*, as everyone in London did. But of course, Emanuele was a Savoy, and they recognized her father as King of France.

"Of course I remember." They had met at Sophie and Tino's wedding in Athens, the night that Hélène had ended things with Eddy. Emanuele, the Duke of Aosta, was King Umberto's nephew. Because the king only had one, rather sickly teenage son, and because Emanuele's father had died years earlier, Emanuele was second in line to the throne of Italy.

Though it would have been in poor taste to say so aloud, many people expected him to be king someday.

"Why weren't you at dinner?" Hélène asked, curious.

"If I'd known you were here, I would have rushed back," Emanuele said smoothly. "Alas, I was at the Grand Prix in Turin."

"Oh, who won?" Hélène hadn't heard of Turin's Grand Prix, but there were so many horse races these days, especially on the Continent.

"A Daimler." Emanuele sighed. "At least it wasn't a Peugeot; the French drivers are intolerable when they win. No offense, Your Royal Highness," he added with a wink.

Hélène stared as comprehension sank in. "You're talking about a motorcar race?"

"Just wait, these races are the future of Europe. Far more exciting than horses."

"A horse is far grander, far more noble and more interesting to watch, than a bunch of gears and a wheel," she said dismissively. "How fast can your cars go? Five miles per hour?"

"Fifteen, actually."

"A horse can go up to thirty at a gallop!"

"But can your horse sustain this gallop for a hundred miles?" Emanuele shook his head. "If you ever visit Turin, I promise to take you out in my motorcar, and you'll see what I mean."

"Thank you, but I'll pass," Hélène said crisply.

"On the motorcar ride, or on more time with me?"

He really was an incorrigible flirt, the sort of man who charmed and teased as naturally as breathing. Hélène deliberately walked past him. "Do you know where the kitchens are? I should like some tea."

"Of course I know where the kitchens are." Emanuele

hurried to keep pace with her. "I spent much of my childhood in this palace, you know."

Hélène knew the story. After Emanuele's father died, his uncle had begun sending for him every summer, quietly preparing Emanuele to be king—just in case.

"I'm sorry about your father," she said clumsily. "It must have been hard for you, growing up without him."

They had paused halfway down the corridor. Massive windows revealed the gardens behind the house, full of shadowed hedges and white marble statues.

"I loved going out in those gardens. I used to hide there, actually," Emanuele admitted.

"From your tutor?"

"Oh yes. He had this awful habit of trying to teach me arithmetic." Emanuele shuddered.

"For me, it was the dictées. My brother Philippe and I loved climbing the old oak in our garden to escape them. My governess would eventually find us there, but we just pelted her with acorns until she went to get my father. Poor Madame de Morsier," Hélène added, "I don't think she liked the dictées any more than we did."

"Forgive my ignorance, but what is a dictée?" Emanuele asked.

"You never had to do dictées? Sentences designed to be purposefully hard to spell. Like, *Charlotte et son chat chantent dans leur chambre*?" She glanced over at Emanuele's profile. "Is there no such thing in Italian?"

"Not in the Italian I speak, but more than half of Italy speaks a regional dialect. That is why French is our court language, because at least we can all understand each other." He grinned. "Perhaps I should make everyone start doing these dictées you speak of."

"Prepare to be wildly unpopular," Hélène warned.

She should have guessed that the Italian language was as unruly and disorganized as its various regions. After all, the nation that Emanuele's uncle ruled was only a generation old. The political movement known as the Risorgimento had united all the Italian kingdoms, Lombardy and Veneto and the Two Sicilies and the Papal States, into a single entity under the Savoys, who had previously been the Kings of Piedmont.

Rome might be one of the most ancient cities in Europe, but it was part of one of the newest countries.

"You know what?" Emanuele declared, turning to her. "I think we should climb a tree."

"Now? Are you mad?"

He unlocked the doors and stepped onto the palace's back terrace. "Why not? You just said that you used to love it."

Because she couldn't. Hélène had pushed the boundaries of ladylike behavior so many times: riding with the men, taking off her gloves more often than she should, eating too much dessert. Climbing a tree was so far beyond appropriate, it was like . . .

Like sleeping with a man for over a year, and falling in love with him against your better judgment, and then losing him to a scheming manipulator?

What did it matter if someone saw Hélène climbing a tree? What punishment could she possibly be given that was worse than losing Eddy?

"You're right," she declared, and strode outside.

Emanuele looked momentarily surprised by her agreement;

then he grinned. The moonlight gilded his handsome features, his aquiline nose and bright hazel eyes. "Excellent."

They headed into the grove of leafy trees—magnolias, perhaps, though Hélène wasn't much of a gardener. Emanuele interlaced his fingers and held out his hands in a makeshift stirrup, like a groom offering to lift her into the saddle. "May I help, Your Royal Highness?"

"Thanks, but no." Hélène reached around the trunk, getting a solid grip, before placing her foot on one of the knots of the tree. Her thin slippers were surprisingly good for climbing, letting her curl her toes for balance. She stretched a hand toward a lower branch and hoisted herself up.

Emanuele chuckled approvingly and headed to a neighboring tree. "I'll see you up there."

Hélène only glanced over once on the way up. Emanuele was making faster progress than she was, his movements brisk and deliberate. Well, perhaps he'd climbed a tree more recently than she had; she moved slowly, choosing her handholds with care. The last thing she needed on this sea journey was a broken leg.

But then, Hélène felt herself settling into the movement. Her thighs were sore, her hands covered in small scrapes from the bark. It was glorious. She'd forgotten how liberating it was to do something entirely physical. Her brain was too absorbed to think or wonder or fret about anything, even Eddy.

When she reached a strong branch, Hélène sat back, leaning against the trunk, one leg to either side. The skirts of her nightgown were past repair. This was undoubtedly scandalous, and probably quite dangerous, too, but she didn't care. It felt so good to *do* something, to push through the anger and sorrow that had numbed her these past weeks.

"How are you feeling?" Emanuele asked, perched on a branch of his own. Behind him Hélène saw the palace, moonlight winking on its great glass windows.

"I'm enjoying myself, actually."

For a moment there was just the sound of wind raking through the leaves, branches rustling around her. Then Emanuele cleared his throat.

"Do you want to talk about it?"

Hélène's heart skipped. "I'm not sure what you mean," she said quickly.

He leaned back, bracing both hands behind his head as if he were lying on a chaise, not on a tree branch suspended in midair. He was so cavalier, so at home there, that it struck Hélène as vaguely piratical. The way a marauder might look while poised up high in the ship's rigging.

"Very well, we don't have to discuss whatever has upset you. We can just talk as our families do, discussing things that do not truly matter. What did you hear about at dinner?" Emanuele asked flippantly. "The weather? The size of your yacht? Or perhaps you'd like to debate the merits of Verdi's operas?"

Hélène's grip on the branch tightened. It was unnerving, hearing Emanuele voice the things she had thought so many times.

"It's not my yacht," she replied, matching his nonchalance. "It belongs to the Romanovs."

"Are the Romanovs the ones who made you so angry?"

Emanuele clearly hadn't heard the rumors about her and Nicholas. Perhaps word of their flirtation hadn't spread as far as Hélène had thought. Or perhaps Emanuele simply didn't care about gossip.

"I don't know you. Why do you even care?" she asked bluntly.

"Because you are a beautiful woman in distress. I wouldn't be Italian if I didn't want to help." The words were flippant, but Hélène heard the genuine concern, and curiosity, beneath.

"Besides," Emanuele went on, "it's *because* you don't know me that I should be easy to talk to. Just as confession is easier when you can't see the priest's face."

"Confession up in the trees," Hélène muttered. "The Church could learn a thing or two from you."

"Alas, I am too sinful to become a priest," Emanuele quipped.

Hélène's gaze drifted downward. Her feet dangled in the open air, giving her an unnerving sense of vertigo. Perhaps that was why this all felt as surreal as a dream.

"I made some mistakes," she admitted.

"Haven't we all?"

"Perhaps, but did yours cost you the person you love?"

Emanuele drew in a breath. "I am sorry. Affairs of the heart are indeed serious." He hesitated, then added, "May I ask of whom we are speaking?"

"Prince Eddy."

"Prince Eddy. Of England," Emanuele said slowly, as if to be sure. "You and he were—"

"We aren't anymore."

"Because you made these mistakes you spoke of, and he disapproved?"

"No, he wouldn't care. But the *world* would disapprove."

Emanuele waited for her to elaborate. When she didn't, he cleared his throat. "I'm afraid I don't follow."

How could she phrase this without giving away her secret? "Somehow May of Teck learned what I had done."

"She's that relative no one has ever heard of, the one with the German father? The distant cousin Eddy got engaged to?"

Hélène was quite pleased to hear May spoken of so vaguely. "Exactly. May learned of my mistakes, and told me that if I didn't end things with Eddy, she would tell the queen. She has proof," she added, so he would understand how dire things were. "An incriminating letter."

"*What?*" Emanuele demanded, so loudly that Hélène looked over at him. He was staring at her in shock. "Are you saying you've been *blackmailed?*"

"Yes." Hélène held tight to the branch beneath her, though the bark was angrily biting her palms. Good thing she could hide her hands beneath gloves.

"You can't let her get away with it," Emanuele said indignantly. "If there's a letter, then you need to steal it back."

"I tried that! I snooped through May's room, but she doesn't have it!"

"Well then, who *does* have it?"

"I don't know. But . . ." Hélène fell silent, thoughtful.

"But what?" Emanuele prompted.

"But there is someone who might know," she said slowly. Why hadn't she realized this before?

Because she didn't like thinking of him. Because it reminded her of her own foolish, costly, devastating mistake.

"Well, what are you waiting for?" Emanuele swung his legs off the branch. "Shall we go talk to this person?"

"He's in France."

"Then you must write him!"

"Yes," Hélène agreed, shaking her head in surprise, or perhaps in disbelief. "I need to write him."

"I'll get paper and pen," Emanuele promised, already halfway down the tree.

As Hélène started back down, the silk of her dressing gown snagged and torn past repair, she felt something in her chest, like a soap bubble that might burst at any moment. It was, she realized, the feeling of hope.

CHAPTER TWENTY-ONE

May

"MAY, I NEED A MOMENT WITH YOU," HER FATHER GROWLED.

May willed her smile not to slip as she murmured an excuse to the society women who were cooing over her. It was shallow, obviously, but she couldn't help enjoying the new attention, after so many years of being shunted to the side. She was only human, after all.

"Of course, Father."

Francis grunted in response, then grabbed her arm and dragged her out of the reception room. May tried not to wince as the boning of her stays cut into her side.

She should have guessed that Francis would be in a black mood. This party—the queen refused to call it a ball, though almost two hundred guests were in attendance—was for Eddy and May, to celebrate that their engagement had been officially proclaimed in Parliament. And Francis detested anything that honored other people, especially May.

Things had been a whirlwind since May's return from Osborne several weeks earlier. White Lodge, normally so drab and dreary, was bursting with activity: full of dresses and hats and delicate squares of lace, sent by merchants all over England vying to make the royal trousseau. Invitations arrived by the dozens, to balls and charity bazaars and private boxes at the opera. So many telegrams were pouring in that the local post office had taken over part of the schoolroom, with its own staff of telegraphers, to handle the volume of messages.

There were practical matters to consider, too. May needed to start interviewing candidates for the posts of private secretary, and lady's maid, and housekeeper. She'd begun selecting wallpaper for the rooms that she and Eddy had been granted at St. James's Palace. And just yesterday they had met with the Archbishop of Canterbury to begin discussing the wedding ceremony—except that Eddy had left after a mere ten minutes, claiming a sore throat. The only thing he'd actually made it to all week was their engagement photo shoot, where they had posed for a picture that would soon be reprinted in newspapers around the world.

It was fine. May was used to doing things on her own.

"Did you see the announcement?" Francis demanded, once he and May had reached the corridor. Thankfully, it was empty, the sounds of the party muffled behind great double doors.

"Yes, Father," May said carefully.

"They listed me after your mother! Without a Royal Highness!"

Because you don't have *one!* May didn't dare say. The official text had read, *Her Majesty is delighted to announce the engagement of His Royal Highness Prince Albert Victor, Duke of Clarence and of Avondale, to Princess Victoria Mary, Daughter of Her Royal Highness Princess Mary Adelaide and of His Highness the Duke of Teck.*

Which was quite correct. May's mother was the royal one.

"I'm sorry," she murmured, which only seemed to irritate her father more.

"*Sorry?* You should have *done* something to prevent my embarrassment!"

"Can't you just enjoy this moment of triumph for our family?"

Francis's eyes narrowed at her audacity. His hand curled as if he meant to strike her.

May flinched, and her father saw it.

He stretched his fingers, releasing the fist. "Some family triumph, if it means your father is humiliated."

"I promise it won't happen again," May hastened to assure him.

"I'm afraid you'll need to do better than that. Once you're married, you will ensure that I get the dignities and styling of a Royal Highness. And I think, as father of the future queen, I am due an official post. Nothing that requires work, of course," he added, with a sharp-edged smile. "But one of those made-up positions that have a great income attached. The kind that you can only get by being intimate with the royal family."

"I'm not sure I can—"

"I think I'd like to be Earl Marshal," he announced. "Or something even greater. Keeper of the Privy Seal, perhaps?"

The nerve of him. "I wouldn't know how to ask for such a thing."

Her father barked out a caustic laugh, rocking back on his heels and looping his thumbs into his belt. "You're a clever girl, May. I'm sure you'll figure something out. Or else."

"Or else what?"

"Or else I'll make sure it all comes crashing down around you," he threatened. "Do you think Victoria would want you in the family if she knew the truth of how you got here? The way you clung around like a snail, slimy and ugly and toxic. Not to mention that you threw yourself at Maud last year, begging for her friendship," he said dismissively. "As pathetic as when you took cast-off clothes from that American brat."

For a moment May just stared at her father. He never seemed to pay any attention to her—how much did he really know? Or was this all just guesswork? "You wouldn't risk it. Not when our family is so close to the throne," she said, but she wasn't certain.

"That's just the thing, May. *You're* the one marrying Eddy. If our family is about to be close to the throne, it needs to be all of us." He smiled bitterly. "Not just you."

He would do it. Looking at his expression, twisted by years of resentment and jealousy—by whatever hopes had long ago been shattered—May knew he would. Francis was far past being ruled by logic.

If he didn't get what he wanted, he would gleefully watch his daughter's life burn instead.

"These things take time," she said quickly. "I'm hardly in a position to ask favors of Her Majesty just yet. Perhaps in a few years—"

"A few *years?*" he bellowed.

May winced and glanced down the corridor in both directions, though luckily, no one seemed to have noticed. "When I've provided an heir. Then I'll be in a stronger negotiating position, and can help you get what you deserve."

"An heir." Francis paused at the thought that his grandchild would someday be King of England. Then he shook his head, brows furrowed. "You still must correct the announcement before it reaches the papers. It will be reprinted throughout Europe! What would my cousins in Württemberg think if they saw it worded thus?"

May highly doubted that they thought of him at all.

"Of course, Father," she said placatingly.

He was still angry, his rage coiling like a snake about to strike, but at least his ire was no longer directed at her.

"Perhaps we should return to the party?" she ventured. Francis grunted in assent, and she hurried back into the ballroom.

When May reappeared, the conversations nearest her broke off. A few guests cast her ingratiating smiles; others looked at her with something like surprise, as if they were still trying to puzzle out how she'd done it. May was too rattled from her father's threats to enjoy their jealousy. She scanned the dance floor, rising on tiptoe to see through the crowds.

"Are you looking for Eddy?" Queen Victoria asked, coming to stand near May.

May must have been more flustered than she realized, because as she sank into a quick curtsy, she told the truth without a second thought. "For George."

The queen blinked in surprise.

May hurried to fabricate an explanation. "I need to ask him something. I'm planning a gift for Eddy, and would like his advice."

Victoria smiled wistfully. Thank heavens she was too sentimental to realize how illogical that was. Why would May seek George at an engagement party to discuss a wedding present, which was hardly an urgent problem?

"Albert gave me a lovely brooch when we were married," Victoria reminisced. "He designed it himself. He commissioned dozens of pieces for me over the years—using the baby teeth of our children, pebbles we'd collected on the beach at Osborne, antlers from the first deer he hunted at Balmoral."

"How lovely," May replied, though it was ludicrous. The ruler of the entire British Empire, who had access to some of the most spectacular jewels in the world, wearing seaside pebbles around her neck?

Victoria nodded to the middle of the dance floor. "I'm afraid George is with Missy. They make a lovely pair, don't you agree?"

May's stomach soured as she watched the two of them. There was no denying that they looked handsome together. She saw George murmur something, at which Missy tipped her head back and laughed, before he spun Missy in an effortless twirl.

"I don't know. Missy is so young," May said daringly, over the hammering of her heart. "And a bit impetuous for such a great role."

"She doesn't have what it takes to be queen, of course," Victoria observed, with her typical bluntness. "But it is hardly the same, marrying the younger son."

The woman who married George would need to accept coming in second. Wearing the smaller crown jewels at state occasions, attending foreign weddings in the duller, more out-of-the-way countries while May and Eddy represented Britain at the big events. Taking on the obscure patronages that May had rejected.

Somehow May didn't see Missy being totally content out of the spotlight.

"I think Missy could be good for George. He's so withdrawn, so quiet," Victoria went on. "Missy is headstrong, certainly; but she will push him to be bolder. Just as you will push Eddy to be more serious."

"I'm worried they aren't a good match." May knew she was overstepping but couldn't help herself; the words seemed to pour from her mouth of their own volition.

It wasn't that May wanted George for herself. She was going to marry his *brother.* But she knew, with certainty, that Missy was wrong for him.

Everyone assumed George was shy, but he was really just wise in his choice of words, and careful to whom he spoke. He was so unlike his red-faced, spoiled, overgrown child of a father. So unlike May's own father, with his petty vindictiveness and cruelty.

George needed a true partner, an equal. Someone who understood him, who listened to his thoughts and worries and helped him solve them. Not a seventeen-year-old who batted her eyes at every man in arm's reach.

"I appreciate your concern, May, but I know what's best for my grandchildren." There was a new, testy note in the queen's voice.

"Please, forgive me," May said hastily. "Should we expect an engagement announcement soon?"

The queen chuckled. "Now I understand your concern! Fear not." She reached for May's hand and gave it what she probably thought was a reassuring pat. "I would never let Missy's wedding overshadow yours. The heir must marry first, and then the nation can turn its attention to the spare."

"I see." May swallowed against a dryness in her throat.

"I think we can sell George and Missy as quite the love match. The nation could use one after all these complaints about grain prices and so on." Perhaps the queen realized the implication—that Eddy and May were *not* a love match—because she added, "The marriage of a future king is different, of course. Your wedding to Eddy is an Act of State."

"Of course," May replied dutifully.

The queen murmured her goodbyes and turned to greet another guest, leaving May to stare out at the dance floor, where Missy was still spinning about in her pink dress with its endless flounces.

As if he felt her watching, George glanced up. His eyes locked on hers.

May had a sudden urge to march onto the dance floor and rip him from Missy's hands. That girl was as flighty as an incandescent moth. She wouldn't make George happy. And she didn't deserve him—his selfless devotion, his warmth.

Before May could doubt herself, she turned and walked with bold strides toward Aunt Vicky. Her Majesty's oldest daughter and the Queen of Prussia, Aunt Vicky could always be counted on to share gossip. Or to ruffle feathers.

May was thinking of what Missy had said back at the Waleses' anniversary party: *You wouldn't* believe *how obvious Ferdinand of Romania was. He followed me around all week like a puppy, talking about his hunting.*

Aunt Vicky's son Wilhelm, May recalled, was friends with Prince Ferdinand.

Aunt Vicky mustered up a half-hearted smile at May's approach. "My dear May. Congratulations!"

May allowed herself a moment to relish Vicky's envy. Once upon a time, Vicky had turned up her nose at May as a potential bride for her son Henry. Well, that was Prussia's loss. Forget being the wife of a younger prince; May was going to be Queen of England.

"Thank you. How are Moretta and Margaret?" May asked sweetly. Aunt Vicky's oldest daughter, Sophie, was the only married one. Margaret was still quite young, but it must have been galling, seeing May chosen for Eddy over Moretta—whose real name, of course, was Victoria.

"They both send their regards," Aunt Vicky replied, with an unmistakably pinched expression.

May nodded to where Missy and George were dancing. "And from the look of things, we will have even more to celebrate soon."

"Missy and George? Oh yes, Mummy has been fixated on their wedding since they were children." Vicky sounded distinctly bored.

"It seems inevitable, doesn't it?" May paused for effect. "Unless Missy gets snatched up by some other suitor."

Predictably, Vicky perked up at the hint of drama. She had always been meddling, a trait that May could only assume she'd gotten from her mother. "What do you mean, another suitor?"

"I'm sure they're just rumors," May said swiftly.

"May." Vicky adopted her sternest voice. "If you have heard something untoward about Missy, you must tell me."

"Nothing untoward! It's just . . ." May glanced away, biting her lip. "She *did* speak rather freely about His Royal Highness Prince Ferdinand of Romania."

Vicky's eyes gleamed with interest. "Oh, he's a friend of Wilhelm's. What did Missy say?"

"She told me that Ferdinand behaved in a distinctly forward manner." In case this was ever traced back to May, she didn't want to be accused of lying. "Though I suspect she might have encouraged his attentions. She giggled when she spoke of him." That part was true.

"Missy encourages a great deal of attention, doesn't she?" Vicky sniffed. "I would never let my own girls behave in such a manner, but Marie has raised Missy and Ducky with far more leeway than is appropriate. Who knows, perhaps such behavior is common enough in St. Petersburg. Or Romania." Vicky spoke the word as if she wasn't quite sure of the pronunciation. Of course, no one in the British royal family would ever even visit Romania; to them it was a distant country in a remote, inconsequential corner of Europe.

"I'm sure it was nothing. We all know that Missy and George are destined to marry, after all. Please, don't repeat what I said," May added, thereby ensuring that Aunt Vicky would do exactly that.

Both women looked at Missy, who was galloping down the dance floor with wild abandon, sweat dampening the armpits of her gown. How typically Missy. Something about her reminded May of Hélène: the way she laughed and frowned and pouted and generally overreacted to everything, as if she were alone with George and not in public.

"I have so loved our chat, May. It has been quite illuminating," Vicky said at last, with a nod of farewell. "Now if you'll excuse me . . ."

When she'd gone, May allowed herself a small smile of victory. Already she was doing it: moving people about like pieces on a chessboard, managing the world as she saw fit. As Queen Victoria did.

May knew she had no claim on George, of course.

But she was pleased to think that Missy might not get him, either.

CHAPTER TWENTY-TWO

Alix

"ANOTHER LETTER HAS ARRIVED FOR YOU," ERNIE ANNOUNCED, coming to join Alix on the front steps.

It was chilly out; the majestic spruce trees that lined the driveway had already shed their needles onto the paving stones. In another month snow would begin to dust the tops of their branches, gathering on the gabled roofs of town like icing on a cake.

"From Maximilian? Or Hélène?" Alix guessed. Both had become regular correspondents of late. It had been hard at first, staying close with Hélène after everything that had happened, but it wasn't Hélène's fault that the tsar and tsarina approved of her when they were so opposed to Alix. Besides, Hélène and Nicholas had already informed their parents that the hoped-for engagement would not happen. Hélène had written that her parents were livid: that they blamed Nicholas, since he was the one who'd officially ended it. Now Philippe d'Orléans was telling Hélène not to worry, that it was better she hadn't married Nicholas, since he was apparently such a cad.

At least Hélène had a protective father. But then, Alix thought fondly, she had Ernie.

Her brother paused, his eyes searching hers. "Alix, this letter is from St. Petersburg."

She closed her eyes. "Burn it, then. Just like the others."

"Are you sure? Because I really think—"

"Please, Ernie," she said heavily.

Nicholas had written her a few times since Cowes, more frequently at the beginning and then, as time passed, less often. Alix had allowed herself to read the first letter, hoping foolishly that it might contain good news. What if Nicholas had finally convinced his parents to let them marry?

Nothing had changed, of course. All he wrote was more of the same: *I promise that we will find a way to be together, but there are a number of difficulties and it may take time. I have never in my whole life been so sure of anything as I am of you. . . .*

Alix knew that Nicholas meant his promises. She just wasn't sure he could actually follow through on them. And if she kept on believing him—letting Nicholas have everything, loving him in secret despite the cost—it would keep hurting her, every time she had to let go of him. To watch him with someone else, even if that someone wasn't Hélène.

Not to mention that if they were caught, Alix was the one who would suffer for it. Not him.

Perhaps it would have been easier if she and Nicholas had never met. Or if she'd ignored her attraction to him, pretended there was no spark. But she was here now, and as much as she loved him, she had to protect her heart.

Already it was getting easier to dismiss him from her mind. Time had done that, and the quiet routine of Darmstadt.

"Very well. I'll burn it." Ernie wrapped an arm around Alix's shoulders and gave her a quick squeeze.

At least one good thing had come out of the whole mess: she and Ernie were closer than ever. There were no secrets between them anymore. He knew everything about Nicholas, and what had happened with Hélène and Eddy, and Alix's unexpected new friendship with Maximilian.

Maximilian's first note had arrived in Darmstadt a few days after the regatta. It began innocuously, with a question about literature—had Alix read the new German translation of Livy's *History of Rome*, and what did she think? To which she'd replied, half joking, *I will attempt the monstrosity that is Livy if you will read Trollope.*

In the months since, they had exchanged stories and confidences, becoming friends quite without Alix realizing it. She'd learned all about Maximilian's family: his father, Wilhelm, was the third son of the previous grand duke, Leopold. Maximilian's oldest uncle, Louis, would have been the current grand duke, but he was, as the family said, "not right in the head." Maximilian had been shockingly open about his uncle's mental state, how he suffered from delusions, forgot where he was or even his own name.

It was all so strange to Alix, who had been taught from a young age to *never* speak of her shameful episodes.

Their letters rambled, by turns serious and superficial.

Alix: *I hosted a dinner with Father again last night; we had the deacon over for pork schnitzel. Ernie and I snuck off to play billiards, and when the deacon caught us in the game room, we had to pretend we were looking for the Bible so that he could lead us in evening prayer. Needless to say, that room doesn't contain a Bible. . . .*

Maximilian: *Remind me to tell you of the time I got caught stealing apples from the rectory's orchard. As punishment, I had to spend the next five years serving as an altar boy. The punishment seemed more excessive than the crime. . . .*

Alix: *Does Baden celebrate Oktoberfest? Though it's nothing like Munich, Darmstadt has been quite taken over with the festival spirit.*

Maximilian: *Oh yes. My cousin Frederick has been practicing Hammerschlagen, and claims he will compete in the county games.*

Alix had heard of *Hammerschlagen*, a game where men raced to hammer nails into a tree trunk, though she'd never seen it.

"Alix? Are they here yet?" Her father, Louis, emerged from the house, sounding slightly bewildered. "I still can't quite understand why they're coming. It's not as if they visited often before."

In this house, *before* only ever meant one thing: before Alice died.

"You know Aunt Marie delights in being unpredictable," Alix said evasively. She and Ernie had already discussed their suspicions that Queen Victoria had sent the Coburg cousins to report on Alix.

The letter from Aunt Marie had arrived a few days ago, announcing that her family would be "passing through Hesse" on a train voyage and would be staying for a few days. It had turned the household quite upside down, maidservants hurrying to wax tables and air out guest bedrooms and wipe down furniture that had acquired a fine sheen of dust. "We've gotten lazy," Alix had whispered to Ernie, who laughed.

The clatter of hoofbeats at the end of the drive made them all look up. A pair of carriages trotted toward them, the horses' bridles jangling.

When the carriages pulled to a stop, Uncle Alfred emerged with a strained smile. Clearly, he didn't want to visit the home of his dead sister any more than Louis wanted him here. Aunt Marie came next, and then Ducky and Missy were spilling from the carriage like pumpkins falling out of a cart, muslins and silks fluffing up as they pushed past each other. There was a breathless string of exclamations all running together: *Alix, we have missed you, where are your stables, we brought presents from Grandmama, will it be this cold all week because I shall need to borrow a coat!*

In spite of herself, Alix smiled. "The stables are out back, and I'm sure Ernie would love to ride with you tomorrow. Of course you're welcome to any of my coats."

Missy stepped forward. "Look at your hair, Alix! Let me guess, you didn't use any hot tongs at all? These curls are all natural?"

As always, Alix was discomfited by remarks upon her beauty. It had never really felt like it had anything to do with her. "No hot tongs," she said hastily. "What is the news from London?"

"London? We came from St. Petersburg! Ducky in particular *enjoyed* herself," Missy teased.

Ducky came to loop an arm through Alix's as they ascended the stairs. "Missy always says too much. Though I suppose I should thank her. If she hadn't told May about me and Kiril, May wouldn't have helped me wriggle out of that engagement to Eddy. I believe you and I have that in common, right, Alix?"

"I . . . what?" The Coburg girls' frankness continued to surprise Alix. She was never so forthright. And who was Kiril?

"Forgive me, I thought you knew. May said that you and Eddy had been promised, but you got out of it," Ducky murmured, too quietly for anyone to overhear. "I got out of the same engagement. May gave me wonderful advice."

"It's not as if she had selfless motives. Now she's engaged to Eddy herself," Alix said testily.

"Yes, she wanted to be queen. I wish her joy of it." Ducky shuddered. "I have no desire for that life, and I can tell that you don't, either."

Alix was spared from replying by Aunt Marie. "Alix, we have a surprise!" she called out. "Look who we ran into on the train! We insisted that he come say hello, of course."

Alix turned around to see that a third carriage was rattling down the driveway. Somehow she knew, even before it drew to a stop, that Maximilian would step out.

His gaze darted to hers for an instant before he quickly bowed to her father, then to Uncle Alfred and Aunt Marie. "I am just stopping by on my way to Prussia," he explained. "I'm afraid I have business with Emperor Wilhelm."

"We are headed to Prussia as well, if you'd like to keep traveling with us," Aunt Marie offered loudly.

"Maximilian, you must stay!" Ernie insisted. "Surely the kaiser can wait a few days."

Maximilian looked to Alix, a question in his hazel eyes. She knew that he would stay or go as she commanded.

"Of course you should join us," she said gently.

A smile tugged his mouth upward. "It's settled, then."

LATER THAT EVENING, MAXIMILIAN WAS THE FIRST TO ENTER THE drawing room, where everyone would gather before dinner.

Alix looked up guiltily; she was ensconced in an armchair, her feet curled up under the skirts of her loosely corseted dress, a book on her lap. When she saw that it was Maximilian, she let out an amused breath.

"You caught me in the act," she said, holding up her copy of *History of Rome*. "My progress through Livy has been slow; I'm still only at the Gallic invasion. I must say, though, it makes me want to visit Rome."

Hesitantly, Maximilian took the armchair next to her. "You've never been to Rome?"

"No. We are mostly here in Darmstadt, aside from our annual trip to London." And the occasional visit to Ella in Russia, but for some reason Alix didn't mention that.

"We are even, then, as I'm not finished the Palliser novels. Though I must admit, I expected happier stories for some of the characters," Maximilian told her.

"Oh, I know. Poor Alice!" Alix agreed.

"Poor Alice?" Maximilian lifted an eyebrow. "Surely you didn't want her to marry George? He was awful."

"But she loved him!"

"Perhaps she shouldn't have," he said softly.

Alix opened her mouth to answer—then closed it again, suddenly unsure. She'd always thought that Trollope did wrong by Alice, marrying her to John, who was steady and reliable and just a teensy bit boring, when she'd had such a passionate romance with George. Then again, Alice's relationship with George was volatile, with moments of anguish as much as joy.

"You may be right," Alix said slowly. "Perhaps I should reread it with the benefit of experience."

Maximilian looked at her curiously, but refrained from

asking what experience, exactly, she meant. Instead he merely said, "Thank you for all the letters."

The words were polite, but there was something intimate about the way he spoke them, as if the letters were a shared secret.

Alix swallowed, suddenly flustered. "I have enjoyed our correspondence very much."

This was the same Maximilian she had met months ago, who'd taken her on that quiet walk in the Buckingham Palace gardens, and yet he felt like an entirely different person. There was *history* between them now, anecdotes and opinions and jokes.

"How was the journey?" she went on, to hide the strange, almost restless feeling beneath her rib cage.

"Quite easy. The train from Karlsruhe is only a few hours."

Funny to think that Baden was so close and yet she'd never visited. When Alix and Ernie went to London, it took the better part of a week. Her trip to St. Petersburg, to see Ella, had been even longer; the Russian railways had snaked up the coast for days, past dozens of small villages centered on a single unpaved street.

"I'm glad you're here," she replied, and Maximilian smiled.

The door swung open, and Ducky and Missy spun into the room in a whirl of chatter. As Alix stood to greet them, Maximilian rose to his feet at the same time, and their arms brushed. It was such a small moment of contact, her sleeve brushing against his jacket, but Alix couldn't help wondering if it hadn't been accidental.

And more surprisingly, a part of her wondered if it might happen again.

CHAPTER TWENTY-THREE

Hélène

HÉLÈNE HAD NOT COUNTED ON SEEING EMANUELE, THE DUKE OF Aosta, again so soon. Part of her had thought she might *never* see him. But that was unmistakably his voice, announcing to a bemused footman that he had a delivery for the Princess Hélène.

"Emanuele!" she cried out, hurrying to the entrance hall.

At the sight of her, Emanuele grinned. In his embroidered waistcoat, with a cravat tied in a Continental knot, he looked every inch the visiting prince. Hélène felt a clang of cognitive dissonance seeing him this way, when the last time they'd been together, they had been climbing trees in the moonlight.

The very next morning, the Orléans party had left for Malta; and then Hélène's parents must have decided they were done sailing, because they'd sent the yacht on to Livadia. They had returned to England the slow way, overland, still making stops to see family members and friends—Prince Baudouin in Belgium, King Ferdinand in Bulgaria.

Hélène had been back in London for a week now. She hadn't attended any balls or social events; she couldn't bear to witness the farce that was Eddy and May's engagement. Her parents were hardly pushing her to go out; they now knew that she and Nicholas would not get engaged, since a letter from the tsar had been waiting for them at Sheen House. "Romanovs," Philippe had said dismissively, tossing the letter in the trash. "So painfully snobbish. Good riddance."

Her father seemed to have assumed that Nicholas thought Hélène wasn't good enough. Hélène let him think that, because there was no way she could explain the truth.

For now, she was happy enough to stay home. Everything in London felt too painful to face. Just yesterday she'd ventured out shopping with her mother, only to see an eau de cologne labeled PRINCESS MAY'S SCENT. It took all of Hélène's self-restraint not to shatter the bottle right there on the paving stones.

At least Eddy was currently out of town. He'd gone to Scotland with his sister Louise and her husband for some autumn shooting, leaving May to swan about London alone, playing the role of the royal bride-to-be. Hélène liked to think that Eddy had gone specifically to avoid May—that the wedding fever that had taken over London was as disgusting to him as it was to Hélène.

"What are you doing here?" she said now, coming to greet Emanuele. "I didn't know you planned on visiting London!"

"I was in Menton, and wanted to stop by," he offered, as if the south of France were a block away instead of several days' journey. "I have something for you," he added.

Hélène tugged him into the airy blue-and-white sitting room down the hall. She left the door open for propriety's sake, then whirled on him eagerly. "Well? What is it?"

Emanuele withdrew an envelope from his pocket. "I would have forwarded it through the post, but after your previous experience with letters getting stolen— Well, I wanted to deliver it myself."

It was from Laurent.

"Finally," Hélène exclaimed, ripping it open.

That night in Rome, when they'd come down from the trees, Hélène had written Laurent to ask about his conversation with May. At last, she had his reply.

"I'm sorry," Emanuele was saying. "Your Laurent must not have known to send his reply to Sheen House, because he posted it back to my uncle's palace in Rome. It's amusing, really, that the letter went from France to Italy and then back to me in France. . . ." He trailed off when he realized that Hélène wasn't listening.

Your Royal Highness, Laurent had begun—a title he had never used while he and Hélène were together. He had finally learned to be circumspect, though it was a little too late.

Please allow me to express my deepest apologies for any distress I may have caused you. The conversation to which you are referring occurred between myself and a Miss Agnes Endicott, an American. I was under the impression that she was a friend of yours. I have never met Her Serene Highness the Princess May, and was not aware that she was involved in any of your affairs. . . .

"Well?" Emanuele prompted. "I must admit, the suspense is torturous."

Hélène showed him the note. "He says that he gave the incriminating letter to someone named Agnes Endicott."

"Endicott, as in the steel family?"

"Who are they?" Hélène asked.

"Wealthy Americans."

Hélène cast her mind back, trying to put a face to the name, but she never paid all that much attention to other young women.

"So, how are we going to retrieve your letter from Agnes?" Emanuele settled back on her family's cushions with decided purpose.

That *we* caught Hélène's notice. "I wasn't . . . You don't need to help."

"But London is so *boring*, and I promised Giuseppe I would stay for at least a few days." Emanuele's eyes glinted mischievously. "Please allow me a part in your plan."

"Who is Giuseppe?" she asked, stalling for time.

"Tornielli. Our ambassador to England."

Emanuele, second in line to the Italian throne, was staying at a bachelor's townhouse near Whitehall. That struck Hélène as something oddly admirable. He could have visited any number of family friends, calling upon the endless skein of relations and obligations that tangled all of Europe's royalty—could be at a grand estate, being fêted with champagne and caviar.

Instead he was staying with an ambassador, the way a statesman would. Not a prince.

"I need to make some inquiries about this Agnes Endicott," Hélène mused aloud. "You're welcome to join me, of course, but . . ."

"Oh, I intend to do more than make inquiries. You are going to need my help if you hope to sneak into Agnes's home and steal that letter back."

Hélène was torn between amusement and confusion. "And what role will you play?"

"I shall be the diversion, of course," Emanuele announced. "If we were fishing, you might call me the bait."

HÉLÈNE WAITED UNTIL EMANUELE WAS ON THE ENDICOTTS' FRONT steps before ducking into the alleyway. Behind her, she heard the inward swing of a door, and the low tones of a butler's puzzled voice.

"Good afternoon," she assumed the butler would say, studying Emanuele with confusion.

Though she couldn't hear her friend's reply, she could guess at it: "Please tell His Grace that his friend the Duke of Aosta has arrived."

She and Emanuele had agreed on this approach, knowing that news of his arrival would travel rapidly through the house, as exciting things always did.

Hélène imagined the butler repeating loudly, "His Grace . . . the Duke of Aosta? But, sir, I'm afraid you have the wrong residence. . . ." At which point a footman would whisper it to a lady's maid, who would run up within seconds to tell Mrs. Endicott. And hopefully put the whole house in a bit of an uproar.

"My apologies," Emanuele would reply, "I'm looking for His Grace the Duke of Sutherland, and am clearly mistaken in my address. I shall trouble you no further."

"But wait, sir, let us assist you!" the butler would exclaim, trying to detain him.

There was no time to waste; Hélène held her breath and walked down the half flight of stairs that led to the Endicotts' staff entrance. As she'd expected, it opened directly into their kitchen.

Hélène was dressed in an outfit borrowed from Violette, a starched white shirt and serge skirt. While it didn't quite match those of the Endicotts' maids, she hoped that no one would look at her closely enough to notice. This was a large household, and probably had a good deal of turnover among the staff.

A woman stood at the sink, elbow-deep in dishes; she barely glanced up at Hélène's arrival. Hélène murmured something vague and turned a corner. She needed to walk briskly, head ducked down, like a maidservant on an errand—

She collided with a real maidservant holding a stack of plates.

"Oh no!" Hélène grabbed the edge of the stack, which was swaying precariously, then lifted the plates from the girl's grasp. She looked a few years younger than Hélène, with frizzy blond hair escaping from beneath her bonnet.

"Thank you," the girl breathed. "I know I shouldn't have carried so many at once, but I still haven't swept the stairs, and Mrs. Travers will be so angry. There's a gentleman just arrived, and Jane said he's dressed like a king!" She paused, seeming to notice that there was something slightly off about Hélène's uniform. "Anyway, thank you . . ."

"Violette. I'm new." Hélène set the plates in the pantry, alongside all the others in the same china pattern. She hoped that was the right spot.

"Violette," the girl repeated, sounding unconvinced. "I'm Annie."

Hélène started up the back stairs before Annie could detain her. The staircase emerged into a hallway with multiple doors, ending in a much wider grand staircase toward the front of the house.

"Good afternoon, Your Grace!" Hélène heard a female voice exclaim downstairs. "I'm Mrs. Endicott. You're looking for the Duke of Sutherland? We must help you track down his address! Won't you have a cup of tea while you wait?"

"You're too kind," Emanuele replied. Hélène could picture him bowing with a little flourish, causing Mrs. Endicott to swoon. "I'm in town from Italy, and still don't know my way around London very well."

"*Agnes!* Come down!" the woman bellowed up the stairs. *Never shout in company,* Hélène's mother would have said. *You sound as coarse and loud as a fishmonger's wife.* Poor Mrs. Endicott didn't know that the appropriate course of action would have been to send a footman to fetch Agnes.

Hélène kept moving down the hall, briskly opening each door in succession: a linen closet; an empty bedroom, probably meant for guests; another closet, this one full of cleaning supplies—

A door swung violently open down the hall. A young woman stormed out, green eyes flashing.

Hélène shuffled to one side and bowed her head, but she needn't have worried. Agnes didn't notice Hélène. She was too busy tugging the neckline of her dress lower over her breasts until she showed a healthy amount of cleavage.

Of course. The type of person capable of such cruel blackmail was also the type to look past domestic servants as if they were furniture.

Hélène waited until Agnes's footsteps clattered down the staircase. She glanced in both directions, then darted through the door Agnes had emerged from.

The bedroom inside was all rococo gilding and swirls, with mirrors on every wall, as if Agnes needed to constantly look at herself from every possible angle. The bed was hung with tasseled silk curtains, and the footboard was carved with *AIE*, presumably Agnes's initials. It was all a bit ostentatious for a bed that was supposedly not visited by any gentlemen.

Just as she'd done with May's room at Osborne, Hélène began searching as quickly as she could, starting with the most obvious hiding places: drawers in the side tables, the space underneath the mattress, the liner of the cushioned window seat. Nothing.

When she opened the armoire, her eyes were immediately drawn to a locked wooden box bolted to the shelf. It could, of course, be Agnes's jewelry. Yet something told her that it was more.

"What are you doing, Violette?"

Hélène whirled around to see Annie in the doorway.

"Please, let me explain. This isn't what it looks like," Hélène hurried to say.

Annie hesitated, which Hélène took as a good sign. At least she wasn't shouting *Thief!*

"Really? Because it looks like you snuck into this house, disguised as a maidservant, in order to steal."

"Well, yes," Hélène admitted. "But the thing I'm stealing is *mine*! Your mistress took something from me, and I need it back!"

Annie stepped farther into the room, pulling the door shut behind her. "You're not a maid, are you." She didn't phrase it like a question.

"Please, Annie," Hélène's words were rushed, frantic. "Have

you ever been in love? The thing Agnes stole—it's not jewelry, or money. It's a love letter. If I don't get it back, I will lose the man I love forever."

Hélène's heart pounded. Then, to her relief, the maidservant nodded.

"We have a few minutes. Miss Endicott is busy with a Spanish duke downstairs."

"An Italian duke, actually," Hélène told her. "He's my friend."

Annie's eyes widened at that. She turned and gestured to the locked box. "Your instincts were good; this is probably where Miss Endicott keeps your letter. But she has the key on her person at all times."

Disappointment flooded Hélène. She had come so close. Was there any way to steal the entire box—but it was bolted into the armoire itself, and even if she managed to pry it free, someone would see her absconding with it. Could she attempt to steal the key from Agnes's pocket? Or did she wear it on a ribbon around her neck?

She blinked, realizing that Annie had reached beneath her bonnet to withdraw two hairpins.

"Are you—"

"Shh!" Annie hissed.

Hélène held her breath, watching as the maidservant stuck the pins into the lock, tugging them back and forth, periodically ducking closer and listening. Finally she gave the lock one last turn, and it sprang open.

"American machine-made locks," Annie said dismissively. "They're so easy to pick. Our old handmade British locks are much better."

They both peered eagerly into the dark interior.

There were a few jewelry boxes, but mostly the box contained a disorganized sheaf of papers: scribbled notes, newspaper clippings, old invitations. And there, crisply folded on top, was Laurent's letter.

Finally, after all this time—after months of heartache, of scheming against May and failing, of nearly giving up hope—Hélène had succeeded.

She snatched the letter, unable to stop herself from scanning it. Scattered phrases jumped out at her—*the first night you came to me, when it was raining* and *Remember that day in the carriage*—and she winced. How could Laurent have been so foolish as to put all this to paper? It was even more incendiary than she'd realized.

"Thank you," she breathed.

"You helped me. It's only right that I do the same." Annie gave a weary shrug. "That's how I knew you weren't a maid. It's everyone for themselves in this house."

Hélène folded the letter, tucking it into her bodice. "Annie . . . do you wish to leave?"

"More than anything, but I need work."

"Go to Sheen House. The housekeeper is Mrs. Archer. I'll tell her to look for you."

"Sheen House," Annie repeated. Then she gasped. "Wait, does that mean you are—"

"Thank you, Annie." Hélène smiled and ducked into the hallway.

It took all her self-restraint not to run down the back stairs two at a time. When she was safely in the alley, Hélène allowed herself to fully breathe at last. Her blood pounded with the thrill of success.

I did it, she kept thinking, in a wild, delirious refrain. She could have Eddy back. He was engaged to May, yes, but royal engagements had been broken before. Surely he would brave any scandal, once he knew that she still loved him. Once she told him all the reasons for what she had done.

A few minutes later, Emanuele emerged through the Endicotts' front door, accompanied by Agnes, who seemed to cling to him with the determination of a barnacle. Emanuele detached himself from the American as gracefully as he could, then finally made his way to the street.

"You look happy," he observed, falling into step alongside Hélène. "I take it our endeavor was successful?"

"I need to telegraph Eddy!"

Hélène pressed her hand against her bodice, where the letter made a reassuring crinkling noise. She felt positively giddy. A childlike joy was bubbling up out of her, making her want to twirl right there in the street.

"Excellent." Emanuele held out an arm. "To the post office, then?"

Hélène started to protest that they couldn't be in public without a chaperone; then she remembered that she wasn't dressed like herself. Today she was a maidservant, and the ordinary rules were off.

"I suppose Violette can cover for me a little bit longer."

For once the London weather—normally fickle and disagreeable—seemed inclined to match Hélène's mood. They strolled toward a grassy area at the end of the street, where a few nurses pushed babies in perambulators. Several older boys were flying a kite, its crimson color vibrant against the robin's-egg blue sky. Hélène was well aware how mismatched they looked, her in the maid's uniform and Emanuele in the full trappings of prince attire, the better to awe Mrs. Endicott. People probably thought she was his mistress.

Hélène didn't care. She was planning exactly what she would say to Eddy. She would have to be circumspect; the telegram would almost certainly be read by someone else before it reached him. She just had to trust that he would know her intent, no matter how she phrased it.

"London is prettier this time of year than anyone gives it credit for," Emanuele mused, admiring their surroundings.

"Don't let today fool you. Usually at this time of year, it's rain and more rain."

"You haven't seen Siam in the rainy season. It's relentless," Emanuele teased, and Hélène's bubble of joy deflated ever so slightly.

"You're right," she said softly. "I haven't seen Siam, and I probably never will."

"Oh, but surely you'll go with Eddy someday?"

Hélène doubted it. Even if this plan worked, and she got Eddy back, their future would always be confined. He was the future King of England.

"Any travel we do will be similar to what I recently did with my parents," Hélène admitted. "Venturing from one royal court to another, repeating the same conversation at every dinner, with different hosts."

They turned onto one of Mayfair's high streets; the black awning of the General Post-Office loomed at the corner. Hélène felt Emanuele slow his steps, as if he wanted to prolong their walk. She matched her pace to his.

"It's impossible to escape, isn't it?" he asked quietly.

"Our families?"

"All of it. The tangle of relations and connections that keeps drawing us in." Emanuele shook his head. "It's why I hope that things will stay as they are, that I will never be king. I want to *extricate* myself from the web, not become one of its major axes."

"My feelings exactly," Hélène remarked.

He cast her a sidelong glance. "And yet you fell for the Prince of England."

"All the more proof that I love Eddy for himself. I love him despite his position, not because of it." It felt strange, and at the same time a relief, to speak about her feelings for Eddy. She hadn't been able to really talk about him since she'd seen Amélie all those months ago.

They walked for a few more moments in silence. Emanuele seemed lost in thought. Hélène found herself curious as to what was distracting him.

"Are you all right?"

"I'm afraid I wasn't completely honest just now." Emanuele sighed. "In truth . . . there are times I also feel the opposite. That I *do* want to be an axis in the web—that I want to someday be king."

His confession seemed to hang in the air between them. Hélène started to reply, but before she could quite find the words, Emanuele kept talking.

"It's a terrible thought, obviously. I love my cousin. And when I catch myself feeling this way, I am so ashamed, because I am wishing his death—"

"That's not true! You are merely wishing to play a greater role in things. It's not your fault that monarchy is set up this way," Hélène said resolutely. "It's a ridiculous system, really, that the heir to the throne must always be waiting for his predecessor to die."

The corner of Emanuele's mouth twitched upward. "Don't tell me that you, a French princess, are secretly a republican."

"I just don't want you to take personal blame for an entirely understandable feeling!" Hélène exclaimed. "You know, when I was little, I used to dream of my father becoming King of France again."

"And now that you are a future Queen of England, you no longer dream of such a thing?" Emanuele supplied for her.

Hélène shook her head. "I no longer dream of it because I'm not sure my father would actually *like* being king." It was shocking of her to say this aloud, and she would certainly never voice such words to her father, but that didn't make them any less true. She sighed. "My father is a good man, and I love him dearly. But he has trouble deciding which jacket to wear to a social outing. How on earth would he ever make decisions about a country? If all the monarchist plotting actually came to fruition and he found himself on the throne—I don't think he would have the slightest idea how to rule France. No," she mused aloud, "he is well suited to the life he leads."

"And what about you? Are you well suited to the life you lead?"

It was a rather personal question. But then, she and Emanuele had entered strange territory, collaborating on breaking into someone's home.

"I wish being a princess allowed for other things," Hélène

admitted. "Seeing the world. Meeting people—real people." Not just the ones in the narrow circle of her existence, so proud of the heraldic emblems on their carriages, of their six-foot-tall footmen in livery, of their gowns and yachts and tiaras.

"I hope that you will think of me as a real person," Emanuele replied, surprisingly earnest.

Hélène stopped, then, and turned to face him. "I don't know how to thank you for what you did today. You were incredible."

"As I said before, I'm Italian. We are constitutionally required to help damsels in distress." Emanuele winked, but she knew that his bravado masked a very real kindness.

Smiling from ear to ear, Hélène pushed open the door to the post office. She had defeated May at last.

And now it was time to bring Eddy back.

CHAPTER TWENTY-FOUR

Alix

CONVERSATION FLOATED CHEERFULLY AROUND THE DINING table as everyone dug into their roast beef with mushrooms, forks scraping over Darmstadt's finest porcelain. The so-called two-night visit had stretched into a week. Alix was pleasantly surprised how much she enjoyed hosting her cousins and Maximilian. Most mornings, Ducky and Missy went out riding with Ernie; Maximilian usually stayed back with Alix, reading or walking around the village.

Just that afternoon they had all piled into a pony cart and driven through the countryside. Alix had been eager to show Maximilian her childhood landmarks: the fields where she and her mother used to pick daisies, the crumbled old house that Ella had always said, in a spooky voice, was inhabited by a witch.

"We need to discuss the water chute." Maximilian turned to Alix with a twinkle in his eye. "How long has *that* been around?"

"My father hired some loggers to build it when we were young." Alix smiled, wistful for the days when their mother would climb with them into a rowboat at the top of the slope. Their boat would hurtle down the chute into the pond, drenching them all with the splash. Alix had adored it.

"I'd like to try it," Maximilian declared.

"You'll get quite wet," Alix warned.

He smiled, unconcerned. "I wonder if one could build something similar for a sled in the snow? I have three nephews, you know; the princes of Sweden. What a delightful Christmas present for them . . ."

Maximilian trailed off as, across the table, Ernie rose to his feet.

"Thank you all for a lovely visit," he began, and paused, waiting for conversations around the table to die down.

Alix shot her brother a curious look; she hadn't known he was planning a toast. Though it made sense, since all their guests would be leaving for Potsdam the next day.

"The past week has reminded me of the importance of family, and of good friends," Ernie added, nodding to Maximilian. "Which is why I wanted everyone here to be the first to hear our fantastic news. Ducky?" He gestured across the table, and their cousin stood, tossing her unruly dark hair over one shoulder.

Like Ducky, Ernie was smiling, but the smile didn't seem to reach his eyes. "Today I asked Ducky to marry me, and to my great delight, she said yes."

There was a moment of startled surprise, and then the table erupted in noise. Uncle Alfred grinned, pumping Ernie's hand in both of his, while Aunt Marie laughed and ran around the table to hug Ducky. They were clearly thrilled that their oldest daughter had chosen such an easy match—not the future King of England, perhaps, but a known quantity, a cousin who would keep her close to home. Even Alix's father seemed to have livened up a bit at the news, clamoring that one of the footmen needed to come at once.

When the footman arrived, it was Johann.

"Bring several bottles of champagne from the cellars!" Louis exclaimed, looking at Johann. "Ernest has proposed! We have a future Grand Duchess of Hesse!"

Alix saw the blood drain from Johann's face—saw the way he glanced over at Ernie, hurt and bewilderment on his face. But Ernie was still smiling that broad, social smile, looking anywhere but at Johann.

IT WAS ONLY LATER, AFTER ENDLESS TOASTS AND CONGRATULAtions, that Alix found her brother alone. He was walking down the hallway toward the front staircase, his steps slow, as if he'd depleted all his energy on that celebratory dinner and had nothing left.

"Ernie!" she whispered. "Are you all right?"

He turned around, heaving a sigh when he saw her. "I suppose the news must have caught you by surprise. I'm sorry I didn't warn you."

"What happened? Did Grandmother arrange this, or Father?"

Ernie nodded to the formal sitting room—the one at the front of the house that they almost never used. Alix followed him inside, not bothering to sit.

Her brother shut the door, then leaned against the frame, bracing his palms on the wood behind him.

"I know this is unexpected, but it's for the best, really.

And I have you to thank! You gave me the idea the other day, when you told me that Ducky is in love with her cousin Kiril."

"I was just guessing!" Alix had told Ernie of Ducky's strange comment about *me and Kiril*, and how May had helped her *wriggle out of that engagement to Eddy.*

"Well, your guess was correct. Ducky confirmed it for me."

"Ernie. What did you say?" Alix asked, staring at him.

"I told her that I was looking for a wife who would not expect fidelity from me, and that in return, I would offer her the same courtesy." He let out a breath, seeming amused. "It was so nice, speaking frankly with the opposite sex, instead of all the useless social niceties we were taught. Honestly, you should try it."

"Surely you didn't tell her about . . ."

"About Johann?" Ernie's expression fell, just a little. "I'm not a fool, Alix. I merely said that I suspected she held affections elsewhere, and that I was in a similar situation. That it could benefit us both to be married. I intend to keep pursuing my own relationships, and will make no objection if she does the same." He shrugged. "I told her that she can invite Kiril here all she wants, entertain him personally."

That was a shocking offer—and far more than any other husband would give Ducky. Alix bit her lip. "Are you sure?"

"What other options do I have? Follow Grannie's orders and marry Maud?"

"Grandmother won't make you marry her if you don't wish to!"

"Of course not." Ernie seemed to slump lower against the door. "But if it's not Maud, it will just be someone else. Princesses will keep being paraded before me, 'coincidentally' invited to Balmoral when we are there, turning up unexpectedly at Darmstadt." He refrained from pointing out that Maximilian had done exactly that, turning up on Alix's doorstep uninvited. "The matchmaking won't stop until I marry. Ducky is the best option available to me."

"Oh, Ernie." Alix felt tears pricking her eyes.

"I don't understand. Why aren't you congratulating me? This is a good solution for me, and for Ducky."

"Because you're talking about your marriage as if it will suffocate you, as if it's a—" Alix fumbled for the word. "A prison!"

"Don't you get it? For me, it *will* be a prison."

The bleak truth in his words made Alix's heart ache. She looked out the window at the darkened sky. Far overhead, the moon was a pale sliver.

"I would have expected a little more understanding, from you of all people," Ernie said impatiently.

"What's *that* supposed to mean?"

"That you know what it's like to resign yourself to the inevitable!"

"I thought you said I did the right thing, walking away from Nicholas!" she shot back.

"Because you might fall in love with someone else!" Ernie exclaimed. "Maybe Maximilian—who adores you, by the way, and seems like your perfect match. Or maybe someone you haven't met yet. But at least you have a chance of marrying someone without the whole thing being a lie."

Alix ignored what Ernie had said about Maximilian, though some part of her tingled with awareness at the thought he might adore her.

"You should have seen Johann's face when he heard the news," she said softly. "He was devastated."

Ernie ran a hand through his hair, frustrated. "What do you want me to do, Alix? Put a tiara on Johann's head and tell everyone he's the Grand Duchess of Hesse?"

"I want you to be *happy*!"

At her outburst, Ernie's tension seemed to deflate. He nodded in acknowledgment of her words.

"Maybe someday the world will be different, and people like me will have a chance at real happiness," he said softly. "In the meantime, I'm lucky to have found Ducky. She fits all the criteria that I need in a wife, and has agreed to let me live on my own terms. She won't ask any inconvenient questions. As for Johann—I'm doing this for *us*, to give us more time together. To protect us. He has always known the demands on me, and what is possible."

As well as what is impossible, Ernie didn't need to add.

There were a thousand things Alix longed to tell her brother: *Please be careful*, and *I worry for you*, and *I hate to see you settling for a pale imitation of love when the real thing is within reach.*

But of course, a real relationship—a real marriage—wasn't within reach. Not for him.

"If you're happy, then I am happy for you," Alix promised.

Ernie stepped forward then, pulling her into a hug. She was startled to realize that he was close to tears.

"Thank you, Alix," he mumbled, his words muffled. "I don't know what I would do without you."

"You'll always have me," Alix swore. Her arms closed tight around her brother—as if somehow, against the odds, she could protect him from society, from the world. From the future that was careening ever faster toward them both.

CHAPTER TWENTY-FIVE

May

SEVERAL WEEKS LATER, MAY STARED AT HERSELF IN THE FLOOR-TO-ceiling mirror, which reflected back the opulence of the private shopping area. The few times she'd come to Linton & Curtis with her old friend Agnes, May had seen luxury, but this was something else entirely. Even the excruciatingly wealthy Agnes was just an ordinary person.

May was now a future queen, and had transcended into the realm of magic.

The entire store had shut down for May's appointment. Mr. Curtis himself was overseeing her fittings, along with the two women Queen Victoria had sent: the Baroness Churchill and the Marchioness of Ely, both the queen's dear friends and ladies-in-waiting—and, incidentally, both named Jane. May hoped that their presence meant the queen would be *paying* for today's purchases. Though of course no one had mentioned anything as plebeian as the bill. May suspected that her mother—currently taking up a whole section of the sofa in the private dressing area, giggling her schoolgirl laugh—hadn't even considered it.

May had felt obligated to bring her; it was hardly appropriate to get fitted for a trousseau without one's mother. But she wasn't exactly asking Mary Adelaide for fashion advice.

A cluster of seamstresses and attendants had buzzed around May all morning, recording dozens of highly specific measurements, helping her into sample gowns so that she might select her favorite necklines. And of course, showering her in relentless flattery.

"Mr. Curtis," the Marchioness of Ely commanded. "Please remind us of the items ordered for Her Serene Highness's trousseau thus far."

The boutique owner smiled, his walrus-like mustache curling upward. "Of course, Lady Ely. The selections include fifteen tea gowns, ten matinée gowns, ten traveling capes, twelve pairs of gloves—"

"Twelve pairs of gloves!" Lady Ely cut in. "Think of how many places Her Serene Highness will go, to parades and to visit coal mines and to the harbor when the navy decommissions a vessel! She will need at least two dozen."

Mr. Curtis murmured in agreement, and May nodded at Lady Ely in thanks. The sheer size of her trousseau order was reassuring. With each bolt of fabric, each ostrich feather or ruffled blouse, she felt safer, more secure. These clothes were like armor, protecting her from the world and all its cruelties.

"Why don't I gather some more fabric selections," Mr. Curtis offered. "In the meantime, Your Serene Highness, would you try on this sample ball gown? Just to see the style on you," he added quickly. "Yours will, of course, have more embellishment."

May started into the changing room—and, to her surprise, her mother rose to her feet.

"Shall I help you undress, May?" she offered.

It was a bit strange, sharing this sort of moment with her

mother when they had always kept their distance, but May couldn't exactly say no. Mary Adelaide followed her behind the curtain and helped unhook the buttons of her striped day dress, so that May could step out of it wearing nothing but her corset and bloomers.

"I can't believe you're getting married," her mother murmured. "And to Prince Eddy! I'm so proud of you, May. You look beautiful."

May was surprised to feel a lump of emotion in her throat. She quickly blinked it away. "Thank you, Mother."

Carefully, Mary Adelaide removed the dark green evening gown from its hanger. "I can see that things are already changing for you. You are going to increasingly be in demand, and I hate to be another person asking a favor of you, but there's something we need to discuss."

May bit back a sigh as she stepped into the gown. "What is it, Mother?"

"Could you get your father a diplomatic posting? Perhaps something in a foreign office?"

"I assume Father put you up to this? Because he already asked me, and as I told him, these sorts of things take time."

Her mother's head dropped morosely. "Francis did mention it, a number of times, but that's not why I asked. I was hoping that if he went abroad, I might stay here."

May stared at her mother, irritation rapidly melting into something like pride. At long last, Mary Adelaide was standing up for herself.

Though a few divorce cases had made their way into the courts, it was still out of the question that the Tecks would divorce, especially now that they were the parents of a future queen. But separations were tacitly tolerated by society. Mary Adelaide could remain here in London, at White Lodge, while her husband was stationed abroad.

"I see," May said meaningfully. "Maybe Brussels? Or somewhere even farther afield, like Rome?"

There was unexpected humor in her mother's expression as she replied, "What about India?"

May snorted. "Can you imagine Father in India? He would despise it."

"Perhaps we would get lucky, and a tiger would eat him."

May gave a strangled laugh at that. Mary Adelaide met her daughter's gaze in the mirror, and then she was laughing too.

It was a bittersweet, aching sort of laugh, the sort of laugh tinged with years of sorrow. May hated that it had taken them so long to finally talk about Francis, even in a roundabout way. Why had they never acknowledged his cruelty to each other? They should have joined forces against him long ago, instead of allowing him to drive a wedge between them. He had clearly known that they were weaker and more vulnerable apart.

"I'm sorry," May told her mother, when their laughter had faded. "About Father, I mean."

Mary Adelaide glanced down at the floor. "Oh, May, it's not your fault. But this is why I'm so glad to see you happy. I want your marriage to be . . . well, a success." *Unlike mine*, was the silent afterthought.

"Of course," May said quickly. She *was* happy. What did it matter that she didn't love Eddy? One need only look at Mary Adelaide to see the consequences of marrying for love.

A commotion out in the store shattered the tentative moment between them. Now fully dressed in the evening gown, May tugged aside the curtain to glance out.

"I'm so sorry, Miss Endicott," Mr. Curtis said hastily. "As always, we are delighted to see you, but I'm afraid the store is closed today."

"May will want to see me," Agnes commanded. Then she looked up and met May's gaze. "May! Can we speak in private? I have news."

What choice did May have? Agnes still knew too much. May couldn't afford for the American to be angry with her, a loose cannon who could detonate in May's direction.

So she smiled as wide as she could and said, "Agnes! What an unexpected pleasure." Then she turned to the boutique owner, still smiling. "Mr. Curtis, I must admit, my head is overwhelmed by all our decision-making! Would you mind if Miss Endicott and I took a turn through the store?"

"Of course! We want you to be comfortable, Your Serene Highness!" he simpered.

May looped an arm through Agnes's as if they were still the best of friends. Together the two young women wandered toward the displays of gloves and ribbons, all eerily devoid of salespeople or shoppers.

"You shouldn't have asked him that," Agnes muttered.

May tensed. "Excuse me?"

"You're a future queen. You shouldn't have asked permission from Mr. Curtis. *He* works for *you*," Agnes explained. "Next time you don't say *Would you mind*; you just inform him what you are doing. He will accommodate you."

May suspected that Agnes was right, but she didn't want

to admit it. "Did you just come here to criticize me, or did you have something you wanted to discuss?"

"I thought you might want to know that it's missing," Agnes said testily.

"What's missing?"

"The letter from Laurent, of course! The one we blackmailed Hélène with!"

"*You* blackmailed Hélène," May corrected her. "Not *we.* I had no part in it."

"Oh, please." Agnes waved away May's protest. "You were more than content to benefit from my blackmail. From what I can see, you're still benefiting from it," she added with a meaningful glance around the store.

Perhaps May *was* equally culpable in the blackmail. She could have told Hélène the truth about the letter. There had been a moment, last fall, when she thought that she and Hélène understood each other—a tentative heartbeat of friendship that could have become something more.

Instead May had let Hélène go on thinking she was blackmailed, ensuring that the French princess hated her.

"A maidservant named Annie stole the letter," Agnes was saying, her voice tight. "She quit, and then a few days later I opened the box where I had kept it, and the letter was missing!"

"She must be working with Hélène." Briefly May recounted what had happened at Osborne, how she'd caught Hélène snooping through her things.

Agnes's face fell. "If Hélène has it, she might feel brave enough to take Eddy back from you. That letter was our insurance policy, our proof. Without it, all you have is slander."

"You didn't hear? Hélène and Eddy are done. She's been flirting outrageously with Nicholas, the Tsarevich of Russia." May sighed. "She stole the letter back because she didn't want me to blackmail her a second time, not when she's about to get engaged to a Romanov."

Agnes stared at May. "Hélène has moved on to *Nicholas*?"

"They aren't formally engaged yet, but I'm sure it will be announced soon."

"You're saying that I had a letter in my possession, a highly personal letter incriminating the *future tsarina* of Russia—and it's out of my grasp?" Agnes seemed outraged.

"I should think that it was enough to have one future queen in your pocket," May snapped.

"Yes, but I should prefer to call on favors from two."

Agnes said it so matter-of-factly, without an ounce of compunction, that May huffed out a laugh. "You'll never change, will you?"

"I hope not. And I hope you don't, either," Agnes said resolutely. "I know you won't believe me, May, but I really have been rooting for you this whole time. I'll let you get back to your trousseau," she added, with a fond glance toward the fitting rooms. "I just wanted to warn you about the letter in case it was a problem. You know, for old times' sake."

May must have been getting soft after that conversation with her mother, because to her own surprise she asked Agnes, "Would you like to stay?"

Agnes smiled broadly. "I would love that."

As they headed back toward the private fitting rooms, they heard a shocked gasp from Lady Churchill, followed by a swift *shh* from Lady Ely.

May and Agnes exchanged a wordless glance, then both slowed their steps, listening.

"It is quite scandalous behavior for a granddaughter of Her Majesty," Lady Ely hissed. "And with the Crown Prince of Romania!"

"That girl has thrown away her future," Lady Churchill agreed. "She could have been the second-highest-ranked woman in England!"

"Poor George . . ."

May stepped into the sitting room with deliberate calm, though her pulse was racing wildly. The two ladies-in-waiting immediately cut off their whispers as she appeared, which only confirmed her suspicions.

Though it was the height of rudeness to admit to eavesdropping, she had to say something.

"My friend Agnes will be joining us for the rest of the fittings." May gave her most demure smile, proud of herself for, as Agnes put it, telling instead of asking. "Forgive me," she added, "but did I hear you mention Missy? I hope she's all right."

Both women stared at her. May's smile never faltered, though she began frantically thinking back through what they'd said. Wait—had they mentioned Missy by name?

Lady Ely glanced at Agnes, as if sizing her up. "Quite shocking news arrived by telegram this morning. But you might as well hear it from us, since it will be common knowledge soon enough." The lady-in-waiting sighed. "Alfred and his family are visiting their cousins in Potsdam. One evening, the kaiser had a grand dinner at the Neues Palais. Over a hundred people in the dining room, which has all been newly renovated and electrified."

"I'm sure everyone was busy congratulating Ducky—you know she recently got engaged," Lady Churchill chimed in helpfully. "Young women can act a bit strangely when they fear that a friend, or a sister, has overshadowed them."

May had heard the news of Ducky's recent engagement, though she didn't understand it. Why would Ducky refuse to marry Eddy, claiming she was in love with her cousin Kiril, and then agree to marry *Ernie*—who was only the son of a minor grand duke? There had to be some key detail May was missing. It didn't make sense otherwise.

Lady Ely waved a hand in distress, picking up the thread of her story. "Some time after the dinner, Missy's mother realized that Missy was nowhere to be seen. Groups of people went out with torches into the gardens. They found her there, alone, kissing Prince Ferdinand of Romania!"

Agnes lifted a hand to her mouth. "Oh my!" she exclaimed with admirably pious shock.

May couldn't say anything. Her stomach had twisted with sharp, acrid guilt.

When she'd mentioned Ferdinand to Aunt Vicky, she'd hoped that the Romanian prince might flirt with Missy, perhaps distract her from George. It wasn't her fault that headstrong, impulsive Missy had walked off with him into the gardens . . . right?

"They are engaged now, of course," Lady Ely went on. "What else could be done? A dozen people saw them together!"

May swallowed over the dryness in her throat and forced herself to chime in. "At least Missy's reputation is saved."

Lady Churchill nodded in agreement, but Lady Ely sniffed. "You'd think that girl would have caused enough trouble, except now she is refusing to marry Ferdinand! She says that *he* kissed *her*, and that her cousin Wilhelm engineered the whole thing—that he suggested she show Ferdinand the greenhouse after dinner." Lady Ely sighed. "Whether or not that is true, Missy was raised better. She should have simply told her cousin no."

"Nothing good comes of being with a young man in the dark," Agnes agreed solemnly. Lady Ely and Lady Churchill nodded, seeming pleased by Agnes's show of decorum.

But once the queen's ladies-in-waiting turned their heads, Agnes lifted an eyebrow at May, as if to say, *You did this, right?*

She had seen May's growing feelings for George last year, after all. And she knew better than anyone what May was capable of.

"I have heard that Ferdinand is quite handsome," May added, as if that might make things better.

"Oh, that he is. He just lives halfway around the world," Lady Churchill said dismissively.

Agnes nodded. "Romania is so far! It might as well be Tokyo!" Somehow she managed to sound sincere, though May knew she was secretly mocking Lady Churchill's small-mindedness.

"Poor Marie, to have both daughters married in the same year," Lady Churchill went on. "My own younger daughter waited a full year after her older sister's wedding before getting engaged. As is quite appropriate."

"Poor Marie?" Lady Ely exclaimed. "I think you mean poor George!"

"Yes, I suppose Her Majesty shall have to find another match for him," Lady Churchill said loyally.

Her friend nodded. "Perhaps one of Helena's girls?"

Another match?

Mr. Curtis chose that moment to reappear, surrounded by assistants carrying stacks of fabric. "Your Serene Highness!" He held his hand dramatically to his chest. "You look stunning in this cut. Perhaps we just lift the neckline an inch or so?"

"That sounds lovely." May tried to ignore the distress she'd felt at Lady Ely's words. Would the queen really find a replacement for Missy so quickly? Not that she cared, of course.

She was engaged to Eddy. George was not hers to worry about. He was nothing to her, really, except a future brother-in-law—and it needed to stay that way.

CHAPTER TWENTY-SIX

Hélène

HÉLÈNE WAS SEATED AT HER VANITY, VIOLETTE RUNNING A BRUSH through her hair, when she heard Prince Eddy in the hall.

"I know she's here!" he cried out.

Hélène and Violette exchanged a glance in the mirror, and then Hélène shot to her feet, stumbling forward.

She heard a harried footman trying to stop Eddy's progress. "Your Royal Highness, if you'll please wait in the parlor, I shall summon mademoiselle. It is quite early."

It was indeed early; Hélène hadn't yet dressed for the day, and was only in a chemise and loose dressing gown. She was halfway to the door when it flung open, and Prince Eddy strode into her room.

"I'm sorry, mademoiselle," the footman stammered, averting his eyes. "I tried to stop him, but he insisted on, well . . ."

"It's all right." Hélène's gaze was locked on Eddy as she said, "Violette, you may go."

The lady's maid hesitated, clearly aware of the impropriety of leaving them alone, and with Hélène half-dressed. Then she curtsied and walked out, muttering something about too many princes showing up unexpectedly these days.

"Eddy. You came." Hélène's heart was pounding wildly.

"What did you mean by that telegram?" He took an angry step forward.

Hélène's dressing room was small, with gilt blue wallpaper and a Louis XVI mirror. The vanity was covered in crystal scent bottles, pots of rouge, the silver-backed hairbrush that Violette had abandoned. There was something discordant about seeing Eddy here, his crackling male energy sucking all the air from the room.

"I meant exactly what I wrote. That I wanted to speak with you," Hélène said softly.

"So you could torture me some more? Whatever game you're playing, I want no part in it."

"I assure you, it's not a game to me—"

"Then why do you keep playing with my feelings?"

"Because I had no other choice! I love you!"

Eddy's expression didn't shift; he might have been staring at Hélène across a battlefield. And in fact, his ancestors had been *her* ancestors' enemies five hundred years earlier.

"I love you," she said again, fiercely. "And I will fight for us with every last breath in my body. That is, if you still want me."

"How can I believe anything you say? You gave up on us," Eddy said accusingly.

"*I* gave up on us?" she repeated, incredulous. "*You're* the one who went and got engaged! And to May of Teck, of all people!"

"I thought I was engaged to *you*!" Eddy broke into a cough for a moment, hand to his mouth. His voice was raspy and hoarse when he spoke again. "Then, without any warning, you decided you couldn't be with me anymore. I offered to give up the throne for you, and you told me to walk away and *forget* you!"

"It looks like you had no problem taking my advice, given how quickly you moved on!" she shot back.

"As if *you* didn't move on to my *cousin*!" Eddy crossed his arms over his chest. "Were you already sleeping with Nicholas when you ended things with me?"

Hélène drew in a sharp breath. "Nicholas and I were never even formally engaged. It was all just pretend."

Eddy didn't seem to have heard her. "I saw you two together, that morning on the yacht! You weren't exactly subtle about it, Hélène. Embracing right there on the deck, for anyone to see."

Oh *no*. Hélène's heart ached at how fundamentally he had misunderstood. "There was nothing romantic about it, Eddy. Nicholas is my friend, and embraced me because I was crying about *you*. As I said, we were only pretending to court."

"Pretending?" Eddy paused, seeming less certain of himself. "But the night before—I thought—you two left the party at Osborne House early. Together."

"We did leave the party early, but Nicholas and I both snuck back into the house. He went to see Alix, and I snooped through May's room," Hélène said softly.

Eddy frowned. "May? As in my May?"

"*Your* May?" Hélène repeated testily. Oh, she hated that phrase.

"You know what I meant! May of Teck, the woman I'm supposed to marry! What does she have to do with anything?"

"Quite a lot, given that she blackmailed me into leaving you!"

Eddy stared at her, stunned. He placed a hand on the back of her chair, a small feminine thing tucked up to her vanity, and held it so tight his knuckles turned white.

"What do you mean, May blackmailed you?"

"She had proof of something I had done, something indecorous, and was holding it over my head. I thought it best not to tell you," Hélène said haltingly. "I was worried that if you knew, you might confront May, and then she would expose me. I'm sorry it took me so long to figure out a solution," she added more softly, "but I never thought you would get engaged to someone else."

"I only got engaged to May because I'd seen you with Nicholas that very morning." Eddy cursed under his breath. "Come to think of it, May was with me when I saw you two together. She's the one who pointed out that you'd left the party together, who made me think that you had . . ."

Why am I not surprised? Hélène thought wearily. Somehow May had gotten her tentacles into all their lives, influencing their very thoughts.

"Eddy. I would never betray you like that," she said intently. "Nicholas and I let people think we were courting, but only because it benefited us both. I wanted May to stop considering me a threat, and Nicholas used me as an excuse to see Alix. We've already told our parents that there will not be an engagement."

"You had me convinced," he said, voice raspy.

"I *needed* to be convincing, to throw May off the scent! It destroyed me a little bit every day, pretending that you meant nothing to me. Trust me when I say that I never stopped loving you." Hélène's voice broke; tears threatened to slide down her cheeks, but she needed him to hear this. "I will never stop, for all the days of my life. There is no one for me but you, Eddy."

Eddy ran a hand over his features, then looked back up. His eyes flicked around the room as if seeing it for the first time. He seemed to finally register that they were alone in her dressing room—that Hélène was standing before him, her bare legs visible through the sheer skirts of her dressing gown. The distance between them was only a few feet, and yet at the same time it felt impossibly vast.

"There is no one for me but you, either," Eddy finally said, then stepped forward to pull her into his arms.

Hélène tipped her mouth eagerly up to his, her hands wrapped around his shoulders. She wished she could stay here forever, inhabiting this moment—this kiss—for the rest of her life. Heat coursed through her, and she knew that Eddy could feel it too: how well they fit together. How utterly *right* it was.

When they finally broke apart, Eddy tucked her head into his shoulder. "God, Hélène, how I've missed you."

THAT EVENING, THE TWO OF THEM WERE INTERTWINED IN BED, IN the rooms Eddy kept in north London. As much as Hélène would have loved to do this at her parents' house, she knew better than to push her luck. After their conversation this morning, Eddy had slipped quietly away. They had agreed to meet up at night, as they used to.

Hélène had forgotten how good this felt. Not just physical intimacy, but afterward: when you could drape yourself over your lover's body, letting your head rest on his bare chest. Listening to the steady and reassuring beat of his heart. All the pins had been tugged loose from her hair, which fell about her shoulders, wild as a lion's mane.

"You said May used something you had done and blackmailed you," Eddy began, lacing his fingers with hers. "What happened?"

So Hélène started from the beginning. She told him how she'd had an affair with Laurent years ago, before she and Eddy were ever involved—and then, when she and Eddy were secretly engaged, how she'd gotten a threatening note from May.

"*What?*" Eddy sat upright, his expression thunderous. "What did the note say?"

"She told me that I needed to end our engagement 'before it was too late,' or else she would tell the queen about me and Laurent! She had a love letter that he wrote me," Hélène added, her cheeks flaming. "That American friend of hers, Agnes, tricked Laurent into writing it. So May had proof. Even back then, she was clearly planning to swoop in and marry you herself."

Eddy wasn't really listening anymore. He slid out of bed, reaching for his shirt as if he meant to storm White Lodge at that very moment. "How *dare* she. I'm going to tell her exactly what she—"

"Eddy, I have the letter!" Hélène sat up. "Just relax for a moment, all right? I stole it back!"

Reluctantly, Eddy sat back on his bed and listened.

Hélène told him how she'd been in Rome when she wrote Laurent, how he'd sent his reply back to the Quirinal Palace. How Emanuele had come to London, and helped her break into the Americans' rented house in Mayfair. Eddy listened in silence, his expression unreadable.

"You seem upset," Hélène said at last, twisting the sheets in her lap. "Are you angry that I didn't tell you any of this?"

Eddy sighed. "It certainly would have made the last year more bearable, knowing the truth instead of thinking that you had stopped loving me."

Hélène placed a hand tentatively on his shoulder. "I'm sorry," she told him, knowing how utterly inadequate the words were. "I worried that if I told you, you would have revealed it to May, and she would have shown the letter to Her Majesty. Then we *never* would be able to get married."

"But now I'm publicly engaged to May," he said flatly.

Well, yes. Hélène hadn't imagined that he would take such a drastic action so quickly.

Eddy shifted farther back on the bed, tucking an arm around Hélène's shoulders and pulling her next to him. "You were probably right not to tell me. We both know I don't exactly have a delicate touch when it comes to things like this." He shook his head. "I just . . . I keep thinking of all the time we lost. We had finally gotten my grandmother's blessing, and then to lose it because of May . . ."

"I'm sorry," Hélène said again, and Eddy turned, brushing a kiss on her temple.

"Don't apologize. I'm just relieved to have you back."

They sat like that for a moment in silence, her head nestled into the crook of his shoulder. Then Eddy asked, "So who is this Emanuele character, exactly?"

Hélène felt a laugh bubble out of her. "Don't tell me you're jealous. You, the future King of England, cannot envy an Italian prince who is second in line to the throne."

"I can be jealous when you're off scheming with him, telling him secrets you didn't even tell me."

"I promise you needn't worry about me and Emanuele," Hélène assured him. "It might seem strange that I shared so much with him, but I really do trust him. He's back in Italy now, anyway. What would it benefit him to tell anyone that May was blackmailing me? He doesn't even know what the blackmail was about."

"I still don't like it." Eddy let out a frustrated breath. "In any case, I should request an audience with Grandmother, and let her know how wrong she was about May. Once she knows exactly what May has done, she will agree that we need to call off the engagement."

Hélène hesitated. "Are you sure that's the best plan?"

"Why else did you go to all the trouble of getting the letter back?" Eddy's voice faltered. "That is—you still want to marry me—don't you?"

"Of course I do!" Hélène pressed a swift kiss to his brow. "I just worry about your grandmother. You know she'll demand the whole story, in all its ugly detail. You can't tell her that May wrote me a threatening note and leave it at that. Which means that she'll end up learning about me and Laurent anyway." And Victoria wouldn't be nearly as forgiving of Hélène's indiscretions as Eddy had been.

"What other options do we have?" Eddy asked, confused.

"We can go to May, confront her face to face. If we offer her a dignified retreat, we might *all* escape this mess unscathed."

"Then she'll get away with it!"

"I don't care if she does, really. As long as I get to be with you." As much as Hélène would have loved to destroy May, she wanted to marry Eddy far more than she wanted revenge. There was no use setting May's life afire if Hélène would be caught in the flames.

Eddy nodded slowly. "I suppose you're right. Actually, I'm supposed to see May tomorrow, to sit for our first official portrait." He made a face. "I think I'll show up late. I don't exactly trust myself not to shout the moment I see her."

"I'll come with you," Hélène promised.

Eddy turned to Hélène with a wicked gleam in his eye. "Good. Now, I want to hear more about the disguise you wore at the Endicotts' house. You really pretended to be a French maid?" He grinned. "Do you still have the outfit, by chance?"

"You're incorrigible!" Hélène started to laugh, but then Eddy's mouth was on hers again, and she was far too distracted to laugh about anything.

CHAPTER TWENTY-SEVEN

Alix

ALIX KNELT IN THE MIDDLE OF A SITTING ROOM DOWNSTAIRS, which had recently transformed into her command center for reorganizing the house. She hadn't realized that their home was in such an appalling state, items tucked haphazardly into closets, fine linens moth-eaten and mismatched. Well, she was determined to fix all that before Ducky came to live here. It would be an embarrassment if a new mistress took over a home in such a state.

Because that's what Ducky would be soon enough—the new mistress of their estate in Darmstadt. Once Ernie got married, Alix would be in the way. Ducky would take over all the responsibilities of hostess, all the charitable works and social obligations, that had been Alix's since her mother died.

When the cousins were departing for Potsdam, Ducky had pulled Alix into an embrace. "I promise, you'll always be welcome here," she'd murmured into her future sister-in-law's ear. It had thrown Alix wildly off-balance.

In all her worries about whether Ernie was making a mistake by getting engaged, she'd hardly considered what his marriage would mean for her. That she would be extraneous. Unneeded. An awkward third party, always hovering around the dinner table, trying not to disrupt her brother and his wife.

Alix sighed and reached for another trunk that the footmen had fetched from an upstairs closet. As she opened the lid, a fine sheen of dust floated into the air.

Her eyes stung when she saw what lay inside. These were her mother's old things.

So many of Alice's possessions had been burned after her death—to prevent the spread of smallpox, the doctors had said. But here were a few items that must have escaped the blaze. Alix pulled out a Bible, its spine creased from frequent use; a polished silver hand mirror emblazoned with roses.

Underneath, wrapped in tissue that crinkled pleasantly, was a white gown. Alix's breath fragmented in her chest as she unwrapped it.

The gown was lovely, reams of satin unfurling as Alix lifted the bodice. The lace veil beneath was yellowing with age, its stitching painfully delicate.

Outside in the driveway, hoofbeats sounded. Alix ignored them.

Would she ever get the chance to wear this veil? Once, she had dreamed of wearing it as she walked down an aisle toward Nicholas. She should probably offer it to Ducky, she realized; but wouldn't Ducky want to wear the Coburg veil?

She held the lace up to the light, studying its delicate pattern. Were those petals or leaves? It was hard to make out, her vision blurry—from tears? No, it was a haziness that seemed to have invaded her vision, making the world fade into black at the edges.

Not again.

It had been so long since one of Alix's episodes, but the old familiar panic settled over her now, like a heavy blanket of smoke, suffocating her. She set down the veil and fumbled to close the trunk, but her hands had frozen into claws, her fingers stiff and useless.

All her worries—about Ernie, about doors closing, about being lonely or foolish or not good enough, about *Nicholas*—they all seemed to turn into blades, slicing wildly at her chest. Alix looked down, expecting to see blood seeping through the bodice of her gown, but there was nothing there.

"Alix?" She heard Maximilian's voice as if from a great distance. "Alix, are you all right?"

"I get like this sometimes." She tried to say more, but her throat felt like it was closing. She struggled valiantly to swallow. "Maximilian, when did you . . . ?"

"I'm sorry that I didn't warn you that I was coming. I left Potsdam early. Missy and Ferdinand . . ." Maximilian trailed off at the look on Alix's face. "You are unwell. I'll fetch Ernie or your father—"

"Please, don't. I can't let them worry. . . ."

Maximilian didn't hesitate. He scooped Alix up in his arms, the way one would carry a child, and held her against his chest as he started upstairs. She wanted to wrap her arms around him, too, but her hands were still frozen, immobile.

Alix didn't question how he knew which room was hers, though there were no brass plaques on the doors here, as there were at Balmoral and Osborne. Of course Maximilian knew. In her overheated mind, it felt natural that he would have been paying attention to her movements.

He set her on the rug before the hearth, then grabbed

the bedcovers from her bed—a bit scandalous, Alix thought faintly, though she didn't mind—and wrapped them tight around her, tucking them under her chin. Once he'd stoked the fire, coaxing it to a pleasant crackle, he sat on the rug next to Alix and tugged her hands free.

"I'm here," he kept saying over and over, like a mantra, as he massaged her hands. His thumbs felt scratchy with calluses, the hands of a man who rode without gloves, who was too impatient for the proprieties. "I'm here, you're not alone, you are safe, it's okay." His words repeated on a loop, soothing and soft.

Eventually, Alix felt her frozen hands unclench. Her chest loosened; her breathing steadied. She looked down at the coverlet wrapped around her, playing with its stitching to avoid meeting Maximilian's gaze.

"I'm sorry," she forced herself to say. "You weren't supposed to see that. Those episodes . . . I suppose you could say they are my cross to bear. My dark secret."

"Dark secret?" Maximilian repeated, frowning.

Alix flushed from shame. "This has happened to me ever since my brother Frittie died. Not very often, but once it begins, I cannot stop it. My body goes into a state of shock, or perhaps it is panic. I don't know what causes it," she added miserably.

"Your suprarenal glands." Maximilian's tone was so reasonable, so conversational, that she looked up.

"My what?"

"Your suprarenal glands. The ones that control your fear," Maximilian explained. "They can malfunction when your body or mind is under stress. It's nothing to be ashamed of," he added gently.

Alix stared at him. "How do you know all this? Have you seen these episodes before?"

"No, I've only read about them. I like to keep up with the latest medical journals." Maximilian blew out a breath. "I keep hoping that someone, somewhere, will find a cure for my uncle."

Once again, his thoughtfulness—his unbearable goodness—struck her to the core.

"Let me know if you encounter a cure for *me* in one of those journals," she said darkly.

"You don't need a cure; you need treatment. There's a difference." Maximilian looked steadily at Alix. "These attacks are a symptom of your anxiety. When your life is calmer, when you feel steady and safe, they will start coming less and less frequently. And perhaps someday you'll look up and realize that you don't have them anymore at all."

"You're quite the doctor," she observed.

Maximilian smiled shyly. "Not a doctor. Just a man armed with logic and observation."

Alix shrugged tighter into the coverlet. The warmth of it felt so good around her, as if it were anchoring her in place. "Please, don't tell Ernie. He'll think it was his fault," she murmured. At Maximilian's confused look, she added, "This usually happens when I'm worried, or upset, and Ernie . . . he knows I have concerns about him and Ducky." She shouldn't have said that, she realized. It was just so *easy* to talk to Maximilian.

"You don't approve of her?"

"They don't love each other!" Alix exclaimed. "And I'm upset for my own reasons, too, because of—because I—"

She broke off and met Maximilian's gaze. He did not

interrupt or ask questions; he just waited patiently, giving her the space to elaborate if she wanted.

"Remember how I told you that I didn't wish to be courted because I was in love with someone else?" Alix asked.

His eyes flashed, as if he'd noticed her use of the past tense. "I remember," he said, his voice carefully neutral.

"Well, that young man and I—we are done."

"I'm sorry." Maximilian seemed to mean it. "Of course I am here, if you need a friend."

It must have been the aftereffects of that gland Maximilian had spoken of, the panic ebbing from Alix's system like a poison. Or perhaps it was the instinctive way he'd carried her, letting her lean on his strength, his warmth. Whatever it was, Alix heard herself say, "If I need a friend, I'll turn to Hélène or to my cousins. I have no use for another friend, Maximilian."

He shifted slightly toward her. "Are you saying . . . ?"

"I don't know if you even wish to court me, but if you'd like to, there are no more obstacles. Unless you were frightened off by all this." She gestured ruefully to the blanket, indicating the whole awful episode that had just happened.

Maximilian's mouth lifted in a smile. "Alix of Hesse, I have wanted to court you for a very long time."

"I— All right, then," she said, suddenly nervous.

"All right, then," he repeated evenly.

Perhaps he had more experience in courting than she did; because even though she'd been forced into those awkward interactions with Eddy two years before, even though she and Nicholas had slept together, Alix felt suddenly uncertain. She'd never been truly courted by a young man—not like this, with everything done by the book, in the proper order.

Maximilian reached over and took one of her hands in his. "And please, stop feeling so ashamed about these *episodes*, as you call them."

Her fingers laced around his. Then they both seemed to realize at the same moment the situation they were in—a man and a woman, alone, in her bedroom.

"I'll check on you later, if that's all right," he said, standing. Then he leaned over to drop a quick, eager kiss on her mouth.

Alix lifted a hand to her lips, startled, as he walked out the door.

Maximilian had seen her. He knew her most shameful secret, and instead of being repelled by it, or disgusted, he had stayed with her through it. Had fought it with calm rationality.

He had walked right into the darkness at the core of her, and he hadn't run off. He'd just lit a torch and started burning the darkness away.

CHAPTER TWENTY-EIGHT

May

MAY FROZE HALFWAY DOWN THE STAIRS. HER FATHER STOOD IN the entrance hall, glaring at the carriage in the driveway—one marked with the queen's crest, pulled by a pair of perfectly matched white horses.

"You are heading to Buckingham Palace?" Francis demanded.

May started tentatively down the stairs again. "Today is the first sitting for my official portrait with Eddy."

"I will join you," her father declared, crossing his arms over his chest.

To May's surprise, her mother strode in from the drawing room. "Come now, Francis, May can go alone. After all, you're not the one sitting for the portrait."

"Neither are you," Francis said viciously. "As if anyone would even *want* a portrait of you, you cow."

Mary Adelaide sagged a little. The morning light fell on her face, underscoring the lines around her mouth, the weariness on her features.

The sight of it broke something in May. Before she could think twice, she clattered down the last few steps, throwing up an arm as if to shield Mary Adelaide.

"Don't talk to Mother that way."

Like some ancient predator that had stumbled across a new victim, Francis turned his head slowly in May's direction.

Behind him, May saw Mary Adelaide shaking her head in warning. *Don't do it,* her eyes pleaded. *Don't provoke him.*

But May was done cowering. Why else had she done all this, schemed and plotted and left a trail of hurt in her wake, if not to become stronger than her father? To protect herself, and her mother, from his cruelty?

Adopting her boldest, most imperious voice—the one Agnes used, the one *Victoria* used—she stared her father down. "You will not be joining me at my portrait sitting. And now you will apologize to Mother."

An excruciating silence echoed through the house.

Francis stared at May; then slowly he smiled. Somehow it was more chilling than all his blustering anger. "Well, well. Look who learned to fight back. I wondered if you would ever be brave enough to turn on me, or whether you would stick to terrorizing other young women."

May felt the blood drain from her face. "I have not terrorized anyone. I have tried to plan ahead, to be clever—"

"Do you deny that you went after other young women, tore them down in order to pave your rise?" he bellowed. May said nothing, and he nodded. "I knew you did something to that Hessian girl. And you and your tawdry American friend were always whispering together. Whose life did you destroy? That cousin of Eddy's, the one from Coburg? No," he mused, watching May's face. "You might have gotten rid of her, too, but you also did something else. Something bigger."

So he did know the truth. Her father had discovered her sabotage of Alix, and had guessed at her blackmail of Hélène, even if he didn't know precisely what it was.

"May, what is he talking about?" Mary Adelaide asked shakily. May ignored her.

Icy fear snaked through her core. How had Francis figured out what she'd done?

Had he seen right through May because, deep down, they were the same?

"You will not repeat such things ever again, to me or to anyone else," May insisted, though her voice shook a little.

"Don't forget that I can still hurt you," Francis threatened.

"You wouldn't dare! I am the future Queen of England. Someday my son will be king!" May took a step forward—and to her surprise, her father retreated. Just a few inches, but it gave her the courage to keep going.

"*I* am the one who can hurt *you* now. Which is why I insist that you leave the country," she commanded.

May heard her mother's shocked intake of breath. Francis went dangerously still.

"You will leave, Father," May continued, her voice hot. "Go to Rumpenheim, to Württemberg, to Mecklenburg-Strelitz—I don't care, as long as you are far from me and Mother."

They stared at each other for a long moment, their eyes locked. May swallowed, refusing to lower her chin, even to blink.

Finally Francis growled, but she saw now that he was more like a caged bear than a wild lion. Embittered, defeated, all teeth and no bite. "Fine. It's not as if I want to stay here, anyway."

He spun on one heel and was halfway to the door when May's next words stopped him cold.

"You still haven't apologized to Mother."

A roaring silence seemed to echo through the room. Francis didn't turn around, but he did mumble, "I'm sorry I ever married you, Mary Adelaide."

It was probably the only apology they would ever get from him.

When he'd gone, May's mother turned, her expression torn between gratitude and confusion. "May, you shouldn't have— Thank you for sending him away," she said haltingly. "But those things Francis said about you, what was he—"

"I'm sorry, Mother. I'm late." May averted her gaze, hurrying out before her mother could ask any more questions.

Safely inside the waiting coach, May sank her head into her hands. She was trembling as if she'd survived an earthquake. *I'm nothing like Father,* she told herself. *He and I are not the same.*

It wasn't as convincing as she'd hoped.

She had grown up conditioned by Francis's cruelty. What if, unwittingly, her own mind had adopted the same shape?

May wanted to be proud of herself for making him leave, but she couldn't shake the sense that she'd succeeded only because her teeth were sharper than his.

Because he was no longer the greatest monster living at White Lodge.

SIR JOHN LAVERY, THE QUEEN'S OFFICIAL PORTRAIT PAINTER, frowned in concentration. Then he stepped forward to adjust May's ermine cape, letting it fall dramatically over the arm of the chair. "Perfect," he muttered.

They were in the White Drawing Room at Buckingham Palace. Sir John had painted all of Her Majesty's portraits here, insisting that it offered the best natural light. May had arrived an hour earlier to sit for her and Eddy's official engagement portrait.

So far, the groom hadn't shown up.

No one had dared remark upon it. A bevy of maidservants whirled about May, smoothing her hair, adjusting the skirts of her white-and-gold gown, helping Sir John set up his easel. May was just wondering if they would begin the painting without Eddy when the sitting room's door burst open.

"Your Majesty!" Sir John bowed, flipping a paintbrush behind his back with a flourish. "As always, it is an honor to commemorate these historic moments for your family."

May hurried to stand and curtsy at the queen's arrival, knowing that Sir John would have to restage her entire pose.

"We are still waiting for His Royal Highness Prince Eddy," the painter apologized.

Then another pair of footsteps approached the door. "Don't worry, I'll be standing in for him."

George strode into the room, wearing the Robe of State—a massive thing of purple velvet, embroidered and trimmed in ermine, linked across his chest by a heavy gold chain. Underneath, he had on a gold brocade waistcoat of the same fabric as May's gown. The garment was a bit long on him and straining at the shoulders; it had been cut for Eddy, and George had always been the stockier brother. Beneath all those layers of fur and chain, his chest was broader than Eddy's.

May flushed a little at the realization that she was thinking about George's bare chest.

"I'm afraid Eddy won't be joining us." Queen Victoria said this carelessly, as if she were remarking upon the weather, but May sensed her annoyance. As Eddy's fiancée, she probably should have been irritated, too. But May didn't care all that much—not when George had come instead.

"Georgie has agreed to fill in for his brother," the queen explained. "John, I trust this won't present a problem?"

"Not at all. I'm just beginning initial sketches today," the artist assured her.

Victoria nodded. "As we discussed, our jeweler will arrive later with the Imperial State Crowns."

May didn't mean to gasp. When the queen turned to her, one eyebrow raised expectantly, May stammered a reply. "I'm sorry, I just—I didn't know we were to be painted in crowns."

Victoria eyed May with unmistakable disapproval. "Sir John here will study the crowns so that he can sketch them atop your heads, but under no circumstances will you or Eddy *wear* the Imperial State Crowns. A crown is not a *bonnet*, May, to be *tried on* at a milliner's shop. It is a sign of the divine power that God grants you through the sacrament of coronation, and only after you have been anointed with sacred oil may you put it on your brow."

"Of course, Your Majesty." May looked down, her cheeks flaming.

Victoria stared at her a moment longer, then shook her head and turned back to the painter. "Sir John, please leave your sketches on the easel before you depart. I will stop by this afternoon to review them and ensure your progress is satisfactory. Do make sure that Eddy"—she hesitated—"that is, George, is standing. I despise portraits of kings sitting on thrones. I'd like to see him in a commanding frontal pose, with a hand on a table. Or holding a saber, as my own dear Albert did in his first portrait."

Sir John bowed in silent obeisance, and the queen swept from the room.

There was a flurry of hushed murmurs as the various attendants helped May sit back down, adjusting her skirts and the fall of her robe. Sir John attempted several poses for George before settling on one that was surprisingly intimate: standing behind May with a hand on the back of her armchair. Then the artist retreated behind his easel, and the only sound was the scrape of charcoal over paper.

May kept her gaze resolutely forward, though she was hyperaware of George standing just behind her. She imagined that she could hear the rhythm of his breaths, could feel his hand mere inches from her head, close enough to play with a few strands of her hair.

"Don't worry about Grannie," George murmured, once Sir John had turned aside to sharpen his charcoal. "She's in a bad mood. Eddy has been acting strangely, and then—" George hesitated. "She got some unexpected news. And you know Grannie never handles the unexpected very well."

May decided to say it. "The news about Missy?"

"You heard?" George whispered.

"Lady Ely told me. Are you all right?" May dared to look back at him, ruining her pose. "I know you and Missy were . . ."

"Grannie always wanted us to marry, which is why she's so upset. But Missy and I were never more than friends."

"But you were always so affectionate with her!" Dimly, May was aware that she shouldn't say this aloud, but she was still rattled from that confrontation with her father and couldn't think clearly. "That day at the Earl of Stafford's house, when you rushed to help her . . ."

George looked confused. "Of course I rushed to help. Missy was stung by a wasp."

May didn't understand why her chest felt suddenly tight, why her mouth had gone dry. It made no difference that George didn't love Missy—that his running after her that day was just George's innate sense of chivalry.

Belatedly, she realized that she needed to reply. "It seems like I misread things between you and Missy," she whispered.

The silence between them felt suddenly weighty, heavy with something new—something that May wasn't sure she dared look in the face.

And yet she wanted to.

"I do worry about Missy, running off with Ferdinand like that, so soon after Ducky got engaged. She probably wasn't thinking clearly." George's voice was gruff. "And none of us knows much about Romania, or this Ferdinand fellow. He's, what? Five years older than Missy?"

Eight, May thought. Guilt fluttered in her chest like a moth.

"I want to make sure Missy wasn't taken advantage of," George went on, oblivious to her turmoil. "It strikes me as a bit unfair that she should be forced to marry Ferdinand because she went into the gardens with him in the dark. From the sound of things, *he* kissed *her*."

Missy wanted the attention, May could have pointed out. *She is flighty and impulsive. Aren't you glad you aren't marrying her?*

"I'm sorry," she said instead.

George's hand lifted, almost as if he meant to reach out and touch her, then thought better of it.

"It's sweet of you to say that," he replied. "But it's not as if this is your fault."

How little he knew.

"Please, Your Royal Highness, Your Serene Highness." Sir John Lavery's voice was clipped. "I must request that you remain quiet, or our session will take twice as long."

George inclined his head graciously and resumed his pose, leaving May no choice but to turn and face the easel once more.

"I BELIEVE THAT'S ENOUGH FOR TODAY," SIR JOHN ANNOUNCED, setting his pencil down.

May blinked. The past few hours had passed in a stupor, the only sounds the scratching of charcoal on paper and the rustle of fabric as one of them shifted position.

"What a relief." George stretched an arm, crushing the ermine trim on the Robe of State. "My legs are prickling with pins and needles."

"I'm sure they are. You had the more difficult pose by far," May agreed.

"Yes, it was harder." George smiled, very softly. "How could I be expected to remain still when you were here distracting me?"

May's heart skipped a beat. He wasn't *flirting* with her . . . was he?

"On second thought, I might have preferred to stand," she declared. "I was in danger of falling asleep for a moment there, and you would have been forced to wake me." There. That was just playful enough without being reckless.

"I could always do what Grandpapa Albert did when Grannie fell asleep during one of their sittings for Winterhalter."

"Her Majesty fell asleep in a portrait sitting?" It was so unexpected from the ruthlessly controlled Victoria.

"Oh yes. Grandpapa woke her up by dumping water on her head."

May was shocked into barking out a laugh. "Don't even *think* about pouring water on me."

"I can't make any promises." George's blue eyes gleamed.

May loved when she saw this side of him, the George who wasn't just a dutiful son, always falling in second place behind Eddy. This George was playful and lighthearted and *fun*.

"Many thanks, Your Royal Highnesses," Sir John announced, having apparently forgotten that May was only a Serene Highness. "I shall see you again tomorrow—or perhaps your brother, if he becomes available," he added awkwardly, with a nod at George.

Then to May's surprise, the artist walked out, leaving them both alone.

May stole a glance around the room to confirm her suspicions, but there were no attendants or maidservants in sight. She and George were totally unchaperoned.

"Should we take a look?" George started toward the easel, the Robe of State dragging behind him.

"Isn't it bad luck to look at a portrait before it's finished?"

"Bad luck?" George snorted. "That sounds like a superstition invented by Renaissance painters who wanted to keep their patrons away from a work in progress. Artists hate being told what to do."

May smiled at that. "Fair enough."

Sir John had thrown a drop cloth over the canvas. May came to stand behind it; then together, she and George pulled back the fabric.

May's first thought was that the woman on the paper didn't look like her. This was only a pencil sketch, of course, but this woman was a cipher: a graven image pressed into a backdrop of furs and jewels. And really, it didn't matter who she was, only that she was a future queen.

She had expected Sir John to capture some of her personality, the clever curve of her mouth or the impatience in her eyes. But that would have been a personal portrait, not an official one.

"You look beautiful, of course." George's voice was gruff. "As for me . . ."

That was when May looked at the left side of the painting. Where George had been standing, Sir John had sketched a male-shaped figure, George's body filling out the robes and jewels and chains of state. The man in the portrait was slightly taller than George, and slimmer—because, of course, this was actually a portrait of Eddy.

"I'm glad I could make a small contribution to the Crown," George joked, but something in his tone betrayed his hurt.

She swallowed. "George . . ."

"I mean, this is the closest I'll ever be to becoming king. To actually mattering."

What reply could she possibly make? George was right. He was a second son; in the eyes of history, he didn't matter. He would be forgotten.

Then May found the right reply.

"You matter to me," she said quietly.

Somehow her hand found his. She was wearing leather gloves, but the sensation of their clasped palms still sent a shiver down her spine. His shoulder nudged against hers as they stood there, studying the sketch together; or perhaps she nudged him in silent support. May was no longer sure of anything.

Certainly, she wasn't sure how her face tipped up. How her lips were hovering so dangerously close to George's.

Then her hands slipped up around his shoulders, tangling on the chain of state, and she brushed it impatiently aside to settle her grip around the back of his neck. May felt dizzy and delirious and rather like she might stumble, but it didn't matter. George was warm and solid and she could hold tight to him.

This kiss had hovered between them for months, for years. And now, finally, it would happen.

George stumbled back, a horrified expression on his face.

"I'm so sorry," he rasped.

"No." May stepped toward him, desperate. She didn't want him to be sorry; she wanted him to kiss her.

"I take full responsibility for all lines that were crossed," he said swiftly. "Please, let's act as if this never happened."

Pretend it never happened? May shook her head. "But I—"

But I love you. But I did everything wrong. But I can still fix things, if you'll let me.

If only May had known that George didn't want to marry Missy. If only she hadn't thrown herself so ruthlessly into this campaign for Eddy. If, if . . . Her entire existence seemed to hinge on so many chances, so many possibilities that May had—through sheer willpower—forced into reality.

"Please, George . . ."

Before May could say anything more, the door flung open.

Prince Eddy stood there, looking handsome and tall and so acutely at ease with himself. Somehow he made George—in the full trappings of state, the robe and chain and gold brocade waistcoat—seem vaguely ridiculous.

Once upon a time May would have been drawn to Eddy for this. Now she resented him on George's behalf. He was handsome, yes, but distant and cold and utterly unlike George, who was gentle and endearing and loving. How had she ever thought she wanted to marry Eddy?

Still, an engagement was not a marriage. There might be a way out of this, a chance for her and George to find happiness after all.

Surely May wasn't the first woman to have gotten engaged to the wrong brother.

"May. Here you are," Eddy said curtly. As if this wasn't the place they were both supposed to be all morning. Apparently, he was oblivious to the aching tension between his fiancée and his brother.

May tried to sound calm as she asked, "Are you feeling better? You must have been ill indeed to miss the sitting for our first official portrait."

"Looks like you sat in for me just fine. Thank you." Eddy ignored May, nodding at his brother.

"I'm sure you have much to discuss," George said awkwardly. "I'll just, um— I need to get out of this robe."

May willed him to look at her, to acknowledge that they had almost kissed, but George refused to meet her gaze as he left.

Eddy turned to her then, his expression flat. "We need to talk."

He was brusque, even rude, but May was still too flustered to notice. She just followed Eddy to the sofa and sat opposite him, absentmindedly fluffing out her skirts so that the elaborate embroidery on the hem wouldn't fold under.

"Well, May, I would say it's good to see you, but that would be a lie."

May jumped from the couch and turned as the door opened once more.

Hélène d'Orléans walked into the room.

For a moment they were all still, as utterly immobile as the charcoal figures in that sketch. Hélène looked well, May thought dazedly. Her eyes were bright, and there was angry color in her cheeks, setting off the magenta stripes of her tea gown.

Moving slowly, Hélène came and took the seat next to Eddy, putting a hand on his arm in an unmistakably proprietary gesture.

It struck May, then, how completely Hélène had outwitted her—making her think she had moved on, that she wanted that letter for the Romanovs' sake.

"You're not getting engaged to Nicholas, are you?" May said into the silence.

Eddy replied on Hélène's behalf. "You should refer to him as His Imperial Highness the tsarevich, and no, she isn't. She's already engaged. To me."

A bit blasphemous of you, being engaged to two women at once, May longed to say. But she didn't dare.

She looked at Hélène instead, her stomach churning. "Agnes told me you stole back the letter—"

"I'd hardly call it stealing, since it was mine to begin with!"

Eddy squeezed Hélène's hand in support, then glowered at May. "May, I can't believe the things you did. Digging into Hélène's past, *blackmailing* her? It's despicable."

"That was Agnes!" May met Eddy's gaze, pleading. "I would never have done something like that, truly."

"But you just admitted that you knew about the letter! Even if what you claim is true, and you didn't send it, you still let the blackmail unfold. You let Hélène leave England, then manipulated me into an engagement!"

"I didn't *manipulate* you!" May exclaimed. "All I did was offer you what all men want—a relationship with no expectations and no consequences! *You're* the one who signed up for a marriage where you had permission to sleep around, just like your father!"

She would pay for that dig at Bertie, most assuredly. But May was gratified to see Hélène flinch. Clearly, Eddy hadn't told his beloved all the details of their engagement.

"What about Alix?" Hélène cut in. "Do you deny that you spread rumors about her?"

"They aren't rumors! Alix really is sick!"

"And Ducky!" Hélène continued ruthlessly. "You gave her atrocious advice, telling her that she should be whining and weak, when you knew it would push Eddy away!"

"Wait—that was you?" Now it was Eddy's turn to look surprised. He stared at May, brow furrowed. "I wondered what was going on; Ducky had never been so dull-witted before."

"She *asked* for my help!" May spluttered. "Ducky didn't want to marry you because she's in love with her cousin!"

"She's in love with Ernie?" Eddy shook his head. "Why didn't she just say so?"

May bit her lip to keep from explaining that she'd meant Kiril. For whatever reason, Ducky had chosen to get engaged to Ernie. May might not understand it, but the least she could do was keep Ducky's secret.

"Even if that's true, and Ducky didn't want to marry Eddy, you have still behaved deplorably. Toward Alix, toward Eddy, and toward *me*," Hélène cut in.

Eddy nodded in agreement. "May. It goes without saying that I no longer consider us engaged."

"Yes, of course. I understand," May said swiftly.

Both Eddy and Hélène seemed startled by her rapid agreement. They couldn't have known that May was already thinking along these very lines—wondering if she could break off her engagement to Eddy and pursue her feelings for George.

"I apologize for all the damage I caused. Please know that I heartily regret it, and I will do whatever you ask in order to call off our engagement," May assured him. "I am as eager as you are to put this all behind us."

Eddy leaned forward, bracing his elbows on his knees. "We will indeed be putting it behind us. Because you are going to leave the country."

May's blood stilled. "Excuse me?"

"As Hélène said, your behavior has been unconscionable. By all rights I should tell Grandmother everything you've done."

May stifled a cry of outrage. Eddy saw this, and lifted an eyebrow.

"But I am *not* going to tell Grandmother, because Hélène has persuaded me otherwise. She has shown you far more mercy than you ever showed her. I will let you leave this whole sordid situation with your reputation intact, which is more than you deserve." He shook his head. "You are going to leave England and never come back."

"No!" May said automatically. "You cannot exile me as if I'm a medieval traitor!"

Eddy rose to his feet, fists clenched. "Then don't consider it a formal exile. Consider it a promise that if you stay here, I will personally ensure that you and your family are ruined."

There was a cruel, dramatic irony in this, May thought over the roar in her ears. Now that she'd finally mustered up the courage to challenge her father, told him to get out of England—the very same thing was happening to her.

"Leave, May." Hélène didn't sound angry anymore, only weary. "Go to Austria, Greece, I don't care. Just get out of this country. We will tell everyone that you are in poor health and have decided not to marry Eddy." She lifted one shoulder in a shrug. "If you find a European prince someday, none of us will stop you. We'll all proclaim how grateful we are for your miraculous recovery."

May felt empty with shock, as if a shard of glass had scraped out all her insides, carved out her tongue. She should speak. She should fight back. Yet she could do nothing. She wondered if this was how men felt when they were struck down in battle, a sort of hollow bewilderment—knowing they were wounded but not how acutely. Wondering if they would die.

Perhaps she and Francis could leave together. They could

drift together from one royal court to the next, belittling each other, feeding off each other's relentless cruelty.

Then May thought of George, and something inside her stiffened.

She might have been shaped by her father, but she had not *become* him—not yet. She would see this through somehow. There had to be a way.

May inclined her head to Hélène as if bowing before a queen. "I would just ask one favor of you."

"You are hardly in a position to ask favors," Hélène snapped.

"Do not forget, I still know about you and your coachman," May warned. "Agnes may not have the letter anymore, but you and I both know that even a rumor could do you immeasurable damage. Especially a rumor based in fact. *Especially* if you and Eddy plan to announce an engagement soon."

Hélène's entire body stiffened. Eddy's voice was low and dangerous as he asked, "What do you want, May?"

"Please, can we keep this between us for a month? Let me sort out my next steps, figure out how to tell my parents. After that, I swear I'll go quietly. You'll never hear a word from me again."

Hélène and Eddy exchanged a glance. Then Eddy turned back to May.

"Two weeks," he warned. "Grandmother is meeting us at Sandringham in two weeks' time. If you haven't left town by then, I will tell her everything."

Hélène looked at Eddy with unmistakable annoyance. Clearly, she hadn't wanted to grant May any concessions.

"Two weeks," Hélène warned, before walking angrily into the hall.

Eddy started to follow Hélène, then paused. "May . . . I am angry with you, but also confused. I can't help thinking that you are a better person than this situation would indicate. What happened?"

May's lips parted. For a wild moment, she considered telling Eddy everything—her father's hateful behavior, the narrow confines of her quiet, constricting life. The sensation of waking up each morning gasping for air. Knowing that she was only a woman, and getting older, and that her options were narrowing by the day. Realizing that she was utterly and completely alone.

She wished she could tell Eddy how much things had changed for her, and for Mary Adelaide, since his proposal.

But Eddy wouldn't understand. He was a man, and a future king. From the moment he was born, he'd lived a charmed life. He had been protected, valued. Loved.

George might understand, but George was probably lost to her too.

"I am sorry" was all May replied.

Eddy shook his head and walked out, leaving her in the White Drawing Room in her queenly robe and gown.

May let her head fall back onto the sofa, tears pricking at her eyes. Just half an hour earlier she had been electrified with the possibility of kissing George, and now this? Eddy wanted to *exile* her?

For so many years she'd been certain of what she wanted—a marriage that would provide an escape. A safe haven. She had used deception and cruelty and betrayal, and now, on the brink of getting what she'd wanted, she saw that she could have so much more. She didn't have to settle for safety; she could have affection, trust.

As foolish as it was to think it, she could have *love.*

May couldn't leave England. That would mean leaving George.

Which meant that she had two weeks to find a way out of this mess.

CHAPTER TWENTY-NINE

Hélène

HÉLÈNE WAS NO STRANGER TO BREAKING THE RULES AND RISKing her reputation. She had slipped out at night plenty of times to see Eddy, had dressed as a maid at the Endicotts' house, but this—going into London in disguise, simply for fun—was Eddy's idea.

"Thanks for agreeing to this," he murmured, looping an arm around her shoulders as they navigated through the crowds.

"Of course. We're celebrating!" Hélène smiled at him, positively giddy with relief.

She had seen the look on May's face the other day. May had no more ideas, no more schemes to pull. Finally, they had beaten her.

It was an occasion worth marking in a very memorable way, Eddy had declared.

Which was why they'd come to Greenwich Fair tonight, dressed like ordinary workers. Eddy had borrowed clothes from his manservant, a simple shirt and pants beneath a plain wool coat, and Hélène wore the same maid's uniform as the day she'd stolen back Laurent's letter.

The streets were flooded with ordinary people: men who

worked at the docks or in stables, women who labored behind sewing machines or as maids. They held hands, laughed, clutched cups of ale. A Harlequin danced past, his costume a patchwork of colorful diamonds; a man with a scar along one cheek juggled flaming torches. Women in form-fitting clothes contorted their bodies, tying their legs and arms into shocking knots. Vendors proclaimed their wares above the din of the crowds—oysters, sweet buns, gingerbread. Amateur theater troupes used squares of dingy carpet as a stage, acting out sword fights or scenes of romance. It was a riot of sound and color and some distinctly pungent odors.

Hélène adored it. She had never been anywhere this vivid, this gloriously alive.

She tugged Eddy toward the river, where a cluster of musicians performed popular drinking songs. Couples danced in an open space nearby. Hélène didn't recognize the dance—a polka, perhaps, or something imported from America?

Eddy grinned. "Care to dance?"

"But we don't know the steps." Hélène faltered, nervous at how quickly the dancers were moving. And there was a lot of jumping.

"Since when has that stopped us? We can fake our way through!" Eddy insisted.

And then Hélène was laughing, spinning in the wrong direction, stepping on her neighbors' feet and mostly on Eddy's. None of her dancing master's training proved useful here. This resembled the Scottish dancing she'd done at Balmoral last summer far more than the staid quadrilles of a London ballroom.

At some point she realized the dancers were forming two lines, hands clasped overhead to make a sort of tunnel. Couples ducked their heads to race down the tunnel amid raucous cheers.

When it was her and Eddy's turn, they ran so fast that Hélène nearly stumbled, until Eddy reached his hands around her waist to steady her. Her breath caught. She thought back to that long-ago afternoon in Richmond Park when she'd been out in a storm, and Eddy had lifted her into the saddle.

That was the very first time Hélène had felt it—this insistent, combustible, impossible attraction between them.

Eddy must have been thinking along the same lines, because he leaned down to kiss her. An unhurried, easy kiss; not rushed or hidden behind the closed doors of Eddy's apartment. *It will be like this from now on*, Hélène thought, and wanted to cry out with joy. They had the letter from Laurent; there was no way May—or anyone else—could blackmail her now. It wouldn't stick without proof.

In two weeks' time May would be out of their lives for good. Eddy would tell Queen Victoria that he was marrying Hélène after all. And eventually, when the hubbub over his broken engagement to May had died down, Hélène would stand up in a church and proclaim it before everyone: that she was Eddy's, and Eddy was hers.

When the song ended and the dancers all paused to catch their breath, Eddy drew her to one side. He looked so handsome like this—happy, carefree, damp with exertion.

Feeling bold, Hélène let her hand drift under his coat and beneath the loose hem of his shirt, to skim over his abdomen. It was so easy to touch him without all the normal hindrances of gentlemanly attire, waistcoats and shirtfronts and cuff links snapping everything together. "I rather like these clothes. Normally, you're so bundled up."

"*I'm* so bundled up? You're the one in corsets." Eddy tugged at the ribbon along the neckline of her white blouse. "You should dress like this more often. Far more convenient."

Hélène swatted playfully at his hand, and Eddy caught hers, lacing their fingers. Then he lifted her hand to his mouth and placed a gentle kiss on her palm. It was such an uncharacteristically tender gesture that she felt a strange urge to cry.

He released her hand as the band struck up another song. Soon everyone around them was singing, clinking glasses as they belted out the words. Hélène hurried to join in.

" 'Oh, the boy I love is up in the gallery! The boy I love is looking at me!' " When he remained silent, she hissed, "Eddy, can't you sing along? You're ruining the mood, standing there frowning during a drinking song."

"I would sing if I knew the words!" he whispered back. "This is hardly the national anthem, Hélène."

"Yes, it's a bit more fun than your stodgy anthem."

Eddy chuckled at that—then suddenly his laugh dissolved into a cough. Hélène looked at him in concern. When the cough deepened, she drew him farther away from the crowds, into a relatively quiet corner near a side street.

"Eddy, are you all right?"

"Yes, of course. Just a bit of a cold. You know, the change in weather." His voice was still hoarse, his eyes glassy.

"Perhaps we should get a drink." Maybe some ale would bring the color back to his face.

"I'll do it. You stay here." Already Eddy sounded better. Nothing to worry about, Hélène told herself.

Hélène watched him retreat toward one of the stalls that sold wine and warm ale. Even in his plain-spun jacket, he looked like a prince: it was clear in the way he walked, the bold directness of his gaze. The crowds around him seemed to part instinctively, as if they, too, knew on some level that he was different.

"Excuse me, miss!" a voice chirped behind her.

Hélène turned to see a young woman near her own age. Her heart-shaped face was flushed with exertion, probably from the dancing. "I had to ask—I heard your accent—are you French?"

"I am." Hélène smiled and gestured down to her clothes. "I'm a lady's maid, in a house off Belgrave Square." Many lady's maids *were* French, after all; it was quite fashionable to have one's hair styled by a Frenchwoman.

The girl's eyes widened. "In Belgravia! Oh, but you must work for a countess at least!"

Before Hélène could reply, a young man stepped forward. "Frances is a milliner, and dreams of making hats for duchesses someday." He cast an affectionate smile in Frances's direction.

"I work at Mrs. Astley's shop. Do you know it? Just last week I made a hat that the mayor's sister wore!" Frances sighed wistfully. "It was trimmed with real ostrich feathers. Someday I'm going to open my own shop."

"I have no doubt that you will," Hélène agreed, smiling. She caught sight of Eddy coming back toward them and hurried to exclaim, "Anthony! There you are!"

She doubted that anyone here would recognize Eddy; the closest they would have ever gotten to him, after all, was at a parade. And he didn't exactly resemble the pictures that had been printed in the newspapers, not dressed like this. Still, it was better not to call him by his real name.

"Violette," Eddy greeted her, his eyes bright with amusement. The ale he handed her was a dark amber color, with foam along the top. Hélène took an eager sip.

When she looked back up, she realized that Frances was staring at Eddy with marked interest. "Do I know you? You seem so familiar. . . ."

Eddy gave a theatrical bow, flipping out his jacket behind him as if it were a cape. "You must have seen my performance earlier today," he said without missing a beat. "I was in one of the tents, doing *Romeo and Juliet*."

Hélène nearly choked on a laugh, then took a quick sip of beer to hide it.

"An actor," the young man with Frances scoffed.

Ignoring him, Eddy fixed his eyes on Frances as he recited, " 'With love's light wings did I o'erperch these walls, for stony limits cannot hold love out, and what love can do, that dares love attempt.' "

"Oh my." Frances looked as dazed as Hélène felt.

The young man held out a hand. Eddy hesitated just a fraction of an instant—no one ever presumed to shake his hand—then took it with a hearty smile.

"John Sheffield," the man introduced himself. "I work as an engineer on the London and North Western Railway."

"He once saw the queen's private car!" Frances cut in.

"That's incredible. What was it like?" Eddy's question

sounded sincere, but Hélène saw the twitch of his lips. He was fighting back a smile.

"Ah. Well, I couldn't see much past the blue curtains." John cleared his throat and nodded at Hélène. "I wonder sometimes if we should follow your country's example. Exile the royal family and stop paying for all their nonsense."

"Why do you say that?" Eddy asked carefully.

"The queen is, of course, exemplary," John insisted. "But what will happen when she dies? We all know the Prince of Wales is dissolute and lazy. It's too early to know about his son, but my guess is that the young prince will be more of the same." John shrugged as if none of this mattered to him all that much. "And that young woman he got engaged to; who is she? No one had even *heard* of her before this month."

Hélène cast a worried glance at Eddy, who seemed like he was about to say something he might regret. "If you'll excuse us, this is my favorite song! It was good meeting you," she added, tugging Eddy away.

They skirted the edge of the dance floor, reemerging into the main streets of Greenwich Fair. It was getting late. The vendors' stalls were now lit by torchlight, which fell over towers of boiled oranges, cheap glass beads, and bottles of wine. Eddy was uncharacteristically silent.

"Eddy, you can't worry about what John was saying."

"I *should* worry, if that's what people really think about my family."

"About your father," Hélène corrected him. "You are not your father, or your grandmother. You are going to be a different sort of king, the kind that can talk to ordinary people, and dance at a fair, and recite Shakespeare! How did you even know that speech?"

Eddy shrugged. "You know I can never remember things I read, but hearing them is different. And I went to the theater a good bit with George, back before you—back when I thought I'd lost you. He said I was sulking, and needed to get out."

"You do have an unfortunate tendency to sulk," Hélène teased.

"Well, I missed you."

The raw grief in Eddy's tone took her aback. She leaned closer, nuzzling her head into his neck. "I'm so sorry."

"It's just, facing a life without you . . ."

"You don't have to. I'm here now," Hélène assured him. "I'm here, and I'm not going anywhere. I swear it."

CHAPTER THIRTY

Alix

"UNCLE MAX?" A THREE-YEAR-OLD BOY, A STUFFED BEAR clutched tight in his hand, stared solemnly up at Maximilian. "Can you help me build a house?"

Alix watched Maximilian kneel, bringing himself level with the toddler. "Of course, Erik. What would you say to a pillow fort?"

She smiled as Maximilian began constructing a house for Erik out of sofa cushions and throw pillows. "If you want your walls to be structurally sound, you need to think about support," Maximilian was saying. "Each pillow should have something holding it up, like so. . . ."

"Typical Maximilian, trying to teach my son engineering before his fourth birthday."

The Crown Princess Victoria of Sweden, Maximilian's cousin, came to stand next to Alix. She nodded in Maximilian's direction before taking a hearty sip of her coffee. Grandmama wouldn't have let Alix walk around holding a coffee like that—*Go sit at the table! You look like a railroad worker, walking around with it in your hands!* she would have said. Not to mention that Grandmama would *never* have let Alix build a fort out of her decorative, tasseled silk pillows.

Things were delightfully casual here in Baden-Baden.

"It's easy to see how much your boys love their uncle Max," Alix remarked, amused. Maximilian looked so endearingly ridiculous, kneeling on the carpet in his shirtsleeves as pillows tumbled down around him.

Back in Darmstadt, after he'd seen Alix's episode—after they had decided to start courting—Maximilian had invited Alix to Baden-Baden, the famous spa town on the edge of the Black Forest. It was several hours from Baden's capital city of Karlsruhe, but Maximilian's family had owned an estate there for over a hundred years. It was customary for the Grand Dukes of Baden to take the waters every summer.

This was new territory for Alix: being courted the proper way, with chaperoned trips and the approval of both families. She knew that Grandmama, in particular, was bursting with excitement at the match—so delighted, in fact, that she hadn't even insisted that Ernie join this visit to Baden-Baden.

And really, the house was quite full of chaperones. Alix had already known that Maximilian was close with his family: because of his oldest uncle's mental illness, he and his sister had spent a great deal of time with their uncle Frederick, the acting duke, and Frederick's children. Maximilian's three cousins were like siblings to him.

Somehow, all those cousins had come to Baden-Baden at the very same time. The ducal estate was full to bursting with boisterous laughter and the shrieks of children.

Alix sensed that they were here for her sake. Not to pass judgment on whether she was good enough, as the Romanovs had done, but simply because Maximilian wanted them to meet her.

"Mama," Erik called out to Princess Victoria, gesturing to the rather haphazard pillow structure. "Look at our fort!"

As if on cue, his two older brothers barreled in from the kitchens and began attacking the pillow fort with loud hollers. Erik laughed and joined them, kicking pillows to the floor, apparently eager to destroy what he had just so painstakingly built.

Victoria started toward her sons as Maximilian came to join Alix. He'd gone to swim laps at the baths very early that morning. Now that she stood closer, Alix realized that his beard and hair were still damp, curling softly around his ears, his lips.

"I didn't know your hair was so curly," she breathed.

"That's because you've never seen me bathe." Maximilian instantly seemed to realize what he'd said, and flushed. "I mean—that is, it gets this way when wet, and I was up so early. . . . I'm afraid I've never been a late sleeper. . . ."

Alix could see the pulse at the center of Maximilian's throat. She imagined she could smell the thermal springs on him, the mineral scent of the water mixing with a warm scent that was purely Maximilian. His eyes darkened, and she knew he felt it too—the pulse of attraction between them.

Then he took a step back, seeming to collect himself. "Are you ready to visit the Trinkhalle? The morning rush should be slowing by now."

She nodded, allowing Maximilian to lead her out the front door and into a carriage. "I'm excited to see it. I've never taken the waters before, not even at Bath."

"Do not mention Bath here, or you will find yourself quite unpopular," Maximilian teased. "We in Baden-Baden think that Bath is by far the lesser spa town."

The Trinkhalle was a massive neoclassical building, with thermal baths in the basement where men and women could—separately, of course—immerse themselves in the natural hot springs that had made Baden-Baden so famous. But most of the grand structure was taken up by the fountain room.

It was an enormous hall, all white columns and marble floors. Morning light spilled in through the skylight, falling on potted plants and sofas arranged in small clusters. Side tables held stacks of newspapers and magazines; and though a few visitors did recline to read, most were walking—strolling with their friends, exchanging gossip, all clutching the same metal cups filled with the healing Baden-Baden water.

Maximilian and Alix went to fill their own cups from the tap. Maximilian watched as Alix took a careful sip.

"Well?" he prompted.

"It's not what I expected." Not salty, exactly, but it didn't taste like any water Alix had consumed before.

"That would be the high mineral content. It is said to cure many ailments: gout, rheumatism and joint pain, rickets . . ."

"Can it cure me?"

Alix asked the question in a whisper, but Maximilian huffed out a breath.

"There is nothing wrong with you, and your episodes are not something to be ashamed of. They are at most an inconvenience," he declared. "I will keep telling you this as many times as it takes, until you believe it."

"I . . . thank you."

Alix drank again from the metal cup. Already she felt calmer, more centered. Maybe the waters really were curative; or maybe it was this time with Maximilian, who accepted her as she was. It was so nice, not trying to hide her condition.

Letting go of the anxiety that had strummed through her blood for so long, as frantic as a second heartbeat.

Maximilian started to lead her toward the mosaics on one wall, but Alix's steps faltered. Her entire attention focused on the older couple walking toward her.

It was the Tsar and Tsarina of Russia. Nicholas's parents.

They must have been traveling incognito, because they weren't surrounded by their entourage of servants and footmen; and they were dressed in clothes that, while well cut and clearly made of expensive fabric, were unembellished. They looked like any other aristocrats on holiday. To add to the disguise, the tsar had shaved his famous beard. He looked thinner without it.

Alix saw the moment that Minnie caught sight of her—how she grabbed Sasha's elbow and hissed something under her breath. Then the two of them started toward Alix with obvious intent.

"I seem to have spotted an old acquaintance," Alix told Maximilian over the pounding of her heart. *They can't hurt me anymore,* she reminded herself.

As they approached, Alix began to sink into an instinctive curtsy, but a quick hiss from Minnie recalled her. She paused, letting the tsar set the tone of things.

Maximilian stepped forward first, holding out a hand to shake.

"It's lovely to meet you," he said. "Welcome to Baden. I'm Maximilian."

The tsar looked at Maximilian's hand with evident bewilderment, as if someone had offered him a dead animal. Then he seemed to remember what to do, and shook it.

"I'm the Grand Duke Ivan, and this is my wife, Natasha. We met Alix when she was last in St. Petersburg, visiting her sister."

So they were pretending to be Russian aristocrats. That made sense; it would have been hard to convince people they were from anywhere but Russia.

"Maximilian, dear," the tsarina pleaded. "Would you mind fetching us more water? I would so love to catch up with Alix in private. Just some family matters about her sister."

Maximilian glanced to Alix for confirmation; when she nodded, he went to do as they asked.

The moment he'd gone, Alix rounded on Minnie. "Is everything all right with Ella?"

"What? Oh, yes." The tsarina waved a hand dismissively. "I just wanted to get you alone. Sasha and I are actually glad we ran into you. There are some things we'd like to discuss."

"I'm not sure what business we could possibly have together," Alix replied, with a touch of impertinence.

Minnie glanced at her husband. She was fidgeting, playing with a strand of blue-gray pearls around her neck. When she realized Alix was watching her, she let out a little breath. "These were a wedding gift from Sasha, if you can believe it."

"It took five years for the jeweler to assemble the pearls. They're from the Nile," the tsar explained. "I told him to match Minnie's eyes."

The pearls were an exceedingly rare color, a deep azure that reminded Alix of a summer storm. And they were exquisitely matched. Each was the exact same as the others, each perfectly round. They were not diamonds, yet she suspected they cost nearly as much.

The tsar and tsarina stared at each other for a moment, their gazes full of love. It was disorienting and a bit disarming, seeing this side of them—knowing that they were more than judgmental parents who'd made her miserable. That they loved each other, too.

Then Minnie seemed to recall where they were, and stepped back. "Sasha, since we found her, you can go ahead and make the offer in person."

The offer?

The tsar grunted, turning to Alix. "I was going to approach your father, but it's quite convenient, actually, that we ran into you. What would you say to a hundred thousand rubles?"

It was such a blunt, unprecedented question, Alix just stared at him. "Excuse me?"

"I don't know what that would be in German marks." He shrugged carelessly. "Suffice it to say, it's a small fortune."

"You could add it to your dowry," the tsarina offered. "Or think of it as a wedding gift!"

"What?" Alix asked, bewildered.

"Marie told me that you are courting that German fellow," the tsar explained, as if he couldn't be bothered to recall Maximilian's name.

"You and Maximilian could use the money to build a new home," the tsarina said, evidently striving to sound reasonable.

The tsar snorted. "Or save it for your daughters' dowries. Perhaps one of them might make a grand marriage—to an English prince, as you failed to do."

Alix stared at them as comprehension sank in. "You're trying to *bribe* me to marry Maximilian?"

"Of course this isn't a bribe," the tsarina said smoothly. "As I said, it's a gift."

Alix still felt dizzy with the strangeness of it all. "Not that it's any of your business, but Maximilian and I only just started courting."

"Perhaps, in that case, you wouldn't mind writing Nicholas a quick note?" the tsarina insisted. "You could tell him that you have moved on, and that he should too?"

"We will send the money directly to you once Nicholas receives your letter," the tsar chimed in. "You have my word."

Shock, and outrage, snapped through her like a whip.

"I am afraid that I'm no longer corresponding with His Imperial Highness," Alix said coolly.

"We know! He won't stop talking about it!" the tsar bellowed, then lowered his voice. "We had so many options for him. Hélène of France, Alexandra of Greece, Marie Louise of Hanover—"

"He says that he will not marry," Minnie cut in, perhaps sensing how utterly rude it was to list all the women whose worth they ranked above Alix's. "He insists that he will rule alone, let Misha be his heir, and then Misha's children can carry on the throne after him."

"I'm sorry for your troubles, but I don't see what this has to do with me," Alix said stiffly.

The tsarina hesitated, then seemed to decide that there was no other way to say this. "We fear that he is refusing to marry because he is still pining for you, Alix."

Something snagged in Alix's chest. Though it had hurt, burning Nicholas's letters, she had convinced herself that it was for the best—that Nicholas would move on, as she was attempting to do. That he might find someone who made sense for him, as Maximilian did for her.

To learn that he was refusing to marry, defying his parents . . .

No, she couldn't think about him. That path only led to heartache.

"Are we agreed, then?" the tsar pressed. "You'll write Nicholas, telling him that you have chosen someone else, in exchange for our very generous gift?"

"No," Alix said slowly. "We are not agreed."

Sasha's expression grew thunderous. "Don't be foolish. This is a lot of money. More than you'll ever see in your lifetime, girl."

"That makes no difference to me." She spoke carefully, each word deadly crisp. "I am a granddaughter of Queen Victoria. I cannot be *bought*."

The tsar's face had grown bright red with rage. "I *command* you to write my son! Tell him that you two are over!"

"I'm afraid you're in no position to command what I will or will not do. I am not your subject." Alix tilted her chin up stubbornly. "You may control all of Russia, but as you constantly remind me, I am just a minor princess from Hesse. You have no dominion over me."

Minnie's lips pursed in disapproval, but Alix saw a different expression flit across the tsar's face, something that might have been respect.

She should have waited until she was dismissed. After all, they were the Tsar and Tsarina of All the Russias, and she was just Alix of Hesse.

But that no longer mattered to her.

"I believe we have nothing else to discuss," she declared. "Now, if you'll excuse me . . ."

Alix turned and walked away. Not far off she saw Maximilian, balancing the four metal cups of water. He hurried to catch up with her.

"Are you all right, Alix? I have your friends' water cups. . . ."

"They were just leaving." She plucked the cups from his grasp and set them on a side table. "And to be honest, I should like to leave as well."

"The mineral water doesn't sit well with everyone," Maximilian said sympathetically. "Can I show you the gardens?"

As Alix headed out with Maximilian, she refused to let herself look back at the tsar and tsarina. They could watch her retreating form, knowing she had done the unthinkable.

She had told them no.

CHAPTER THIRTY-ONE

Hélène

WHEN THE TELEGRAM ARRIVED AT SHEEN HOUSE, HÉLÈNE OPENED it eagerly, hoping it was from Eddy. Instead it had been sent by his sister Louise, asking if Hélène could come to Sandringham.

Finally, Hélène thought in relief. Eddy had left town a few days ago: he'd insisted on going to Sandringham first, "to soften Grandmother up before we tell her our news," as he'd put it. Then a cough had racked his chest, and he'd given a watery smile. "And it seems that I'm still ill. Better that I recover in the country instead of passing this sickness along to you."

"Norfolk will have you better in no time," Hélène had agreed. "My mother always says that country air will heal you faster than a city doctor."

She needed Eddy back at full health so that they could decide together how to handle May. The two-week deadline was fast approaching, and May still hadn't left London.

Hélène folded the telegram and looked at her parents across the breakfast table. "I'm headed to Sandringham with Prince Eddy," she said. "Violette will accompany me, unless you have any objections?"

Her parents stared at her, then exchanged a surprised, confused glance. Hélène saw all the questions they were valiantly swallowing back: What did it mean? Were she and Eddy together again? But they seemed to decide against asking for details—ever since the Romanovs had written, informing them that there would be no engagement between Hélène and Nicholas, they had skirted the topic of courtship or marriage.

"Have a good trip," her father said simply. But Hélène saw his smile of cautious hope.

When her train pulled up to Wolferton Station that evening, Hélène saw a solitary woman waiting on the platform, dressed in a fur-lined cloak and matching hat.

"I hadn't expected a personal welcome," Hélène exclaimed, giving Princess Louise—now the Duchess of Fife—an airy double kiss, the French way.

Louise didn't smile, and an odd shiver traced up Hélène's spine.

"Come on," Louise said simply, pulling Hélène toward a waiting carriage and gesturing that Violette should follow in the buggy cart. "I hope you don't mind, but I've arranged for you and your lady's maid to stay with our neighbors, Lord and Lady Wyclif. They are most eager to host you."

Hélène blinked at Eddy's sister. "I'm not staying in the main house? Did Her Majesty refuse to see me, or are you keeping me a secret?"

"Grandmother isn't at Sandringham. You know how she is about illness," Louise explained. It was true; Queen Victoria abhorred illness, and was always fleeing London when there were outbreaks of scarlet fever or influenza. "I just . . .

I acted somewhat on my own, bringing you here. I didn't want to alarm Mother."

"I take it Eddy still hasn't told anyone about our engagement, then?" Hélène asked carefully.

"Ah, so you did reconcile!" Louise nodded sharply. "I thought so."

Hélène glanced out the window to hide her confusion. When she'd gotten the telegram, she'd assumed it was all Eddy's doing, that he had asked Louise to send for her. But he clearly hadn't told Louise anything. Why had Louise summoned her here, then?

They turned up the front drive, and Hélène caught her first glimpse of Sandringham, a sprawling brick structure with stone gables and cupolas that gleamed in the evening light. The estate had not been in the royal family long; it was the last property that Prince Albert purchased before his death. He'd gifted it to the Prince and Princess of Wales, supposedly in the hope that it would strengthen their marriage: that its remote location in Norfolk would keep Bertie away from all the temptations of London—namely, all his mistresses.

As it turned out, Bertie only came here for shooting weekends. But Alexandra loved it. Hélène suspected that she thrived in this English country air, in a way that she never did in Scotland. This was her house, after all, and Balmoral was the queen's.

"Eddy has told me so much about Sandringham," Hélène said, in an attempt to break the silence. It seemed like one of the happier places of his childhood. He'd described skating parties on the lake, lit by colored torches, where servants handed out mugs of mulled wine or steaming chocolate. He'd told her about the pranks he and his father had pulled every

Christmas morning, leaving pudding in people's shoes or filling bicycle pumps with water and squirting his sisters. With the royal family's typical quirkiness, Sandringham was one of the places they were most relaxed, yet they held tight to rigid court etiquette. Dinner was ruthlessly formal, requiring women to wear diamonds, men to wear their full decorations and orders.

Louise sighed heavily. "Hélène. You know that Eddy is quite ill, don't you?"

No. There was a note of something in Louise's voice, but Hélène refused to hear it. "Oh, influenza has been everywhere this winter. Have you all been taking your daily dose of quinine? It will cure most anything. . . ."

She trailed off as their carriage approached the front of the house. Louise didn't wait for a footman to open the door; she hopped out, jerking her head toward the front steps. "Why don't I take you to him now."

Hélène had a vague impression of the hallways they walked through: scrolling wallpaper hung with swords or suits of armor, painted porcelain plates arranged in circles and mounted to the walls. In one sitting room she saw a stuffed bird in a glass case.

Finally Louise paused at a wooden door. "He will be so glad to see you. Yours is the only name he keeps saying."

Hélène nodded in reply, her throat dry, and turned the door handle.

Eddy lay in bed, the covers pulled up around his shoulders. He was so pale. For a terrifying moment Hélène thought the worst—until she saw the soft rise and fall of his chest, and her heart was able to beat again.

"Excuse me, miss." A nurse who'd been seated in an armchair quickly stood. She left with a curtsy.

Hélène rushed to the side of Eddy's bed and pressed a hand to his brow. He was too cold, wasn't he?

"Hélène." His eyes opened, and he smiled, the old winsome smile that lit up his face. Seeing it made her feel better.

"Eddy! I'm sorry I didn't come sooner. I had no idea you were this sick," she insisted.

He reached for her hand, lacing their fingers. Hélène pressed a kiss to his knuckles, fighting back tears. How had so much changed in the span of a week? Eddy looked like he didn't have the strength to get out of bed, let alone talk to his grandmother about their engagement.

"You should leave," he said weakly. "I would never forgive myself if you got ill. . . ."

"Please, I'm as strong as a horse. I don't get ill."

"That makes sense." He started to say more, but dissolved into a fit of coughing. Hélène hated that she could do nothing. She just stood there, helpless, as he gasped for air, his hands clawing at the bedcovers.

"Damn this sickness," he said at last, in an old man's voice—high, wheezing. "You're here, alone in my room, and I can't even enjoy it."

This time the old flirtatious smile was strained.

"Let's see what we can manage," Hélène said, with forced lightness.

They were already flirting with impropriety, having her in his room unchaperoned, under the roof of a royal residence. A residence that Hélène wasn't even supposed to *be* at.

She didn't care. If they found her like this, she would suffer the consequences.

Hélène sat back on the bed, moving slowly so as not to

disturb Eddy, then stretched out until she was lying next to him, on her side. She reached an arm around his torso, settling against him the way she did so often when they were in bed together. He sighed a little in contentment, shifting to make space for her.

It was strange. When she tucked her head into his shoulder, she could smell the illness on him—a caustic, medicinal smell—but his body was as taut and strong as ever. He certainly didn't resemble the patients she had seen at the hospital, frail or wasted away. Why, from the feel of his muscles, you would think he was in perfect health.

You just had to ignore that his skin was slightly cool to the touch.

"The nurse might come back. Or the doctor," Eddy said softly.

"So what?" Hélène kept tracing her fingers in light circles over his skin, the way her mother used to do when Hélène was little and felt sick. "If the doctor walks in, I'll say that I'm helping to cure you."

"Ah, yes, physical touch. The oldest cure known to man."

"And you said you weren't French," she teased.

They lay there for a while in silence, just listening to each other's heartbeat. Then Eddy said, "Tell me something."

"What?"

"Anything. I just want to hear your voice."

Hélène tried to adopt her most upbeat tone, thinking of what might distract Eddy. "We had quite an eventful night on Saturday, leaving the Devanes' reception. Lord Lawrence almost got into a brawl with my parents over our carriage."

"He never could handle his whiskey," Eddy remarked. Hélène tried to ignore how thin his voice was.

"It was quite amusing, honestly—Lawrence was so drunk that he couldn't tell his coat of arms from ours, kept trying to shove my parents away from the door. In the end my father decided it was easier to give him a ride home than to forcibly kick him out."

She went on like that for a while, talking about nonsensical things. When Eddy's breathing had become more even, Hélène fell silent. But she didn't move. She stayed there, her arm still thrown over his body.

Here was her happiness, she thought. Here was what she cared about most, held within the circle of her arms. She could not bear to lose it.

She began whispering again, but in French this time. Saying things she never dared tell Eddy when they were awake. That she believed their souls had been cleaved apart in the moment of creation, as the Greeks thought, and that now they were reunited. That she couldn't wait to have children with him. That she hoped they had his eyes and his laugh, and his sense of mischief, too. That those children would be raised in a new way—not to resent the throne, or to fear it, but to accept it as a privilege and a responsibility.

"Are you praying?"

Eddy's question startled Hélène. She'd thought he was long since asleep.

"In a fashion," she agreed, and leaned over to kiss his brow. She had been proclaiming her love for him, after all. Surely God had heard. Surely He would answer.

"I love you," Eddy murmured. He drifted off again, and this time she knew he was truly asleep.

He was far more ill than she'd realized, Hélène thought nervously. No matter. She was here now, and she would bring him back to health through sheer force of will.

He would get better. Hélène had youth and determination and stubbornness on her side, and she refused to even think about the alternative.

CHAPTER THIRTY-TWO

May

MAY SLID INTO THE FRONT PEW OF THE CHURCH OF ST. MARY Magdalene, crossing herself before she lowered onto the kneeler.

She'd been at Sandringham for two days now. When the summons had come—a note from Eddy's mother on her personal stationery, sent by special messenger, informing May that Eddy was ill and she needed to come as soon as possible—she'd devolved into momentary panic.

Did she dare show up at Sandringham when Eddy clearly didn't want her there? The last time she'd seen him, he'd told her in no uncertain terms to *leave the country.*

But if she ignored a direct request from the Princess of Wales, then she might as well pack her bags and leave for Rumpenheim, because she would abandon any chance at a future in England.

Besides, what if Eddy's illness had changed things? People tended to feel forgiving after a brush with death, didn't they? At the very least it might buy her some time. And in the best-case scenario, Eddy might recover and decide that it was no use punishing May for her transgressions. They could find a tactful way to break off Eddy and May's engagement, then part ways amicably.

But once May had arrived at Sandringham, and realized

that Hélène was there, too, she had known that her hopes were futile. Eddy might be willing to forgive and forget, but Hélène never would.

The two young women hadn't actually spoken. Hélène was here illicitly, stashed away with neighbors like some kind of guilty secret. But May was paying attention. She'd heard the servants whispering, had figured out that a young woman who was decidedly *not* Eddy's fiancée was visiting him in his room.

When she saw Hélène slipping out a side door one day, May had actually ducked—as if Hélène might look back and see her through the window. Should she return to London? No, May decided; her instincts told her to stay put. There were too many moving pieces right now. She didn't need to retreat, not yet.

Still, May knew enough to avoid a confrontation with Hélène. Which was why she'd come to St. Mary Magdalene. At the Sandringham estate she was too busy playing the role of the concerned fiancée to actually take a moment for herself. Here in church, May had space to think, to plan. To try to plot a way out of this mess.

And of course, it didn't hurt that praying at church, hands clasped before her, contributed to her image of piety.

"I thought I might find you here."

Something in May loosened at the sound of George's voice. She shifted off the kneeler and met his gaze.

He didn't seem happy to see her. Of course he wasn't happy, May chided herself; his brother was ill. And yet. George hadn't tried to be alone with her since that afternoon at the portrait sitting. Whenever they saw each other in person, he was distant, as if his mouth hadn't hovered a breath away from hers. She might have thought she'd imagined the whole thing, except that the memory of the almost-kiss kept replaying in her mind, over and over.

She glanced around the church; they were alone. Then she patted the pew next to her.

George hesitated for a moment before sitting, then lowered his head into his hands. "I don't understand! Just last week we were on the train, and Eddy said he was tired and didn't want to play cards. The next thing I knew, he was in bed, surrounded by doctors who began saying—saying I need to start preparing myself, just in case I need to—" He broke off, staring at the enormous mural of Christ behind the altar.

May shifted closer to him on the pew. "I'm so sorry."

"No, I mean— I'm sorry, too. You must fear for Eddy's life as much as I do."

She blinked. For a few minutes there, she had utterly forgotten that she and Eddy were engaged.

"George, Eddy and I . . . You must know that we are not . . ." How to say this without sounding insensitive? May faltered, changing tack. "I can't imagine what you're going through."

George was silent for a long moment. It was warm inside the church, but he still hadn't shrugged out of his heavy wool coat. May wondered if he'd walked there.

"Did you know I didn't speak until I was nearly two?" he said at last.

"No, I didn't," May replied, confused.

"My parents were worried about me. Not about my hearing; I could follow instructions, so they knew I was listening and understanding. I just didn't say anything in reply."

"Perhaps you were keeping your opinions to yourself," she ventured.

"I think that I didn't learn to talk because I had Eddy to do it for me," George explained. "From the beginning he took care of me. He made himself my interpreter for the world, telling everyone 'George wants this' or 'George doesn't agree,' and I would just nod along. If we ever got into trouble, he would say it was his fault so that he took the caning from our tutor."

"I'm sure whatever prank got you into trouble was Eddy's idea," May pointed out.

George smiled, but it quickly faded. "May . . . I can't bear the thought of losing him. We may have drifted apart since childhood, but he's still Eddy. He's still my brother."

May longed to tell George a soft, palatable lie, like *Of course you won't lose him*, but she knew better. That kind of lie hurt more than the truth.

It had always struck her as unfair, that George had grown up in Eddy's shadow—that his family had showered Eddy with attention and concern while leaving George to his own devices. But that distance from the throne had also granted George a measure of freedom. He'd been able to grow up quiet and introspective because Eddy had taken center stage; had been able to make choices for himself that Eddy never would.

If George had to step into the spotlight, and actually take on the burden of being the heir . . .

May shouldn't even think it. It felt wrong to sit here imagining her fiancé's death.

Yet the fact remained: if Eddy were gone, all of May's problems would vanish with him.

Hélène would never tell Queen Victoria about May's blackmail without Eddy to back her up. And even if she did, May could always say that Hélène was lying—that she was jealous and grief-stricken, and had imagined things.

If Eddy died, Hélène would have no choice but to leave May alone. And then, after an appropriate mourning period, May could find a way to be with George.

It might shock some people if she married her dead fiancé's brother, but there was royal precedent. That was the nice thing about royal history: there was precedent for everything. Just look at the current tsar and tsarina. Minnie had originally been engaged to the tsar's older brother, Nicholas, but when he died, she went on to marry Sasha. And everyone knew that Catherine of Aragon had been married to Henry VIII's older brother, Arthur, first.

As long as Queen Victoria approved, May felt certain that she and George could find a way.

"Should we head back to the house?" May suggested gently. "We could go visit Eddy together?"

George shook his head. "Actually, I'd like to pray for a while. Would you stay with me?"

"Of course." May shifted back onto the kneeler and dipped her head, her earrings swaying with the movement. She folded her hands and closed her eyes.

She did not pray for Eddy's swift recovery. She prayed for him to forgive her, for him to end their engagement without harming her, and for some miracle that might allow her to be with George, despite the mess she had made. All her choices had seemed like the right thing at the time, but May saw now how mistake had built on mistake, until she was tangled in such a knot of hurt and betrayal that she couldn't break out of it.

That was what she prayed for now—a way out.

As long as Eddy's fate hung in the balance, then so did May's.

CHAPTER THIRTY-THREE

Eddy

"WE NEED TO TELL GRANNIE," GEORGE WAS SAYING. "HASN'T anyone told her? Is she coming?"

Tell her what? *Eddy tried to ask his brother, but the words felt clunky in his mouth. And he was so cold. He must be at Balmoral; it was the draftiest, coldest castle. There were never enough fires there, and if you did try to start one, the wood would hiss in angry protest. . . .*

"Grannie is going to be so angry." George glanced nervously over his shoulder at the door. "We really shouldn't."

"Don't you want to feel how heavy it is? I've never held a real sword. Have you?" Eddy asked, well aware that George had not.

A flicker of longing darted over his little brother's face. "Fine. But let's hurry."

It was almost too easy, convincing George to do something illicit. And really, what else were they meant to do on a rainy day at Balmoral if not explore these dusty old sitting rooms? Eddy and George had wandered through the familiar spaces, rapidly deciding that this one—with its assortment of traditional Scottish weaponry and clan insignia on the walls—was their favorite. Then their eyes had caught on Grandpapa Albert's old sword.

Eddy stood on tiptoe, straining his fingers toward the sword, but he wasn't tall enough.

"I'll have to lift you," he muttered, kneeling down. "Get on my shoulders, all right?"

It wasn't the first time Eddy had carried George in the name of a prank, like when Eddy had convinced George—draped in an oversized bedsheet—to ride piggyback into the kitchens on All Hallows' Eve, moaning like the dead. Chef was so startled he'd dropped an apple turnover onto the floor.

George obediently climbed onto Eddy's shoulders. Eddy stood with a groan, and George grabbed the sword by the hilt. "Got it!"

Eddy winced as he knelt back down. "You're getting heavier."

"I *am* six," George said defensively. He clambered down from Eddy's shoulders, holding tight to the sword. "Do you think Grandpapa ever used this?"

Eddy reached for the weapon, and George handed it over without protest. "No. It was probably just a ceremonial gift. But that doesn't mean *we* can't use it," he added, adopting a fencing stance. "Get back, you evil knight!"

George didn't jump into a fighting stance the way Louise would have. He gave a very put-upon sigh. "Why do I always have to be the villain?"

"Because I'm older," Eddy replied, stating the obvious. "Grab one of the pokers from the fire; that can be your sword."

George looked annoyed but did as Eddy asked, brandishing the poker like a weapon. "Get back, knight! I will destroy you!"

Eddy and George moved about the sitting room, their weapons colliding in various jabs and ripostes. They jumped over sofas, climbed up onto ottomans as they fenced and parried their way around the room, which had become their own personal battlefield. The sword was heavy, and Eddy's arm was starting to get tired, but he refused to trade with George. This had been his idea; he should get the better weapon. And besides, he was the big brother. The stronger one.

But George must have gotten stronger than he realized, because he landed a particularly solid blow, and Eddy dropped the sword.

The impact of the metal hitting the wooden floor echoed through the whole house.

He and George exchanged a worried glance, then dropped to the floor, both reaching for the sword. George got there first—

"What on *earth* is going on here?"

The brothers shot back up, both bowing at the waist. "Sorry, Grandmother," they chorused.

"Is that your grandfather's sword?"

George held out the sword and closed his eyes, bracing himself for the worst.

Victoria took it, lips pursed, and placed it lovingly back on the wall. Then she stared at the two of them. "George, go find a book to read. Eddy, come with me."

She gestured to the sofa, which was the same red-and-white plaid pattern as the curtains. Eddy reluctantly took a seat opposite her.

"I'm disappointed in you, Eddy. You acted discourteously, and worse, you talked George into your poor behavior."

"How did you know it was my idea?" he asked sullenly.

"We both know that George follows in your wake." Grandmother's reproof was gentle. "He wants to be just like you, Eddy. It is a heavy responsibility, isn't it, being the elder brother?"

"Is that why you're punishing me, and not George?"

Grandmother shook her head. "I am not punishing you, but I want you to understand that you must take care, even more so than George. You are the future king, and he is not. Do you know what that means?"

"Yes," Eddy said impatiently. "I will wear the crown, and ride in the first coach in parades, and my face will be on money!"

"There is so much more to reigning than what you've described. You will need to listen to your advisers and your Parliament, and sign laws. You will lead the Church." Grandmother must have seen Eddy's focus drifting, because she reached for his hand. "But yes, you also get to wear the crown, and ride first in parades."

"What about George? What will he do?"

"He will be a duke, and remain a valued member of this family. But he will never be king, not unless—" Grandmother broke off, shaking her head as if she shouldn't have spoken.

Eddy knew what she'd been about to say. "Unless I die, like Grandpapa Albert."

"You are young and healthy," the queen said solemnly. "Let us pray that such a day never comes."

"WE NEED TO HELP HIM GET WARM," A MALE VOICE WAS SAYING.

"Get him warm?" That was Eddy's mother. "You came all the way from London, and the best advice you can give my son is to add a blanket? I thought you were an expert in pulmonary illness!"

"I am doing all I can, but His Royal Highness's decline has been precipitous. I'm afraid it is in God's hands now. Perhaps, Your Royal Highness, you might join Her Serene Highness the Princess May at chapel. Your prayers will do as much for His Royal Highness as any medicine. . . ."

EDDY PROWLED THE CADOGANS' BALL IN HIS MUSKETEER COStume, ignoring everyone who attempted to greet him, searching for Hélène.

It had been torture, not speaking to her for the past several weeks. Eddy hadn't realized that one's happiness could be so utterly dependent on another person. Really, this whole falling-in-love business was much riskier than anyone had told him.

Then he saw her dancing with Tino.

She looked impossibly lovely and out of reach, wearing an ordinary riding habit instead of the fancy dress that the invitation had called for. How typically Hélène, to buck convention by wearing something she already owned instead of an elaborate gown in the style of Cleopatra or Marie Antoinette. The riding habit showed off her figure, and her cheeks were flushed pink. She tipped back her head and laughed at something Tino said.

She glanced over as if she felt Eddy staring, and their gazes locked.

He jerked his head toward the double doors that led to the terrace. Hélène hesitated for a moment. Then, to his relief, she murmured something to Tino and followed Eddy.

When they'd reached the shadowed privacy of the orangerie, Eddy cleared his throat. "Have you read my letters?"

Hélène crossed her arms over her chest, shaking her head. He should have known. Her stubbornness was one of his favorite things about her, as long as it wasn't directed at him.

"I want to talk to you," he pleaded, but Hélène cut him off.

"I don't think we should be speaking at all, not when you're going to marry Alix!"

"But that's just what I want to talk to you about! I want to marry you instead!"

The words had taken up residence in his mind long ago; it was high time he spoke them aloud.

Hélène just stared at him, saying nothing.

"I'm sorry, I'm doing this all wrong." Eddy hurriedly fell to one knee, willing her to know how serious he was. It was a strange sensation, kneeling: he'd never done it before anyone, not even Grandmother. But in this moment, as he begged Hélène to spend the rest of her life with him, it felt utterly right.

"Marry me, Hélène," he breathed.

She stepped closer and pulled him to his feet, her eyes smoky and soft with emotion. "Eddy. You know we can't."

"Why not?" he demanded. "Just because we're royal, we have to be bound by laws and precedence?"

"In this instance, yes!"

He frowned. "Then we'll elope—"

"I love you too much to pretend that I'm ashamed of you!"

Eddy inhaled sharply. He loved Hélène, more than he'd ever imagined that he could love another person, but he hadn't said it aloud. He had no experience with grand declarations of love. Funny, that he could be willing to scale mountains or stay above deck on a ship in a storm, yet the prospect of telling this woman he loved her was terrifying.

He was secretly glad that she'd been the first to say it.

"Oh, Hélène. Surely you know that I love you too."

Eddy opened his arms, and she stepped into them, where she belonged.

He hadn't known that this was what he was looking for—or more accurately, he hadn't been looking at all. Yet now that he'd found it, he knew there was no letting it go.

It wouldn't be easy, but then, nothing worth having came for free. He could either marry some nameless princess picked out by his grandmother, and regret the loss of Hélène for the rest of his days; or he could fight for her with every fiber of his being. Even if it cost him everything.

He would give up his title for her, if it came down to that.

"You still haven't given me a real answer," he murmured. "Will you marry me?"

"Of course I will," she replied.

Eddy felt almost lightheaded with joy. *This is it,* he thought, *the moment that the rest of my life begins.*

"MISS, YOU REALLY MUST GO," A VOICE WAS SAYING.

"I beg your pardon, but I really must not." Hélène's voice was clipped, tense. "Now if you'll please let me return to my prayers? *Notre père, qui es aux cieux, que ton nom soit sanctifié . . .*"

Eddy smiled to himself. Hélène must have seen, because she broke off abruptly.

"He is awake! Doctor, look!"

Eddy forced his eyes open, glanced around the room. Why was he at Sandringham?

"Your Royal Highness." A doctor he didn't recognize stepped forward. "May I—"

"No. Please leave me and mademoiselle in peace."

It was unmistakably a command. The doctor hesitated, then bowed and left the room.

Eddy looked up at the woman he loved. Her face was suffused with tenderness and concern and a hesitant, tentative hope. "Hélène . . ." He hated how raspy his voice sounded. "Do you remember the day I asked you to marry me?"

"The first or second time?"

She was joking; that had to be a good sign. "I don't remember there being a second time," he managed to say. "The second time was implied."

Hélène reached for his hand and gave it a gentle squeeze. Her voice grew serious. "Of course I remember. Now no more talking. Just rest."

"How long have I . . . ?"

"A few days," Hélène said with false lightness. Eddy suspected it was longer, a week at least.

"And you've been here the whole time?"

She hesitated. "I'm not here, technically speaking. I've been staying with the Wyclifs. But I've come to see you as much as possible." When he didn't reply, she valiantly kept talking. "I've kept busy, you know. I've been wandering the grounds, planning a surprise project for Her Majesty. I was thinking we could make a Scottish garden here, with some thistles, bluebells, sweet violets." She kept talking, explaining that she'd already sent to Balmoral for seeds, that the gardeners had festooned off a corner of the greenhouse to start. Her words were quick and almost frantic, as if she might fend off what he had to say next.

An uncharacteristic calm had settled over Eddy. He knew, with grave certainty, that he wouldn't live to see the Scottish garden.

He wouldn't live to see any of it. All the things he had barely let himself dream of: Hélène in her wedding gown, meeting his gaze with a knowing smile as she walked down the aisle. Traveling with her, somewhere wild and unexpected like Udaipur, where they would sail the cold mountain-locked lakes, eat naan in sandstone palaces. The children they might have had. Oh, what troublemakers those children would have been, half-French and half-English—or really, half Eddy and half Hélène.

Eddy had hardly begun to want all these things, and now they were slipping out of his grip. *Everything changes*, his grandmother always said. *That is the one thing you can count on, constant change.* But he hadn't expected that change would mean loss.

"Hélène," he said weakly. "I would ask something of you."

"Name it."

"You need to let me go."

Her grip on his hands tightened. "What?"

"You must promise that when I am gone—"

"Stop! Don't say such a thing!"

He forged resolutely ahead, mustering all his strength. "Promise that you will not mourn me too long. You must go on and live your life."

The room was very still, the only sound the deceptively cheerful crackling of the fire. "Eddy." Hélène's voice broke. "You are my heart's desire. I will never love anyone else."

"That's not true." It was so hard to say these things, yet Eddy forced himself to, for Hélène's sake. He loved her so much it hurt. He loved her enough to want her to find someone else, to find happiness without him.

Never had he imagined that such a love was possible.

"You have a wonderful heart, with so much love to give. Someday you'll meet a man you're ready to share that love with. Of course, he will have to be quite special, to be worthy of you." Eddy attempted a smile through the cracking of his heart. "Adventurous, and brave, and kind, and strong. Someone who makes you laugh. When you meet that person, I want you to give him your love wholeheartedly. Don't hold any back out of respect for me, all right?"

"You can't speak like this." Tears streamed down Hélène's cheeks. "I don't want to meet someone else. I want you!"

"Promise me." Eddy's voice was urgent. "You deserve a wonderful, long life, full of all the joy that the world has to offer. You deserve to *see* the whole world. And if you can't do it with me, I need to know that you will still do it, even with someone else. You must promise."

The force of his command seemed to echo in the room. Miserably, resentfully, Hélène nodded. "I promise. But I'm angry with you for extracting such a promise while you are ill and I have no choice but to say yes."

Negotiating to the bitter end. Eddy loved her for it. He felt such pride in that moment that she had been his, if only for a short while.

What a formidable Queen of England she would have made.

"I love you," he told her. "Never forget that."

"I love you, and I always will." She sniffed, holding his hands so tight that he could barely feel them. "Always."

There was so much more Eddy wanted to tell her, but the

words flitted like restless birds around his mind. George . . . That was one more goodbye he needed to say. He wanted to tell George how sorry he was for leaving him with a burden he'd never expected. And wait, wasn't there something he wanted to warn George about? May. That was it. He wanted to tell George about May's true nature, how cruel she had been to Hélène and Alix and Ducky. George needed to be wary of May. . . .

He would call for his brother in a moment. For now, Eddy needed to close his eyes. That conversation with Hélène, extracting that promise from her—it had been taxing. Dreams swirled in his vision, beckoning him back to the warmth of the orangerie, the night she'd agreed to marry him. And further back, to his childhood, when he still hadn't understood what it meant to be a future king. Now it would be George's turn. . . .

"WE HUMBLY COMMEND THE SOUL OF THY SERVANT, PRINCE ALbert Victor, into the hands of a faithful Savior. . . ."

There was the sound of weeping. Eddy sensed that people were holding both of his hands. One was in the familiar grip of his mother, but who had the other? It was a woman, but not Hélène.

Hélène. He tried to form her name with his lips, but no sound came.

"Teach us who survive, in this and other like daily spectacles of mortality, to see how frail and uncertain our own condition is; and so to number our days . . ."

His mother let out a wail.

"Here now, Mother," George said gruffly. Eddy was glad that George was there. He thought he heard Louise weeping in the corner. And was that Grandmother? She might keep death at bay, he thought, with something like amusement. Nothing could fell Queen Victoria.

But where was Hélène?

He needed her here. She was his everything, the axis his whole world spun on. He had wanted to share the rest of his life with her; if he couldn't have that, she should at least share his death.

With monumental effort, Eddy summoned every last vestige of strength in his failing body. He forced his lips to form the word that he held dearest in the whole world, one he had said so many times, in passion and despair and impossible love.

It came out a whisper, but everyone in the room heard it with utter clarity.

"Hélène. Hélène."

CHAPTER THIRTY-FOUR

Hélène

IT WAS NEARLY DUSK, BUT HÉLÈNE DIDN'T CARE. SHE RODE HARD, mud flying up from Odette's hooves as the mare hurtled down the paths of Richmond Park. Hélène wasn't normally such a reckless rider, but she had no regard for safety right now. She didn't really care what happened to her anymore.

The forest rushed past in a shadowed blur. Wind whipped at her face, bringing tears to her eyes. They were the only tears she had shed in the past week.

Eddy was gone, and Hélène still hadn't wept.

It seemed impossible that he had died, that a young man in the prime of his life could be felled by an illness, just like that. Hélène couldn't bear it. She wanted to howl with grief, to scream at God for His unjustness in taking Eddy from her. For the fact that there was an Eddy-shaped hole in the world where he should have been.

So she did exactly that: tipped back her head and let out a wild, ragged scream.

Odette reared in protest, her hooves waving in the air; then she fell back down and slowed to a walk. "No," Hélène muttered, and dug in her heels once more. Maybe if she kept running fast enough, she could outpace reality. Could run away from what had happened.

Hélène would never forget the earth-shattering moment she'd heard the news. She'd been at luncheon with Lord and Lady Wyclif, wondering when Louise would send for her: Louise had been coming daily to sneak Hélène over to Sandringham. A footman had entered the dining room and murmured something to Lord Wyclif, whose gaze instantly darted to Hélène.

"Tragic news," he'd said gravely, and looked down with a sigh. "His Royal Highness has passed."

The message was wrong, Hélène had immediately thought. The footman was mistaken, because Eddy couldn't be dead.

Later, she would read every detail about his final hours; the account was printed in newspapers all over the country, along with some awful photo Eddy had previously posed for with May. It didn't even *look* like him, Hélène thought each time she saw that image. He seemed so miserable. Or constipated. Yet the papers kept printing it anyway, recounting how he had died peacefully, surrounded by his family, with his beloved fiancée, Princess May of Teck, holding his hand.

Somehow Hélène had made her way back to London. She felt numb with shock. None of this felt real—except, impossibly, it was. She knew because she came back to a city in mourning. Church bells clanged in the cold winter air; shops were closed and shuttered. Even the hansom cabs put black felt on their windows and black ribbons on the bridles of their horses. *He was so young,* everyone murmured in hushed, somber tones; *and to think that he died just a few months after getting engaged!*

He *was* engaged, Hélène wanted to scream. Not to May, to *her.* But May had become the personification of the nation's grief: a desolate, romantic figure at the center of an epic tragedy. There was even a drinking song making its way through the nation's beer halls: "A nation wrapped in mourning, shed bitter tears today, for the noble Duke of Clarence, and fair young Princess May."

Fair young Princess May—more like, the manipulative and heartless Princess May. As if it wasn't enough for May to steal Eddy in life, now she'd stolen Hélène's rightful place of grief.

Hélène was the one who should ride in a carriage at his funeral. *Hélène* should be the first to place flowers at his tomb. Not May, who'd never loved him at all, who had only ever wanted him for his title.

It was getting late. Hélène could barely see the trees to either side of the path. A chilly mist hung in the air, making the path feel otherworldly, matching her mood.

When hoofbeats sounded behind her, she cursed under her breath, twisting in the saddle. No one else ever rode this time of day. Then she saw who it was, and slowed.

"Maman?" she croaked.

Marie Isabelle was mounted in a man's saddle, as Hélène was, rather than the sidesaddle that she should have been using. She was wearing a very loose gown that would have earned her a few raised eyebrows if anyone had seen.

"Hélène. It's time we headed back," her mother said gently.

Hélène just stared at her. "I didn't know you rode astride."

"There are many things you don't know about me. Mothers don't tell their daughters everything. Perhaps we should,"

Marie Isabelle mused as she pulled up alongside Hélène. "I kept things from my past from you, but you are not a girl who needs to be sheltered. You are a woman. And perhaps if I'd told you of my mistakes, you would not have repeated them."

Hélène's hands tightened on the reins. "Eddy was not a mistake."

"I'm not saying he was," Marie Isabelle said evenly. She waved in Hélène's direction. "But riding alone in the dark, at top speed, when Odette could stumble over an obstacle she can't see—that is a mistake. Come home with me."

Hélène's lips pressed together, but she tugged Odette's head around, starting back toward Sheen House. Her mother fell into quiet step alongside her. The sun had set; Marie Isabelle's profile was more shadow than person. It was easier this way, perhaps. Hélène could ignore her mother and pretend she was alone. Or better yet, pretend that Eddy was the one riding alongside her.

"It's all right to cry, you know," her mother finally said. "Don't keep it bottled inside the way these Englishwomen do; the pain festers and turns to poison, burns you from within. You need to let it escape your body. Even if you must scream again."

"You heard that?"

"I was tempted to join in," Marie Isabelle said flatly. "You think you're the only woman who's ever screamed into a forest? I am a daughter of Spain. My ancestors, when they grieved, used to shout into the Pyrenees with such anguish that people thought dragons lived there."

"Eddy and I were engaged." Hélène was surprised to hear

herself speak. "We had reconciled and were once again planning to get married. We were about to ask permission from his grandmother."

"Oh, Hélène. I'm so sorry." They walked in silence for a few moments, and then her mother added, "I suspected that there was no lovers' quarrel. That something else was going on, something you couldn't tell me." She paused, offering her daughter the opportunity to speak if she so chose. But Hélène wasn't ready.

"I loved him so much," she said simply.

"I know."

They walked quietly in the direction of the stables. The horses sensed that they were almost home; they grew restless, tossing their heads, their hooves prancing lightly over the ground.

Hélène's mother let out a breath. "I will not do you the disservice of saying that everything will be all right. I love you too much to tell you a lie."

Startled by her mother's words, Hélène looked over. Marie Isabelle was staring into the distance. "A loss like this . . . It cleaves your life in two. There will be the time before and the time after. I wish I had a way of making it easier. If I could trade my life for Eddy's, I would."

That last had been spoken simply, without drama, as if Marie Isabelle had been remarking on the weather. Hélène knew her mother loved her, but to hear her say such a thing—it made that love fiercely, wildly clear.

"You will always carry him in your heart, and it will always hurt. But eventually the pain will lessen. Eventually, someday, you will be able to smile again."

Hélène couldn't imagine wanting to smile ever again. Her very soul felt splintered in two.

"After the funeral, I want to leave London," she told her mother.

"I assumed as much. Your father and I have already started making the arrangements."

Hélène nodded, aware that she should be grateful, but her gratitude was buried too far beneath the pain.

"I was wondering if we could go to Rome. I'd like to enter a convent."

At that, Marie Isabelle looked over sharply. "Hélène, no. You aren't serious."

"I won't marry, all right? I refuse to do it! You *cannot* make me!" Hélène's voice had become wild, erratic.

Her mother leaned out of her saddle, reaching across the shadowed distance to put a hand on Hélène's arm. "I won't ask you to get married. But, Hélène, you would hate being a nun."

"It sounds like a relief, escaping from the world. Living in quiet isolation."

Marie Isabelle made a skeptical sound. "All those rules and restrictions, bells chiming at all hours, labor with no reward? You would hate it."

As if marriage wasn't all about rules and restrictions, and labor with no reward. But Hélène hadn't minded any of that, back when she was marrying Eddy.

Everything had felt different with Eddy. He made the entire world seem brighter, livelier, full of promise. Hélène couldn't begin to imagine how she would move forward without him.

She felt grief sinking its claws into her. As if some feral

animal had awoken in her chest and wanted to shred her heart from the inside.

"I cannot even publicly mourn him," she said helplessly. "I was his fiancée, his *real* fiancée, and instead everyone is grieving with May!"

"When did you start caring what everyone else thinks?" her mother demanded. "Eddy knew what was in your heart, and so does God. What else matters?"

"It matters because I want to *mourn* him!"

"Who says you cannot? You are mourning him now, here, in a place he loved. Which is far more appropriate for Eddy than a grand funeral procession."

Her mother was right. They had reached the stables; it was fully dark, and peaceful, the only sounds the whickering of horses and the wind rustling the branches. An owl hooted deep in the forest.

Hélène dismounted swiftly. A stable hand stepped forward, but Marie Isabelle caught his gaze and shook her head.

"The Princess Hélène and I will stable our own horses tonight," she murmured. "You may go."

Sorrow was rising sharp in Hélène's throat as she unsaddled Odette, found a set of combs, brushed her coat until it shone. There was something soothing about the repetitive motion. Odette leaned around, sniffing Hélène's hands in search of a treat, her breath warm.

The shock or anger, whatever was holding back Hélène's tears, began to crack.

Hélène sat down on the ground. And there, in the warm darkness that smelled of hay and horses, she wept at last.

CHAPTER THIRTY-FIVE

Alix

ALIX HEADED TO SHEEN HOUSE THE VERY AFTERNOON SHE ARrived in London. She felt anxious to see Hélène, to tell her friend that she wasn't alone in her grief—that someone, at least, knew what Eddy had meant to her.

London was unlike Alix had ever seen, the entire city shrouded in mourning. Windows were hung with black crêpe, church bells echoing through the silent streets. A massive pile of flowers had formed at the gates of Marlborough House, and was growing by the minute; weeping strangers kept stopping by to add their own arrangements. Alix knew they weren't really grieving Eddy. How could they, when none of them had known him? They were thinking of someone else who had died too young—a daughter they had lost in childbirth, a friend who'd gone to war and never come home. Eddy became that person for all of them. His funeral would be an outpouring of national grief, and yet it wouldn't be about him at all, because that was the point of the royal family—to let people channel their emotions somewhere. To give them a focal point for their joy or anger or heartbreak.

When she reached Sheen House, she asked the butler to please announce her to the Princess Hélène.

"I'm sorry," he stammered, "but mademoiselle is not at home—"

"Alix? Is that you?"

Hélène stood at the end of the hall. She looked pale, her eyes shadowed. Her dark hair floated in a tangled cloud around her head.

"I just got to London this morning. I wanted to see you," Alix said hesitantly. She wasn't sure whether her friend was ready for company.

"Come in, then." Hélène turned without preamble and headed down the hall, leaving Alix to follow.

The sitting room they entered felt stale; there was a pale green coverlet tossed on the sofa, and various glasses of water and bowls of uneaten food on the coffee table. "I've been sleeping in here." Hélène flopped down on the sofa. "My room is . . . Well, Eddy was in there, at least, in my dressing room. Not long before he died."

"Oh, Hélène." Alix sat next to Hélène and pulled her into a hug, wrapping her arms around her friend's body. She felt thin, almost frail.

"Excuse me, miss." A maidservant ducked into the room and began stacking glasses with quiet efficiency.

"Annie! It is *my* job to look after mademoiselle!" hissed a French lady's maid, hurrying into the room after the maid. Hélène waved them both away.

"I'm fine, really." When they had left, she looked at Alix with a pale smile. "The two of them are like a pair of hens, clucking over a single egg. I can't get rid of them."

"I'm glad someone is looking after you. Where are your parents?"

"They're making preparations for us to leave."

"You're going away?" Alix asked, startled.

"Right after the funeral. There's nothing left for me in England," Hélène said heavily.

"You're welcome to come see me in Darmstadt—all of you," Alix offered, but Hélène shook her head.

"Thank you, but I need to go farther afield. Italy, or perhaps Turkey. Somewhere warm, where it doesn't rain."

"Of course." Alix understood. Hélène needed to flee, to find a place that didn't make her think of England.

Hélène's next words were quiet. "I keep forgetting that he's gone, you know. I'll want to tell him something, and then suddenly I'll remember that I can't, and the pain of it hits me all over again."

"Sometimes I still forget that my mother is gone, and I lost her thirteen years ago," Alix confessed. "When there's something I want to tell her, that's what I do. I talk to her."

"At her gravesite?"

"I talk to her portrait. We have a picture of her in the library." Alix felt a little foolish admitting this, but Hélène would understand. "Even when I'm not in Darmstadt, I whisper things to her. I always get the sense that she's listening."

"I don't have any portraits of Eddy. I'm sure May does," Hélène said resentfully.

Alix's heart ached. "I would say that I'm sorry, but I know it's a useless thing to say. When people used to tell me how sorry they were about my mother, it made me irrationally angry. As if they shouldn't just be sorry, they should *do* something."

"I don't think there's anything you can do, Alix, unless you have the ability to turn back time."

Alix reached for a silver-backed brush, which by all rights belonged on the surface of Hélène's vanity yet had been abandoned on a side table. "You know what I can do? I'll brush your hair. You need it, honestly."

"Oh, very well." Hélène shifted, pulling her feet up onto the cushions so her back faced Alix.

They were silent for a while, the only sound the swish of the hairbrush as Alix teased knots from Hélène's dark mane. Then Hélène said, "You know what else you can do? You can distract me."

"Distract you?"

"You never told me what happened with Nicholas!" Hélène drew in a breath as if remembering something, then twisted to look at Alix over her shoulder. "I hope you didn't misinterpret— That is, Eddy told me that he'd seen me with Nicholas on the yacht, and he assumed the worst."

"I knew that there was nothing between you and Nicholas." Alix sighed. "Still, it didn't work out between us."

"I think you can convince his parents! It will just take time," Hélène insisted.

Alix shook her head. "Actually, Maximilian of Baden is courting me now."

"That German man from the regatta?"

"He makes me happy, Hélène."

"Oh. Well." Her friend seemed to be struggling to remember Maximilian. Finally she settled on, "He *is* rather tall, I recall."

"He's more than tall. He's kind, and earnest, and . . ." Alix trailed off as Hélène stood and crossed the room to a mahogany cabinet. Light refracted on all the crystal decanters within.

"What are you doing?" Alix demanded.

"Getting us a drink." Hélène reached for a crystal square-cut decanter full of amber liquid. She poured it into two tumblers, then handed one to Alix.

"Is this brandy?" Alix had only ever had sherry, or wine.

"It's what Eddy would drink if he was here." Hélène took a large sip. Alix hesitated before doing the same.

She choked, coughing. The brandy burned her throat.

"I'm all right," she managed, then took a much smaller sip. It felt less abrasive this time, curling in her stomach like liquid fire.

"You don't really break the rules, do you?" Hélène almost sounded amused.

"I broke the rules that time with Nicholas," Alix said unthinkingly.

"I *wondered* what happened that night! I assumed you were together, but I wasn't sure how far things progressed."

"Oh, they progressed." Even now the memory of that night brought heat to Alix's cheeks. "But then I realized that Nicholas would never get his parents' permission to marry me. That I couldn't keep waiting for the impossible."

Hélène seemed to consider that thoughtfully; then she huffed out a breath.

"It's funny, isn't it? That we were engaged to both of them at different times?"

"Both of them?" Alix repeated.

"Eddy and Nicholas! We made quite a tangle of things, didn't we? The only way it could be messier is if May had been engaged to Nicholas, too." Hélène rolled her eyes. "Honestly, if she could have figured it out, I'm sure she would have been."

Alix surprised herself by taking another sip of brandy.

When had Hélène refilled her tumbler? The alcohol was seeping into her mind, loosening her limbs, casting everything in a golden glow. "I don't think my engagement to Eddy should really count," she protested.

"Your grandmother considered it real enough."

"And you were never actually engaged to Nicholas!"

"True. We could barely manage a pretend courtship." Hélène pulled the green coverlet onto her lap, glancing over at Alix. "All I'm saying is that it's amusing, that you and I were connected to the same two men. Especially because we are so different."

"We are certainly different," Alix agreed. "But perhaps that's why we are friends. Perhaps friends who are too similar come into conflict."

"I wouldn't know. I don't have any female friends, except my sister. And you," Hélène declared.

"Me too. Just you and my sister," Alix murmured.

Hélène tilted her tumbler, letting the liquid slide from one corner to the other, lost in thought. "I suspect most women wouldn't become friends the way we did. Sharing fiancés, fake courtships, secrets."

"I don't know *how* most women make friends," Alix admitted. "It's not really covered in the etiquette books."

"Because society doesn't want us to work together. We are taught to think of each other as enemies. As competition in the marriage market."

Hélène's words saddened Alix, primarily because they were true.

"Tell me more about this Maximilian," Hélène declared, changing the subject. "How long has he been courting you?"

Alix recounted the story of Maximilian's courtship, how easy and bright it had all felt. She told Hélène how his family adored her, how Maximilian had seen her in the throes of an attack and helped her manage it. How they both wanted the same things from life: a simple home in Germany, full of books and children.

"You said a lot of words, just now," Hélène replied at last. "None of them were *I love him*."

"We haven't been courting all that long!"

"So?" Hélène pressed. "How long did it take you to fall in love with Nicholas?"

Alix said nothing. She had loved Nicholas from the very first visit, probably the very first moment.

Hélène sat up straighter, gesturing to Alix's expression. "See! That look on your face—you didn't look like that when you were talking about Maximilian, not once! Instead you kept telling me how *nice* he was, and that if you married him you would live near Darmstadt."

"What's wrong with *nice*?" Alix demanded. "At least if I got engaged to Maximilian I would be better off than Ernie! At least I would have a *chance* of loving Maximilian someday!"

She immediately winced; she shouldn't have said that, shouldn't have hinted at Ernie's secret, even in the vaguest of terms.

Hélène seemed confused. "What does this have to do with your brother?"

"Nothing," Alix said hastily. "It's just—he and Ducky are not well matched."

Hélène shrugged. "I suspect they'll do better than most.

Alix, just because your brother's marriage was arranged for convenience doesn't mean yours has to be. You can have more than *nice* or *easy*. You love Nicholas, and despite all the obstacles in your way, he loves you, too."

"Yes, I love Nicholas, but it has always been so volatile, so—difficult!" Alix shook her head, tears pricking at her eyes. "With Nicholas I felt overwhelming joy, and at the same time, so much pain. I may not love Maximilian yet, but I know I could come to love him someday. And it would be a more adult love, based on affection and trust. Not a wild storm of emotions."

"A more adult love, or a safe one?" Hélène challenged.

"The kind that doesn't leave you heartbroken!"

Alix could picture the love she might feel someday for Maximilian: the kind of love where two people pass a wailing baby back and forth, smiling over its head; where their lives grow so entwined that they know each other's sleeping patterns, how they like their coffee. The kind of love you could *rely* on.

"Perhaps that kind of love is enough, if you never know the other kind," Hélène said at last. "But you do, Alix. You have felt it—the combustible, overwhelming, heartbreaking kind. Which means you can't give up on Nicholas."

Alix ran her fingers over the tracery on the crystal tumbler. "You wouldn't say that if you knew how much we've hurt each other. It's hopeless."

"You think Eddy and I didn't hurt each other?" Hélène exclaimed. "We made all kinds of mistakes! But I would give anything, would feel all that hurt a million times over, for just five more minutes with him."

Alix felt her eyes burning with tears. "I'm sorry. I didn't mean . . ."

"Don't apologize," Hélène said heavily. "You want to do something for me? Go find Nicholas, tell him how you feel. I know he hurt you—but maybe, when you love that hard, some pain is inevitable. Maybe that kind of joy *has* to be balanced by heartache and grief. I don't know," Hélène said helplessly. "All I know for certain is that *you* still have a chance at that kind of love, because Nicholas still walks this earth. Eddy is gone forever! So don't go telling me that you and Nicholas are hopeless, because you're both very much alive."

WHEN ALIX RETURNED TO BUCKINGHAM PALACE, WHERE SHE and Ernie would be staying until the funeral, Ernie greeted her carriage. "What's wrong?" he asked, perceptive as always.

"I saw Hélène. She said some things that I can't stop thinking about," Alix admitted.

Her friend's words kept echoing in her mind: *I would give anything for just five more minutes with Eddy* and *You still have a chance at that kind of love, because you're both very much alive.*

Alix used to be so certain of her and Nicholas. She had been ready to give up everything for him, to move to Russia and change her religion and her language, to say farewell to all she knew and loved.

Now there was Maximilian, and the feelings that were growing between them. The life they built together would be so easy, so familiar. Alix wouldn't have to change anything for him.

"I'm sure Hélène is heartbroken," Ernie murmured sympathetically.

Through wordless agreement, the siblings started up the stairs, lowering their voices. "She's devastated. It made me wonder . . ."

"About Maximilian?" Ernie prompted.

"No, about Nicholas." Alix sighed. "I never told you that I saw the tsar in Baden-Baden."

She explained how she'd run into the tsar and his wife in Baden-Baden on holiday, taking the waters. How they had offered her a small fortune to write Nicholas a letter, telling him that she had moved on, and he should, too.

"Now I've seen Hélène, and hearing her talk about Eddy . . ." Alix trailed off.

Ernie filled in the blanks. "It made you realize that life is short and unpredictable, and you need to fight for true love?"

"She reminded me that Nicholas and I are not impossible. No matter how hard it might feel." Alix glanced down. "I wish I knew what he'd written in all those letters he sent after the regatta. But we burned them all."

Ernie looked distinctly sheepish. "I wouldn't say *all* of them."

"*What?*" Alix demanded.

"I saved two of them, in case you changed your mind. Do you want to see them?"

"They're here?"

"Yes. I've been keeping them in my writing case, on the off chance you would—"

He hadn't even finished the sentence before Alix was running up the stairs two at a time. She heard Ernie's footsteps behind her as she reached his room and began tugging open his writing case, revealing loose papers, a wax seal, scattered pens.

"And you said you didn't want to hear from him ever again," Ernie declared from the doorway, watching her.

"I don't *want* to feel like this, all right? But I do!" Alix's voice shook as she found a pair of envelopes stamped with the distinctive red and white of the Greek mail system.

"Looks like they were posted from Greece," Ernie explained. "My guess is that Nicholas enclosed the letters in a larger note to Tino, and Tino reposted them."

"He was forbidden to write me." And yet he'd still managed to send the letters. In his own way, Nicholas had fought for them, tried to vanquish the obstacles between them.

She sank onto Ernie's rug, her skirts pooling around her in ripples of charcoal-colored silk, and tore open the first letter.

Alix,

I know you said to forget you, but I cannot. Send just a word, I beg you, so that I may know whether or not to hope. I have told my parents that I will not marry Hélène, that in fact I won't marry anyone except you, and that if I cannot have you then I will remain unwed until the end of my days. It might be enough to convince them, in time. . . .

The second letter was more of the same, but Nicholas's normally precise handwriting had disintegrated into a frantic scrawl. There were smudges in the ink, thumbprints.

"Was I wrong to keep them?" Ernie sank onto the floor next to her and looped his arms around his knees.

"No, I'm glad you did. It's just . . ." Alix lowered the letter, carefully smoothing the wrinkles from the page. "Remember the fairy tales Mother used to tell us when we were little?"

"About handsome princes and love that defies the odds?" Ernie asked, only a little teasing.

"Exactly. In stories, the lovers always end up together, no matter how hard it seems." Alix's voice fell as she added, "Do you think it's the same in real life? That true love finds a way, no matter what?"

"I don't know."

They both sat with that for a moment; then Ernie blew out a breath. "I do know this, Alix. Hélène was right; you and Nicholas are not impossible. She has *lost* the man she loves, and as for me and the man I love . . . I can never be with him, not in any real sense. But Nicholas is still alive, and he loves you. You have a chance at happiness. Don't squander it."

Alix shifted closer, opening her arms to hug Ernie—but he paused, wrinkling his nose. "Alix. Have you been drinking brandy?"

"Hélène and I opened some," she admitted. Perhaps that explained why her emotions felt so close to the surface right now, hope and hurt and love all swirling about.

Ernie chuckled. "I'm telling Grannie that you're indisposed. Then I'm bringing you some bread and cheese, maybe some tea, and you are going to bed."

"Why?"

"Because you've never had brandy before, and if we don't act now, you'll be facing a rather brutal morning tomorrow. Come on." Ernie stood, holding out a hand.

Alix let him pull her to her feet. Then, still holding her two letters from Nicholas, she followed her brother to her room.

It was quite nice, actually, being taken care of like a child. Ernie brought her food, as he'd promised, and called a lady's maid to help Alix into her nightgown.

She went to sleep, the pages of Nicholas's letters crinkling beneath her pillow.

CHAPTER THIRTY-SIX

May

MAY SHOULD HAVE BEEN WEARING BRIDAL WHITE. INSTEAD SHE was dressed in a high-necked black gown, a black veil covering her features, her hands—in their black gloves—clasped in her lap. She was inside St. George's Chapel, at Windsor, but not for her wedding to Eddy. For his funeral.

Everything had happened so fast: his illness, his sudden death. The entire nation still felt thunderstruck by it all. The fact that Eddy had gotten engaged, and then died, in the span of a few months—it felt like a storyline from a novel, the sort of melodramatic thing that Alix would read.

Except that May was living it.

A winter sunbeam arced through the stained-glass windows, falling on the wooden floors of the chapel. May shivered. It was cold in here, and protocol didn't allow heavy coats at a funeral.

Today had felt endless. The procession, with all those soldiers and drummers and gun salutes, and Eddy's beloved horse—what was its name, again?—walking in a black harness, with Eddy's boots and spurs reversed in the stirrups. May had ridden in a carriage after the coffin, behind George and Uncle Bertie, who walked the whole way.

May forced herself to swallow a yawn; she couldn't let anyone see her disrespecting Eddy like that. But lately it had been impossible to sleep, her dreams full of shadows and accusations.

I didn't kill him, May reminded herself yet again. Just because she'd sat in the church of St. Mary Magdalene and thought that things would be easier without Eddy . . . She hadn't *prayed* for his death, not technically. She wasn't some medieval witch cursing her enemies. It was coincidence.

Of course, everyone assumed she was devastated. They were all watching her with furtive glances, wondering what she would do now. May suspected that some of them—the ones who'd been slightly resentful of her rise, the ones who'd never thought she deserved to marry Eddy—were secretly glad to see her brought low. Not that they were glad of Eddy's death, but they were pleased that May would never be queen.

She was right back where she'd started: an unmarried woman, stuck under her father's roof. Except that wasn't quite true anymore. Now that Francis was gone, White Lodge was, unofficially speaking, Mary Adelaide's house.

May kept worrying that her father might reappear. What if he realized that Eddy's death meant May's political influence had dwindled, and he came back to torture her? But so far, at least, he had stayed away. She'd heard he was currently in Württemberg, pretending to lord it over his distant German cousins.

Without him, White Lodge felt almost cozy. May spent a lot of time with her mother now, quietly working through the mountain of condolence letters that had arrived, many from complete strangers.

And there was her trousseau to sort through. So many beautiful things—tea dresses and garden dresses, evening gowns with crystal beading and rhinestone embroidery, all with handbags and shoes and gloves—meant for a honeymoon and national tour that she and Eddy would never take, for parties May would no longer attend. May kept half expecting someone to show up and take it all back. And who would pay for it? Eventually, there would be a bill, and May didn't dare ask the Waleses. It would have been the height of rudeness.

Now the organ music swelled to a crescendo, and the queen—stone-faced and stoic in her grief—started down the aisle. May sank into a painfully deep curtsy. At last, the funeral was over. She let the crowds sweep her out of the chapel and into one of Windsor's reception halls, where everyone milled about, sipping on wine and exchanging whispers. Alix of Hesse had come with her brother, May saw—and was that Hélène d'Orléans with her parents? Surely she wouldn't dare say anything to May, would she?

Then May caught sight of George, standing across the room with the Prince of Wales.

For a moment May forgot to hide her emotions. She let everything she felt for him, all the hope and yearning, run wild on her face.

All she needed was a few moments with George, just to make sure he was all right. To tell him that she was here if he needed her. May and George hadn't truly spoken since their murmured conversation in the pew at St. Mary Magdalene. She'd seen him often enough since then: at Sandringham after Eddy's death, and then here at Windsor once the family had arrived for the funeral. But she hadn't exactly had an opportunity to find him alone.

May started across the room with purpose. A few people approached, but she put them off with gentle nods, murmuring that she needed to speak to her late fiancé's family. She saw the moment George registered her approach, the way his expression softened at the sight of her, just a little—

"May! There you are!" The Princess of Wales stepped between them, holding a spray of flowers in one hand. "I have something for you. I had to special order it, but I told the gardeners to spare no expense."

May realized that they weren't just any flowers: they were the exact ones she had ordered for her wedding bouquet. Orange blossoms and camellias and white roses, tied with the signature white ribbon of a bride.

"I was thinking you could place it on Eddy's coffin," Alexandra sniffed. She was talking quite loudly but was clearly too distraught to realize. "Since you didn't get to carry it on your wedding day . . ."

It was such a performative, dramatic gesture. The type of thing that May normally would have thought of herself, except that she no longer cared about putting on a show.

Actually, she was getting quite tired of pretending to mourn someone she had never loved.

More people were glancing over, their eyes bright with sympathy and curiosity. What other choice did May have? She nodded in agreement with her almost-mother-in-law. "What a lovely thought."

The two of them drifted back toward the chapel, dreary and melancholy in their black gowns.

May dared a single glance at George over her shoulder, and saw that he was watching her leave.

TWO DAYS LATER, MAY WAS STILL AT WINDSOR, AND STILL HADN'T spoken to George alone.

There was always someone around—one of the Waleses, or some extended family member, or even the Archbishop of Canterbury. He had patted May on the head as if she were a stray puppy and murmured that she needed to resign herself to the will of God.

As if May had ever resigned herself to anything.

She had just spent hours with the Princess of Wales, answering the seemingly endless mountain of letters, writing on that awful black-edged stationery until her hand cramped. Now, as she headed through an upstairs hallway, May paused.

George was walking out in the frozen garden.

She hurried to her room and shrugged into her overcoat, then clattered down the stairs and outside. The winter air was bitter cold, but May forced herself to loop around the path in the opposite direction from George, so that they would run into each other by the marble fountains.

He didn't look up, even as her footsteps crunched loudly over the gravel.

Finally, when they were only a few feet apart, May gasped in surprise. "Oh, George! I hadn't expected to see anyone out here."

"Nor did I." He wasn't making eye contact; his tone was distant, formal.

"I imagine you need to be alone right now, but if you'd like company . . ." May tipped her head toward the path.

"Very well." Still not looking at her, George fell into step beside May, past the frozen parterres where roses would bloom come summer. The crenellated battlements of Windsor rose up against the slate-gray sky, reminding May of the castle's original function—to keep enemies out.

"I'm so sorry." The words felt useless, but she needed to say them. "I know you must be bewildered, and hurting, and in shock. If you need to talk, or . . ." May trailed off, suddenly uncertain.

George was silent for a moment, his breath puffing out little clouds of steam in the freezing air. "I do want to talk," he agreed. "And we need to do it now, since I leave for Cap Martin tomorrow. Who knows when I'll see you again."

"Oh, I might go to the Riviera too!" The words tumbled out of May. "Lady Wolverton offered Mother the use of her home at Cannes. It's not so far from Cap Martin. I have never seen the Riviera; I hear it is lovely, even if the orange and lemon trees are all dead this time of year. . . ." She bit her lip, realizing she was babbling. "What I mean to say is, you don't have to carry this weight alone. There are so many people who love you, who are here to help."

When he replied, George's voice was tight with warning. "I think you and I should keep our distance from each other."

"No." The word came out as a reflex; she swallowed. "George, you must know by now Eddy never loved me. He never wanted to marry me. You heard him—he said Hélène's name on his deathbed!"

May knew everyone in the room had heard him speak Hélène's name, clear as day. No one mentioned it to *her*, of course, but she suspected they were all writing it in letters to various family members, wondering exactly what drama had played out behind closed doors.

"You shouldn't feel guilty for being friendly with me," she added. Though she hoped he would want to be more than friendly.

George's eyes narrowed. "I don't feel guilty. I blame *you* for manipulating me, just as you've done to everyone else."

May was so startled that she tripped. George didn't hold out a hand to help her.

When she righted herself, May looked him in the eye. "I never manipulated you. I meant every word I ever told you."

"Of course you would say that. From what I've heard, you're a liar—"

"I love you!"

She hadn't meant to blurt that out. May knew it was a terrible mistake, knew that it was too soon after his brother's death to be talking of romance. But now that she'd admitted the truth, she found that she couldn't stop.

She had been silent for too long, burying her feelings for George down deep. Suddenly, she couldn't bear the thought of him not knowing the truth.

"I love you," she said again. "I have loved you for so long, George. Since the open-air market at Osborne, when you gave me the mayflower. No, since last summer, when we were together at Balmoral—or even since we were children! I can't pinpoint an exact moment," she added helplessly. "All I know is that I love you. I love your smile, and your generous heart, and your stubborn pride. It's a bit like mine, you know. I love that you make me want to be a better person. You make me want to deserve you."

They had reached a walled garden with an obelisk at its center, a grand marble thing with gilded numbers on its face. The flowerbeds, bordered in low limestone bricks, were iced over with frost.

May held her breath and waited.

"I won't lie; for so long I hoped to hear you say those words," George told her at last. "Now I don't know whether to believe them."

"Of course you can believe them! Like I said, Eddy and I should never have gotten engaged. I only wanted to because I thought you and I—I thought Missy . . ."

"Is it true, what you did?" George asked quietly.

"Missy's marriage is not my fault!" May protested. "All I did was tell Aunt Vicky that Prince Ferdinand had flirted with her! I can't be blamed for recounting a simple story!"

George went very still, and May instantly realized her mistake. She should not have confessed. Not without knowing what she'd been accused of.

She placed a gloved hand on his arm, tentative. "Please, just let me explain."

George stepped back, shoving off her touch. "Explain what? That you manipulated and threatened your way into getting engaged to Eddy? I didn't even know about Missy," he said bitterly. "But it's good to know how much cruelty you're capable of."

It felt like a vise was closing over May's chest. "I made a few mistakes—"

"Mistakes? Is that what you would call it, spreading rumors about Alix? I'd call it slander."

"I may have told a few people about the fainting spell I witnessed, yes. I was worried about Alix!" Worried she might marry Eddy, in truth, but George didn't need to know everything. "There's no crime in recounting a true fact."

"What about Hélène? Did you blackmail her?" George demanded.

May longed to deny it, to dismiss the whole thing as a misunderstanding, but Eddy had clearly spoken to George before he died. She knew George might forgive her mistakes, but he would never forgive her for lying to his face.

"I didn't write the letter, but I did know about it. A friend impersonated me. I only found out after the letter had already been sent."

"If that's true, why didn't you tell Hélène to ignore it?" George pressed. "You were perfectly happy to let her leave the country, so that you could swoop in and convince Eddy that he wanted a marriage of convenience!"

Yes, he'd definitely spoken to his brother.

"And now Eddy is dead, and you're claiming that you loved me the whole time? Are you going to make me the same offer you made my brother? Tell me that I can sleep with anyone I want and you'll never hold it against me?"

May stood up a little straighter, hands clenched. "I shouldn't think I need to. You are not like him."

"No, I'm not," George agreed, in a caustic tone. "I'm just the younger brother, the one you flirted with as a precautionary measure—a backup plan—in case things with Eddy didn't work out."

"You know that's not true!"

"I don't know anything about you anymore, May! I thought you were different. And I did love you."

The past tense of that statement seemed to echo viciously around the garden.

"When Eddy got engaged to you . . . that's the only time in my life I remember truly hating him." All the fight seemed to have drained from George's voice. "Eddy always got everything he wanted, and I had never minded before, but then he had *you*. And he didn't even appreciate you! He saw you as a placeholder, a person to wear the crown while he did as he pleased. Eddy had no idea what a gem you are—at least, that's what I thought at the time," George went on gruffly. "Now I'm not sure."

May dared to step forward, taking his hands. To her surprise, he let her.

"You can be sure of this, George. I love you. I did some things that I am not proud of, but we are here now. You and I can have a second chance. I'm sorry about Eddy," she added hastily, not wanting to sound insensitive. "I hate that this is how we got here. But don't you think we could start over? We still have each other."

Gently, George pulled his hands from hers.

"No, May," he said with heartbreaking finality. "I will continue to be cordial to you in public, which you deserve, as my late brother's fiancée. But do not speak another word in this vein. I refuse to hear it."

He was angry with her for hurting Hélène, and Missy, and Alix. Or perhaps he still didn't trust that she loved him for himself, rather than his title. Either way, he was telling her no.

May wished she hadn't waited so long to tell George how she felt. She could have professed her love for him a thousand times over, but she had always held back, out of . . . what? A fear of being rejected, as she was now?

"I am sorry," she said again.

George nodded once, curtly, then turned on his heel and walked off.

May stayed in the garden until her hands grew numb from the cold, even in her leather gloves. For so long she had been proud of herself—of her cleverness, her foresight. Now she just felt a hollow sense of regret. She had made so many mistakes, mistakes that were still playing out their consequences.

When she finally started back toward Windsor, May noticed icicles hanging from the branches of a nearby tree. They looked like frozen tears.

CHAPTER THIRTY-SEVEN

Alix

"CAN YOU HAND ME SOME TWINE?" ERNIE WAS POISED ON THE top step of the ladder, positioning a candle on the fir tree.

"Not until you move that candle higher," Johann insisted.

"It's perfectly spaced!"

"Alix, tell your brother how wrong he is," Johann pleaded, turning to her. "We have a better view of the tree than he does."

Smiling, Alix reached for the box of twine. "Sorry, Ernie, but Johann is right."

"Of course. I'm always right," Johann teased.

Ernie barked out a laugh as he caught the twine that Alix tossed to him.

The three of them had spent a lot of time together lately. In another household it would have been impossible, but here in Darmstadt, in a smaller house with a close-knit staff, they could get away with unusual behavior.

When they were alone, Alix treated Johann the way she would treat anyone that her brother loved. And so Ernie and Johann were open with Alix, letting her see the things they would normally have kept hidden—the way they laughed together; the glances they exchanged in amusement, or exasperation, or affection.

No one spoke about the fact that this would all have to stop once Ernie married Ducky.

Alix tried not to think about that. Or the fact that this was her last Christmas as the mistress of Darmstadt. Next year Ducky would be the one pulling out the decorations, arranging them in their proper places, wrapping them away at the end of the season with loving care.

Alix paused, glancing out the window at the town's familiar streets. Smoke rose up from chimneys in the distance. So far the snow had only been a light dusting, but Alix knew that heavy snowfalls would come soon enough, the streets vanishing beneath a glittering blanket of white.

She blinked; a rider had turned down the avenue toward the house. He sat his horse easily, a dark cloak fluttering out behind him.

It was Maximilian.

"Looks like you have company, Alix. Johann and I will make ourselves scarce," Ernie said meaningfully. Johann nodded, folding the ladder before following Ernie out into the hall.

Alix ran a hand nervously over her dress, then walked out to greet Maximilian.

After that conversation with Hélène, after rereading those letters from Nicholas, Alix had agonized about what to do. In the end, she'd written to Maximilian, asking him to come see her.

"Alix!" Maximilian was off his horse in a fluid movement, then bounded up the stone steps toward her. A groom silently emerged to take his steaming horse to the stables.

"Thank you for coming." Alix opened the door, gesturing him inside, to the warmth.

Maximilian surprised her by pulling her into a hug, right there on the front steps. He brushed a kiss on her brow. "I'm sorry about your cousin. I wish I could have gone to London with you." He'd been stuck in Potsdam doing business with the kaiser, who was increasingly coming to rely on Maximilian as a statesman. Probably because German politicians were usually known for their bluster and swagger, rather than their tact. Maximilian, reasonable and logical, was something of a rarity.

Alix led Maximilian to a sofa in the main drawing room, where the half-decorated tree stood proudly in a corner. "You know, I haven't been to many funerals," she said clumsily. "This one felt different from the others I've seen, my mother's and Frittie's. Those were quiet, whereas Eddy's was all gun salutes and battalions of marching soldiers."

"And yet I'm sure you felt it all over again, didn't you? The loss of your mother, and Frittie."

Of course she had. That was the nature of loss; it compounded itself, made you think of other losses, other griefs. Alix had wept at the funeral—for Eddy and for Hélène, but also for her mother. For her tiny baby brother, who'd hardly gotten a chance to live.

"I was wondering if we could talk," Alix began, feeling awkward.

Maximilian frowned in concern. "Of course. Is everything all right?"

Looking at him, in that moment, Alix saw everything he felt for her written plainly on his face. It almost made her second-guess her decision. He was so warm, so sincere. So true to himself and the people he loved.

No. She had to do it now, before she lost her nerve.

"I am sorry, Maximilian, but we cannot keep courting," she said as gently as she could.

The silence between them pulsed with hurt and confusion. Maximilian didn't speak right away. He was looking very steadily into the distance, working something out in his mind.

"You are back with him, aren't you?" he guessed. "The other young man, the one you loved?"

Alix shook her head. "I will probably never see him again. But that doesn't change the fact that I cannot keep seeing you."

"Alix." Maximilian clasped her hands in his. "If things with him are truly over, then what is keeping you from seeking happiness elsewhere? Because I know we could be happy together, you and I."

He was right; they could have been happy together. Maximilian had wooed her so beautifully, from the very day they met, when he'd walked with her in the Buckingham Palace gardens and given her the space she'd asked for. He had always given her what she asked, had respected her wishes the entire time she'd known him.

Things were so *easy* with Maximilian, so safe. Free of heartache and pain and secrets and lies.

But Nicholas had always hovered between them. No matter how hard Alix had tried to forget him.

If she had never met Nicholas, Alix might have been so happy with Maximilian. But for better or worse, she *had* met Nicholas. Hélène was right; Alix couldn't let herself settle for anything less than . . . true love? Passion? She didn't know how to describe what she felt for Nicholas; it was wild and limitless and impossible and heartbreaking and deliriously wonderful. Even when it hurt.

"You are such a good man, Maximilian. You deserve someone who loves you wholeheartedly, and I could never give you the whole of my heart."

He was watching her intently. Alix knew he could read the emotions on her face, the anguish and regret.

"I see," he replied, though she knew that he didn't see, not at all.

"For what it's worth, I hope we can remain friends," she added.

Maximilian's voice was sharper than she had ever heard it as he said, "Alix, don't do me the disservice of pretending I can be your friend. You know I will never think of you as just a friend."

"I'm sorry," she said again, voice breaking.

Maximilian stood stiffly. "I should be getting back now. Of course, if you are ever passing through Baden, you are always welcome."

"Thank you." They both knew that Alix would never be passing through Baden. It would be cruel to strain his hospitality in that way.

This was goodbye, for good.

As he started toward the door, Alix realized belatedly that he had a long ride ahead. "Wait! Before you go, can I get you some water, or a glass of wine? And doesn't your horse need to rest? You don't need to leave just because I—"

"It's all right, Alix. Give Ernie and Louis my best." Maximilian cast her one last look, and then he was opening the front door, his steps echoing with a hollow finality.

Alix walked to the window. She watched as he called for his horse, remounted, rode off into the darkening streets of the city.

Only a few minutes later, Ernie and Johann reappeared, holding a bottle of claret. "I thought I heard you calling for wine, so I opened this," Johann said, without an ounce of remorse for eavesdropping. "Looks like you need a glass."

"I can't believe Maximilian didn't stay." Alix accepted the glass, distracted, and took a sip. "He can't mean to go back to Baden tonight?"

"Let him go, Alix," Ernie said gently. "He'll head to an inn, get himself some ale or perhaps a bourbon, ride back in the morning. A man needs some time to himself after a rejection like that."

"So you were listening?" She tried to sound angry, but found that she was too weary, too sad, to be upset.

"No, we weren't, but if you hadn't rejected Maximilian, he would have stayed," Ernie said evenly. "Besides, I can see the guilt on your face."

Alix set down her wine and collapsed onto the sofa. "I do feel guilty. I know this was the right thing to do, but still, I wish . . ."

She trailed off, not knowing what she wished. That she loved Maximilian as much as he loved her? That she hadn't spoken to Hélène? That she still had a chance with Nicholas?

"What will you do now?" Ernie asked.

Alix tried to sound flippant as she replied, "As much as I'd love to stay here forever, playing the eccentric aunt to your and Ducky's children, I think I should leave once you're married. You will want your own space."

"No one would ever call you eccentric," Johann said loyally. "You're too beautiful."

Alix laughed at his blatant attempt to cheer her up. He was wrong, of course; often beauties were labeled the most eccentric, but she appreciated the sentiment all the same.

"I was thinking that when we go back to England to see Grandmama next month, I would offer to be her secretary," Alix said tentatively. "Aunt Beatrice is always begging for someone else to take on the role."

Their aunt Beatrice, Queen Victoria's youngest child, was in her early thirties. For years, Beatrice had served as the queen's personal secretary; Victoria didn't trust her correspondence with anyone outside the family. Beatrice was now married with three children, yet she still showed up each morning to read Grandmama's letters and write out her responses.

"We all know you'd make an excellent secretary. You are painfully organized," Ernie agreed. "But let's not rush to take on Aunt Beatrice's life, all right? You are always welcome here. You know that."

Alix decided to change the subject. "Can we finish the tree? It's looking quite lopsided with only a few branches done."

Johann hurried to retrieve the ladder while Alix sorted through the candles.

The rest of the evening, as the three of them decorated the tree and sang Christmas songs woefully off-key, and ate so much salted toffee that they all claimed stomachaches, Alix thought how lucky she was to have a family like this: warm, accepting. Full of love.

She could survive any heartache, as long as she came home to this.

CHAPTER THIRTY-EIGHT

Hélène

"A CARRIAGE JUST PULLED UP THE DRIVE." VIOLETTE STOOD AT the window of Hélène's dressing room, lifting a corner of the drapes to peer out. "It has no crest. Who would come in an unmarked carriage?"

Hélène didn't reply. She tilted her head back on the chaise longue and closed her eyes. Various satin-lined trunks were opened around her, gowns and stockings spilling out in frothy abandon.

She didn't care about the carriage, or what Violette packed, as long as they left. Hélène couldn't bear another day in England. The entire country felt saturated with memories of Eddy. Wherever she went—walking through Mayfair with her mother, on a ride through Richmond Park—she kept expecting him to appear, grinning mischievously. It was even worse at social gatherings, where all anyone talked about was Eddy and May, and how their brief engagement had ended so tragically. The only bright spot lately had been the night she and Alix sat up drinking brandy, speaking of Alix's romantic affairs. For a brief moment, it had distracted Hélène from the howling storm of her grief.

Perhaps she would take Alix up on her invitation, and visit her in Darmstadt. She could attend Ernie and Ducky's wedding later this spring. Not that Hélène was in the mood for a wedding—but Alix had seemed so worried about her brother, and Hélène wanted to be there for her friend, just as Alix had been there for her.

Besides, it wouldn't be all that difficult to travel to Darmstadt from Eu.

Eu. Hélène still couldn't quite believe it, but miraculously—impossibly—the Third Republic had lifted the terms of exile for her and her mother. Her father and brother were still banned from the country, but the Orléans women had apparently been deemed nonthreatening enough to visit.

Hélène and Marie Isabelle were going to Portugal first, to collect Amélie and her new baby: a girl this time, named Maria Ana. Then they would all make their way to Normandy, to spend some time at the Château d'Eu. A house full of Orléans females; if Eddy were here, he would joke about how loud and chaotic it would be.

If only Eddy had ever gotten to visit Eu. But perhaps it was better this way; it didn't contain any memories of him.

Hélène's chest loosened as she thought of the house. The great bay windows where she used to hide. The apple orchard, where she and Amélie would sneak away as children, to eat tarts stolen from the kitchen. The cool green of the woods in summer. The salt air that lingered on the breeze. Hélène used to love visiting the port, watching the sailors come in on their ships, imagining that they had come from wondrous faraway lands.

"Mademoiselle." A footman appeared at the door, looking flustered. "Forgive my interruption, but your presence is requested downstairs."

Hélène sighed. "Please tell my parents I'm indisposed."

She couldn't bear the prospect of another mindless social visit. Another tea where some society matron would go on and on about Eddy's death, about what a terrible loss it was for the country, and what would poor May do now? Hélène hated nodding along as if she, too, viewed Eddy's death with the dispassionate view of an outsider. As if she believed May's show of well-rehearsed grief.

Most painful of all had been the funeral.

After the service, Hélène had waited in the long line to approach the coffin. Then at last she'd been standing next to Eddy. Looking at his beloved face one more time.

He lay there so peacefully; still so handsome, even in death. Hélène had mouthed the words *I love you,* her fingers itching to reach out and touch him—

The person behind her, some gentleman with a gray beard, had let out a pointed harrumph of impatience. And Hélène had torn her gaze away, her heart shattering.

"Your parents were quite insistent that you come downstairs," the footman said now, cutting into her thoughts.

Hélène stood, feeling rather put-upon. This had better not be another suitor. If her father had summoned Nicholas, or worse, some other prince . . .

"Shall I redo your hair, mademoiselle?" Violette suggested. "Or perhaps you might change?"

Hélène glanced at her reflection for the first time in days. Her face was pale, making her brows and golden-brown eyes seem darker than usual.

"No, I'll head down like this." In the privacy of her home, Hélène had been wearing black. She couldn't do so in public; she wasn't technically entitled to grieve Eddy. But here, she was dressed in the full mourning that befitted a woman who had lost her fiancé.

Downstairs, Hélène hesitated at the threshold of the sitting room. The footman must have been mistaken; no one was there.

Then she heard an all-too-familiar voice: "Don't dawdle, Miss d'Orléans. Come in, and shut the door behind you. I would speak with you in private."

The Queen of England was at Sheen House.

Hélène did as Victoria had asked, and shut the door. The sitting room felt eerily silent, dust motes dancing in the morning light.

"Your Majesty. I hadn't expected such an honor," she murmured, and sank into a curtsy.

This was positively unheard of. Queen Victoria hadn't gone out on a social call in decades. She attended balls, or events in town; but if she wanted to speak to someone, she summoned *them* to *her*, at Buckingham Palace.

In answer to Hélène's unspoken question, the queen nodded toward the unmarked carriage outside. "This is why I keep such a carriage. There are times when I wish to see someone, and don't want it advertised."

Victoria gestured to the opposite sofa, and Hélène took a seat.

"I know you are grieving." The queen's gaze drifted to Hélène's black gown. "I spoke with Eddy before he died, and he told me that he was desperately in love with you. That the two of you hoped to get married after all."

"Yes," Hélène said levelly. "Eddy was planning to speak with you. He wanted to break things off with May, and eventually, once the scandal had calmed down, announce our engagement."

"I won't lie, it would certainly have been a scandal. But we could have weathered it. Stranger things have happened in this family," the queen added, almost to herself. She drummed her fingers in their black silk gloves against the arm of the sofa, thinking.

Hélène realized the silence had stretched on an inappropriate amount of time. "Your Majesty, shall I ring for some tea?"

The queen ignored her. "When Albert died, people told me such nonsense. That God had drawn Albert back to Himself because Albert's soul was too good for this world. 'His death makes a link between you and heaven,' the Archbishop of Canterbury said." Victoria huffed impatiently. "Albert was certainly not too good for this world. He was a good man, with a strong moral code and a kind heart; but he was still a man. He was not flawless. As for a link with heaven—I did not want that. I wanted my husband with me, alive."

Hélène nodded, her throat closing up, and the queen met her gaze.

"What I am trying to articulate, perhaps poorly, is that after I lost Albert, there was nothing anyone could say to make it better. So I will not waste your time with any such useless sympathy."

"Thank you," Hélène said softly.

"For what it's worth, I am sorry." The queen spoke clumsily; she clearly wasn't used to giving apologies. "I regret the role I played in keeping you and Eddy apart. It would seem that I'm not as good at matchmaking as I once was."

That last was said lightheartedly, but Hélène didn't smile.

"Given the circumstances, I wanted to bring you this," Victoria added, holding out a hand.

Hélène rose and walked over; because even here, in a private audience, Victoria would never do anything so indecorous as *lean*. When the queen dropped a gold band onto her palm, Hélène stared at it in shock.

"Eddy's wedding ring," Victoria said unnecessarily. "He would want you to have it."

"I don't know what to say. Thank you." Hélène held the ring so tight that it dug into the flesh of her palm.

"It is devastating, is it not?" The queen's voice broke. "I keep regretting that I was so hard on him."

Hélène didn't argue with that. Instead she said, "Eddy loved you."

The queen shot her a grateful look. "Someday, if you have children, you will understand. You do your best as a mother; and then you grow older and notice all the mistakes you made. Your grandchildren feel like a chance at doing things differently, correcting those mistakes. Albert and I were far too indulgent with Bertie, and look how he turned out," Victoria observed, with shocking disloyalty. Hélène suspected she would never have made such a remark to anyone else—that they had entered some strange territory where they could both speak frankly.

"After Bertie, I thought I would do things better with Eddy, take a stronger hand. But I fear that I never gave him the credit he deserved. Certainly I never understood him the way you did," Victoria added, nodding at Hélène.

"You had a hard role, playing both monarch and grandmother," Hélène said magnanimously.

Silence descended in the sitting room once more. Hélène wondered, suddenly, where her parents were. What did they think of this strange audience between herself and the Queen of England?

"If you'll forgive an old woman's meddling, I should like to give you some advice," Victoria went on, after a beat. "You were the great—the only—love of Eddy's life. But that doesn't mean he needs to be yours."

Hélène looked up defensively. "Of course he is. I will never love again."

"Eddy would not want you to drown in grief, as I did with Albert." Victoria sighed. "Trust me when I say that I know how you feel. When Albert died, I could not get out of bed. It felt like the entire world had collapsed in on itself, like I was suffocating. But at least I got twenty years with Albert. You and Eddy had not even started your life together, had not yet tasted the joys of marriage."

Hélène tried to imagine what Victoria would say if she knew the truth—that Hélène and Eddy had indeed tasted some of the joys of marriage. *Tell her*, she imagined Eddy goading her. *Grandmother could use a bit of shock.* The thought made her want to laugh.

And then, half a heartbeat later, she wanted to cry.

"I almost didn't give you that ring." Victoria gestured to the gold band, which Hélène was still holding tight. "I didn't want it to become an obsession for you, the way Albert became for me. It all happened before you were born, of course, but you must have heard what a recluse I was after Albert's death. I retreated to Balmoral, shut all the blinds, saw no one."

"What drew you out of it?" Hélène whispered.

"I realized that I had the other great love of my life to think about."

"Your children?"

"My country."

There was another beat of silence. Victoria's bright blue gaze met Hélène's, and for a moment, Hélène felt like she was looking into Eddy's eyes.

"You are so young, Hélène. I know you loved Eddy, but don't do as I did and bury yourself alive. Keep living, for his sake. Here, or abroad, it doesn't matter. Just promise that you will live, since Eddy cannot."

Hélène stared down at the ring in her hand to avoid the queen's gaze. "As it happens, I am leaving England. My mother and I are going to Normandy."

"Of course. It is too bad that the lift on your exile did not extend to your brother and father, but you know, it would be quite difficult for the Third Republic to allow the Pretender and his heir back in France."

Hélène started to nod—then she realized what the queen had said. How did Victoria know about the terms of her exile? Unless . . .

"Your Majesty. Did *you* get our exile lifted?"

The queen shrugged. "Republican governments are so hard to deal with," she said vaguely. "I make it a point never to negotiate with France. That is Lord Salisbury's job."

"Thank you," Hélène said fervently. How wondrous of Victoria, to know exactly what Hélène needed and provide it.

The queen gave a slight, enigmatic smile. "Speaking of your

brother, how is he? I keep hearing good reports from Lord Roberts, his commander in chief."

For the past four years, Philippe had been stationed with the Royal Rifle Corps in Bombay.

"You may not have heard, but he is leaving Your Majesty's service," Hélène admitted. "He and my father are going on a tour of the United States. You know my father fought in the American Civil War, as part of the Union Army? He wanted to show Philippe all his old battle sites, introduce him around."

They were also going to Canada, to quietly muster up support for the Orléans cause among the French inhabitants of Montréal and Québec. But Victoria didn't need to know that.

"A trip to America! I cannot wait to hear about it." The queen's eyes danced as she added, "Does Philippe have any plans to marry?"

Hélène was almost amused; the queen was incorrigible. "Who were you thinking to match him with? Maud?"

"Not Maud! She needs someone quieter—one of the Danish princes, perhaps. I was thinking of Thora. She could use someone adventurous, and of course it would help Philippe greatly if he married into this family—" Victoria broke off, shaking her head. "I said I would swear off matchmaking, and here I am, doing it again. Old habits die hard, I'm afraid." She smiled sadly. "In any case, I don't need Philippe to marry into my family. I have you."

Hélène looked at the queen, startled.

"You may not have been able to marry Eddy, as the two of you so ardently desired, but I will always consider you one of my own," Victoria said fiercely.

"Thank you, Your Majesty. That means the world to me." Hélène stood and curtsied again—but the queen held out a hand, stopping her mid-motion.

"Don't bother with the formalities, please. And I would be honored if you stopped calling me Your Majesty. You must address me as Grandmother, the way you would have if you and Eddy had wed."

"I shall say it in French, if that's all right with you." Hélène paused before saying, "Grand-mère."

Then, to Hélène's utter shock, Victoria stood and pulled her into a hug. Her arms wrapped around Hélène's torso and she held her close, as if she was pouring all her love for her late grandson—all the affection she had failed to express in his lifetime—into this single gesture.

When they pulled apart, both women's faces were wet with tears.

Victoria took a moment to compose herself, then nodded to Hélène. "This is farewell, my dear, but I hope not goodbye. Or as you would say, au revoir." *Until we meet again.*

When the queen had left, Hélène remained standing for a long while, holding Eddy's gold wedding ring to her chest. She needed to find a ribbon, so she could wear it close to her heart.

And then she would go to France.

CHAPTER THIRTY-NINE

May

ONCE UPON A TIME, MAY WOULD HAVE BEEN THRILLED AT A PRIvate summons to Buckingham Palace. Now she just viewed it with a sinking sense of dread. She was so sick of acting like a melancholy national mascot, wrapping herself in funereal black crêpe, only invited to parties as an object of maudlin curiosity. Queen Victoria would probably want to talk about Eddy, and May would have no choice but to nod along as if she had, in fact, been in love with him.

As if she didn't love his brother, who was very much alive.

When she reached the palace, May followed a footman into a sitting room. He offered her a cup of tea, which she accepted, mainly for the simple joy of holding the mug. It was so beautiful and delicate, painted with snowdrops and winter thistles.

What a pleasure it would be to have beautiful things like this. To offer your guests snowdrop mugs in the winter and bright floral ones in the summer.

"Hello, May."

The queen glided into the room, wearing her signature black gown and a black lace coif. May hurried to sink into a curtsy.

Victoria sat, gesturing for May to take the seat opposite her. "I would ask how you are doing, but I'm sure the answer is *not well*."

May bowed her head in dutiful agreement. "It has been a tragic time indeed."

"We are all deeply aggrieved." The queen perched on the edge of her sofa, straight-backed and alert. "However, I did not ask you here to talk about Eddy. We are here to discuss your future."

"My future?" May repeated. No one had spoken of her future since Eddy died, as if she had been buried alive right alongside him.

There was a pause as the queen considered her next words. "I see that beneath your placid surface, May, you are a fighter. As I have been my whole life. A difficult childhood will do that to you," she added under her breath.

May suspected, then, that the queen knew about Francis. Perhaps she didn't know the extent of it, but she sensed his true nature.

"I aspire to be as strong as Your Majesty," she replied softly.

The queen nodded, and it seemed to May that a moment of kinship passed between them—across the generations, bridging rank and wealth and love and loss. They both knew what it was to be a woman with her own mind, in a world shaped by men.

Even a queen had to fight for what was hers.

"There has been too much upheaval of late," Victoria mused aloud. "Eddy's death has shaken the nation to the core. To lose a young man who would have been king, uprooting the line of succession . . . Our role as the royal family is to maintain stability, to be steady and immutable even when the world changes around us. Now that Eddy is gone, we cannot afford any more disruption."

"Of course," May replied, though she didn't quite see what this had to do with her.

A knock sounded at the door, and satisfaction settled over Victoria's features. "Oh, good. He's right on time."

May turned to look, and her heart skipped a beat. Standing in the doorway was George.

"Georgie, dear. Come join us," the queen requested.

May tried to catch his gaze, but George was deliberately looking anywhere but at her as he settled into a nearby armchair. He didn't reach for a tea mug, just leaned back and crossed his arms over his chest.

"I shall, as Lord Salisbury would say, get to the point," Victoria declared. "You two now have my permission to court."

May's heart soared in delight—but before she could say anything, George let out a strangled cry of protest.

"Grannie, you can't mean that. It would be disrespectful to Eddy."

"On the contrary, it would be disrespectful not to! She didn't *marry* him, after all," the queen pointed out, with brutal practicality. She frowned at her grandson. "I thought you'd be thrilled, given that you asked to court May first."

"You asked to court me?" May blurted out, eyes on George. He still didn't acknowledge her.

"Yes, back at Osborne, the day before you got engaged to Eddy. George came to me and asked for my permission to court you. I would have granted his request, except that Eddy declared the very next morning that he would marry you or no one else." Victoria shrugged. "Naturally, since Eddy was the older brother, his desires came first. I told George that he had to step aside. He was very dutiful, of course, and obeyed me."

Eddy's desires came first—this was said so matter-of-factly that May winced. She tried again to meet George's gaze, but he was staring down at his shoes, jaw clenched.

George had wanted to court her. If only he'd asked his grandmother's permission a day earlier. If May had known, she would never have gotten engaged to Eddy.

They could have all been spared so much hurt: her, Eddy. Hélène.

"May, your engagement to Eddy, short as it was, introduced you to the nation," the queen went on briskly. "People already think of you as a future queen. It's quite a touching story: you and George, sharing your mutual grief at Eddy's death, slowly realizing that you care for each other. The nation will love it."

"I'm sorry, but I can't," George said flatly. "I regret to say that I no longer feel about May as I once did."

It stung, hearing that.

The queen sniffed. "I don't see why. Really, Georgie, you and May are far better suited than she ever was with Eddy. And if I'm being honest, she's better for you than Missy—"

"What happened to Missy is May's fault!"

There was utter silence, broken only by the sound of Victoria tapping her spoon against her teacup. May knew she had mere seconds before the queen decided her fate.

She sensed that a lie, however clever, would hurt her cause.

"I'm sorry, Your Majesty," May said quickly, turning to the queen. "Missy had once told me about Prince Ferdinand—that he was flirtatious with her. She giggled, and seemed quite fond of his attention." May hung her head in shame. "I mentioned this to Her Royal Highness the Queen of Prussia, and I fear that she may have related it to Ferdinand, who acted on it."

George finally looked up, his blue eyes bright, but he said nothing.

The queen sighed. "So, you relayed a bit of gossip to my daughter Vicky."

"Yes," May murmured. "Again, I am sorry."

"My dear, I appreciate the apology, but Missy's marriage is hardly your fault. Did you make her walk in the gardens with Ferdinand? Did you insist she linger there, kissing him for so long that they were discovered? I'm afraid Missy has only herself to blame for this turn of events," the queen said crisply. "Though, May, I will expect you to exercise more discretion in the future. A future queen does not engage in idle gossip, especially not about a family member."

May nodded, her heart pounding. "Of course, Your Majesty."

"What about Alix?" George demanded, looking from May to his grandmother.

"What about her, George?" the queen asked, with mounting irritation. "Are you saying that you would rather marry her? She did just break things off with that sweet Maximilian of Baden, but still . . ."

"No, I'm talking about how May kept Alix from marrying Eddy!" George blustered. "May has been cruel, and heartless, and—"

"Alix never wanted to marry Eddy! Quit spouting nonsense, George," the queen snapped. "You are going to marry May. That is my final decision."

"But I do not love her!"

Victoria set down her teacup with a loud clatter. May flinched.

"George, you are a future king now! You are no longer the second brother who gets to do as he wishes! You have a responsibility toward this family and this nation, and I command you, as my heir, to fulfill both!"

There was another long silence. May waited for George to deliver the killing blow, to tell the queen that May had blackmailed Hélène.

But he just stood, his expression blank, and bowed at the waist. "Very well, Your Majesty. I will do as you command."

The queen sighed. Morning light streamed in through the windows, illuminating her face. For the first time May could remember, Victoria looked like an old woman, rather than the ageless queen who had led this nation for over half a century.

She turned to May. "You have said nothing, my dear. Are you opposed to this, as well?"

"Oh, no—I mean, I would be honored to marry George." May looked at him, willing him to meet her gaze, but he was still staring pointedly away. "Not because you are a future king, George, but because I love you. My engagement to Eddy . . . Well, you know we never loved each other. It has been different with you, from the beginning."

"It's settled, then," the queen declared, with quiet satisfaction. "This will make the nation so happy. A joyful ending to a very tragic story. Now I think I shall leave you two." The queen rose; May and George both bobbed to their feet, like marionettes tugged on a string, so they were not seated while Her Majesty stood. "Georgie, dear, I'm sure May would appreciate a real proposal, not one from me," Victoria added. Then she swept into the hall, leaving them alone.

May would have been shocked at the lack of propriety if every fiber of her being hadn't been focused on George. On his nearness, the rise and fall of his chest. She waited, her every nerve alight, for what he would say next.

"May, would you marry me?" he asked.

This was all wrong; George wasn't looking at her, his gaze fixed on the wallpaper behind her, as if he were reciting a script.

"Yes," May agreed, "but please, George, look at me? I want us to be happy—"

He gave a caustic laugh. "It has never mattered in this family whether I was happy. Her Majesty has commanded me to marry you, and if there's one thing I always do, it's my duty. That's me, the reliable second son until the end."

His voice was flinty and hard and unyielding. It hurt some quiet and vulnerable place deep within her, hearing him speak to her without the usual tenderness.

"George, I love you!" May wrung her hands fiercely. She was still wearing her engagement ring from Eddy; it dug angrily into her skin. "I love you, and while I regret the things I have done, I don't regret a moment I've spent with you."

"You can spare me whatever speech you've rehearsed," he said wearily. "I'm sure it's very pretty, but it's wasted on me. I loved you so much once. Not anymore."

"Please, I don't—"

"You can *stop*, May. You're going to get what you've always wanted; you're going to be queen. Isn't that enough?"

"But it isn't what I want anymore! I want *you*!"

May couldn't believe she was here. That after all she'd done, she would somehow get everything she'd wanted—George, and the Crown.

Except that she didn't actually have George. Not in the way that mattered.

She had his hand, but not his heart. And it was his heart she wanted: that sweet, thoughtful, wondrous heart, which had loved her for so long, without reservations and without constraint.

And she had managed to throw that love away. She would have a loveless marriage after all, just like her parents.

As she watched the man she loved walk away from her, May realized, for the first time in her life, what it felt to be truly, achingly alone.

CHAPTER FORTY

Alix

THE STADTKIRCHE, THE LUTHERAN CHURCH OF DARMSTADT, WAS only a stone's throw from the ducal manor; Alix could see her own front door through the stained glass. The window depicted a pastoral Jesus, holding a shepherd's staff and surrounded by sheep. When Alix got restless as a child, her mother used to walk her over to the window, where she would press her daughter's chubby toddler hands to the glass. *Red, blue, yellow,* her mother would murmur, naming the colors as Alix touched each one—and then again in German, *rot, blau, gelb,* and then in French, *rouge, bleu, jaune.* Alix could hear the echo of her mother's voice even now, whispering past the stone font where Alix had been baptized, past the tarnished bronze candlesticks and the faded Gobelins tapestry on the wall.

Looking around the chapel, Alix felt that she could see the entire circle of her existence. This wedding probably seemed quaint to some of the wedding guests—to Aunt Marie in her furs and glittering tiara; or to Aunt Vicky and the cousins from Prussia. Or to May and George, who sat near Uncle Bertie in one of the front pews, both oddly subdued and seeming to avoid each other's gaze. George wore a black armband on his sleeve, and May's gown was the pale lavender of half mourning, as if anyone here was in danger of forgetting that they were still grieving Eddy. According to the official narrative, that shared grief was what had drawn them together. Their own wedding was set for later this year—though they didn't seem especially lovestruck to Alix.

Alix glanced a few rows back, to where Hélène sat with her parents. She was so surprised, and grateful, that her friend had made the trip from Normandy. *I needed to see where you grew up!* Hélène had exclaimed last night, when they stayed up far too late, exchanging stories about the past months. *Besides,* Hélène had added, with a ghost of her old playfulness, *it was getting a teensy bit boring, being in the country. There's only so much apple picking one can do.*

Darmstadt was hardly a great urban destination, but Hélène didn't seem to mind. After the wedding, the Orléans family was going on an extended tour of Italy. The sunshine would do Hélène some good, Alix thought—though she suspected, in some small way, that her friend was already healing.

She looked to where Ernie stood at the altar, waiting for the ceremony to begin. Alix saw him glance at the church's main double doors—then he stared at Alix, his eyes bright with concern.

Somehow, even before she turned, she knew she would see Nicholas.

He wasn't supposed to be here. Alix's sister Ella had come from St. Petersburg a few days ago, along with her husband Sergei, who had given the couple a wedding gift on behalf of the Romanovs.

Yet here was Nicholas, achingly handsome in his uniform and knee-high boots.

He met Alix's gaze as he settled on the bride's side of the church. Which was only fair, since Ducky was his first cousin.

The wedding passed in a blur. Alix felt like her heart was hammering the entire time, her body tingling with awareness at Nicholas's nearness. Before she realized it, the priest was intoning the final blessing and Ernie and Ducky were walking down the aisle, amid applause and a crescendo of organ music.

As the guests began filing out of the Stadtkirche, a hand brushed Alix's elbow.

"Please, Alix," Nicholas said softly. "Walk with me?"

She nodded, not trusting herself to speak, and gestured toward the back of the church. Its pillars were wreathed in ivy and rosemary—there should have been white roses, except that it was impossible to get roses in Germany this early in the year. Beneath the flagstones lay the crypt where her entire family was buried: her grandparents, her brother Frittie. Her mother.

"Nicholas, I—"

"I came to—"

They had both spoken at the same time, clumsy and flushing. Alix held out a hand, gesturing that he should go first.

"It was a lovely wedding," Nicholas began, seeming unsure of himself.

"You didn't need to come."

He flinched at her bluntness. "Of course I came. I wanted to see you." He hesitated, then added, "Is it true, about you and Maximilian of Baden?"

"We were courting, but I ended things."

Nicholas's deep blue eyes met hers, cautious, hopeful.

"Dare I hope . . . Is it because of me that you broke it off?"

Of course it is, Alix thought, tears rising to her eyes.

Everything *is because of you. No matter how hard I try to forget you, no matter how easy things were with Maximilian, I keep running back here. To you.*

"Yes," she said simply.

Nicholas stepped forward then. He seized Alix's shoulders with both hands—roughly, almost desperately—and lowered his mouth to hers.

Alix felt like she'd been hibernating all these months without him. Like she'd been half dreaming, and now she'd been brutally shaken awake.

She still loved Nicholas. She would probably always love him, with a love that terrified her, and thrilled her, and shook her to the core.

When they pulled apart, Nicholas fell to one knee, dust motes dancing around his head in the afternoon light.

"I love you," he said fiercely. "Please, marry me."

Alix stared at him. Misreading her silence, he kept talking.

"I know that I am asking a lot of you. I wish that I were an ordinary man, and loving me was simple and uncomplicated." He gestured to his uniform, with its sash and brass buttons and high Romanov collar. "But I was born into this family and these responsibilities. My future, narrow as it is, was laid out for me the moment I was born. You, of course, are still free to make a different choice. Selfishly, I hope that you don't."

Alix tugged him to his feet. "But—your parents. Did you convince them to change their minds?"

"*You* did that," Nicholas said proudly. At her confused look, he explained. "My father is very ill, Alix. The doctors say it is kidney disease."

"What is the treatment?"

Nicholas's expression faltered. "There is no treatment. He might live weeks, perhaps months, but we are saying our goodbyes."

"Oh, Nicholas. I'm sorry."

The tsar was so formidable, a bear of a man: it seemed impossible that he could be struck down by illness like any ordinary mortal. Surely he could only be killed by some mythical weapon that was guarded by dragons.

Now, though, Alix understood why the tsar had gone to Baden-Baden. He wasn't just taking the waters; he'd been searching for a miracle cure.

"After we left the regatta last summer, I told my parents that I refused to marry Hélène. That I refused to marry anyone but you, actually. I said I would remain a bachelor forever, and the Romanov line could continue through Misha. I think I was starting to wear them down," Nicholas admitted, "until I heard about you and Maximilian."

He sighed, staring down at his shoes. "I know how much you love your home. He seemed so perfect for you, and I thought—you deserved to be happy, even if that happiness was not with me."

Alix reached a hand instinctively toward Nicholas, and he laced their fingers gratefully, as if she were a lifeline.

"I told myself that the right thing to do was to let you go. That I was being noble by staying away," Nicholas went on. "But I couldn't stop loving you, and wanting you, and missing you. Even if I knew that you belonged with Maximilian, in a life that made you happy."

"*You* make me happy," Alix assured him.

"My father must have taken a turn for the worse, because

he called me into his room and gave me this." Nicholas let go of her hand so that he could withdraw a velvet pouch from his jacket pocket. "He said I should give it to you, that you would know what it meant."

Alix took the pouch from Nicholas and slid its contents onto her palm. She realized, startled, that it was the tsarina's pearl necklace. The pearls gleamed an unearthly blue-gray in the dim light.

"Father told me that he saw you in Baden-Baden. He said that he and Mother talked to you, asked about you and Maximilian—I'm sorry about that, by the way," Nicholas added, wincing. "Father told me that you stood up to him. Did you really shout that you aren't his subject, and he couldn't tell you what to do?"

"I'm not sure I *shouted*, exactly." Alix let the pearls slide through her fingers, the stones cool and heavy. Nicholas didn't seem to know that his parents had tried to bribe her, but she decided not to mention it.

"My father was impressed. He said that I was right about you—that you're made of stronger stuff than he had realized. *Go get her*, he told me. *I'd like to see you married before I die.*"

Nicholas spoke of his father's death so matter-of-factly that Alix couldn't help it. She threw her arms around him, pulling him into a hug.

How strange that Alix's impertinence, her sheer rudeness, was the reason she finally got the Romanovs' blessing. But then, wasn't that what people said about bullies—that they only responded to a show of strength?

"Please, Alix." Nicholas murmured into her ear. "I wish I could undo all my mistakes. I should have fought harder for us; I should never have taken you for granted. I know I don't deserve you, but also—I don't know how to face any of this without you."

Alix was still holding the pearls, balled up in one hand. It hit her then, in a way it hadn't before: how deeply permanent this decision was. How absolutely certain she needed to be.

Nicholas would be tsar. Not someday, but soon.

Choosing him meant an entirely new life, leaving behind everything that felt safe and familiar. Moving to Russia. Taking on public appearances, which always triggered her episodes. Learning a new religion, a new language; organizing grand court balls and visiting the sick, and doing it all in a country she knew nothing about.

Alix looked at Nicholas's face, so handsome and hopeful, and she knew that she would do anything—make any sacrifice—to be with him. It simply wasn't a question.

"Yes," she whispered.

Nicholas braced his arms beneath her and lifted her into the air, spinning her around and around so that her skirts belled out around her.

"You mean it?" he exclaimed, covering her face with kisses.

"Yes!" Alix's smile mirrored his own, and she repeated the word over and over again, for the sheer joy of saying it. "Yes, yes, I will marry you!"

The tapers flickered, making Nicholas's smile shimmer; it was as if the candles themselves were celebratory. Alix couldn't help thinking that her mother was present. She could *feel* Alice here, as surely as if her mother's arms were wrapped around her.

Her mother was here, and Nicholas was here; and in this moment, Alix felt utterly surrounded by love.

CHAPTER FORTY-ONE

May

MAY OF TECK STILL HATED WEDDINGS.

Or at least, she regretted accepting the invitation to this one. The ducal estate in Darmstadt was decidedly too small for so many guests—though no one else seemed to mind the cramped ballroom, since they kept lining up for jostled, sweaty dancing.

What had Ducky been thinking, choosing Ernie when she could have had a future king? There was simply no understanding some people.

But the real reason for May's irritation was standing a few feet away.

George had stayed dutifully near her, though he was currently talking to the widowed—and very beautiful—Crown Princess of Austria. May knew he wasn't actually flirting; he was just expressing sympathies for the death of Stéphanie's husband, but still. Couldn't he pay a fraction of that attention to *her*?

When Queen Victoria had asked if she and George would like to attend this wedding—chaperoned by Uncle Bertie, of course, since they weren't married—May had jumped at the chance. A trip might be just what she and George needed. Surely he couldn't ignore her for all those hours of travel, together onboard ships or on railway cars.

And yet he did. He was invariably, perfectly polite: he sat next to May at dinners, strolled around the deck of the ship with her, held out his arm to accompany her into a party. But he had become a quiet, withdrawn version of himself. Nothing like the George who used to confess his daydreams with a shy smile.

May almost wished he were cruel. At least she knew what to do with cruelty, could fight back against it. This studied indifference cut her to the quick.

A prickle of awareness traced down May's spine. She glanced up—and her eyes met those of Hélène d'Orléans.

Yet another reason she shouldn't have come. If May had known her enemy would show up, she would have let George and Bertie handle this wedding on their own.

Still holding May's gaze, Hélène tilted her head in unmistakable invitation, then walked out into the corridor.

May could have ignored her, of course. But a contrary part of her itched for this confrontation. So she followed Hélène down the hall, to a room filled with armor, where bayonets and swords hung on the wall. How appropriate.

Hélène placed a palm on the back of an armchair, studying May through narrowed eyes. "My condolences to George. Dare I ask how you tricked *another* prince into proposing?"

"Yes, George and I are engaged," May said evenly. "Don't expect a wedding invitation."

Hélène scoffed. "I wouldn't dream of attending such a farce of a wedding."

Before May could reply, a third figure entered the room. "Hélène? I saw you marching off, and you looked so angry,"

Alix began—then she caught sight of May, and her expression hardened. "Oh. It's you."

"It's me," May echoed, slightly sarcastic.

"Alix!" Hélène took a step forward. "What happened with you and Nicholas? Are you . . ."

Alix burst into a smile. "We're engaged."

Well, May thought, there seemed to be a lot of engagements happening lately.

"Oh, I'm so glad!" Hélène pulled Alix into a fierce hug, and the two women stood there, embracing like sisters. They seemed to have forgotten that May was in the room at all.

May watched them with confusion, and something like regret, or perhaps yearning.

She cleared her throat, suddenly exhausted. "Hélène. Did you want something, or shall I return to the party?"

The two other young women stepped apart, and Hélène turned to face May, fists clenched at her sides. "I do want something, as it happens. I want you to admit how despicable you are. It wasn't enough for you to ruin my life, and Eddy's? Now you have to set your sights on George, too?"

May felt an unexpected urge to cry. "I love George," she protested weakly.

"You don't know the first thing about love! What Eddy and I shared, the willingness to do anything for each other—*that* is love. Did you know he offered to give up the throne for me?" Hélène exclaimed.

Alix reached a supportive hand toward Hélène, who squeezed it gratefully.

"I didn't know, but I'm not especially surprised. Eddy was always impetuous," May said softly. *Like when he got engaged to* me *just to hurt you*, she didn't need to say aloud. That had been the most reckless, impetuous thing of all.

Hélène frowned, as if thinking along the same lines. "I don't know what hold you have over George, for him to marry you despite knowing what you did."

Despite knowing what she'd done? May blinked as the realization hit her.

"You told George, didn't you." She'd always assumed that *Eddy* had shared everything with George before he died. But, no, it had been Hélène.

Of course, she thought, with a hollow sense of regret.

The marriage game had always been a match to the death—between women, between her and Alix and Hélène. Because that was the way the world worked. It pitted women against each other, kept them divided.

"Yes, I told George," Hélène said triumphantly. "I saw you two making romantic eyes at each other when you thought Eddy wasn't looking. Then after Eddy died"—there was only the slightest catch in her voice as she spoke the word *died*—"I decided that George needed to know the truth about you."

As if you *know the truth about me*, May wanted to say, but the words lodged in her throat, sticky and hot.

It seemed so simple for other people—Hélène, Alix, George—this notion of doing the right thing. When had it become complicated for May? How had she waded into such murky, gray territory, justifying all her actions, no matter the cost?

She fixed her gaze on Hélène. "You're right; I never loved Eddy. The truth is, I didn't *believe* in love back then. I thought it was a fairy tale, invented for those novels you read." She waved a hand in Alix's direction. "Or worse, a hoax that parents tell their daughters in order to convince them to marry cruel men. Like my father."

That last was spoken in a near whisper. May wasn't sure why she'd said it. Perhaps because nothing else seemed to matter anymore—not the lies, or the great game of pretend that she had played for so long. What was the point of any of it, when she had lost George?

She wanted someone in this world to know the real her, and it might as well be Hélène and Alix.

"What do you mean, cruel like your father?" Alix asked carefully.

"Neither of you would understand. I've seen you with your parents, Hélène, the way they look at each other—and at you." May's next words were directed at Alix. "And you—do you remember what you told me two summers ago, on the train to Balmoral? How your parents were so in love that your father has never recovered from the death of your mother?"

Alix nodded. Hélène stared at May, something shifting in her expression.

"My father is nothing like that. The complete opposite, in fact." May sighed. "At least now he's living on the Continent, far from me and my mother."

Alix made a low, distressed sound. "Are you saying that he . . ."

"He does not hit us," May explained, because she didn't want to lay claim to injuries she hadn't suffered. "But for as long as I can remember, he has treated us in an ugly and hateful way." She thought of the years of shouting, the candlesticks hurled at Mary Adelaide's head. The insults, the constant belittling, the mockery.

These young women would never understand, because they hadn't grown up around that sort of vicious cruelty. They had grown up cherished, loved.

"My brother Dolly left home the moment he could, but what could I do? Sandhurst does not accept female recruits," May said bitterly. "Why do you think I was so determined to marry, and marry someone higher born than my father? I needed to get away, and protect my mother from him."

To May's surprise, Alix stepped forward and hugged her, the way she had hugged Hélène. It brought unexpected tears to May's eyes.

"I'm sorry for telling Maud about your fainting spells," May murmured, voice breaking.

"It's all right," Alix assured her. "I never wanted to marry Eddy."

And now Alix was engaged to Nicholas. Once upon a time May wouldn't have believed Alix could be tsarina: she'd thought of Alix as so shy, so timid. Now she saw that beneath Alix's stillness lay a quiet blade of strength.

She felt suddenly desperate to say all her sins aloud, as if voicing them would earn her absolution, like a Catholic at confession.

"I told Aunt Vicky about Missy," May said, wincing. "That's why Ferdinand kissed her that night."

Alix tried to assuage May's guilt on that point, too. "Missy is excited to marry Ferdinand, did you know that? Ducky tells me that they are happily planning the wedding."

May had saved the most difficult apology for last. She turned to Hélène and, tears stinging her eyes, said, "I'm sorry that I kept you apart from Eddy."

Hélène's eyes flashed. "That seems a very easy thing for

you to say, now that Eddy is dead. Now that you're engaged to his brother. You *won*, May."

"It doesn't feel much like winning, since I'm in love with a man who doesn't love me back!"

May wasn't sure why her eyes kept betraying her like this, sending tears sliding down her cheeks. She wiped at them angrily. "I love George," she repeated, looking back at Hélène. "You may not believe me, but it's true. I have done so many things that I regret; I schemed and manipulated, and in the end I wound up, impossibly, engaged to a man I love. But thanks to you, he despises me. So perhaps *you* won."

"I did not win! The man I love is *dead*, or did you forget that?" Hélène exclaimed, and May flinched.

Of course. That had been thoughtless of her to say.

"I think we're done here," Hélène said heavily. "Goodbye, May."

May twisted her engagement ring back and forth beneath the leather of her glove. "Goodbye," she repeated.

The three of them stood there for a long moment. They had been so many things to each other over the years: enemies, rivals, and for a fleeting moment—before Eddy came between them, before May made all her mistakes—friends.

But Eddy was dead now, and there was nothing connecting them anymore. May would run into Alix at family events over the years, since Nicholas and George were cousins, but she suspected that they would keep their distance.

As for Hélène, May doubted they would cross paths again.

May knew, with sudden certainty, that the three of them would never again be in a room together. They had reached the end of it—the era where their lives had been so hopelessly, heartbreakingly entwined.

Hélène was the first to go; she stormed from the room in a whirl of satin skirts and outrage. But Alix lingered on the threshold. Her enormous blue-gray eyes met May's, luminous with sympathy.

"I'm sorry about George," Alix said softly. "For what it's worth, I think he still loves you. He's just hurting from everything that happened, and perhaps he feels that he needs to punish you, for Eddy's sake. But I saw the way you two were together, when you thought no one was looking. He just needs to remember that feeling."

Then Alix was gone, and May was alone, Alix's words echoing through her mind. *I think he still loves you.*

What if Alix was right, and some reluctant corner of George's heart still cared about her? After all, he'd never told the queen about May's blackmail of Hélène. Surely if he despised May, he would have unearthed that secret—would have listed every last one of May's transgressions in an effort to avoid marrying her. But he had held it back. May had assumed he'd done so to prevent further scandal . . . but what if he'd been protecting May?

If he'd loved her for as long as he said he did, then surely there was something left. Surely he would fall in love with her again, if only he remembered.

May would *make* him remember. She hadn't survived this long and climbed this high to fail when it really mattered.

She tilted her chin up in a gesture she'd unconsciously learned from Hélène, and headed back into the party to find her fiancé.

She was May of Teck, after all, and could do anything she set her mind to.

CHAPTER FORTY-TWO

Hélène

"PERHAPS WE SHOULD REJOIN YOUR PARENTS?" VIOLETTE walked alongside Hélène, valiantly attempting to hold a parasol over her mistress's head, but Hélène was moving too quickly.

"Just a bit farther. I want to see the ships headed to America."

The docks at Genoa were hardly the sort of place a young lady should stroll about, but then, Hélène had never been like other young ladies. She felt a restless flutter in her chest that only movement could dispel. Which wasn't surprising, after the events of the previous week.

"Move along!" barked a man, ducking past her as he held one end of a heavy wooden crate. Along the docks, massive steamships loaded and unloaded their cargo: boxes labeled in Italian or French or English, trunks monogrammed with their owners' initials. Hélène saw crates of chickens and livestock on lead ropes. Travelers hurried to nearby inns or onto ferryboats that would take them upriver; sailors clustered in groups to smoke cigarettes, gossiping in half a dozen languages. Everything was rowdy and dirty and wonderfully full of life.

It felt so cosmically unfair that she was here without Eddy. He would have loved this, would have been running ahead of her, eager to show her around.

"Hélène?"

She turned around in surprise, shrugging deeper into her heavy cloak. "Emanuele?"

Violette drifted aside to give them privacy, stubbornly taking the parasol with her.

"What are you doing here?" Emanuele looked just the same as when she'd last seen him, when he and Hélène had been sneaking around Agnes's house. Had that really been just six months ago?

"My ship leaves in an hour. My parents are at the *albergo*, where they are almost certainly complaining about the wine selection." Hélène tilted her head in the direction of the dock-side inn. "We were in Germany earlier this week, at the wedding of Prince Ernest to his cousin Ducky."

Emanuele smiled softly. "Ah, yes. There are not many ports near Hesse."

Hélène's parents had been startled when she suggested they attend Ernie and Ducky's wedding. They had nodded eagerly, exchanging a hopeful glance, clearly thrilled that she wanted to be in society again. Hélène's only thought had been of Alix—until she'd seen May at the wedding.

Of everything she'd expected—vitriol, accusations, perhaps even shouting—she'd never imagined that she would see the version of May she had encountered: deflated, defeated. For so long Hélène had dreamed of confronting May; and in the end, it hadn't been worth the fight.

In the end, she'd felt sorry for May.

Emanuele gestured toward the harbor. "You're not traveling on the *Himalaya*, by chance?"

"As a matter of fact, we are." Hélène paused before asking, "Are you also headed to Rome?"

"I'm actually not disembarking there. I'm staying on board all the way to Alexandria," Emanuele told her.

Alexandria. The word broke through the haze of grief that Hélène had been shrouded in for months. It conjured up visions of adventure, of wandering through cobblestone streets, visiting the lighthouse that had guided travelers since Caesar. Sailing up the Nile, past crocodiles, to see the pyramids.

"If you're not busy, would you like to accompany me?"

For a moment Hélène thought that Emanuele was inviting her to Alexandria. She was seized by a bizarre impulse to say yes—but then she realized he was gesturing to his shoes. One of them was in tatters, its sole peeled back from the stitching. A rather remarkable amount of bright red stocking was visible through the leather.

"As you can see, I'm in dire need of a cobbler. I'm told there's one two streets away," Emanuele remarked.

To her surprise, Hélène fell into step alongside him. "Surely you don't travel with only a single pair of shoes?"

"Oh, I had others, but I lost them in a game of cards," he said airily.

"You gambled for *shoes?*"

"Of course I did. It's only a sin when you gamble for money," Emanuele joked. "Besides, I was playing against the crew. Shoes seemed like the great equalizer, the one thing all of us had."

"Until you lost yours."

"Sailors are alarmingly good at whist. All those hours out at sea, you know."

Hélène chuckled. "Gambling away your shoes—that's something Eddy would have done."

The moment the words left her mouth, she froze. Had she really just done that, just spoken about Eddy with *laughter*?

Emanuele clearly saw her shock, because he said, very gently, "He would want you to think of him with happiness."

Hélène nodded and took a deep breath, not trusting herself to speak. The salt air felt somehow calming. Out in the harbor, gulls wheeled and dived among the foam-capped waves.

She knew, deep down, that Emanuele was right. Eddy would want Hélène's grief to be balanced by joy.

Something was shifting within her, like tectonic plates moving and resettling. Perhaps it was because of what Queen Victoria had said when she'd given her Eddy's wedding ring; or perhaps it was the end of her years-long feud with May. But for the first time since Eddy's death, she felt like she could breathe again.

She would always miss him. Yet it was nice to know that she could think of Eddy with laughter, and not just tears.

"I worry that I am losing him," she admitted, so quietly that Emanuele had to lean forward to hear. "That I am forgetting him."

Already Eddy's features were blurring in her mind. There were photos of him, of course, but they were so painfully official: he was always in uniform, his jaw set, expression neutral. Hélène didn't miss Eddy, the Prince of England. She missed the *real* Eddy: his wicked smile, the impatient way he tucked back his hair when it fell forward, the irreverent edge to his humor. The boldness in his voice when he spoke of the things he truly cared about. The light in his eyes when he caught sight of her.

At night, in her dreams, Hélène would see Eddy with perfect clarity—and then she woke up, and the images would drift away like smoke, no matter how hard she tried to clutch at them.

"You are not forgetting him," Emanuele assured her. "Not in the way that matters. That is the thing about losing people; even if their faces blur in your memory, you will retain the important thing: the love you shared."

"I know," Hélène murmured.

"It is because you loved him so dearly that you hurt so much. But also, this great capacity to love is what will heal you."

Hélène shot him a look. "You sound very wise."

"Oh no," Emanuele said swiftly, the old irreverence returning to his tone. "I just make a point of seeming that way."

He was right, though. Hélène knew that she would never forget the important things about Eddy, no matter how much time had passed.

"I'm coming, too," she declared.

"Thank you. It really is quite chivalrous of you, given the circumstances." Emanuele's shoe was now in such disrepair that he was half hobbling. He winked at Hélène. "If I don't get this fixed soon, I may spend our entire voyage with bare feet, which would *really* cause a scandal."

"I'm sure you can win your shoes back," she replied. "But I wasn't just talking about this visit to the cobbler. I'm coming to Alexandria."

A slow smile spread over Emanuele's face. "Really?"

"I'll have to convince my parents, but I'm sure I'll find a way. I can be very convincing when I need to."

"I have no doubt of that." There was a huskiness to Emanuele's voice that made her look over at him, but he was turning onto a side street, where vendors sold things from temporary stalls or from the tops of overturned barrels. They shouted their wares in rough voices—bolts of cloth, rope, honey, wax.

Eddy would have loved all of this, Hélène thought. Already it hurt just a little bit less, remembering him.

She glanced back over her shoulder at the harbor. The ocean seemed to stretch out forever, limitless and wild and full of possibility.

"Hélène!" Emanuele stood at a cobbler's stall. Atop the makeshift counter, Hélène saw rows of men's shoes, all ruthlessly durable and meant for travel, all the same practical shade of brown.

"I need your help deciding upon the color. Brown, or brown, or . . . dare I suggest brown?" Emanuele asked.

Hélène made a show of deliberating. "I must say, the brown is quite handsome."

There was something about Emanuele that reminded her of Eddy. They were both devilishly handsome, though Emanuele's hair and eyes were darker, his grin a little bolder. No, it was more than that: it was the way they inhabited each moment to the fullest, no matter what other people thought.

Eddy had asked her to live. To explore new cities, and climb more trees, and continue to defy convention. She would do all of that, for his sake.

And perhaps someday—not soon, but eventually—she might even love again. For the first time since Eddy's death, such a thing felt possible.

But there was no rush. For now Hélène felt the world unfurling before her, vast and wondrous and ready to be explored.

AUTHOR'S NOTE

The story told in *A Queen's Game* and *A Queen's Match* is based on real historical events—namely, the tangled engagements and marriages of Alix, May, and Hélène. I have always been an avid reader, but I had never heard this particular chapter of royal history until I stumbled across it in a biography of Queen Victoria. The real history was so dramatic, I knew at once that I had to write it as a historical romance.

As with all historical fiction, I have tried my best to stay true to the historical facts, embellishing and inventing when needed.

The marriage of Prince Albert Victor Christian Edward, called Eddy, was a source of great frustration for his grandmother, who initially tried to match him with his cousin Alix of Hesse. Alix refused to marry Eddy, and soon afterward, Eddy embarked upon a love affair with Hélène d'Orléans.

Though I took liberties in imagining just how far Hélène and Eddy's relationship progressed, physically speaking, this sample of a letter from Eddy to Hélène should give you a sense of just how much they adored each other:

> *I feel you are more than half mine already, and it would take a very little to make you mine altogether and for*

good and all . . . very little persuasion would induce me to carry you off . . . and then people might say what they liked and I would gladly bear the consequences.[1]

Given the overwhelming passion of their letters and the sheer romance of their story—rings exchanged in secret, permission reluctantly granted by Queen Victoria—I never quite believed the "official" reason that the engagement was broken off. Hélène claimed that she could not convert to the Church of England as she had promised. Was that true, I wondered? Perhaps something else, or someone else, had come between these two people who loved each other so desperately. . . .

Eddy's engagement to May of Teck came as a shock to contemporary observers, royal and commoner alike—primarily because May, as a Serene Highness, was considered just barely royal enough to be queen. Eddy himself wrote of the engagement in a letter, "It can't be helped."[2]

Meanwhile, Eddy and Hélène were still corresponding in secret. Eddy's death in January 1892, just a month after getting engaged to May, came as an utter shock to the nation. May was present at Eddy's deathbed, but it is widely documented in family letters that Eddy's final words were "Hélène, Hélène!"

After she ended things with Eddy, Alix of Hesse fell for Nicholas of Russia, but his parents denied them permission to marry. It is true that Nicholas's parents and Hélène's parents

1. Prince Michael of Greece, *Eddy and Hélène: An Impossible Match* (Rosvall Royal Books, 2013), 23–4.

2. James Pope Hennessy, *Queen Mary* (Hodder & Stoughton, 1959), 240.

entered marriage negotiations on their children's behalf (Hélène's suggestion of fake-dating was my addition, but who knows—it's not impossible!). Alix and Nicholas were finally able to marry in 1894, immediately following the death of Nicholas's father. Though Nicholas and Alix were very much in love, their marriage was strained by growing political unrest and violence in Russia.

After bearing four daughters—Olga, Tatiana, Maria, and Anastasia—Alix finally gave birth to a much-desired son and heir, Alexei. It soon became clear that Alexei had inherited the "bleeding disease" that had killed Alix's brother Frittie, and Alexei was kept closely watched behind palace doors.

Alix, Nicholas, and all their children were massacred in Yekaterinburg in the Russian Revolution, though rumors persisted for years that their daughter Anastasia had escaped.

Queen Victoria did not live long into the new century. She died in January 1901, leaving behind five of her nine children and thirty-one of her forty-two grandchildren.

Prince Ernest of Hesse became Grand Duke of Hesse soon after he and Ducky were married. They divorced in 1901, less than a year after Queen Victoria's death. Ducky went on to marry her maternal cousin Kiril, whom she had loved passionately since she was a teenager. Ernie's relationships with male valets are well documented among family diaries and letters.

Queen Victoria did send Maximilian of Baden to court Alix in 1891, but Alix was too in love with Nicholas to accept his proposal. Maximilian did, in fact, go on to inherit the duchy, as his male cousins' marriages all remained childless. He married Marie Louise of Hanover, and they had two children. Maximilian continued his political rise during World War I and served as the final chancellor of the German Empire before Germany became a republic in 1918.

Hélène d'Orléans married Emanuele Filiberto, second in line to the Italian throne, in 1895. They had two boys, Amedeo and Aimone. Hélène and Emanuele traveled far more widely, and adventurously, than was typical of royal couples in that era—the Sahara, the Congo region, Shanghai, Palestine, Alaska. Hélène was actively involved with the Italian Red Cross during World War I.

Emanuele never did become King of Italy.

May of Teck, known to history as Queen Mary, was married to King George V for forty-three years and is generally considered to be the matriarch who shaped the modern British royal family—and who kept it together during times of great crisis. May and George's oldest son, David, abdicated the throne to marry a divorced American woman named Wallis Simpson. May's second son then assumed the throne as George VI.

May died at age eighty-five after seeing her granddaughter Elizabeth become queen.

William, Prince of Wales, is May's great-great-grandson.

ACKNOWLEDGMENTS

Wrapping up a story is always bittersweet, and this one in particular has been a passion project from the very first moment. I am so grateful that I got to chase my dream of telling this (mostly!) true historical story. Thank you to the talented and wonderful people who made it all possible.

Caroline Abbey: It feels surreal to think of our very first phone call back in 2018! I knew at once that you and I would love working together. Thank you for the countless hours you have spent with me, chatting about royals and history and character arcs and romance. These books are so much better because of your thoughtful notes and guidance.

Joelle Hobeika: Thank you for always being my biggest cheerleader, my very first reader, and my outline guru. There is no one else I would rather have in my corner!

I'm grateful to continue working with the fantastic team at Penguin Random House, especially Barbara Marcus, Mallory Loehr, Kelly McGauley, Elizabeth Ward, Adrienne Waintraub, Tricia Lin, Katie Halata, Lauren Stewart, Tiffany Liao, Clare Perret, Rebecca Vitkus, and Barbara Bakowski. A special thanks is due to Noreen Herits and Cynthia Lliguichuzhca for always doing such a wonderful job publicizing my books, and to Ana Hard for yet another beautiful cover!

Thanks also to everyone at Alloy Entertainment: Josh Bank, Les Morgenstein, Romy Golan, Matt Bloomgarden, Kat Jagai, Elysa Dutton, Chelsea Kardos, Sarah Campbell, Kyle Stivers, and Malini Narayan.

I am fortunate to work with the talented foreign sales team at Rights People: Charlotte Bodman, Alexandra Devlin, Harim Yim, Claudia Galluzzi, Hannah Whitaker, Annie Blombach, and Amy Threadgold. Thank you for helping to share these books with readers around the world.

Thank you also to the Penguin Random House audio team—Orli Moscowitz, Joseph Ward, and Imogen Wilde—for bringing this story to life in audiobook form.

This job would be a lonely one without my friends. Eliza, Alexandra, Sarah, Julia, Emily, Biz, Stacy—thank you for being my experts on British life, for planning book launches and writing retreats, for listening to countless plot points, and for letting me plunder your best one-liners for my characters.

I'm grateful for the constant support of my family. Mom, Dad, Lizzy, John Ed, and MK: Thank you for making it possible for me to write, whether by running my carpools, helping organize my house, or trying to keep me on schedule (the hardest task of all). I couldn't do this without you.

Alex—as always, you brought out the best of this book by bringing out the best in me. Thank you for being my greatest support system and my best friend. William, Edward, and I are so lucky to have you!

And finally, I want to thank the readers! It means so much to me that you were willing to join me on another royal adventure. Thank you for making it possible for me to do a job that I love.